KING PENGUIN

THE TWYBORN AFFAIR

The author was born in England in 1912, when his parents were in Europe for two years; at six months he was taken back to Australia, where his father owned a sheep station. When he was thirteen Patrick White was sent to school in England, to Cheltenham, 'where, it was understood, the climate would be temperate and a colonial acceptable'. Neither proved true, and after four rather miserable years there he went to King's College, Cambridge, where he specialized in languages. After leaving the university he settled in London, determined to become a writer. His novel *Happy Valley* was published in 1939; *The Living and the Dead* in 1941. During the war he was an R.A.F. Intelligence Officer in the Middle East and Greece. After the war he returned to Australia and is currently living in Sydney.

His other novels are *The Aunt's Story* (1946), *The Tree of Man* (1956), *Voss* (1957), *Riders in the Chariot* (1961), *The Solid Mandala* (1966), *The Vivisector* (1970), *The Eye of the Storm* (1973) and *A Fringe of Leaves* (1976). In addition he has published two collections of short stories, *The Burnt Ones* (1964) and *The Cockatoos* (1974), which incorporates several short novels. In 1973 he was awarded the Nobel Prize for Literature.

PATRICK WHITE

THE
TWYBORN
AFFAIR

A KING PENGUIN

PUBLISHED BY PENGUIN BOOKS

Penguin Books Ltd, Harmondsworth, Middlesex, England
Penguin Books, 625 Madison Avenue, New York, New York 10022, U.S.A.
Penguin Books Australia Ltd, Ringwood, Victoria, Australia
Penguin Books Canada Ltd, 2801 John Street, Markham, Ontario, Canada L3R 1B4
Penguin Books (N.Z.) Ltd, 182–190 Wairau Road, Auckland 10, New Zealand

First published by Jonathan Cape 1979
Published in Penguin Books 1981

Filmset, printed and bound in Great Britain by
Hazell Watson & Viney Ltd, Aylesbury, Bucks
Set in Garamond

TO JIM SHARMAN

What else should our lives be but a series of beginnings, of painful settings out into the unknown, pushing off from the edges of consciousness into the mystery of what we have not yet become.

David Malouf

My suspicion is that in Heaven the Blessed are of the opinion that the advantages of the locale have been overrated by theologians who were never actually there. Perhaps even in Hell the damned are not always satisfied.

Jorge Luis Borges

Sometimes you'll see someone with nothing on but a bandaid.

Diane Arbus

PART I

'Which road this afternoon, madam?'

'The same, Teakle – the one we took yesterday.'

'Bit rough, isn't it?' her chauffeur ventured.

'We Australians,' Mrs Golson declared, 'are used to far rougher at home.'

It was an assertion she might not have made in company politer than her chauffeur's. She detected in her voice a sententiousness she found distasteful, particularly since the life she led at home was more comfortably cushioned than that of almost any Australian. Joan Golson had never known it rough.

'Rough – I bet it is – from what I hear.' Teakle was in the mood for divulgence.

So discreet, so English, such a dedicated member of the serving class, he surprised his employer by his remark. She would have liked to know what he had heard, but would not be so indiscreet as to ask. She suspected that English servants were given to taking liberties in the service of Colonials. It made her feel inferior.

In the circumstances she raised her chin, moistened her lips, and adjusted her motoring parasol, a collapsible one in tussore lined with bottle-green.

'The air of the pine forests,' she remarked, 'is so refreshing, I find, after that stuffy town. That's why I thought of taking the same drive as yesterday.'

'Yes,' agreed Teakle, very upright, very steady, 'the air at St Myool is pretty sewerish – what you'd call French.'

Not sure whether this was a remark she should accept, Mrs Golson did not reply. Instead she looked about her at the landscape in a manner befitting the owner of a 1912 Austin in bottle-green, like the livery of her temporary chauffeur and the lining of her little parasol.

To be strictly accurate it was *Mr* Golson who owned the high-set bottle-green Austin. If Mrs Golson overlooked the fact, she was hardly aware. She was unconscious that she lumped her husband in with her very considerable material possessions, perhaps because Mrs Golson was wealthy in her own right (not to be compared with E. Boyd Golson in his, but rich) and because, in her heart of hearts, she considered a women could face the world with more panache than a man, anyway an Australian one.

'Mr Golson don't seem to care much for motoring.'

'He'd rather sleep off his luncheon!' Mrs Golson laughed, but she also frowned as though she had invited her chauffeur to share her vision of her husband asleep in a deep armchair in a public room.

'He likes to motor,' she added, 'but when there is a purpose.'

She hoped the man would leave it at that. For Mrs Golson was preparing to enjoy her own purpose in having herself driven down this rutted road, past these smelly salt-pans, through the grove of ragged pines, where the air was far less restorative than she had implied.

She was nursing the discovery made yesterday, which introduced a purpose at last into their hitherto rather aimless sojourn at St Mayeul. Undertaken as an antidote to several weeks of over-eating and over-dancing in London and Paris, Mrs Golson, and to some more bemused extent her husband, E. Boyd, had from the beginning regretted their stay at the Grand Hôtel Splendide des Ligures. Mrs Golson realized of course that it was Lady Tewkes who was to blame. This formidable personage, with rings growing out of the bone itself, and her casually incorrect version of the English language ('the Hôtel Splendide is an 'otel, dear gel, I can recommend with confidence') intimidated the less than confident Joan Golson of Golson's Emporium, Sydney, and in her own right, Sewell's Sweat-free Felt Hats, which little Joanie had inherited from poor Daddy.

'It sounds charming,' Mrs Golson had assured her mentor.

Though more or less at home with vocabulary (everything not actively 'horrid' was for Joan Golson automatically 'charming') she used it somewhat tentatively abroad. It was her accent which often teetered, or so she heard, however carefully she managed it, and however carefully the eyelids of the Lady Tewkeses refused to bat; the most arrogant among the English were so mercilessly polite. ('Oh no, Joan, not a trace, I assure you, one couldn't tell. . .') It didn't always shore up her smile; she could feel a tic at work in her dimple like a canker in the rose.

Her own accent apart, there was always Curly, the Australian husband. One could hardly call anybody 'Boyd', though his mother persisted in doing so, and 'Ernest' had a habit of becoming 'Ern' when the past cropped up in embarrassing guise, often in the most unlikely places, like the Grafton Galleries or Claridge's. Through sheer lack of defence Mrs Golson had settled for 'Curly', the little boy's nickname and clubland label by which E. Boyd was generally known, and which did not sound outlandish among the Bimbos and Jumbos, the Babies and Pets on the more rakish side of Epsom and Cowes.

Still, the unflinching eyelids, the non-committal smiles of the English when faced with what is regrettably colonial can become a strain. To land at Calais or Boulogne and find oneself simply and unacceptably foreign was by contrast a relief.

Tilting her head, her parasol, at the angle adopted by a lady enjoying foreign travel, Mrs Golson was jolted, swayed, tossed on-ward in her leather-upholstered motor-car along the stony, rutted road, through the straggling pines, and as she was subjected to all of it she mused more sinuously on her experience of the afternoon before, which she did so hope to repeat, at least to some extent. She would like to seize on certain details, perpetuate them in memory. If only she had kept a diary, but she never had; she was far too irregular in her habits. (Write to Eadie. Of late she had neglected Eadie. Eadie would have hugely enjoyed yesterday's 'snapshot'; one could hardly call it more.)

As she imagined sharing with her friend Eadie Twyborn her experience of the previous day, Joan Golson found herself straining against upholstery still new enough to give out some of the perfume of leather, raising herself to the extent where her little motoring parasol might be carried off by the blast created by impetuous motion, while she parted the knotted gossamer protecting her face from wind, grit, and suicidal insects, to anticipate the pleasures of what she hoped to re-discover.

The evening before, Teakle had driven the car with uncharacter-istic dash, a reckless rush, perhaps due to the deep ruts and bumps on the surface of the sandy road. Emerging from the pine-grove as they mounted, they almost shaved what proved to be the containing wall of that charming villa lurking beyond the branches of probable almond trees, less equivocal olives, the clumps and spikes of laven-der, and lesser tufts stained with the flickering colours of faded, archetypal carnations.

The whole effect was faded, she remembered, now that the last mile quickened her vision of the desirable villa, shutters a washed-out blue, walls a dusty, crackled pink. A workaday cottage rather than a villa, one might have decided, if it had not been for those who were presumably its owners.

With almost voluptuous parsimony Mrs Golson proceeded to

restore to her picture of a garden the two figures trailing towards a terrace on which the house stood: the elderly man, a stroke of black and yellow, ivory rather, in a silver landscape, and ahead of him this charming young women (daughter, ward, wife, mistress – whatever) leading her companion through the rambling maze, the carnation tones of her dress dragging through, catching on, fusing with those same carnations which she reflected, while absorbing something of their silver from the lavender and southernwood surrounding her.

The long thin brown arms of this girl, the perfection of her jawline, the grace of her body as she turned smiling to encourage the dispensable (anyway for Joan Golson) man in black. (Yes, write to Eadie, write tonight – who would so much appreciate this graceful creature strolling with unconscious flair through her unkempt garden.)

Mrs Golson realized she was perspiring in anticipation of reunion with the scene she recalled. She started searching for her handkerchief. On finding it, she fell to dabbing where the moustache would have been. And sat forward.

Yesterday, much as she would have liked to, she could scarcely have ordered Teakle to drive slower as they coasted, slow enough, alongside the garden wall, while its owners (tenants?) continued following the path. She could only look and hope it would not be too quickly over. As for the couple in the garden, they turned at one point and looked back with the blank stare of those who cannot believe, and rightly, that strangers passing along the road can enter into their charmed lives.

Not long after the car had passed, Mrs Golson ordered her chauffeur to turn, and they headed back along the road to St Mayeul. Nobody was visible at the villa. Mrs Golson had relapsed against the upholstery, while the prudent Teakle drove into the dusk and the direction from which they had come.

On entering the Grand Hôtel Splendide she caught sight of Curly's head, its hairless dome rising above the padding of the chair in which he was sleeping off a late luncheon, till night should propel him towards his dinner. Joan hoped to slip past, but Curly seemed to sense her presence: he rose and, slightly lurching, asked,

'Enjoy yourself, treasure?'

She might have replied if, in her memory, she had not still been driving up the rutted road beyond St Mayeul.

As she was again this evening, slightly raised against the car's upholstery, furling the collapsible parasol, raising the gossamer veil well in advance of what she hoped to see, knowing that, despite the motion of the car, anyone at all perceptive would have noticed her trembling.

She was in a positive fantod long before hearing the mild explosion which suddenly occurred, when the collapse of nervous stress, and the swivelling, and final listing of the car as the driver brought it to a halt, almost tore her apart.

'Oh, damn – *not*,' Mrs Golson all but shouted, 'surely not a *panne*, Teakle!' A private joke which on another occasion it would have amused her to share with her English chauffeur at the expense of the despising French, it had nothing joky about it today.

'Looks like it,' Teakle replied, and jumped down with an agility she would not have expected of a man his age.

Teakle's virility should have been some consolation to his mistress, but she could only feel irritated – by motor-cars, men, the frustrating of a plan which nobody but herself knew about. She was considering whether to stand around helpless by the roadside, or remain sulking inside the car, when she realized that what had seemed tragic might prove a godsend.

'I am going to walk on ahead,' she announced laboriously while climbing down. 'The exercise – the air – will do me good.'

'Won't be much more than a jiffy,' her servant assured her.

'Oh, but take your time!' she insisted, already starting up the hill. 'Don't, please, exhaust yourself,' she advised with exemplary concern. 'I'd hate *that*,' she panted.

'Nothing to it,' the man grumbled, perhaps put out to think that she might be questioning his professional skill.

Mrs Golson turned. She was looking at her watch. Her voice sounded almost martial as her strategy formed and firmed itself.

'In fact I shall definitely want to walk for at least half – , no, make it an hour. And you needn't pick me up,' she added. 'I'll return when I feel I'm ready. I'll meet you here. By then you'll have repaired this exasperating *puncture*.'

'Only change the wheel,' he muttered, somewhat disconsolately it sounded.

If she had sounded stern, it was that Joan Golson had never felt so much her own mistress. In her naughtiness, she made haste to get away before her servant should offer advice, or turn into a nanny or a husband and exercise some form of restraint. But he did not murmur, and as she escaped up the hill, she was conscious of her foolishness in thinking she might be of importance to him, to anybody, except as a source of rewards (to Curly perhaps, though he, too, expected rewards) least of all to the charmed couple at the villa for whom she was risking, if not her neck, her ankles, to catch sight of once again. So she hurried, and panted, and several times ricked an ankle on the stones, in her rush to humiliate herself perhaps in their eyes as an eternally superfluous character. But did arrive.

After bursting out from the last of the runtish pines, she laid her hand on the containing wall, of roughly mortared, red stone. Where the villa was situated there opened a view of the sea, its hyacinth deepening to purple at that hour of evening, islands of amethyst nestling in tender feathers of foam, clouds too detached in every sense to suggest anything physical, only a slash of brash sunset to warn of the menace invariably concealed in landscape and time.

Still reeling with drunkenness for her triumph in arriving here alone and at a perfect hour, Joan Golson was not at first aware of music. She stood steadying herself against an aged olive, fingering the cork-like striations in its carapace, her attention venturing through the tufted maze of the deserted garden, until caught up, tossed by waves of music dashing themselves recklessly against the solid evening silence. The surge of music, now all around her, was escaping through an open window from the villa farther back. By advancing alongside the wall, she found that she could see inside the house to an interior already illuminated by a single austere brass lamp, its shade, in green porcelain over white, allowing no more than the necessity of light.

Swathed in its translucent cocoon sat the two figures, side by side on a stool as austere as the brass lamp, the man's back rigid and admonitory, the woman's form narrower, more sinuous, but no less dedicated, wearing what could have passed for a habit in grey-to-silver luminous silk, the long trailers of sleeves drifting in the wake of the music the two performers were dashing off.

It was reckless and at the same time controlled (by the man, Mrs Golson might not have cared to admit), it was joyous, with under-tones of melancholy, it was a delirious collusion between two who were, the more she looked, united in their incongruity: the lithe young woman and the stiff, elderly man – the lovers; there was by now no doubt in Mrs Golson's mind.

As she stood by the wall watching the scene through the open window, the tears were streaming down her cheeks, for joy, from the music she was hearing, and out of frustration from the life she had led and, it seemed, would always lead, except for the brief unsatisfactory sorties she made into that other life with Eadie Twyborn; probably never again, since Eadie had been aged by her tragedy.

Then, suddenly, the music was brought to its triumphant close in an upward flurry of unashamedly brazen notes. As they flung them from their fingers the two players teetered on their shared stool, shoulders hunched, torsos inclined backward from the hips, before they turned, facing, laughing at each other, the ivory-skinned, beaky, elderly man, and the lovely lean tanned features of the considerably younger woman.

Joan Golson was inching along to identify herself more closely with every detail of the scene, when the couple embraced. Or at least, the young woman leaned towards the cadaverous man, seeming to rise above him, plunging her mouth into his, dashing her lips back and forth, while his skeletal, veined hands took possession of the sinuous arms, which the grey trailers of sleeve surrendered, the skin deepened by restrained lighting almost to the tone of terracotta. So they sat and clung in what was prevented from becoming perfect union.

The young woman appeared to remember, or realize, or know by instinct. She rejected her elderly lover, left the stool, and practically striding, one would have said, reached the window, where she stood looking out, it might have been in anger, though the watcher doubted she was visible through the dusk. Yet the young woman leaned out, gathered in the shutters, and slammed them shut. Only a crack of light was left to commemorate all that had been desirable.

By the time Mrs Golson reached her car darkness almost prevailed beneath the pines. Teakle must have long since finished changing the wheel. He was sitting in the driver's seat. Unusual for him, he was sulking, or so it appeared. He allowed her to climb up unassisted.

Now it was her turn to sulk. 'I walked farther than I expected. Mr Golson will be wondering.' Whether she had put things right or not she would leave it at that; while Teakle silently changed gears and remained as anonymous as possible.

Unlike yesterday, Curly Golson had shaken off his luncheon, and was standing looking anxious beneath the stucco archway which framed the entrance to the hotel.

'Anything happen, sweetheart?' he asked somewhat angrily.

His wife sounded equally peeved. 'We had a — puncture.'

'What's the cove been up to? Doesn't take all that time to change a wheel.'

'It was something technical – some difficulty over tools.'

Foolish of her not to have been less precise, but she could not care as she led the way to the little gilt cage in which the hunchback liftman hoisted them by a greasy rope to the second floor.

When she had got herself out of her frock, Curly became affectionate: he would have liked to stroke, to kiss her shoulders, till she took refuge in a négligée.

'Aren't we changing for dinner?' he asked with a sudden show of gloom.

'No,' she said. 'I have a headache. I'll get them to bring me something on a tray. Perhaps write a letter or two. Ought to write to Eadie Twyborn.' For the second time this evening Mrs Golson felt she had been unnecessarily precise.

Curly's eyes bulged when he was thwarted. 'Long time since you mentioned Eadie.'

'Yes. I've been neglecting her. For that matter, she's neglected me. Eadie's aged since their tragedy.'

Curly Golson's eyes resumed their milder china glaze as opposed to their accusing blaze of blue. He had resigned himself.

'I'll go down alone then,' he said.

It would be no hardship for him, she knew, and presently he did, to eat his way from caviare to peaches in champagne.

When she had finished her *œufs sur le plat*, she took out her writing-case and rummaged for one of the larger sheets of her own monogrammed letter-paper, then wondered whether she could fill it. She felt too languid, even, in a strange sense, fulfilled. She sat lumped in what she believed was called a *bergère*, in the same style as the rest of their Louis Whichever suite (the Golsons never did things by halves) at the Grand Hôtel Splendide des Ligures. However sincere her intention of writing, for the moment she preferred thinking about her dearest friend Eadie Twyborn: Eadie down on her knees pulling the tops off onion-grass in her Edgecliff garden, Eadie in that grubby old coat and skirt which was lasting for ever, soil clinging to her fingers, her rings, her father's signet, while the little red Australian terriers sat or lay around, blinking, sniffing, licking their privates, barking when they had cause, or more often when they hadn't. In his study Edward, home from circuit, sat looking through a fresh batch of legal papers. Edward smelled of stale cigar. Eadie, too, smelled of cigar, the cheroots she smoked with Edward up in the tower-room, alone. Nobody and everybody knew about Eadie Twyborn's cigars. She and the Judge had what was

16

considered the perfect marriage, that is, until their disaster, which in no way damaged their relationship, only them.

Eadie was drunk when she said, 'You, Joan, are the one I depend on – for some reason. I can scratch my navel and you won't bawl me out. I can blub if I feel like it, and you'll – oh, I don't know.' She did, though; you and Eadie both did.

'Of course my stupid darling judge comes first.' Eadie poured some more into her own brandy balloon; she was quite maudlin – disgusting really. 'It's brought Edward and me closer.'

Joan re-arranged her letter-paper. She wrote in her large bulbous hand – tonight it looked enormous:

Dearest Eadie,

There she stopped as though daunted by that exceptionally stylish comma; and might get no farther.

She was practically snoozing: it was the bland, buttery eggs and the half-bottle of champagne Curly had insisted on ordering; it was Curly's cure for everything. She loved him, she supposed, his generosity, even his baldness: she would lie holding his head against her breast as though brooding on a giant egg.

But as she sat snoozing, or allowing her mind to flicker amongst the tufts and wands of plants, the scents of evening, the silken swaths of colour with which the bay was strewn, the owners came out from the house, in which lights were burning, making its walls, which should have looked less substantial in their dissolution by dusk, if anything more solid, like a hollowed pumpkin with a candle in it. She heaved sniggering in the Louis Whichever *bergère*, but only for a moment; her actual surroundings were too ephemeral, banal, too downright vulgar. Back in the garden the others had reached her side and were supporting her, the cold bloodless fingers of the more controlled elderly pianist, and the terracotta, votive hands of his mistress-wife. They were leading her along the paths of the garden, then through the rooms of their enchanted house, past the upright, 'fun' piano (no, they couldn't be the owners; they were the tenants of the pseudo-villa) the lamp with its porcelain shade lighting them in their solemn progress.

Somewhere in a narrow hall, in the region of a console, above it a mirror, they parted from the man in black. He would stay behind, no doubt reading; yes, he looked a bookworm. She might have turned to thank him had she known in which language to communicate with her friends. So far, she realized, language had not mattered: they relied on touch, glances, and the smiles which united the three of them, as the two on the music-stool had been united earlier that evening by music and a sensual embrace. (Though she had not taken part in it, Joan Golson could feel the warm saliva in her mouth.)

And now, though she should have thanked him for his kindness, she did not turn towards this man standing hesitating in the hall, but allowed the young woman to lead her on, bumping their way, burrowing down passages the villa or cottage had failed to suggest to a common *voyeuse*. Until settling into a room of apparent importance and their evident goal, the woman or girl was helping her out of clothes which clung like refractory cobwebs, and into the bed which she had warmed with a copper warmer conveniently standing amongst a hearthful of glowing pine-knots.

Joan was acutely conscious of the embossed pattern of fruit and flowers on the copper warmer which was first slid between the sheets waiting to receive her. Language was what she could not sort out: perhaps it was the language of silence as the young woman turned her noble head towards her, the invited guest holding in her whiter, plumper fingers a stronger terracotta hand, but from which, in spite of its warmth, she experienced no response, little enough illumination from the white smile in a terracotta face.

Mrs Golson roused herself from a smell of singed or sun-bleached sheets.

On the sheet which she had before her on the table she saw that she had written: *Dearest Eadie* – comma.

She giggled slightly, remembering how on one occasion Eadie had given herself a moustache, dashed off with burnt cork, and they had dressed – or Eadie had – and ordered drinks in a hotel winter garden, and joined in with the guests at a formal dinner dance, Eadie in the Judge's check trousers, Joan in her pale blue charmeuse, everybody staring at them.

Oh dear, write to poor old Eadie Twyborn, tell her about the couple at the villa – if that would ever be possible . . .

7 feb. 1914

A day which should have been idyllic grew increasingly black, ending in storms, after a real Visitation. Could not believe as this sporty motor surged up our hill that it was Eadie's pal J.G. sitting in the back seat. But crikey, it was! Angelos tells me not to worry. I don't, of course. But why should I be persecuted? Eadie has sent her. A. says no, Eadie couldn't have, it's nothing but coincidence. Angelos is always right. Or not always. Only when he isn't wrong.

But just when I'd begun to order my life, perhaps even make it into something believable, this emissary comes to smash it to pieces. Nothing so brutal as a soft, silly woman.

Everything, I now see, has been leading up to this act of aggression. Gentle perfection is never allowed to last for long. The more laboriously it has been built up, the more painfully it is brought down.

Text for every day to come: *I must not dwell on Joan Golson's arrival on the scene.*

Had hardly blundered back to consciousness this morning when A. reminded me that it is my birthday. I hadn't forgotten, but it's pleasant to be reminded. He brought out presents: the fan (spangled gauze — slats in mother o' pearl) and a shawl embroidered with pomegranates. Both extremely pretty. But what I loved best was his less material present, which we shared as never before. Why am I besotted on this elderly, dotty, in many ways tiresome Greek? I can only think it's because we have been made for each other, that our minds as well as our bodies fit, every bump to every cranny, and quirk to quirk. If I hate him at times it's because I hate myself. If I love him more deeply than I love E. it's because I know this other creature too well, and cannot rely entirely on him or her.

It was one of the hyacinth mornings, a sea breeze blowing not only its own salt but all the early perfumes of the garden in at the window. When Angelos had left me and started sponging himself I sat by the window in my pomegranate shawl fanning myself with the spangled fan. Delicious fluctuations on bare skin. Looked at myself in the glass and decided I would pass. As I do! Or at any rate, on the days when I don't hate — when I can forgive myself for being me. So that I'm not purely the narcissist I'm sometimes accused of being — by Angelos on his worst days — and as I am, undoubtedly, on mine.

He comes back into the room rejuvenated by friction, bald head shining, the still black fringes of hair standing out like the spines of a sea-urchin as he rubs himself with his towel. For a man in his sixties his legs are remarkable: muscular, firmly planted on the ground, the old man's usual ganglion of veins scarcely visible in A.'s case.

He said, 'I was wrong to give you these things. You have dressed yourself up like a whore, sitting at the open window by morning light.' We both laughed. His teeth are still brilliant. Mine will crumble before I'm even half his age. I shall hope to crumble, not teeth alone, but entirely. God spare me a gummy old age!

Angelos holding his head on one side as he continues drying the back of his neck, eyeing me with bright, predatory eye, light playing on the polished curve of the ivory beak, a smile coming and going in response to the voluptuous pleasure of friction . . . We might have begun again, devastating, perhaps even destroying each other in the course of one, silken morning if we hadn't heard Joséphine arriving.

When I am clothed and more or less in my right mind I go out to say the right thing. She has brought me the prettiest bunch of flowers — *n'y a que celles qu'on trouve aux champs*. There are wild candytuft, marigold, anemones, a kind of wilting celandine — all tightly bound together by stalks of grass, and warm from the hand of Joséphine: this solid, russet girl, glowing from her walk up the hill from the village on one of the more benign mornings of early spring on this favoured coast. Joséphine looks good, smells good (that smell of innocent soap, unconscious virtue, and honest exertion) *enfin* Joséphine is unmistakably GOOD. How unforced and enviable! This morning she wishes me health and many years of life. Her smiles are genuinely for my future. Yet Joséphine has been sad lately: at times all sighs and sniffs — her sister who is marrying away — the widowed mother who may move back to her native Toulon. Is Joséphine about to leave us? All the symptoms would suggest that. But not today. Joséphine won't dare give notice on a birthday.

Angelos said she will. He says a Greek lives by his heart, a Frenchman — and how much more a French*woman* — according to reason. 'Joséphine has given you this charming bouquet to soften the blow it is reasonable for her to deal us. You do not want to believe this because Anglo-Saxons are by nature — most of you — Christian Science. You cultivate your Science to its utmost — all of you, all — the moment a slave threatens to defect.'

I wouldn't admit that he's right, but he is. Joséphine will defect this evening.

The ruddy skin of this clumsy but touching girl is peppered with little moles which suggest that somebody once let off a shotgun at her. She even smells of gunpowder after the walk up from the village.

When she first came to us I told A., and because he didn't think of it himself he said, nonsense, she only needed a bath. I told him, 'If I found myself alone in the house with Joséphine I might feel inclined to rape her.' He said I was trying to make myself sound

20

experienced, but that he was pretty sure I had never slept with a woman. 'In fact,' he said, 'I know you haven't, my dear Eudoxia, because if you had you wouldn't be blushing now – like an embarrassed schoolboy who hasn't been near the brothel he claims to have visited.'

I expect I had asked for it. I was relieved when he left me alone.

Angelos considers that men are to women as apples to figs, the clean and the messy among fruits. I am not prepared to argue. He disgusts me at times – this sensual Greek whose every hair rouses me.

He says that he never considered himself a sensualist, just a normal man, till I appeared. Whether to take this as a compliment I can't decide. After Anna died he had avoided intimacy with other human beings. His Smyrna family had a puritanical streak: his aunts, some of his uncles, not his mother, most of all his wife Anna, who seems to have set herself up as a professional saint. It was only after a branch of the family business took him to Alexandria that the rot set in, preparing him for his relationship with me after the fatal encounter at Marseille!

I am told this on his worse days. I become the flower of his decadence, the seeds of which were already sown in Nile silt. It is usually a day of rain, of retribution, of family history, when he airs his theories. (As for Greek family history, outsiders cannot hope to penetrate what they are expected to accept.) I shouldn't complain. I wouldn't care to have Angelos burrow too deeply into my past, not that there is much fear of his unearthing shame, only pain.

Anna according to the photograph: plushy figure on a steel framework, pallid skin rather doughy in texture, vague hair, the Greek eyes – a smouldering of masochistic coals. I bet Anna staged a Greek tragedy or two. And he loved her for it. That is what they understand best: masochism on a stony mountain, a white chapel perched on its summit to commemorate a hypothetical saint. So he canonized his Anna.

I expect we are all jealous of the women in their past, but how much less exciting if the women had not kept the bed warm.

I'm not ungrateful, only resentful of certain aspects of life which must remain withheld from me, th   h I try to persuade myself I can experience *all* by efforts of will or imagination. Here I am, 25 today, but fruitless as the moment I was born. How green and vulnerable nobody can suspect, not even my darling Angelos. If I hadn't found Angelos Vatatzes I would have sunk – or might have swum?

I blame Joan Golson for the morbid rubbish I'm writing tonight. I'd be tempted to conjure up my own collection of family snapshots, submit to that sly look which hindsight reveals on innocent faces, like the unconscious cynicism surfacing from childish letters lovingly bundled by a mother with expectations of posterity. I might have enjoyed a painful wallow (talk about masochistic Greeks!) if I hadn't destroyed most of what would incriminate . . .

After lunch we settled down to a siesta, longer than usual and more languid from the pleasures of early morning.

I awoke to hear dishes being slung about in the kitchen — a sound which creates a void in a house at the best of times. Angelos continued lying on his back. Made sure he was still breathing. The eyelids of old, sleeping men can be terrifying.

While dressing I prepared myself for hearing that Joséphine will move to Toulon with that dreadful mother of the weeping ulcer. It is on the left leg, and Madame Réboa loves to roll the stocking farther down, to explain to her victim of the moment *comme je souffre vous n'avez aucune idée et la plaie n'est plus belle avec le pus qui coule tout le temps*. Madame Réboa's ulcer is by no means pretty, but most of us have one, while concealing it. It is Fernande her eldest who is marrying (a carpenter) and will live at Arles. Céleste the youngest (*ma plus belle fille*) has a *matelot* in gaol at Marseille for some offence which is never mentioned.

When I have finished dressing and go out to Joséphine, it is just as we have suspected. She is standing moist-eyed amongst the glistening dishes. The words she uses, like *bonté*, *cœur*, *aimable*, are not her own. One wonders who has lent them. Not Madame Réboa, who never for a moment verges on the abstract. I say that it is very sad, that I have valued her friendship as much as her services. (True, but the truth is not always enough to prevent one feeling a hypocrite.) Has she a friend, perhaps, who will come to us? In fact she has not, but will consider. (I like to think I am acquitting myself with aplomb, as my mother would. I do indeed detect echoes of her in my voice — a distasteful discovery if Mother weren't so professional.)

I tell Joséphine that, as her decision was unexpected, she will have to return for the wages we owe her, and a little present (money of course) which I want to give her. (My mother would have carried off this part of the performance with greater style.)

But at last it is done, and I leave Joséphine arranging, thoughtfully and for the last time, the washed dishes, the scoured pans, in our cupboards, before taking off her apron, preparing to rejoin her mother who is, *sans doute*, behind it all. The good Joséphine of russet cheeks and shot-speckled neck will provide another snapshot to add to my collection of reprehensible innocents.

Angelos looking every inch a spry Greek half his age suggested we walk to the village, to purge ourselves of the effects of Joséphine's 'surprise'. Angelos who can smile his way through any of the less subjective situations was accordingly purged. I was not. Aware of Madame Réboa's plan, the whole of Les Sailles watched us with the complacent expressions of initiates: the postmistress, the baker's wife, Monsieur Pelletier in his newspaper kiosk, even the fishermen mending their nets. Am I absurd? Perhaps I am. I must accept it when people stare at me. Angelos says, 'They are planning what they will do with you, Eudoxia, after dark, when they can enjoy the freedom of their thoughts.'

The freedom of one's thoughts . . . My thoughts were never a joy – only my body made articulate by this persuasive Greek. Then I do appear consecutive, complete, and can enjoy my reflection in the glass, which he has created, what passes for the real one, with devices like the spangled fan and the pomegranate shawl.

(Is it so very different from Joanie Golson? Isn't that what one is aiming at? Ugh!)

When we had bought some stamps, and *Le Figaro*, which A. feels duty-bound to read while never doing so, we return by the coast road. (This was where the fishermen aimed their smiles. Toe-nails in yellow horn . . . Scabby, swollen hands, but each man as finical in mending his net as a broiderer poised above her frame of *petit point*. The dainty fishermen! My coarse mouth lingering over their ignorance of life.)

We walk. It was A. who wanted the coast road. My instincts were against it, but I could not have explained if he had asked me to. Had I known what was in store for us en route and on arrival at the villa, I might at least have made a womanly scene. To introduce Angelos to more than the bare details of my past is something I have always failed to do, just as he feels he cannot convey the essence of his, or nothing beyond stationary figures with traditional features: the photograph of the Smyrna family, the icons of St Anna and the three Emperors of Byzantium-Nicaea. He tries endlessly, God knows, substituting himself for each Imperial Highness in turn, but another person's past can become a joke, then a bore. If I've given up rubbing Angelos's nose in mine, it's not because I might appear a joke or a bore, but because I'm afraid of what I might find.

My Angelos grasps me by an arm as we climb the road through the tunnel of cedars above Les Sailles. 'Beau Séjour' has been taken over by Americans, one hears. A.'s arm and wrist have grown frail, those of an aged man, when he isn't. We climb towards the peak of our evening, which has not yet been hinted at, unless as a vague unease. Twigs snapping under foot, the smell of something — fungus? excrement? a dead animal of some kind? At 'Beau Séjour' tables at which the guests will sit when the places have been set, the candles lit and slewing in the wind. A livery-faced waiter in his yellowed woollen undervest, buttons sewn to a strip of tape, is laying desultory knives and forks.

'Darling . . .?' My lover turns towards me as though wanting something confirmed.

By the light beneath the cedars he has the teeth of an old Alsatian dog — well, why not, if he's devoted to me — nuzzling at my calf, nosing at the hem of my skirt.

Normally Angelos's teeth are a brilliant white, those of a demanding, sensual man.

'Your serve, Rand . . .' From behind the vines screening the *pension* tennis-court one can hear the felted balls flying back and forth, swish swish of starched skirts, the thump and shuffle of blancoed shoes, the straining, the panting of young men leaping at the net, ribs as taut as racquet strings. An unbearable high chirruping from *les américaines*.

'*Ti echeis, agapi mou? Yiati trecheis?* Why — *run?*'

It isn't possible to explain to those one loves the reason for arbitrary fears if shame is involved. Angelos should understand, but doesn't. My flight from the screened tennis-court at 'Beau Séjour' on the coast road above Les Sailles can only seem ridiculous because it cannot be transposed. Beyond the screen nobody, as yet, has run from the court, while his partner stands, hemline stationary, racquet poised for the decisive shot, her enviably shallow blue eyes still only faintly suspicious of what may be a blow prepared for her. While *he* runs up into and through the house.

'What on earth?' She laughs as she slams the ball against the ivy screen frightening the sparrows nesting in it. 'Impossible creature!' Giggling out of her long, elegant, regurgitating throat; it's *de rigueur* that an Australian girl of Marian's upbringing and class should giggle even when the roof is carried away.

The misdirected ball lands bouncing where nobody will ever discover it.

Marian and the others, her born equals, walk off the court to pour themselves glasses of lemonade. Sinewy wrists, not a tremble amongst them, though Marian's sapphire engagement ring may have caused embarrassment to all three. Down below, at Double Bay, the trams can be heard crossing from opposite directions. At dusk their extremities will flower with sprays of violet sparks.

It was ridiculous of me to give way to panic simply at the sound of tennis balls this evening on the road from the village. I pulled free of his supporting arm. I was hurrying towards the safety one always hopes to find ahead. When I hear the cry, and looking over my shoulder realize it was I who had been supporting Angelos. The terrifying despair in his face and the old man's hand outspread against his chest are too explicit. I run back. It is weeks since the last attack. 'Are you all right?' 'I am all right—a twinge or two . . .' We are so clumsy in our concern, our gestures, our questions and our explanations. Our bodies bump, skins flutter. We have seldom been closer than when seated together on a large porous stone at the roadside: grains of sand have become as enormous as pebbles, fern fronds were never more intricate, a single tender cyclamen is clinging by a crimson thread to the cleft in a rock. These, more than inadequate words, are our comfort, the embodiment and expression of our love.

When he has rested we continue up the hill and the questions really begin.

A.: You will never leave me, will you, E.?

E.: Why should I leave?

A.: You're young.

E.: I was born old.

A.: Your body's young [he laughs] and that is what decides.

E.: My body's what you make of it.

[Both laugh]

We walk on. He is stroking my arm, the tops of his fingers lingering on a scab near the elbow. The evening is falling practically in veils around us.

A.: Do you think we'll find anything to eat?

E.: There's the cold veal.

A.: It's drying up.

E.: Yes, it's drying up. I'll make you some *œufs brouillés*.

A.: Dear Doxy, what would I do without you?

E.: Engage a housekeeper.

A.: So much more expensive.

25

Angelos *is* mean; it is one of the scabs on our relationship, on which I linger in our worse moments. Not a sore spot, but an aggravation, like an old man's fart in the next room.

E.: A fart can't blow us apart.

A.: *Qu'est-ce que tu veux dire, ma chère Eudoxie?*

E.: Neither of us could ever walk out on the other. We've explored each other's scabs, experienced each other's airs and graces. I like to think we understand as far as it is possible to understand.

At this point we reached the gate, which will fall off its hinges if nothing is done about it. Our beloved landlady Madame Llewellyn-Boieldieu will do damn-all beyond let her crumbling villa, her 'Crimson Cottage', to the next unwary tenants. So we submit to the indignities this *demi-Anglaise* subjects us to.

My masochistic lover rather enjoys the indignity of dilapidation. Of the screaming hinges at 'Crimson Cottage', he has said, 'At least they will warn us when the Turk is at the gate.' Not always they won't — not this evening.

Anyway, we had reached 'home' — the blistered paintwork, scurfy walls unchanged, the network of threads and suspended hand-mirror to scare away birds from budding branches, all that has shot or died since we left . . . The scents your skirt drags from the borders of a garden: the drag-net skirt is one of the advantages a man can never enjoy.

On the other hand there is not much that escapes those old drag-net eyes of his. Angelos is a specialist in dredging up the moral wreckage of others, while inclined to remain impervious to his own. His eyes will flicker past his worst faults.

I had barely finished kissing those nut-shell eyelids, and he thrusting himself against me, his laughter radiating through my whole body, when we heard a motor assaulting the hill, emerging from the pines, shaving the garden wall. And there is Mrs E. Boyd Golson staring out; one would say 'glaring' if one didn't know her to be myopic and afraid of limiting her social successes by taking to spectacles.

At least her driver didn't toot, but trust the Golsons to have a klaxon disguised as a brass serpent slithering down to rest on a mudguard.

Angelos couldn't know what had descended on us, except that it was something distasteful, something not quite, but almost American.

26

I lead him away, along the path, into our refuge, where we are left to face the night.

Angelos says, 'I would have liked to make music with you, E., if all inclination has not left me.' His tenses go to pot in a crisis. I tell him I have no inclination either. I bring him the *œufs brouillés*, but he has no appetite. I make myself eat his helping as well as mine. As I gobble the eggs I can feel a trickle down my chin. I must look as thoroughly vulgar as the situation and Joanie Golson call for. Poor cow! She can't help it any more than I can.

I know that before long the Emperor of All Byzantium (Nicaea thrown in for good measure — Mistra too) will begin to accuse the Colonies. Rain is battering the shutters. Madame Réboa will no doubt have started showing her ulcer to a fresh victim. For all his Byzantine pretensions A. might have sprung on Joséphine this evening if she hadn't shed the apron along with the servitude she inherited in our house. Instead he sits rocking in the rented *demi-fauteuil style provençal*.

A. says, 'I will never hold anything against you. Nor anybody. Not even that gangster Palaiologos. Where is Anna my wife?'

The rain is sawing at the shutters. He must know how I hate the name of Anna.

'I expect Anna has taken her martyrdom to Heaven by special ladder.'

I don't think he heard.

'A good woman, but without the flair of the Empress Eudoxia.' He arranges his tongue against his palate before going off into his usual tumbled Imperial catalogue. 'She used to wait on the steps . . . along with the Panhypersevastos . . . the Grand Stratopedarch . . . the Primikerios the Constable the Logothete . . .'

During the recitation he slips lower on his throne. I pour my Emperor another brandy.

He asks, 'Did Anna die at Blachernae? Or was it after we moved to Nicaea?'

Or Smyrna? Or Alexandria? Or even Athens? The Stations of the Greek Cross.

I help him upstairs, by now so sloshed he is only for undressing. Old cold feet, like skate on the fishmonger's slab, the feet of my 68-year-old child, the snoring funnel of the aged mouth . . .

The shutter tears free of the latch, and the room is incorporated into the churning night, the garden threatened with uprooting, its only stable feature the immense olive, in the branches of which the moon appears caught for a second or two, and at intervals the scud of cloud.

How enviable this olive tree encased in its cork armour, hardly a tremor in its gnarled arms, its downthrust roots firmly holding. To have such stability — or is oneself the strongest stanchion one can hope for? To realize this is perhaps to achieve stability.

Writing about oneself at night is release of a kind, but no more than of a kind — like masturbation.

8 feb.

Slept v. little as result of the storm and the Visitation. If I had known there was to be a Second Coming I might have abandoned my old child, made for the railway station at St Mayeul, and spent the rest of the night waiting for the first train — whether to Genoa, Nice, Marseille or Perpignan would not have worried the fugitive.

But this morning was again one of those with which we are blessed in these parts and which exorcise the recurring nightmares.

That very real one: the shutter has flown open, the whole cliffside a churning mass of pittosporum and lantana scrub pressing in upon, threatening all man-made shoddiness. The giant emu's head and neck tormented by the wind. As its plumage is ruffled and tossed, its beak descends repeatedly, almost past the useless shutter, almost into the room where I am lying in my narrow bed, fright raised in goose-pimples, when not dissolving into urine.

Last night, to make this dream more disturbing, my father came in: this tall man with droopy moustache and swollen knuckles — not forgetting the eyes. My father's eyes are the most expressive part of him: a liquid, apologetic, near-black, terrifying when faced with any kind of dishonesty, terrified in turn by the grief of others, poverty, children. I never dared call my father 'Dad' — Mother might become, grudgingly, 'Mum', a sulky 'you' more often than not — but my father could never have been less than 'Father'.

I speak of him as though he were dead, when last night he was standing beside me, after the shutter had burst open and the beak of the giant emu was threatening to descend into the room, to tear me open as I cowered in my narrow, sodden mattress (hair, they had decided, on account of the asthma).

Mastering fear of his own child, my father was standing over me, offering a cold, knobbly hand. Which I took in desperation and love. He was trembling. I could smell his fear. It was that of a man, intensified, and overlaid by those other smells of cigar smoke and port-wine. I guessed that my father must be the only person in the house, otherwise he would not have come in, he would have left me to Nanny, or Mummy, even to Emma or Dora. But here he stood in person by the bed, his waistcoat with one of the points crumpled, the watch-chain with its gold symbols, and the miniature greenstone tiki which somebody had brought back from a holiday at Rotorua, and which I would have loved to fondle had I dared.

And now his hand. I did not dare.

'Is anything wrong?' he asked, 'darling?'

He had never ventured on a 'darling' before, and this confirmed my belief that Father was the only person in the house.

'Is there?'

'No.'

When everything was. I was swimming in it.

Then he said, 'Aren't we a bit smelly?' Shall I change you?'

'No.'

I was brimming with love for this man I was privileged to call 'Father', while going through life avoiding calling him *anything* unless it was dragged out of me.

So I repeated, 'No'.

I could see how relieved he was – this tall, stately, scruffy man. Both my parents were given to food-spots, too argumentative, always in too great a hurry to pay much attention to what they were eating. My mother could look the slut of sluts, and did, except when she set out to kill. But the food-spots seemed to dignify my father, like the asterisks in books too technical to read. My father was essentially technical: a closed book if it hadn't been for his troubled eyes.

Not like those of my more than troubled, my dotty 68-year-old child. Again eyes which are as near as anything black, but ready to splinter into hilarity and rages. Vatatzes is protected by malice, madness, the Byzantine armour inherited from his ancestors, and the infallible weapon with which he overcomes his chief adversary's last resistance.

I have often wondered what sexual solace my parents were able to offer each other. This matter of tense when speaking of parents: as far as I know mine aren't dead, yet almost always I speak of them as though they were. They seemed indestructible; it was their child who died, one of the premature suicides.

When I said he need not change me, Father re-latched the shutter, and managed a smile. The night-light made the smile dip and shudder in his long face. Then, incredibly, he bent and, whether by accident, kissed me on the mouth. It seemed to me I was drawn up into the drooping moustache, as though inside some great brooding loving spider without being the spider's prey; if anything, I was the spinner of threads trying to entangle him more irrevocably than his tentative sortie into loving could ever bind me.

Then the moment broke. He tiptoed out, lapped in and dislocated by the elongating light, and I fell back blissful on my bed of piss which the two of us had agreed to ignore.

This morning was so bland I brought the table out on the terrace at the back without asking Angelos whether I should. He accepted without comment. Too much on his mind, I suspected: Byzantium, Nicaea, our Visitor of the evening before. As he sat behind his cigarette smoke, under the trellis which is already fuzzing with green, on his face that expression of irony which so often foreshadows cruelty, I wondered whether he hadn't shared what was either my fantasy or my dream.

To sidetrack my suspicion I launched into the kind of banal remark one makes in the cause of self-protection. 'Isn't it a lovely morning here on the terrace?'

No reply. I sit watching his pointed teeth, the quiver of a veined eyelid, a slight trembling of the hand holding the cigarette.

'Well — isn't it?' My chest begins to pout inside my morning-gown, which normally would have gratified my nakedness, ourselves alone together until the arrival of the recently defected Joséphine Réboa.

'Nobody,' he aims it with precision, 'can talk of loveliness,' he douses the cigarette in his bowl of unfinished coffee, 'who has not experienced Smyrna. This,' he almost screams, 'this French *post-card* is *nothing*! *La Côte Morte*!' Laughing, but unbalanced by his laughter, this horrible desiccated wretch, to whom I am committed by fate and orgasm — never love. 'At this hour we used to sit on the terrace, looking out across the Gulf — our senses drenched with the tones, the scent of stocks at whatever season — the mauve marble of our house on the Prokymea stained with gold — before the blood began to flow . . .'

'Oh, come off it!'

I realize I am trembling with rage. I am nauseated by the cigarette doused in the bowl of half-drunk coffee, roused by the friction of my gown against my skin, drugged by the colours and scents of Smyrna as conjured up by the old magician. (Isn't this how our relationship works?)

'The year she made her pilgrimage to Tinos — before the Turk was driven out of Thessaly . . .'

'Oh yes, we're off now — off to the Martyrs' Stakes, the Orthodox races . . .'

'. . . I went with her, but only to see they treated her respectfully on the steamer — that they gave her the cabin I'd reserved for Anna Vatatzes — that they did not seat boors at her table in the saloon — and replaced the stained tablecloth. Otherwise, I sat on deck, amongst the peasant women surrounded by their bunches of fowls and bleating kids, the cheeses they were bringing to sell receiving the spray from their vomit. This was *my* pilgrimage from Smyrna to Tinos. On arrival I sit waiting for my sainted wife at a café on the *paralia* — because my faith, or lack of it, will not allow me to go up to the church with her.'

'Masochist, Angelos!'

I am enraged, always, at the sight of the saintly Anna's face, herself a walking candle lighting candles in the dark church. I reach for my lover's hand, past the broken crusts, past the used cups. I disturb the surface of cold *café au lait* in which the cigarette has disintegrated. When I have locked his fingers in mine, we sinners sticky with half-dried semen sit and watch as she kisses her own reflection in the glass protecting the jewelled icon from sinners, germs, and thieves.

Then I lean forward, I cannot restrain my impulse, I kiss the hand I am holding, and we are bobbing like two helpless corks on the tide of our emotions.

'At breakfast, E.!'

I bow my head. I am exposed from my divided breast, past the slope on which my navel is embossed, as far as the muslin folds of my lap.

'Why are you crying, Eudoxia?'

'Fuck it — I'm not! Being emotional isn't necessarily crying, is it? If I weren't emotional, you'd call me a cold fish — or worse still, an Anglo-Saxon. Of all the insulting names you call me, that is seldom one of them.'

We sit laughing, legs entangled under the table, his old bony kneecaps eating into me, neither of us aware that this will be the Day of the second Coming of Our Lady Mrs E. Boyd Golson.

All day long the dream of my Father kept recurring. In a series of waking dreams I found myself adding details to it.

Mummy came in. I was lying vaguely telling the rosary of dreams and thoughts while sucking the forbidden lolly I had hidden under the pillow. She rattatted on my bedroom door, only as a joke, because she barged straight in. I thought at first she must have wanted to catch me at something, but soon realized this was the last thing in her head, she was too exhilarated, so excited it did not even occur to her that she was the one who might be caught out. She was dressed in a pair of check pants and coat which could have belonged to my father. Certainly the waistcoat of crumpled points was his, though she hadn't been able to commandeer the watch-chain. She was wearing a hat, its brim pulled low, which I recognized, as a Sewell Sweatfree Felt. Chugging along in the rear was Joanie Golson, her bosom expiring in palest blue charmeuse.

Mummy announced, 'We are going out, darling. If there's anything you want, Daddy'll be here, reading through some — legal stuff.' She gulped down what was turning into a hiccup.

Though the shutters were closed, and only a feeble glimmer from the night-light swimming in its saucer, a green moon could have been presiding over a painted scene. Its most incredible detail was that Mummy had corked on a moustache: the perspiration had worked its way to the surface and was winking through this corked band, while behind Mrs Judge Twyborn, Mrs Boyd Golson glugged and panted, her charmeuse melons parting and rejoining, parting and rejoining.

Having done their duty by Eadie's tiresome child, the couple left, and I began drowsing and waking, drowsing again, to the tune of Joanie's globular breasts.

Though Mrs Golson re-appeared regularly at the Twyborns', she was on my list of avoidables from the night of the corked moustache until she sprang upon us yesterday.

There was nothing to disturb this afternoon's siesta: Byzantium might never have begun falling apart, figments became the reality parents and lovers like to believe they have created. Could one dismiss as figment Eadie's emissary Joan Golson rising through the dusk in her green motor the other side of the garden wall?

Later this evening, under a resonant sky, Angelos proposed to make music. We did, too.

We launched into the Chabrier waltzes, dashing them off too quickly, turning our backs on other eventualities, side by side on

Madame Llewellyn-Boieldieu's stool. I would like to appear less tentative, less receptive of the ruler and the rules. I would love to *splash* music around me, while A. is determined to control my least impulse for extravagance. His hands. His wrist-watch. His veins. Chabrier's oxidized streamers stream out behind us, in my case never freeing themselves because knotted to my wrists, and because the old bastard won't allow me the freedom of music.

All desire for music had left me. I knew I was giving a brazen performance, but saw it through. Blew a raspberry at the end. Overtaken by contrition, I forced an embrace on him. Normally we would have joined also in laughter. Not now. He began what was a visible gnashing: a guard dog's teeth, flared nostrils, not a dog's, those of a frightened man, the gristle in an aristocratic nose rising out of transparency, thickening at a bridge still delicate. There have been times when I could have bitten off this nose.

As he gnashes, he warns, 'I think she has come again, E.!'

Not so soon. It wasn't possible.

'*Comme hier soir . . . Ti zeetahiy afti then xeroh . . .*'

I jump up and look out. There she is, sure enough, against the wall, under the olive which till now was my best protection. Her surroundings and her body make her Paris clothes look ridiculous, giving a couturier's model the stamp of Golson's Emporium Sydney Australia. Whatever the label, Paquin or Golson, it is Eadie's Joanie.

I latch the shutters.

This evening we didn't eat. Neither of us had appetite, thirst only. And as he quenches himself in brandy, the Pantocrator rises, like the phoenix strewing his golden plumage on the head of the one faithful — his hetaira.

He says, 'They shut her in a tower. My wife Anna. Or was it my mother? Or my concubine? Or the Empress Eudoxia?'

'Oh, come off it, darling! My Australian arse won't take any more!'

I try dousing the two of us. My eyelids will only half-open. I am a bundle of sticks and rag, an old battered umbrella.

My darling's skin is turning black.

'They shut her in a tower at Pera.'

'Yesss!'

The ivy alive with Australian sparrows.

I know, I know the smells the feel of a monk's clammy hands candle-wax sweat verdigris cold slimy *kritharakia* in the tower in

33

which I am in-carc-er-ated the cancerous tower of a dying human relationship.

He breaks up. Laying his head on the keys of the piano. To which we have returned inevitably, to be played out.

I ignore my lover and unlatch the shutter. Outside, the past is spread, in pools of blue, in black limbs, in felted voices. I lean against the sash. If only to be drawn back into what I could not endure, but long for . . .

By now she knew the narrow streets by heart. She knew the abridged biographies of the girls who worked for the pharmacist, every fly which crawled on the chicken livers and rabbits at the poulterer's, the almost petrified heap of excrement (human, she suspected) on the paving at the south-west corner of St Sauveur. She had read every novel in the catalogue at the English Tea-room and Library, excepting those withheld from her by conspiracy. At the Grand Hôtel Splendide des Ligures, *ces Anglais Monsieur et Madame Golson* were on the verge of acquiring the status of permanent guests.

Or so it seemed to Curly.

'Don't know what's got into you, Joanie. Why do we have to stay, treasure?'

'But you love it,' she replied. 'And Lady Tewkes would be so offended if she thought we didn't appreciate St Mayeul.'

Curly grunted. He was happy enough eating through the menu, then sleeping it off. He enjoyed paying his respects at the races at Nice, and in the rooms at Monte, where Teakle drove him when Joanie didn't need the car.

She didn't need it all that much, unless on principle, to be driven out for the good of her health like any other lady of means. As she had grown familiar with every detail of St Mayeul's streets, so she was becoming familiar with the roads radiating from the town. She had appropriated, so to speak, even the more obscure lanes. She knew which faces to expect at farm or vineyard. Sometimes young people, children, or the very simple took it into their heads to wave, but Mrs Golson did not return their wave. She was not sure whether she ought in front of her English chauffeur, though in fact it would have been behind his back.

It was really too ridiculous: that she should discover in herself traits belonging not so much to a snobbish woman as a guilty little girl. At the heart of her confusion stood the image of the crackled-pink villa, where the road past the salt-pans burst from the pine-grove and embraced the hill. Actually the road was one with which Mrs Golson was less familiar than most of those which formed the surrounding network, in that she had suppressed her desire to return after her two initial visits. She did not dare, but must of course, eventually. The villa remained so vivid: not the vividness of actuality, more a sensation, a pervasiveness, as in dream landscapes. It worried her. Somehow she must find the strength to break the spell.

She still had not found it when circumstances began the breaking.

She was walking with her husband under the palms in the hotel gardens, an undistinguished though impeccable grid, with its pebble paths, borders in variegated box, and beds stuffed with what Mrs Golson believed are known as French marigolds. She had run into Curly by chance on his return from the races at Nice, where Teakle had driven him earlier that day. Not having the car, she had set out to climb the hill behind the town, and now her feet were hurting. This contributed to the tiresomeness of what Curly was telling about his flutter or two on the horses.

When he went off in another direction. 'On the way back we took a wrong turning, and found ourselves on a side-road Teakle said you particularly fancy. He's driven you there more than once since we came here.'

'I can't think of any such road.'

'We came back through some sick-looking pines—past a string of stinking salt-pans.'

'To be precise, he drove me there twice.' At once Mrs Golson regretted her precision. 'I found it not nearly so attractive as I first imagined.'

'Anyhow, we were almost let in for an accident, not far from where Teakle said you had a puncture.' The way Curly spoke, it was she who had had it, not the car.

Mrs Golson realized she was breathing hard. 'How—an accident?'

'A couple coming round a corner— not looking where they were going.'

'What did this *couple* look like?' Did her enquiry sound too intense?

'Some old Frog, and a girl, walking hand in hand.'

'What makes you think he was French?' she asked.

'Well, he was wearing a beret.'

She was really exasperated. 'Lots of the English wear them—those

35

who have lived abroad. There's Mr Mercer here at the hotel – and Lord Corfe,' she remembered with warmer satisfaction.

'That's right. You wouldn't find a bigger Pom than that.'

Mrs Golson merely frowned.

'Anyhow, this old cove, whatever he was, looked a bit potty. Waved his arms, nearly laughed his head off after we swerved. Likes to live dangerously I reckon.'

Mrs Golson rose above her exasperation, frustration, what amounted almost to misery. 'Did you have any conversation with them – after you'd practically run them down?'

'No question of running 'em down. Teakle's too professional. I wouldn't be paying him otherwise. No, we just drove on. What would we have talked to them in?'

'But the girl – she must have been terrified!'

'I looked back. And she was looking back. She was in a regular paddy, I'd say, like some women get into for no good reason. The girl was a looker, in more ways than one,' then Mr Golson decided to add, 'if you like 'em flat,' and caressed his wife's behind with a hand.

'I do wish you wouldn't do that, Curly!' She might have addressed him as 'Boyd' but propriety did not allow her to go so far.

She was looking nervously from side to side, past the trunks of the abraded palms. There was a smell she disliked, perhaps from the (French?) marigolds.

'I was only being friendly,' he said.

'There's a time and place for friendliness.' Not even then, her tone seemed to imply.

They had reached the stucco entrance archway.

That night Joan Golson developed another headache. She did not go down with Curly to dinner. She refused even to contemplate a tray with *œufs sur le plat*. She was too restless. She unearthed the sheet of paper on which she had written *Dearest Eadie* (comma). She knew she would not bring herself to write, however accusatory that stylish comma on which her will-power had fizzled out. What could she have said? Subtle she might aspire to be, but her intuitions had often let her down.

Curly said a few days later, 'I'll give you a couple more weeks, Joan. We can join the *Simla* at Marseille. If I don't show up soon at the "shop" they'll be wondering what I'm playing at.'

As democratic Australians the Golsons were in the habit of

referring to Golson's Emporium as the 'shop'. His wife might now have suggested, had she been at all malicious, that it wouldn't have occurred to them at the 'shop' to wonder what Curly was playing at. His business duties consisted of little more than initialling the letters they left in his tray, and reading the *Sydney Morning Herald* until it was time to lunch at the club. It was Mr Darling who mattered: they depended on Darling for their considerable income; though no one could deny that E. Boyd Golson, as a member of his family, was a figure, and that he had a gift for jollying the directors at a meeting; anyway they laughed.

As Mrs Golson was to no extent malicious she remained silent; then she said, 'If you really want it, we could leave tomorrow, motor back to London for a last fling, and board the wretched *Simla* at Tilbury.'

'Not if it'll put you out.' He was rather sweet, liable not to want his own way once he had got it. 'It's only a mystery what you find in St Mayeul. I'd begun to wonder whether you were having an affair.'

She was so furious. 'An affair with who?' More furious for having forgotten her grammar.

'I don't know. Somebody. The lift fellow!'

It would have been too ridiculous to go on feeling furious, so she began laughing, rather hysterically it sounded. 'That hunchback? Do I strike you as being so depraved?'

Curly was bellowing back; he had never looked shinier. 'You can take a joke at your expense, darling. Expect that's why I married you. Though come to think,' he began subsiding, 'some of your friends . . .'

'Are hunchbacks?'

'I was thinking of old Eadie Twyborn.'

'Poor Eadie! We know what she's been through.' Mrs Golson felt she must be looking pale under the faintest dash of rouge she was wearing out of deference to France.

'She's got quite a reputation.'

'Eccentric, we know.'

'Bruce Benson swears he's seen Mrs Judge Twyborn dressed in her husband's pants, ordering drinks in the Australia winter garden.'

'Are you sure she wasn't wearing the Judge's wig as well?'

Curly nearly split himself. 'He didn't *say* . . .'

'I wouldn't put it past a male gossip.' Then, as Curly mopped his face, 'Eadie is my friend, and I won't have her traduced by Mr Benson or anybody else,' Mrs Golson asserted sententiously, while hoping the impressive word she had used in poor Eadie Twyborn's defence meant what she thought it did.

'What he did say,' muttered Curly into his handkerchief, 'was that she'd corked on a bloomin' – *moustache*;' and he was off again in the handkerchief.

Mrs Golson announced that she was going to the English Tea-room and Library to look for a novel before the rain set in.

It was a blustery day, by far the most unpleasant since their arrival on the Coast. The wind slapped at her, and worried the tails of her lesser sables. It made her feel nervy, on top of the scene with her husband. Mrs Golson could not be accused of telling a lie in defending her friend; there are the occasions when it is necessary to smudge – 'smudge' somehow made it look dirty – to *blur* the truth. That way Joanie could feel justified, if still unhappy for the blurred thought that she had been defending herself every bit as much as Eadie.

Foolishness no doubt. She composed her mouth, raised her chin, only to be confronted with the image of the pink villa netted in stereoscopic detail by her veil: through branches of olive and almond the faded blue of eaves and shutters, the tumbledown gate, the clumps of lavender and southernwood, the blobs of red or pink pinks. The scene with Curly made what should have appeared romantic, poetic, a refreshing recollection, take on tones which she could only see as sinister. She closed her eyes to dismiss the image, and with it, she hoped, the direction her train of thought might take. There had never been anything the least bit sinister about Joanie Sewell Golson, Daddy's blue-eyed girl, Curly's wife, and Eadie Twyborn's loyal friend.

None the less, she was relieved to arrive at the English Tea-room and Library, except that, as she turned in, she caught sight of a pouting, heavy, middle-aged woman, over-dressed for a walk through a provincial town. (Plate-glass, she reminded herself, never tells the truth; it was a well-known fact.)

Mrs Golson got up her best manner for Miss Clitheroe presiding behind the counter which dispensed rock-cakes and scones together with culture.

Mrs Golson had brought her Hall Caine to exchange for an Edith Wharton long coveted but never secured.

Miss Clitheroe barely glanced at the shelf. 'Edith is out. More probably stolen. She means so much to us at St Mayeul.'

Rather glumly Mrs Golson accepted *The Hand of Ethelberta* while trying to console herself with the thought that some considered Mrs Wharton 'sarcastic'.

Miss Clitheroe was the kind of Englishwoman established in foreign parts who made people grateful for any of the smaller mercies she vouchsafed. She was so thin, so high-toned, so assured, and had lived abroad so long she could afford to be patronizing. Her French exhibited a fluency that nobody, not even the French themselves, would have dared reject, its timbre reminiscent of a struck gong.

Mrs Golson would never have admitted that Miss Clitheroe terrified her. She did not know, poor thing, that others, not only Colonials, but fairly intrepid English, had experienced the same terror while ordering their tea and scones or exchanging their library books. Nor were they reassured by her smile, if she deigned to subject them to it, while staring through her gold-rimmed spectacles along the ridge of what could have passed for a high-born nose, in which was rooted, above the swell of the right nostril, a small but noticeable, tufted mole. Miss Clitheroe was familiarly, and always spotlessly dressed, in a pale brown, or what she herself referred to as a 'biscuit' smock.

Mrs Golson dipped her eyes before the Englishwoman's superior stare. Far too much had happened today; little did she know that more was to happen.

Miss Clitheroe might have known from the way she kept glancing at the clock and tapping her ring on the counter – a father's signet, Joanie realized, such as Eadie wore.

Such an air of prescience in the proprietress made the customer swivel on her heels, and there was the charming young creature of the pink villa walking past the English Tea-room's bow-window.

'Oh,' Mrs Golson began to churn it out, 'who is that young person – just walking past – Miss Clitheroe?' She heard herself generating the unpleasant sound of phlegm she associated with the thick enunciation of certain men, her husband included.

'That is Madame Vatatzes,' Miss Clitheroe replied without hesitation.

Mrs Golson confided, 'I've seen her – or so I believe.' Then, regrettably, she giggled.

Miss Clitheroe went on tapping her father's ring on the counter. 'A charming young woman.'

'Charming – yes, charming.'

They were on about it, *ratatattat*.

39

Miss Clitheroe said, 'I can't say I'm acquainted with her. Nor her Greek husband, who is somewhat – well, eccentric.'

Miss Clitheroe paused in her tattoo.

Mrs Golson said how interesting – 'A *Greek*!'

'Oh, yes,' Miss Clitheroe replied, 'we're near enough to the Near East.'

After which they both fell silent.

Till Mrs Golson asked, 'What is *she*? I mean, of course, her origins.'

Miss Clitheroe hesitated. 'She could be English. She is very well-spoken. But one can't always tell, can one? in a world like this.'

She looked at Mrs Golson, who feared that she was being lumped among the undesirables.

But what the deuce, as Curly might have said. She was obsessed by her vision of the young woman in the velvet toque, the rather ratty stone-marten stole, in transit past the tea-room window. The reflections in plate-glass would never distort Madame Vatatzes as they are reputed to, and do distort those who are in for punishment.

Although Madame Vatatzes was not wearing them, she had left behind her, Mrs Golson thought she detected, the scent, the blur of violets.

Oh, ridiculous!

While Miss Clitheroe had begun a recitative from behind the counter. 'They are out at "Crimson Cottage".' She gave it a French pronunciation, and nobody, least of all Mrs Golson, would have disputed her right to do so: she had lived so long on the Coast, and besides, the spit which flew out through the gaps between her teeth defended her bona fides. 'They rent the place from Madame Llewellyn-Boieldieu – slightly Welsh through the Llewellyns of Cwm. Her husband, Monsieur Boieldieu, didn't recover from an accident.' Here Miss Clitheroe glanced at the clock. 'Are you acquainted with Madame Boieldieu?'

Mrs Golson was going at the knees. 'I know nobody,' she confessed feebly, and ordered a pot of strong tea.

Miss Clitheroe was not amused; she called, '*Geneviève? Un thé.*'

'*Pas de scones? Pas de rock-kecks?*' Geneviève called back from the depths.

'*Rien d'autre*'; Miss Clitheroe was very firm about it. '*Je suis en retard.* You will understand,' she told her customer, 'an invalid friend is expecting me.' She began throwing a handful of *rock-kecks* into a cardboard box.

From her experience of the English Tea-room's *rock-kecks* Mrs Golson hoped the invalid friend would have the strength to cope.

She herself was coping with the tea, which she soon rejected forcibly. 'I too,' she said, and smiled, 'am late. My husband will be wondering.'

Husbands! Miss Clitheroe's stare implied.

When Mrs Golson had paid for the nasty tea she was abandoning (it was the idea of tea more than tea itself that she had needed as a fortifier) she hurried off in the direction taken by Madame Vatatzes. Conscious of Miss Clitheroe's stare boring into her shoulder blades, she would have liked to point out that the direction was unavoidable, since Madame Vatatzes had been heading towards the Grand Hôtel Splendide des Ligures.

Everything today was unavoidable, it seemed, for here on the edge of the hotel garden there had gathered a group of sympathizers, voluble but ineffectual, round one who appeared to have suffered a mishap. The person was seated on the low wall containing the hotel garden, just outside the rotunda where a musical trio of sorts performed at this hour of afternoon.

With joy and dismay Mrs Golson realized that the individual exciting the pedestrians' concern was none other than Madame Vatatzes.

'*Mais vous devez souffrir, madame, si vous vous êtes foulée la cheville,*' said the least vague, though hardly authoritative member of her entourage. '*On doit vous emmener quelque part . . . au moins appeler une voiture . . . votre mari . . .*'

'*C'est rien. Oui, je souffre un petit peu . . . Je resterai ici quelques instants pour me reposer,*' the young woman replied in a low and level voice, apparently practised in the use of the French language and only slightly foreign in the intonation she gave it.

'*Qu'est-ce que c'est arrivé?*' The crisis made Mrs Golson less conscious than usual of her clumsy linguistic carpentry.

On the credit side, as an Australian she was probably more competent to take the matter in hand than any of those standing round expressing formal sympathy. Realization gave her the courage, moreover, to face the handsome Madame Vatatzes, who in turn seemed to be quailing in the presence of Australian competence.

When she suddenly made the effort to reply in perfectly good English, if slightly flattened perhaps, by whatever it was that had happened to her. 'Something minor and foolish. From thinking of other things I stepped half on half off the kerb and twisted my ankle.'

Although now in the position of *dea ex machina* Mrs Golson blushed with embarrassment for the French she had blurted at one who had such command of English.

'Should you see a doctor perhaps?' she suggested, when she had intended to insist with British firmness.

'Oh no, not doctors! They pull you about so!'

Madame Vatatzes sounded so positive Mrs Golson would have felt ashamed of her miserable suggestion, but had what might prove to be a real brainwave.

'Why not let me help you into the hotel — where I'm staying — and our man will run you home in the motor?'

'Oh, I couldn't *really*!' protested Madame Vatatzes with no good reason.

She had the finest eyes Mrs Golson had ever seen: neither blue, nor grey, nor green, but a mingling of them all, changing probably according to mood or light. Her companion imagined how, on a day which loured less, the eyes of Madame Vatatzes might reflect the sun itself.

Mrs Golson must have appeared so entranced, the eyes could have realized their own power, and relented.

Soon after, Madame Vatatzes sighed, and said, 'You are very kind. Perhaps I'll accept your offer.' She glanced up, smiling not quite at Mrs Golson, as though unwilling to admit her own dependence. 'My husband is getting on,' she said, 'and imagines all the worst disasters.'

Mrs Golson was enchanted to help this lovely young creature hobble as far as the rotunda, and to take upon herself some of Madame Vatatzes' weight. The ugly movements to which the young woman was reduced by her mishap gave her companion strength. As they entered a world of sticky cakes and stickier music Mrs Golson might have discovered a mission.

'Absurd this afternoon music always sounds!' She laughed to apologize.

Mrs Golson would have loved it on her own. She thought she could identify the Meditation from *Thaïs*. She would have loved to settle down with an éclair, followed perhaps by a reckless *Mont Blanc*, and let the music lap round memories of a recently established, intricately constructed, relationship.

'Are you musical?' she asked far more recklessly than she would have downed the forbidden *Mont Blanc*.

'My husband says I'm not,' Madame Vatatzes bit her lip for the pain her ankle was causing her, 'only musically ambitious.'

Remembering the two on their piano-stool, Mrs Golson nursed her secret. Or was it? Had Madame Vatatzes seen her standing at the wall under the olive tree spellbound by the music she had been listening to? She could not be sure. She did not care. To help support the weight of this radiant young woman was in itself enough to dismiss doubts. Mrs Golson was so devoted to her mission she would have got down on all fours and offered herself as a mule if asked.

Instead she announced, at the highest pitch of recklessness, 'We'll take the lift up to our suite – away from this appalling din – and sit in comfort – rest your ankle – while I send for the car.' It sounded dashing, to her herself at least.

Madame Vatatzes hobbled and grinned.

Released by the hunchback from the gilt cage in which he functioned, she stumbled and gasped on catching sight of a figure some way down the corridor. '*Je me demande . . . cette femme de chambre . . .*'

'Charming girl. Joséphine. She came to work here just the other day.'

'She is – or was – my maid,' Madame Vatatzes explained, not without bitterness. 'A liar into the bargain.'

'Oh, they all thrive on untruths!'

'Most of us do. Did you never tell a lie?'

'Oh, well, of course one does – *sometimes* – under provocation – tell a fib!' Mrs Golson admitted and laughed.

'But Joséphine – I thought her too good, too innocent to lie like the rest of us.'

'My dear!' Mrs Golson protested. 'I can't believe you tell untruths!'

Madame Vatatzes, on Mrs Golson's arm, had hobbled almost as far as the corner round which Joséphine had made her escape.

'Yes,' Madame Vatatzes confessed. 'I've never been brave enough to live the truth.'

Mrs Golson felt she was being drawn out of her depth. She did not want to be upset. She was ready to be charmed again.

'And Joséphine needed the money, I expect. We couldn't afford to pay her as much as we ought.'

Madame Vatatzes was far too explicit for Mrs Golson. At the

same time the mention of poverty cheered her up; it gave her back her sense of power. She must think of something, valuable but discreet, perhaps a pretty brooch in *semi*-precious stones, to give this attractive young person. She doubted, however, that Madame Vatatzes would allow herself to be bound.

Just then they reached the door of the Golson suite.

'Oh dear, my husband has been smoking – *cigars*!' Mrs Golson rushed at the window.

'I must say I enjoy the smell of a cigar.' Madame Vatatzes' thoughts seemed to make her feel at home, for she sat down abruptly in the Louis *bergère*; it could, on the other hand, have been pain in her ankle forcing her to take the weight off it. 'In fact,' she confessed, 'I like the smell of a man.'

Breathless from the stiff window as well as confused by the unorthodox remark, Mrs Golson replied, 'Well, it depends – surely. I can enjoy the smell of tweed – and leather – and all that – but I can't say I like a man's smelly smells.'

At once she blushed. She had never felt so tactless, stupid, vulgar. She wondered anyone put up with her. No doubt they would not have, if it hadn't been for her money, it was her own bitterest private opinion on sleepless nights and in the company of those she wished to impress.

But Madame Vatatzes did not seem to question her companion's values. 'Even what you call their smelly smells can have a perverse charm. The smell of an old man, for instance. So many layers of life lived – such a compost!'

It was too much for Mrs Golson. 'Wouldn't you like to take off your shoe? I'll put a cushion under your foot. I could even bathe the ankle. A compress . . . Should it be hot or cold? I can never remember.'

'Oh no, thank you – *really*!' It brought Madame Vatatzes back to her senses.

Mrs Golson noticed that, although the ankles were shapely enough, the young woman's feet were on the large side, hands too, for that matter. Madame Vatatzes must have been conscious of her feet. She made a move as though to hide them under a skirt which was not long enough. Mrs Golson was reminded of an injured bird made anxious by the presence of some additional and possibly graver threat.

'I was only thinking of your comfort,' she said.

It restored her own confidence, if only momentarily.

'Are you English?' she ventured to ask.

'More or less,' the young woman replied.

'You speak the language so beautifully.' Mrs Golson paused, and sighed. 'We are Australians,' she informed her recently acquired friend.

'So I gathered.'

'*Ohhh?*' Mrs Golson mewed. 'Most people tell me there isn't a trace. With men, it's different of course. Curly — that's my husband — is unmistakable. But Curly you haven't met — except . . . No, tell me, *do* — how can you tell?'

'By those I've known.' Here Madame Vatatzes smiled her most seductive smile, then veiled her extraordinary eyes. 'By a certain tone,' she murmured, and left it there.

It went on clanging in Joanie Golson's ears, who, nevertheless, had been known for her game of tennis, and who now played a devious shot.

'Your husband, I take it, is French?'

Madame Vatatzes returned the ball out of Joanie's reach. 'No,' she said, 'he is not French'; and sat contemplating her ankle.

Only Curly's arrival could have affected Joanie worse.

Still looking, it was not at her ankle, but into distance, Madame Vatatzes asked, 'Couldn't you, please, make good your offer? My husband's an old man. And sick. He's probably beside himself.'

Remembering the rorty old boy bashing the piano, Mrs Golson was not deceived by Madame Vatatzes' pathos. She only accepted that the shimmer had faded from the present occasion. What she would have liked to know was how much she had been taken in — but ever. Would she remain the plump turkey, a knife eternally poised above its breast? (She was inclined to dismiss those she had fooled or threatened, because hers was surely only a dessert-knife, not to be taken seriously.)

But she hustled herself away from her doubts, disappointments, and any suspicion of hypocrisy. 'Oh, my dear, of course — I must ask them to find Teakle — get him to bring the car round. We'll have you home in no time.'

Mrs Golson smiled at Madame Vatatzes and Madame Vatatzes smiled back. They might have been forking up *Mont Blanc* together in the rotunda below, enjoying that state of perfect feminine collusion, in which advice is given on the falsification of dressmakers' bills, and what He does to them, or doesn't do, is discussed and deplored.

When Curly had to come in.

Mrs Golson decided on cheerful acceptance. 'This is my husband,' she said. 'Madame Vatatzes, Curly, has sprained her ankle. We met in the street soon after the mishap. I promised that Teakle would run her home.'

If Curly recognized the 'looker' he and Teakle had almost run down while she was out walking with her husband, he made no mention of the incident, to Mrs Golson's agreeable surprise. Surely he must recognize her? He was so obviously appreciative of the creature's beauty.

'You can be sure we'll take the necessary steps, Mrs Vatats . . .' E. Boyd Golson's pores oozed visible enthusiasm.

Madame Vatatzes lowered her eyes. It was less likely that she should recognize a man who had whizzed past her in a motor-car. She was simply embarrassed by Curly's native crudity. At the same time Mrs Golson's mind could not help reverting to their conversation of earlier. Was it that Madame Vatatzes, behind her silence and her modest expression, sat testing, categorizing, perhaps even enjoying, the smell of a man? Mrs Golson was at once shocked by her own disgusting thought, even though it had been forced on her by this new acquaintance.

'. . . do something about it at the soonest . . .' It seemed to Curly's wife that his suit fitted him far too snugly, that he was straining at the seams, cracking, almost stuttering with enthusiasm and the formation of a plan to ease Madame Vatatzes' distress. '. . . only thing – Teakle's gone into Toulon by train with some cove he's palled up with at the old hotel.'

'Then I must make other arrangements. I must hire a cab. I *must* go home,' Madame Vatatzes, again in some distress, insisted.

'And so you shall, dear lady,' E. Boyd Golson assured her. 'I'll drive you there myself.'

'That is so kind. Only three or four kilometres along the road to Les Sailles,' Madame Vatatzes informed him. 'Normally, I walk it. We both walk it – in cool weather.'

'You can rely on me, madam, to drive you to the frontier if necessary.'

This was an event Joan Golson had not bargained for. Again she had the impression of straining tweed, bursting flesh, and worse still, her late father-in-law's professional hands dealing with a bolt of calico. The thought of entrusting her precious jewel to Curly's gallantry was almost more than she could bear.

'Oh, do take care!' she gasped. 'Don't talk too much! My husband's inclined to be a reckless driver.'

She stood pleating the skin above her nose, inside their encrustation of rings her white hands plump and helpless at her waist.

'Nobody else has ever complained about my driving. If you feel that way, Joanie, come along for the spin. Lay a restraining hand on my arm whenever you think it necessary.'

'Oh dear, no! In such a wind — and when was my poor advice ever taken?'

She laughed, and so did Curly.

Then Madame Vatatzes advanced, and again thanked Mrs Golson for her kindness. 'Without you, everything might have been so much more disagreeable.' The young woman's handshake was so frank in its expression of warmth that Mrs Golson's rings were driven into her.

Their visitant was going. She was leaving on Curly's tweedy arm. Joanie had not allowed herself the last delicious spasm of a glance into Madame Vatatzes' eyes. She knew she was sulking, a silly schoolgirl standing in the doorway, no doubt looking white about the gills as she watched them down the corridor. That ratty little fur the girl was wearing! For a mad instant Joanie contemplated tearing her sables off the gilded chair-back where she had hung them, rushing down the grey expanse of corridor, to arrive before the lift door opened, and fling her furs round the girl's shoulders, not so much to spite Curly as to offer a token of her own passion.

But mercifully she did nothing so foolish, and the door of the cage opened, and Madame Vatatzes turned to wave, not with a flutter of the hand as one might have expected, but with the whole arm, describing a lovely, leisurely arc. At this distance one could not distinguish the eyes, but the smile opened in the terracotta face. Mrs Golson was glad she could not see the eyes; they troubled memory, and with it most of the certainties of life.

The Golsons did not investigate each other, unless surreptitiously, till the following morning, for Joan had taken a sleeping draught ('too mild to be habit-forming') and Curly was exhausted by too much unexpected excitement, and finally, too much champagne.

Over breakfast, tea and *assiette anglaise* for Curly, chocolate for Joan ('only one cup — so rich the spoon stands up in the stuff') each wondered how best to re-open the situation of the evening before. When Joan was peeved, he knew too well, she might stay peeved for a day or two; while she could not have borne Curly's boots trampling the most refined and complex sentiments of any she had experienced.

It was Mrs Golson, however, who opened the attack, and brutally. 'I do hope the poor thing wasn't cold – motoring – and only that little balding fur.'

Curly had to laugh. 'You don't suppose, precious, that I let her freeze – that I didn't put an arm round her – on our reckless drive.'

His lips looked quite revolting under the blandishment of fat ham.

'You're so heavy, darling, in your humour. I prefer you when you're natural.' Mrs Golson's pout had a chocolate stain in one corner; she could not know about that, only the dob of chocolate on the bosom of her négligée, with which she was now trying to deal.

'You delivered her safe and sound, I take it. Did they ask you in? You were away so long for such a short distance.'

'We had some conversation on the doorstep. The French don't ask you in.'

'He's not French – and she's English – not quite, but sort of.'

'Well, the old bloke's something foreign – nutty as a fruitcake.'

'Greek, to be precise. I had it from the English Tea-room.'

'Well, foreign. And nutty.'

'Did she tell you anything – on the reckless drive?'

'What would she tell me? We talked a bit – as you do with a woman – an attractive one.'

'I'd have thought her rather too mannish for your taste.' It pained Mrs Golson deeply to have to make this accusation.

'She was decent,' he said, forking into his mouth a sliver of red beef from the depleted serving dish.

'The house, anyway, is most attractive.'

'The house? You know it?'

It seemed to Mrs Golson that her whole ethos, the knowing and the not knowing, the necessary lies and the half-truths, was threatened by her unfortunate lapse.

Then she had another of her brainwaves. 'She told me about it. She described it,' she muttered, 'and it sounded charming. Pink. Slightly dilapidated . . .' She went through a whole catalogue for the garden, as Madame Vatatzes herself would never have done, her garden as familiar as the ratty stone-marten stole; but Curly, who never noticed gardens, would not be aware of her subterfuge.

As indeed he wasn't. 'The gate'll fall down if they don't do something about it,' he declared like any practical Australian male (the elderly refined Greek, Monsieur Vatatzes, would certainly give no thought to the matter as, seated on the piano-stool, he dashed off duets with his charming wife).

' "*Crimson Cottage*"!' Curly snorted, and opened *Le Petit Niçois*, which he did on principle, as part of the morning ritual, while unable to read what was inside. 'Did you know there's a war brewing? I bet you didn't, Joanie treasure!'

She was outraged. 'Of course I did! I have it from the English Tea-room that war is inevitable. Kaiser Wilhelm's determined to have one. The French will resist. The English will come to their assistance – though the French don't count on it. So Miss Clitheroe says.'

'Where does that put us – as Australians?'

Mrs Golson hesitated. 'I expect Australia will do the right thing, provided it doesn't go against good sense.'

'But us Golsons!' Curly insisted.

'Do we count?' Joanie answered.

For an instant they looked at each other, trying to decide.

Then Curly ventured, 'I don't want it to look as though we're doing a skedaddle, Joan dear, but I can't see it 'ud be practical to let the *Simla* sail without us.'

'Yes, darling, I know it would only be *sensible* to catch the *Simla*.' Agitation and the division of loyalties caused Mrs Golson to lash her rather large thighs around each other inside the peach chiffon négligée. 'At least you might investigate – run over to Marseille with Teakle and pay a deposit on the cabin.'

Play for time, play for time . . . Surely there would be a letter of thanks? too much to hope for an invitation? at least a formal call when the ankle allows. Even if they missed the *Simla* her passionate desire to renew acquaintance with Madame Vatatzes convinced Mrs Golson that she was ready to face the passions of war – a war which in any case was only rumoured and too remote from the Golsons to affect their lives.

When Curly said, 'You can be sure I've paid the deposit. It only remains to clinch the deal. And that's what I'm going to do. It wouldn't be reasonable, Joanie, if I didn't.'

'Well,' she said, looking down her front into the jabot in beige Brussels in which the dollop of chocolate had lodged, 'you are a man of course, and your attitude is that of a man. Don't think I don't appreciate you, darling.' She raised her head and aimed a ravaged smile, while stroking the necklaces of Venus in the plump throat which he admired and she deplored. '*But* as a foolish romantic

woman I can't help thinking of all the people – the *little* people –
that *femme de chambre* Joséphine, honest old Teakle remaining behind
in poor England – even the abominably superior Miss Clitheroe –
all those we'd be running away from and leaving to be swallowed up
by a war;' then when she had risen, and executed a figure or two
in peach chiffon, 'the Vatatzes too – that old man and his young
wife – who don't belong anywhere, it seems – but will be caught –
subjected to all the terrors – the horrors.'

Mrs Golson had never thought like this before. She could not help
feeling impressed by her own illumination.

And Curly was so proud of Joanie. He would have liked to bed her
if he hadn't decided to run over to Marseille and make sure of their
passage to Sydney – 'home', as opposed to Joanie's 'Home', where
the shops were, the real, Bond Street ones, not Golson's Emporium.

Joan Golson thought she had probably lost. She would be carried
back out of the iridescence into a congealing of life, from which only
Eadie Twyborn had rescued her at brief moments. And she had
neglected Eadie. That letter she had started and never got down to
writing. But what could one say when all was surmise, suspicion,
doubt, or dream? One would never be able to conclude, never live
out the promises.

15 March

The extraordinary coincidence of yesterday! That it had to happen
– my ankle is nothing, a slight twist, today barely noticeable – but
it had to happen: one of those coincidences of which my life, I
believe *any* life, is composed – in this case so that Mrs Golson might
appear as I sat outside the hotel garden, surrounded by onlookers
offering their formal French sympathy, which falls short of practical
assistance. Oh, we Australians are pretty good in a crisis! For once
I'm not speaking ironically. Joanie did not know it, but I could have
fallen on her bosom as she raised me up and led me into that
pretentious Hôtel des Splendeurs et Misères des Golsons Inter-
nationals. The sticky sweets of *le goûter – les gâteaux et le porto*, not
forgetting *le Massenet*, all around us.

What, I wonder, would have happened if I had thrown myself
amongst the sables, the brooches, my face burrowing into that
Medici frill, or deeper, into the powdered cleavage? Would I have
given Eadie cause for jealousy? (They say that women are not the
worst bitches.)

To give Mrs Golson her due, she showed greater kindness and

50

consideration than I've known in years. As I sat in their gilt 'salon' I could have enjoyed a good cry – but kept it cold – and rightly so. All that about taking off my shoe – herself itching to undo the strap. I could not very well have had Joanie Golson pawing at what has always been my worst feature.

That old pair of shoes I gave Joséphine – she said they were big, too big for her mother, her sister's fiancé had tried and almost got them on. Joséphine was always candid, except in giving notice. You could have knocked me over when I saw her scuttling down the corridor at the Splendeurs et Misères des Ligures. Can't blame her for wanting the extra money and thinking us stingy, all foreigners are believed to be rolling in money. However, that did not prevent me wanting to do her some small form of physical violence as she scuttled off and turned the corner, showing distinct signs of *paint*. Is Joséphine perhaps also something of a whore? If she is, *I* can hardly accuse her.

No, I am not. Though the ring I wear may be part of a disguise, my natural lust has never, unless in fantasy and dream, overstepped the bounds of fidelity. And where there is true love, true lust can surely be allowed?

Anyway, Joséphine who gave notice, and who may or may not be a whore, has been dismissed even from my best memories since she scuttled down the corridor.

The smell of a man – that really shocked poor Joan Golson. It came out. I couldn't help it. In spite of her appearance she's probably refined. Her private tastes would prevent her being titillated by what can be a devastating stench. Not that Eadie can't devastate in that old coat and skirt which will last for ever and which would stand up on its own thanks to compost, food-droppings, and hair from the Australian terriers which climb on her when she has passed out on the library sofa after lunch.

But can tart herself up and be a credit to the Judge on any of those social occasions which women married to the Law are allowed to grace. She has her distinction to fall back on, features, the carriage of a head, which even her enemies (lawyers' wives always ready to prosecute) interpret as aristocratic. Eadie in her tarnished gold brocade, the sable hem and bordered sleeves (moth-eaten to anyone who had looked as closely as her child has) but impressive to others, *imperial* (not surprising she gave birth to a Byzantine empress – or hetaira, according to how you size things up) wearing the few ancestral rings (scrubbed of garden soil with a toothbrush before

51

receptions) and her father's signet. It must have been the General's signet which caught the eye of Joanie Sweat-Free Golson. Which led to the corked-on moustache. And drinks in the winter garden at the Hotel Australia.

I must write to that poor cow J.G., thank her for her kindness, which I like to think was more than the steamed-up passion some women seem able to generate for another — as opposed to the freemasonry (so necessary) which also exists, along with trustful feminine affection.

I admire women, and would like to love them — but it isn't always possible. (Angelos, I believe, both admired and loved Anna, but only lusts after me — the hetaira, and Empress Eudoxia in name.)

Poor Joan, I think, does not love her husband, but like that legion of wives, needs him. After apologizing for his cigar smoke and his Australianness, how she glared when he came in. The Joan Golsons of this world spend their lives brooding over accents.

I don't think I ever set eyes on E. Boyd Golson in the past, only indirectly through the conversation of Eadie and the Judge. I could not have heard about him from Joan because I was either away at boarding school or, after the night of the corked-on moustache, hiding under the hydrangeas whenever she came. Eadie would call, 'Joan's here. Where are you, darling? Aren't you a silly old shy thing! Our friend wants to see you.' It made you burrow deeper into the hydrangeas, into the smell of mould and slaters. After that historic night I couldn't bear her. ('You'll have to understand, Joanie, we have a brumby for a child. It must be my fault, Edward would not have got a brumby on any other woman.' Giggle giggle, and the brumby is soon the least of their preoccupations.)

When here was E. Boyd Golson in the flesh, or I should say, his Harris tweeds, his Jermyn Street boots, his bay rum, with a lingering of Havana cigar and Armagnac — every inch a well-appointed gentleman of means. That he was incidentally an Australian would not have mattered to those who, unlike his wife, care for men. Curly Golson is both pretty awful and rather exciting — to those who care. That I might have cared, wrecked poor Joanie's evening. While Curly cracked, and bulged, and shone — stimulated by his encounter with a female.

Again, I must not be a bitch. I'm sure he loves and serves his wife. Does she deserve it? That is another question.

All the way back along the road to Les Sailles in the Austin car he was as full of gallantry as I can imagine a bull moose in the mating season. I almost reached up and touched the horns, velvety but strong, sprouting out of Curly's tweed cap.

Our conversation:

C.: You know, the first time I saw you I thought, damn shame, but I'd never be able to talk to that lady. She's French, or something.

E.: [regrettably as arch as C.] Was there another time?

C.: The time I nearly ran you down — or Teakle, that's our man. When you were out walking with your husband . . .

E.: That time . . . Well, I do perhaps remember. But vaguely. Other cars have almost run us down. Angelos becomes excited talking. We have so much to discuss. And walk too far out.

C.: [glum] Mrs Golson and I sometimes hardly talk for days — unless about what there is for dinner — or whether we ought to get our boots mended.

E.: Really? [Pause] That's sad, isn't it?

C.: Never thought of it as anything but normal.

E.: Still sad.

Oh, the Australian emptiness! At this point I couldn't help laughing, and that made it sadder still. My brutality — wanting to get my own back as we were thrown against each other all the way along the atrocious road through the *pinède*, the ruts reminiscent of those approaching Mittagong. Once, cracking, he edged an arm around me and a rut allowed me to edge him off. Hypocritically. When I could have enjoyed his Harris shoulder.

The difference between the sexes is no worse than their appalling similarity . . .

Just after that, after mounting the rise, the bull moose straining at the wheel, we burst out upon 'Crimson Cottage'. And there was Angelos standing on the doorstep. I could see he must have run out fifty times, wondering whether his 'wife' had been crushed by some vehicle, raped by a peasant, or abducted by a rich man like the one now fetching her back in a motor.

Yet when we descended from this monstrous machine, and he had staggered down the path, almost tripping over rosemary and wormwood, which do disregard the bounds of garden aesthetics, as A., loaded with brandy, oversteps social decency, these two incongruous males, the gallant Curly and lovingly licentious Greek, fell upon each other, I'm sure only from relief at finding male company.

While I was left to hobble, and enjoy the scents of the evening garden, so much subtler if less exciting than the male
stench.

(I would like to think myself morally justified in being true to
what I am — if I knew what that is. I must discover.)

They calmed down eventually, the two, and suspicion began to
set in between the Emperor of Byzantium and the raw Colonial Boy.

A. began clutching me as though the crutch he thought he had
lost might still be snatched away from him.

A.: Thank you, sir, for returning me my . . . wife. I really don't
know how to thank . . .

C.: Not at all, not at all, Mr— Tatzy. A very special occasion — to
make the acquaintance of this charming young lady — your
wife.

(Australian wives with aspirations are so constantly 'charmed', I
have noticed that it rubs off on some of the husbands, especially
when overseas.)

Curly began saying good-bye, Angelos looking gloomier, not for
being separated from this new acquaintance, whom he had accepted
wholly, too readily, and then regretted doing so. Boyd Golson was
not a man one would have to reward materially (not like Joséphine
Réboa) but my dearest husband, when faced with the less tangible
demands, is apt to grow morally poverty-stricken. I could feel his
arm clutching me, not only from relief, but also in a sense asking for
forgiveness, in that he was not prepared to give to one who possibly
deserved some token of recognition.

I must tidy it up later if I can — and in spite of my own unwilling-
ness (most of us are French underneath).

Curly: (jerking at his tweed cap.) Good-bye, good-bye. Perhaps we'll run into each other, Mr— Madame Tatzy . . . again.

Angelos: Oh yes, we must see one another. Oh, we shall — *sans
doute* . . .

Angelos displays a long-toothed smile. E. Boyd Golson is laughing. His open pores. His clear-blue eyes, the lights in them
heightened by the Australian climate and alcohol. Poor Curly, his
boyishness racks me, his manhood disturbs . . .

Finally he is driving off in the bottle-green Austin, and nothing
definite has been arranged. All will depend on me and/or Joan: the
women.

It astounds me that anybody should depend on *me*, that anyone,
even Joanie Golson should expect; and here is this subtle old Greek

lizard, my husband, dragging me towards the claustrophobic evening prepared for us, yet from which he hopes to extract a sense of security, faith (apart from his agnostic/Orthodox one), hope — Eternal Hope.

Animals are more dependable: Eadie's frowzy, till-death-us-do-part Australian terriers. Plants are less detached than they seem, more responsive than many human beings, their insinuating scents, their reasoning habits. I am only I — a plant too, but one the wind spins on its mooring.

All evening we recapitulate the Macedonian and Thracian campaigns. 'The Bulgars, E., are without necks, or not altogether, they have the necks of pigs. They squeal and bleed like pigs when stuck with a Hellene's javelin.'

Oh yes, those Bulgars! Madame Llewellyn-Boieldieu's *mobilier provençal* is threatened by the press of cavalry returning from the wars, the *salon* filled with the clash of metal, a stench of leather and hairy, black, bloodshot men swaying in their saddles.

I await him on the steps, along with the palace officials in strict order of hierarchy, we too, sweating in our robes, collecting the dust blowing out of Asia.

This small, unlikely figure dismounts. 'Where is Her Imperial Highness?'

Nobody dares answer a question so mad.

I break off my novelette to smoke one of his cigarettes. I'm growing as mad as Angelos, who hasn't stopped smoking all night, while slaughtering Bulgars in Thrace and Macedonia.

When we had gone to bed he asked, 'Will your new friends take you away from me?'

'Why should they?'

'Eudoxia was given as a bribe to Grimaldi. They hoped he would help them recapture the City. But it didn't work that way. He shut her up in that tower at Castellar.'

Always these towers! I am the one shut in a tower more fatal than those experienced by other fictions — his Eudoxias and Annas. I bet even Anna the wife is a fiction.

At least the towers usually materialize as a prelude to tenderness. We fell asleep locked together.

However much I need him I must somehow escape.

Waking in the night, he said, 'I could see it in his eye.'

'In whose? And what?'

'The Golson man — that he'll take you away.'

'We aren't living in the Middle Ages. You almost make me wish we were.'

When he had turned his back on me he said, 'He'll take you to Nice.'

'We might all go there together. In the green Austin. Wouldn't it be fun?'

'Nice is the most vulgar place on earth.'

'There are some you haven't seen, *darling*.'

In any case we must return their kindness. Perish the thought! Those who are kind don't, surely, expect their kindness duplicated? Or perhaps they do, a carbon copy, a kind of receipt. I'll write Joanie a letter of thanks, a civil note, the exquisite sentiments of which will fan her passion from a safe distance, Curly's too.

Must stop being a cock-tease.

Mrs Golson was growing ashamed of herself. *'Vous n'avez pas quelques lettres pour moi?'* she heard herself bleat at the porter's desk, not only on returning from an outing, but sometimes less excusably after taking the lift down from her Louis Whichever suite for the express purpose of making her futile enquiry.

'Non, madame. Pas de courrier. Rien.'

At times the porter scarcely bothered to turn his head and glance in the direction of the pigeon-hole. She could see that he, even more than the hunchback liftman, was becoming suspicious, connecting her with the rumours of war; when she was less responsible for its threats and stratagems than anybody on the European scene.

She must restrain herself. But didn't.

'Toujours rien pour moi?'

'Si, madame, il y a une petite lettre.'

Mrs Golson experienced the greatest difficulty in receiving her letter with an indifference to match the porter's own. She knew her skin was glowing, her hands were trembling, and that idiocy had crept into the smile the porter would in any case not have expected from this foreigner he only just deigned to serve.

'Merci,' she barely whispered, and even then it sounded to her ears regrettably Australian.

Grasping her unopened letter, she took the lift. All the way up, while hauling on the greasy rope, the silent hunchback stared at her clenched hand, she was convinced, out of the corner of one suspicious eye. Along the corridor Joséphine stood leaning on a millet broom, smiling, but watchful. They, the servants, were the spies.

Mrs Golson felt downright faint by the time she had unlocked her door and was free to tear at her blessed letter.

18th March 1914

Quite laughable! She had waited three days, not a lifetime. She did in fact laugh now that she could afford to.

My dear Mrs Golson,

The letters one writes to thank for a genuine, spontaneous kindness usually seem forced, their words, and the sentiments the words fail to express, inadequate. That is why I have hesitated these few days to try to convey my appreciation of your help – Mr Golson's too, it goes without saying.

I think it is in part the reclusive life I lead which gives rise to these difficulties – not that I would choose to live otherwise, for I have to consider the needs of an elderly, invalid husband. You must not imagine I am making further inroads on the kindness you have already shown. I have learnt to cultivate my garden! Even the persistent rumours of war have failed to destroy our peaceful existence. (Don't you think the French the worst of all warmongers?)

Again – I hope without appearing effusive – I would like to thank you – and Mr Golson. My husband joins me in my gratitude.

Sincerely
E. Vatatzes

On reading her letter, Mrs Golson fell back exhausted in her gold *bergère*. Deserted by any pretence at deportment, she half-sat, half-lay, her legs stretched straight ahead, her ankles and feet sticking out from underneath her skirt, her heels planted in the balding pseudo-Aubusson. She felt dehydrated by an excess of emotion both concentrated and suppressed.

But what could she believe? 'My dear Mrs Golson . . .' She herself was in the habit of writing 'Dearest . . .' to a mere acquaintance, when it didn't mean a thing. By comparison 'My dear . . .' sounded personal; it had about it an air of warm envelopment (or so Mrs Golson would have liked to think) of unaffected affection. It made her heave in her gold *bergère*, thoughtlessly rumpling her beige zouave.

Madame Vatatzes gave every impression of being sincere. There were the implications, however. 'I have learnt to cultivate my

57

garden!' That exclamation mark. And wasn't Curly dragged in without good reason? Or so Mrs Golson liked to think. Was this young woman begging for a rescue from the far from 'invalid husband', or merely inviting a literary correspondence with sentimental undertones?

Joanie Golson was to no great extent literary. Gruff notes from her closest friend Eadie Twyborn had not exactly encouraged the literary convention.

Come at 8. The Judge dining at the club with fifteen other males. The child atrocious all afternoon. Threw tantrum after tantrum. Nanny useless. Don't know why intuition didn't warn me against conceiving. My darlings are suffering from a plague of fleas. Bathed them in sheep-dip. Hoping.   E.

PS. Child will be under control — asleep.

Mrs Golson was racked. What should she do? What could she expect? Probably nothing. She slipped deeper in the *bergère*, her sporty zouave by now rucked in sculptural folds.

And as always, Curly came in.

'How are we, treasure?'

'I have a throat . . .' She did, indeed, sound hoarse; had he been sufficiently aware, he might have found her proud of it.

But Curly, as the bearer of tidings, was momentarily self-impressed. 'The Russians are the ones we've got to watch.'

'Watch for what?' Mrs Golson asked languidly.

'Been talking to a cove back from St Petersburg. The Russkies will decide whether we're to have a war.'

'I doubt it,' Mrs Golson replied. 'The French are convinced the Boches are the danger. Miss Clitheroe heard from a well-informed source that the Kaiser is planning to widen the Kiel Canal.'

'In any case, I did the right thing — booking our passages in the *Simla*.'

'That remains to be seen,' she said. 'The French,' she asserted shamelessly, 'are the worst of all warmongers.' She seemed to gargle with it, and her throat became so far restored that she consented to go down to dinner with her husband, after freshening up and changing into a pretty frock.

Between the *consommé à l'ambassadrice* and the *blanchaille en corbeilles de pommes pailles* she opened her beaded evening bag and, on clearing her disaffected throat, announced with appropriate nonchalance, 'I've had the most charming note of thanks from the little Vatatzes.' Without awaiting comment, she allowed the letter to flutter down beside the mess Curly was making of his roll.

'The little Vatatzes? I wouldn't care to fall foul of such a strapping young female.'

'I was only speaking figuratively.' She wondered where she had learnt it; perhaps from Judge Twyborn, Eadie's necessary adjunct, as Curly was, less creditably, hers.

'What are we expected to do about them?' he asked when he had read the letter.

'Nothing,' his wife assured him, though it made her bleed (figuratively) to do so. 'We can't go barging in on what is obviously a delicate sensibility.' Mrs Golson was pleased with her own.

Since the whitebait had offered itself for attack, E. Boyd Golson only grunted. He brought down his knife across the heaped fish and the potato basket containing them. It distressed his wife never to have learnt whether one is meant to eat the basket; she would dearly have loved to devour the lot, but restrained herself beyond nibbling at a straw or two, a finger crooked under the weight of a pink sapphire, her defiant frown and arched eyebrows challenging her fellow diners' censure.

Protected by their pink shades the candle-flames stood erect on the island-tables of the Grand Hôtel Splendide des Ligures as the clientele munched, gobbled, sucked up their soup (from the pointed end of the spoon, Mrs Golson felt superior to notice) while any larger-than-life passions, and the mythic war promised by the newspaper prophets and reinforced by Miss Clitheroe's well-informed sources, were dismissed to a safe distance from this illuminated stucco folly inside its perimeter of slatternly palms, box borders, and regimented marigolds.

If war had begun to creep closer to Mrs Golson personally, it was only this evening, and because she had failed to halt her own very private passion. It surged around their island-table causing the candle-flames to flicker, and her vision of this charming girl and a frail old man to submerge in what was becoming a general void.

'There is nothing we can do,' she repeated.

'Do about what?'

'The Vatatzes.'

Having demolished the last of his potato basket, Curly would have felt replete if the main courses weren't still to come. 'What are the Vatats to us?' he exploded through the crumbs of fried potato.

Mrs Golson giggled. 'I thought you were rather gone on her!' She was at once ashamed, not of her husband, as was usually the case, but of herself, for she added quickly and with an earnestness which made her eyes protrude, 'Did you gather from her letter, perhaps, that she might have been holding out her hand asking for help?'

Who wasn't? Mrs Golson's voice implied as it cut out on a note of high interrogation.

'Don't see why *we* . . .' Curly grumbled.

'No,' she agreed. 'There's no reason.'

Reason is the most unstable raft, as Mrs Golson was learning. She suspected that she, and any other refugee from life lashed to its frail structure, was threatened with extinction by the seas of black unreason on which it floated, sluiced and slewing.

The storm the night before, the worst in a succession of storms inflicted on the Coast that spring, had driven Monsieur Pelletier, not unwillingly, out of the conjugal bed and down to his kiosk at an early hour. To exchange the smells of tortured sheets and sleeping bodies, a full *pot de chambre* and the dregs of a *tisane*, for those of damp newspapers, mildewed cigarettes, and coffee brewing on a spirit lamp, gave him a *raison d'être* he had never achieved in marriage, parenthood, vice, or any form of civic responsibility. When he had taken down the iron shutters from the leeside of his constricted stall he began to breathe again, dragging on the air still churning out of the Atlantic, on past Gibraltar, to wane somewhere east of Marseille.

It was natural enough at this hour of morning that Monsieur Pelletier should see himself and his iron kiosk of salt-eroded shutters as the focal point of all existence. As he strode up and down outside the kiosk, thumping his ribs with blue flippers, easing the arthritis from his limb, coaxing his circulation back, working his tortoise-neck so that the rusty chain concealed in it began to grate less audibly, the storm seemed to expire in a series of turbulent gasps in his formerly tubercular lungs.

Once or twice, encouraged by the scent of coffee over methylated spirit, he laughed. There was also the smell of seaweed, the great tresses heaved up amongst the rocks and stranded on the narrow strip of grit referred to in Les Sailles as *plage*.

There was no real reason why Monsieur Pelletier should exist. At times, at dawn in particular, outside his kiosk, this was what he suspected, while never exactly giving in to his suspicion (any more than Mrs Golson gave way to hers, churning on her bed in the Grand Hôtel Splendide at St Mayeul amongst the scum and knotted tresses of dreams). Monsieur Pelletier and Mrs Golson had not met at any point; they would not want to meet; they did not credit each other with existence.

It was only in the figure now clambering down over rocks, that the two might have agreed to converge.

At a distance the stranger's figure was still unremarkable enough, sombre in its long cape, either black, or of a very deep green. Not yet recovered from the storm of the night before, the whole landscape had remained withdrawn in its sombre self, the sea still streaked with oily black, except when throwing itself against the promontory of rock or the strip of gritty *plage*, it flashed a frill of underskirt which would have shown up white if it had not been dirtied, toning with grey concrete, black asphalt, the straggle of palms, saw-toothed blades parrying the last of the wind, a line of tamarisks, their cobweb-and-dustladen branches a dead green at the best of times, now harried to a kind of life, overall the coastal spine covered with a scurf of dead grass and network of black vines.

The figure in the distance climbing down amongst the rocks, their normal, living red dimmed by the neutrality of early morning was very much a part of the storm-exhausted landscape. Himself from Lille, Monsieur Pelletier had come to appreciate the Coast partly because it had returned him to life by driving out the ailment from which he had suffered as a younger man amongst the damp cobbles of his birthplace, but also because he found in the landscape a spiritual refuge from his wife and family, from the intrigues of this village which the more ambitious inhabitants liked to call a 'town', as well as from his own thoughts, doubts, fears, especially those incurred by references in the newspapers he had for sale, which he didn't so much read as flicker through, not wishing his mind to become entangled with their contents, and thus perhaps encourage a return of his malady.

Despite his original interest in the unidentifiable figure climbing down the rocks towards the sea, Monsieur Pelletier now began to shiver, as though one of his less desirable, unidentifiable thoughts was forming in his private landscape. Arrived on the edge of the sea, the unknown person threw off the cape. Whether the stranger, a naked one at that, was a man or a woman, Monsieur Pelletier could not be sure: there were enough *folles Anglaises* along the Coast to make it a woman; there were plenty of romantic Englishmen and pederast-poets to provide a possible alternative. The equivocal nature of the scene made Monsieur Pelletier shiver worse than ever. Had it not been so early he might have run and borrowed Admiral Gandon's telescope or the ex-Préfet Delprat's binoculars, although in those circumstances he would without doubt have had to share the scene with the owner of either instrument, in the one case a lecher, in the other a dry cynic; whereas the newspaper vendor, poetic at heart (he could recite whole yards of Victor Hugo and Chateaubriand) would have wished to keep his incident a wordless poem.

It was all very agitating. There stood the person poised on a rock above the sea. Because a romantic, Monsieur Pelletier saw the naked flesh as white marble, or perhaps ivory overlaid with the palest gold leaf, though if in possession of telescope or binoculars he might have had to admit to its being a dirty grey in keeping with the tonal landscape. Only for a moment, though. The straight figure raised its arms, composed its hands in the shape of a spire or an arrow, and plunged into the disquieted and disquieting sea. At the same moment a wave, more emotional than the majority let loose in the aftermath of the storm, struck the rusted rail separating the *plage* from the concrete and asphalt esplanade, from which the spray was catapulted straight into Monsieur Pelletier's eyes.

Aaahhh! He stood arrested, groaning and grinning with anguish, frustration, astonishment, and some measure of fear, all trickling water, grey stubble, mauve gums, and a few prongs of decalcified teeth. Only for an instant his disarray: intense interest made it necessary for him to locate the swimmer's head.

And there it was, dark against dark. Bobbing intolerably, though the person appeared to be a strong swimmer. It was still impossible for the watcher to decide whether the hair, illuminated by sudden slicks of light, was that of a *folle Anglaise* or *pédéraste romantique*, but in whatever form, the swimmer was making for the open sea, thrashing from side to side with strong, sure, professional strokes. It must be a man, Monsieur Pelletier decided, and yet there was a certain poetry of movement, a softness of light surrounding the swimmer, that seduced him into concluding it could only be a woman.

With this inference in mind, he began spinning on the heels of his coarse boots, their nails grating as they ate into the paving. For some reason, he remained distressed. It could have been the news in the damp papers with which his iron stall was cluttered — *toujours les*

Boches, at work like salt air or termites – or it could be his own rebarbative life: Simone's fallen womb, Violette Réboa's ulcer, his own never wholly reliable sputum – or or – the swimmer headed for the open sea and the single hair dividing this from sky (though a Romantic, the newspaper-seller was not a believer) as life from death.

This was it. As the swimmer toiled farther out, Monsieur Pelletier was convinced to the extent that he began to moan, to fumble, then to thrash at himself inside the pepper-and-salt trousers he had worn on and off over the past twenty years, and as he approached his climax, it was in conjunction with his own precariousness, the activities of *les Boches* in the newspapers, and the action of the obsessed swimmer, so strong, yet so poetic, so hopeful yet so suicidal, as indeed we all are, in our sea of dreams.

At the actual moment when Monsieur Pelletier came in his pants, the light struck through the congestion of oyster tones which had represented the sky until then, and the glistening oyster-forms of cloud slithered apart, so that the waves were streaked with violet and the hyacinth of their normal plumage was restored. Monsieur Pelletier, who had lost sight of the swimmer's head as he relinquished that of his own throbbing penis, again caught sight of hair in long black strands, undoubtedly a woman's, the figure describing an arc as it turned, and returned towards the shore, away from the Sargasso of its intentions.

His relief united with the trickle of his own cooling sperm. A single gob, on reaching his kneecap, struck him cold, disgusting to the extent that he spun round, and there was Violette Réboa limping in the direction of the kiosk.

'*Qui est cette personne, madame,*' he shrieked at the intruder, '*qui nage – sans raison – à cette heure du matin?*'

Madame Réboa's cod lips prepared to protest at the question she was being asked at the same unseemly hour as the swimmer had chosen for a swim.

'*Ma foi!*' she pronounced sulkily.

She had come to buy, or, she hoped, to be given a box of matches.

Neither Madame Réboa nor Monsieur Pelletier believed in each other entirely since the relationship they had enjoyed long ago, before the ulcer started eating into Madame Réboa's leg.

She now demanded her matches, and Monsieur Pelletier led her as far as, and no farther than, the kiosk's perimeter. (There were those who said that Violette Réboa's Joséphine had been got by

63

Aristide Pelletier behind Simone's back; when it wasn't TRUE, Simone insisted.)

The fug inside the kiosk was intolerable: over and above the collaboration of methylated spirit, mildewed tobacco, damp news, salt air and rusty iron, there was a smell, or scent rather, of chestnut trees in flower, which only he could distinguish, Monsieur Pelletier liked to think. Or could Madame Réboa too?

Anyway, he kept her out.

And drew her attention seawards, where the swimmer was nearing rocks refurbished with their familiar porphyry by the increasing light. *'C'est une fille? Ou un gars?'*

Again Madame Réboa was unable to give an opinion, but announced with seeming irrelevance, *'Elle est belle, hein? la femme du fou Grec — qui est elle-même folle — une espèce d'Anglaise — mais gentille . . .'* and added as she stumped away, *'Ils n'ont pas un rond'*; thus declaring herself firmly against beauty, charm, and madness.

Monsieur Pelletier was relieved to see her go, just as years ago he had been relieved when the outbreak of the ulcer gave him reason for ending a relationship which, though passionate enough, was inspired by lust on either side.

Strangely, it did not occur to Aristide Pelletier that the emotions the swimmer aroused in him might have been occasioned by lust, not even taking into account the trickles of sperm still moist on his groin and thigh. Whether the swimmer were the young wife of the crazy Greek or some unknown woman or youth, neither physical passion, nor even a burst of lust, could enter into a relationship which presented itself as a tremulous abstraction, and which must remain remote from his actual life. In one sense disgusting, his regrettable act of masturbation seemed to express a common malaise, his own and that of the swimmer headed for the open sea, as well as a world despair gathering in the sea-damp newspapers.

As the swimmer, as the light, as the colour returned, what could have remained a sordid ejaculation became a triumphant leap into the world of light and colour such as he craved from the landscape he knew, the poetry he had never written, but silently spoke, the love he had not experienced with Simone or Violette — or Mireille Fernande Zizi Jacques Louise Jeanne Jacques Jacques Jeanne — a love he knew by heart and instinct, but might never summon up the courage to express, unless perhaps at the point of death.

He had forgotten the swimmer, who had by now climbed out, glittering with archetypal gold and silver, of light and water — life in fact, before the flesh was doused in the sombre cape. Head bowed, hair swinging, the figure began traipsing up the shoulder of the hill and out of sight.

At the same time as the anonymous being was lost in the fuzz of gold above the hyacinth sea, Monsieur Pelletier remembered, and hurried in to where the coffee was boiling over in a series of expostulatory ejaculations on to the resilient flame of the rickety little spirit lamp.

18 mars 1914

Have done my duty by Mrs Golson. The letter is writ, and delivered. Now we can forget about them.

I find to my astonishment that the minutiae are what make life bearable. Love is over-rated. Not affection – affection is to love what the minutiae are to living. Oh yes, you've got to have passion, give way to lust, provided no one is destroyed by them. Passion and lust are as necessary as a square meal, whether it's only a loaf you tear into, or devour a dish of beans, with a goose's thigh, a chunk of bacon, buried in them.

This is where I differ from my darling. He is nourished by coffee and cigarettes. He provokes passion, but doesn't enjoy it, except its more perverse refinements. I doubt he has ever experienced lust, which is why he could appreciate the sainted Anna, and why he has created the aesthetic version of me – so different, far more different than he could ever understand. For all his languages he could never understand the one I speak. Oh yes, he does, he does, I know. And doesn't.

We read each other's thoughts as clearly as one can follow the snail's track across the terrace. In spite of it, he crushes me – regularly. Do I crush him, I wonder? Of course I do – oh Lord, yes – I do! Knowing will never prevent it.

For this reason it is so important to concentrate on the minutiae: the mauve-to-silver trail of the snail unaware that he's going to be crushed, the scrapings from the carrot which hasn't yet been sliced, the lovely long peeling from the white flesh of the unconscious turnip . . . (I can thank the defection of Joséphine Réboa for most of these revelations.)

All afternoon I was dragooned at the piano: *Jeux d'enfants*. Very upright, rigid. I was not rapped across the knuckles with the ruler, only morally. We are the *chevaux de bois* gyrating, gyrating, the painted nostrils.

65

I *must* break away.

Tonight again we have been over the Bogomil heresy without my coming any closer to what essentially it means. Perhaps it's that way with any heresy, more than most others those of sexuality.

E.: But don't you think it a ferocious act to burn a heretic?

A.: Depending on the times.

E.: But is a human being less human depending on the times?

A.: Who can say? Anna, a correct, a strict woman, believed it necessary to burn Basil the Bogomil.

E.: Anna your sainted wife believed in the bonfire?

A.: Oh dear no, the Comnena — a forerunner.

E.: Forgive me if I'm confused. Past and present are so interwoven in the Orthodox mind.

(Like cigarette smoke in the kitchen after midnight.)

A.: What you will never understand is the Orthodox mind.

E.: Certainly not in an un-believer like yourself!

A.: One might have believed then — as one does now — in the structure of tradition — of Orthodoxy — as one believes in the visible Church of Ayia Sophia.

E.: And in the Holy Ghost no doubt!

A.: Why do you laugh at the Holy Ghost?

E.: You're right. One can't laugh at what is omnipresent.

All the while a storm is raging. One doesn't reckon on the storms which arise along this serene coast. One thinks of it as a place of convalescence, honeymoons, benign airs and perfumes. Not the potential suicide in half those drifting euphorically among those same airs and perfumes. Over which the Holy Ghost presides, even in the souls of unbelievers, as he does over most marriages, A. to E., Boyd to Joanie Golson, Eadie Twyborn to Edward her Judge. Sometimes the Holy Ghost is a woman, but whether He, She or It, always there, holding the disintegrating structure together (or so we hope in our agnostic hearts) and will not, must not, withdraw.

At one stage there was such a crash the largest olive-tree could have been uprooted, thus proving that the Holy Ghost has indeed withdrawn. I have come to need that olive-tree. My lover/husband kisses me on each nipple and in each armpit before falling back asleep. Drunk with heresies, with Orthodoxy, he cannot reach farther. He is growing frail, but of the two, I am the frailer. I used to imagine I could burn for love, but now to drown for it would be the less obtrusive way out.

At least I've written the letter to the Golsons.

66

Got up this morning with the intention of being precise, methodical, final. The storm had withdrawn very early. A.'s death-mask was still snoring on the pillow. So as not to disturb it I leave him for other rooms before unlatching any shutters. It is a moment of false dawn before the real. Wind still blowing, if not so frantically. Such light as there is gives the impression of being visibly blown in different directions. Silver bouquets strewn on the surface of a black sea. As after any violent storm, one's own fears have done the worst damage. My olive-tree is standing. The garden would seem an argument for permanence – only one or two insignificant, dispensable branches lying uncouth amongst the silver tussocks, the hummocks and cushions of lavender, dianthus, southernwood, and thrift. My rented garden. Nothing is mine except for the coaxing I've put into it. For that matter, nothing of me is mine, not even the body I was given to inhabit, nor the disguises chosen for it – A. decides on these, seldom without my agreement. The real E. has not yet been discovered, and perhaps never will be.

Oh yes, only return to the point at which I ran from the tennis court, from Marian's hysterical giggle, her white, sinewy arms, the thud of the felted ball as she drove it at the ivy-throttled screen, disturbed sparrows twittering, ascending.

Around me in this half-light of deserted rooms evidence of the minutiae on which I'm trying to base my doctrine of life. In the false dawn it doesn't work. The Holy Ghost was never such a ghost. I am perhaps the only stereoscopic object to be found – if I could believe in myself, but I can't. Moving very slightly on the bathroom tiles was this little ball of hair-combings, which I had thrown at the waste-basket, and missed. All my misses, if they could be gathered up, embodied like this insubstantial ball of hair, would make a monument to futility.

If there were need for that. The fact that I sit here writing as I do, and *rereading what I have written*, is evidence enough. By now I should be inundated, along with all that I cherish – my old A., our life together, the piano duets, glimpses of thrift and pinks, even my failures in the kitchen (those burnt-out saucepans), sea and light, sea and light.

Already walking down the coast road I regretted my intention, and seeing myself, never more clearly, as I am. I've always hated stubbing my bare toes. I'm neither an Australian nor an Orthodox martyr. If I had taken him by the hand, my dear Angelos might have been walking beside me, far more exposed than I, his old testicles swinging in the grey light, towards fulfilment by immersion. Instead, I am alone. Everything important, alas, can only be experienced alone – the rocks I must clamber down before entering this repulsively oily sea.

Then the plunge. I am swimming. Yes, I can swim as I could never walk barefoot. I am swimming in the direction of Africa, of nowhere. That, surely, is what I have chosen? It is just because I can swim with ease that finally I burst out laughing. Like an amateur, I swallow a gutful of water. And light. All the refractions of light around me – violet into blue blue. I swallow it and spout it out. I am the Amateur Suicide. I turn and snooze back through healing water. I am not ashamed, as I shall be later. For the present, snoozing and spouting. Rising, as Angelos must be rising out of those other, grey waves, to bare his teeth at the bathroom mirror, farting, regardless of whether I'm there or not. This is marriage, I would like to think, enduring marriage as authorized by our version of the Holy Ghost.

But I *must* escape, and not through suicide. I knew it as I dashed the (healing) water from my face and body on those damn rocks, to which I should have had no intention of returning. Was this why I wrote the letter to Joanie Golson? to enlist her sympathy, her help? Can you escape into the past? Perhaps you can begin again that way. If you can escape at all.

When I got back, Angelos said, 'Where were you? I began to worry. What were you doing? Look, your feet are bleeding!'

'Yes, they're bleeding, I'll put iodine on them. That will be hell – but your wife Anna would have approved. Actually, I only went for a swim – nothing less orthodox than that, *darling*.'

A. laughed. 'I wondered where you were, and why you didn't bring me my coffee.'

This is why you can't help loving A. – in the absence of a Holy Ghost, his trust in one frailer than himself.

Mrs Golson had just returned from the English Tea-room and Library where she had succeeded in securing (there was no other word for it) that elusive novel by Mrs Wharton. If Mrs Golson was already intimidated by what she saw at a glance between its covers, she would be proud to sit with it in public places. In fact she had already more or less decided to venture into the rotunda and order tea instead of having it sent up to their suite, when she discovered that it was Madame Vatatzes, no less, standing at the reception desk.

Mrs Golson's spirits soared, which did not protect her from simultaneous confusion.

'Are you visiting somebody,' she asked, 'at our hotel?'

Madame Vatatzes also appeared confused. 'I was passing,' she replied awkwardly, 'and thought I'd look in — to see whether you were still about.'

'What good luck that I am!' Mrs Golson hoped she sounded jaunty rather than rakish.

Madame Vatatzes seemed to find her manner acceptable. They both laughed.

But almost immediately the unfortunate Mrs Golson was faced with another dilemma: whether to take her attractive friend up to her private *salon* and keep her to herself, or to flaunt Madame Vatatzes, far more spectacular than Mrs Wharton's novel, in a public room?

When suddenly she was tossed, with no effort on her part, on what seemed the dilemma's only possible horn. 'Shall we be devils and brave the music in the rotunda?' It sounded most unlike herself.

'Why not?' said Madame Vatatzes. 'We'll have each other to fall back on.' Immediately after, that white smile broke in the terracotta face.

Mrs Golson almost took her by the hand and led her towards the music. If she thought better of the hand-play, she continued to feel extraordinarily daring, as she marched ahead across the gloomy hall towards the more luminous rotunda, where the palms stood quivering in their jardinières under onslaught by piano and strings.

Mrs Golson paused to look about her in triumph and choose a table worthy of her guest. Not neglecting that other alliance with Mrs Wharton, she held the volume flat against her bosom. They made an imposing trio, Mrs Golson saw reflected in panels of amethyst and amber, her own lips slightly parted, Mrs Wharton's lettering at least displayed, Madame Vatatzes graver in expression, perhaps because censorious. It might well have appeared a worldly, and to a refined, reclusive young woman, a vulgar scene.

What if it were? Mrs Golson was thriving on it; she would not apologize any more.

'Shall we take this table?' she suggested. 'Or shall we be deafened?' Almost another apology; she laughed to make it less so.

'More likely seduced by those sticky strings,' Madame Vatatzes remarked.

Memories of their first conversation persuaded Mrs Golson she ought not to feel surprised. So she swam across the short space separating them from the desired table, moistening her lips, lowering her eyelids ever so slightly, conscious of the sounds her movements made, those of silk and feathers, and in regrettable undertone, the faint chuff chuff of caoutchouc.

Madame Vatatzes was following with a charming negligence reflected in the amethyst and amber. Today she was wearing grey, which made her look, Mrs Golson decided, almost a quaker – a tall one. She was so glad Curly wasn't with them. Nor was he likely to nose into the rotunda; he had a passionate hatred of music, especially the violin.

For a moment as they seated themselves Mrs Golson wondered what on earth they would say to each other, but now there was the tea to order – and oh, yes, *gâteaux*; she would insist that Madame Vatatzes eat several, which would give herself the opportunity of eating one, or perhaps two; and there were other eyes to outstare, of those who resented intruders, who despised newcomers, for Mrs Golson and her caller could not but fit, for the present anyway, into this unfortunate category.

'*Thé pour deux personnes,*' she offered in her most sculptured French to a waiter who looked quite contemptuous considering how the Golsons overtipped him for his contempt. '*Et des gâteaux – beaucoup de beaux gâteaux – pour mon jeune ami.*'

Madame Vatatzes was looking so excessively grave that Mrs Golson, in her sincere delight and manhandling of gender, was reduced to appearing the younger of the two. She was conscious of it herself, not only from her friend's face, but from the reflective panels of amethyst and amber. Mrs Golson hoped that Madame Vatatzes did not regret paying her call.

She would have loved to say something reassuring, as from an older to a younger woman. She would have loved to gaze at Madame Vatatzes' disturbing eyes, which she remembered from the previous occasion. But this was a luxury Mrs Golson promised herself for later, after the weak straw-flavoured tea, and the slight but not unpleasant bilious sensation which came to her from indulging in *Mont Blanc*. By then, each of them, she hoped, would be lulled into the requisite state of intimacy.

In waiting, Mrs Golson tapped with her nails on the bland surface of the little table. The nails had been very conscientiously done by a young Scottish widow, a protégée of Miss Clitheroe's. This afternoon, Mrs Golson felt, her half-moons were particularly fine. (The nails themselves were looking paler than they should have been; should she, perhaps, consult a doctor?)

Far more ominous those full moons the eyes of chattering female macaws and parakeets, their stare levelled at interlopers from beneath wrinkled mauve-to-azure lids. In contrast to the females their no less watchful, for the greater part elderly escorts, lids blackened by digestive ailments and insomnia; in more than one instance a single smoky pearl pinned into what must be a grizzled chest. Among the throng of French, a Russian bearing up under a mound of strawberry hair, who continued munching her language along with a *baba au rhum*, on one eyelid a pink wart flickering behind the net veil she had hoisted to the level of glaring nostrils.

There were the hats.

There were the jewelled hatpins.

There were the jewels.

And cigarette smoke, a blue-grey, interweaving yarn; to Mrs Golson, the perfume was intoxicating.

But the eyes: if only they had been less daunting; and the ferocious mouths. All the veils had been raised to allow the parrot-ladies to fall upon *le goûter*, the black, the white, the beige gloves unbuttoned, folded back like superfluous skins for the ivory-skeletal or white-upholstered claws to fork unencumbered at confectioner's custard, whipped cream, chocolate pyramids, and chestnut wormcasts.

Each wearing, in addition to the routine rosette, the aura of an ex-president, -prefect, or minor Bonapartist nobleman, the males were more austere. Their movements groaned as they plied their cigarettes, the more indulgent among them sipping a *porto*. There were signs of congestion, a whiff of saltpetre, and from one quarter — was it the creaking of a truss?

Mrs Golson had begun to regret her daring; herself so middle-aged Australian, Madame Vatatzes so young, so healthy, so untarnished.

'Oh dear, I shouldn't have brought you here!'

'Why ever not?' The younger woman spoke with a huskiness which might have masked the sulks.

'Into this mausoleum!' Unfortunate choice of a word, Mrs Golson

71

sensed at once: that elderly husband, who might be asthmatic, and even wear a truss.

'It's what I'm used to,' said Madame Vatatzes.

She had chosen a *Mont Blanc*, they both had, and were forking them up in what Mrs Golson hoped would become an extended orgy. (She had grown as reckless as Curly on the drive back to Les Sailles.)

When the Russian lady, her eyelid with its pink wart flickering behind the net pelmet, distinctly lowed, if she did not practically bellow through her *museau de bœuf*, the two friends got the giggles. Transformed into two schoolgirls in a tea-room, they sank back to enjoy the waves of their heaving mirth. Joanie Golson saw that her friend had broken out in delicious speckles of perspiration just where a moustache would have been. Gulping. Biting on the already deformed hotel fork as she dealt with the cream and the chestnut worm-casts. Which according to the tea-room code should have been a lettuce and ham sandwich, its thin green strips smelling of vinegar and knife, with even thinner slivers of ham, the whole lolling loosely round expiring lips before the mouth sucked it in.

The girls humped their backs and giggled.

Finally Madame Vatatzes sat up. 'Shouldn't we control ourselves?' she suggested.

But they were off again.

It was Mrs Golson who took control. 'When we were in Paris,' she told, 'and I went to the Louvre, of course I had to find the Mona Lisa. Nobody could help. *Nobody*. Curly— my husband— was *furious* — he'd only come because — well, he's my husband. Then I discovered that what we were looking for is known as *La Gioconde*!'

Ultimately rescued at the Louvre, here Mrs Golson remained lost, long-winded, irrelevant: looking at Madame Vatatzes she realized that she and her close, giggly, schoolgirl friend with the lettuce ribbons hanging out of their mouths were of different worlds.

It is always like this, Joan Golson supposed.

On the dais across the room, the violinist was snatching, half brave, half desperate, at a tangle of hairs hanging from his bow.

The Russian began looking down her front to see why she should have become a focus of attention.

Overhead, the immense nacreous shade shed its light more dreamily, that of convolvulus and sea-pinks. It seemed to revolve, though it must have been the effect of the music, for the shade was in fact stationary.

Madame Vatatzes finished her *Mont Blanc*. She wiped her mouth in determined fashion with the paper napkin, and rummaged in her bag, not much more than a shabby old black velvet reticule such as she might have picked up secondhand, capacious, and probably a comfort to its owner. Mrs Golson herself, fearful of disease and insects, hated anything secondhand.

'What a charming bag! So practical . . .' she murmured.

'Tat,' Madame Vatatzes replied, and even went so far as to confess, 'I got it secondhand at Marseille.'

Mrs Golson loved her; she would have put up with disease and insects.

Madame Vatatzes had found what she was looking for, which turned out to be a little box lacquered in crimson, black, and gold.

'Do you smoke?' she asked her hostess.

'Very rarely. And only in private. I'll sometimes smoke a cigarette to keep my husband company – but seldom finish it.'

Madame Vatatzes offered her box, and Mrs Golson accepted, giggling.

Madame Vatatzes lit their cigarettes after breaking a match or two.

'We smoke constantly,' she said, and her voice had hunger in it. 'Smoking is Angelos's worst vice – and one of mine.'

The cigarettes, Mrs Golson realized at once, were of the cheapest French variety. It made her feel more daring, more foreign. The Golsons liked to feel foreign abroad, while tending to deplore foreignness at home, unless, in Curly's case, it promoted business, or in Joan's, if it impressed those who thought themselves socially superior. But in the rotunda at the Grand Hôtel Splendide des Ligures she was more than anything the wicked schoolgirl. As she drew on her cheap cigarette, some of the nostrils closer to them became aware of an infringement on their code of behaviour.

Mrs Golson crossed her ankles, and said in rather a fruity voice, 'I'd be intrigued to hear, Madame Vatatz – *es*, what you know of Australia. Were you ever there? Or is it only from acquaintanceship with other Australians?'

Madame Vatatzes sank her chin. 'Oh, I was there! But briefly. Long ago.' Her sigh was outlined in blue smoke.

Joan Golson caught something of the blur of blue leaves, blue bay, a motor-boat panting in the distance, reflections distorted by the motions of disturbed water.

Mrs Golson said, 'I'm so grateful, my dear, that you should have offered me your friendship.' But immediately started wondering whether it had indeed been offered.

For Madame Vatatzes seemed to have forgotten her hostess. Her chin still sunken and moody, she sat smoking with defiance which suggested rage rather than pleasure.

Disgusted by the filthy cigarette, and made bilious by the *Mont Blanc* as she had feared she might be, Mrs Golson was billowing helplessly, and in her billows envisaged herself being drawn out of her rubber corset. Would Madame Vatatzes hear the sound of suction? She so slim and uncorseted, so long and lean of thigh when divested of her quaker grey, her nipples a tender beige on the slight cushions of her breasts.

Both crushing and crushed, Mrs Golson roused herself, but spoke from behind lowered eyelids. 'Australia is not for everyone,' she admitted. 'For some it is their fate, however.'

Madame Vatatzes grunted, or so it sounded. 'I've not made up my mind about fate.'

Oh dear, is it ever possible to make it up for anybody else when one almost never succeeds in deciding for oneself? Mrs Golson resolved to try.

It was her turn to rummage in her bag (Curly's anniversary present) to take out the shagreen engagement book, extract the slim gilt pencil, scribble on a page, and call the waiter.

Madame Vatatzes seemed hardly aware until the music broke in on her; then she roused herself. 'This awful thing! Why did you do it?'

'I did it because the day you hurt your ankle it was what they were playing, when I led you in from the street.'

'But so horribly sticky!' Madame Vatatzes was visibly suffering.

While Joanie Golson had crimped her face, clenched her hand, not so much the wicked schoolgirl as the naughty child clutching her forbidden jujube.

'Won't you let me enjoy it?' she implored this stern older girl.

'I can't think why anyone should want to.'

Immediately after, Madame Vatatzes gathered up her smoking tackle and shoved it in the velvet reticule.

'Why I came here this afternoon,' her head was still bent above her operations, 'was because Angelos suggested it. He would like to meet you – Mr Golson too, of course. Thursday – would it be possible? To a glass of something – say five-thirty. At "Crimson

74

Cottage".' She pronounced it as Miss Clitheroe had, and as Madame Llewellyn-Boieldieu would have.

Poor Joanie was thoroughly flabbergasted: the letter, the formal call, the invitation, all as she had dreamed, and rejected as too symmetrical to expect. Today she suspected that fate *is* symmetrical.

'Oh,' she gasped, 'I'll have to ask Mr Golson — my husband — *Curly* . . . Did you say Thursday? I'm almost sure we have nothing on Thursday.' Knowing there wasn't, she did not even bother to look in her book; in any case her hands would have been too helpless.

'I've never gathered,' she gasped, no, her corset wheezed, 'your husband's profession — that is,' she said, 'if he had one before he retired.'

'Spices,' Madame Vatatzes seemed to gnash her strong white teeth; it could have been provoked by the Meditation from *Thaïs*. 'He exported spices, from Smyrna, from Alexandria. Not all that successfully,' she added. 'As heir to the Imperial throne he considered himself above commerce. A Byzantine by birth, he's a Byzantinologist by vocation, and an authority on Orthodox theology, which he admits he doesn't yet understand.' She rose, tall and cool, reeking of her cheap French cigarette. 'His true hobby, I sometimes think, is entomology.'

Still cowering on her gilt chair, Mrs Golson quailed before these biographical details she had been rash enough to encourage. Until her friend's smile and extended hand dissolved the terror in her bones, and she sprang up, or that is how it might have been, had her form been less globular. Now she wobbled on reaching the erect position, but did not fall, thanks to Madame Vatatzes' firm hand, and even more, the protracted smile.

What could one give in return? In her room Mrs Golson had an unopened box of Turkish delight. Too far up, and besides, she was always fobbing people off with presents instead of confronting them.

In the glass panels she saw her own face perspiring mercilessly through its powder and the ritual dash of rouge, while Madame Vatatzes walked, cool, erect, timeless, through the barrage of music, the cigarette smoke, and interrogation by veiled eyes.

When they had reached the dusty hall, calm except for the action of a furtive heart, Mrs Golson asked, 'That evening when I passed by your villa and heard you playing — the two of you — what was it, I wonder?' Mrs Golson did not even pause to wonder at her own courage; on Madame Vatatzes' arm, her question seemed natural, logical, as gilt-edged as a love she had always hoped for.

'Oh, I don't know – it could have been – yes, I think it probably was – we had all three, after coalescing, begun to emerge – to *surge*. Yes, on that evening I think it was probably Chabrier.'

Mrs Golson, who had never heard of the fellow, was relieved her friend had not seemed to find her presumptuous. She was so grateful for *everything* that she lunged forward to set the revolving door in motion for the departing guest.

Ejected by it after a brief but delirious twirl, Mrs Golson leaned forward on her cramped toes, peering at a halcyon sky as though expecting at least a cyclone. 'My dear, I quite forgot,' she remembered, 'couldn't I have our man run you home?'

Madame Vatatzes lashed out with her head, perhaps not yet recovered from the revolving door and already part of Mrs Golson's non-existent cyclone. 'I shall walk,' she said, 'so good for one – and be back in no time.'

What would have become of him all these weeks without the personal objects surrounding him, the appurtenances of a stable life? Whether in London, Inverness (most of all perhaps Inverness; you can feel most foreign where you think you understand the language and don't) or Paris, or here at this damn St Mayeul where they were stuck for one of Joanie's less explicable whims, he derived significant support from his hairbrushes alone, the concave ivory with gold monograms (time the bristles were renewed, time they were washed if Joanie would get down to it, you tried picking out the fluff yourself with a pin) less from the clothes-brush and softer-bristled narrow one for hats, the stud-box, and bottle for hair tonic, a slit in the leather casing to show you the level of the stuff inside. All these *things*: Curly Golson sometimes wondered how they had acquired him. Joanie perhaps: 'Oh, but darling, you ought to *have* one . . .' So they became necessary, his various appurtenances, like the yacht at Rose Bay, the horses in training at Kensington, the bottle-green Austin with brass fittings, even Joanie Sewell, comfortable in her own right. Whether he had acquired Joanie or she him, he had never decided. She was a good investment and luscious piece of flesh (no one would have dragged it out of him.)

Dressing this afternoon she had finished before him for the first time in history. She was in the other room doing God knew what, not putting in time, she never put in time, but whipped it up to what she hoped was the level of her expectations. Which she never reached, while achieving all else, all the solid things in life. Himself for instance: Golson's Emporium, on top of Sewell's Sweat-free Felt.

Along the coast it was an evening of sun after a day of brooding. Clear blue, but brisk. Curly Golson was standing at the bedroom window of his suite at the Grand Hôtel Splendide. In the gardens below and down the Avenue Félix Faure the palms rose slashed and bashed without appearing more tattered than was natural to them. A scent of unidentifiable flowers (he accepted, but did not care for flowers) and horse manure, and France, drifted up as far as his nostrils.

Duty returned him to the dressing-table and he made a pass or two with the brushes at what remained of his hair, reviving it with a slight dash of bay rum and cantharides from the leather-cased travelling-bottle. He got himself into that rather natty sage waistcoat he had picked up in the Burlington Arcade, over it the Harris jacket (it was cold enough for that). The glass told him he was a fine figure of an antipodean gentleman.

Yet on returning to the open window he found his self-assurance sinking. He could not have accounted for it, or not immediately. The same anonymous bourgeois figures were advancing towards and retreating from him between the formal avenue's tattered palms, when suddenly he was overwhelmed by his own anonymity, which did not protect him from a suspicion that the world of menace held him in its sights. He tried creeping out of range, away from the open window at least. Must be this war, which you could otherwise avoid by not understanding the French papers and resisting your inclination to go in search of *The Times*.

There remained the rumours. These were what the open window framed, embodied in the anonymous faces of the French figures dressed in black, traipsing for no revealed purpose up and down the Avenue Félix Faure. Curly Golson hadn't had it so bad since Inverness, though that was different, like contributing a detail to some old, time-darkened painting, harmless enough in theme, but lethal as dreams can be, with their load of buried personal threats; whereas the threat lurking beyond the window at St Mayeul was of a more general nature, at the same time one from which the sleeper's will might not succeed in waking him. He had not experienced anything like this before. He might have discussed it with Joanie to ease his spirit, if he had been able to express himself, but hadn't been born what they call 'clever'.

Joanie called from the *salon* next door, 'What are you doing, darling? I've been wondering whether we ought to take a present.'

'Hadn't thought about it. Could take along a case of champagne.'

'Heavens, no!' She was shocked to visualize Teakle lugging the case in their wake, through the overgrown garden, towards the dilapidated villa.

Curly had come out from the bedroom, and in spite of his tastelessness she was glad to see him, in his Harris tweed, exuding the scent of bay rum, so far removed from what Madame Vatatzes had referred to as 'the smell of a man'. Mrs Golson sat smiling up at him from the Louis *bergère*, almost worshipful had he noticed.

But today Curly seemed moody and preoccupied. 'What about pushing off?' he asked, as though she had kept him waiting, and not the other way round.

Dear Curly, so reliable! When not submitted to the heavy demands of sexuality, in the context of what she understood as marriage, part duty, part economic, Joan Golson loved her husband.

'That's a stunner of a waistcoat, darling!'

But he did not seem to hear her remark. She ought to seduce him more often with little soothing compliments. Titillated by a thought, not quite innocent, and not quite reprehensible, she got up meekly enough and followed his broad tweedy back. Her mood of the moment was what she recognized as fragile. She might brush against him on entering the lift and they would enjoy a delicious reunion of loyalties under the hunchback's malicious gaze.

It didn't work out quite like that. Curly's blenching finger pressed on the button repeatedly. '. . . out of order . . . antiquated . . .' The voice made husky by alcohol and smoke vibrated in her.

'Oh, darling, but how maddening!' she protested. 'It's the man – the hunchback. He goes across and talks to the porter. I've caught him at it.'

It occurred to neither of them to take the stairs. Hadn't they paid for the lift?

So Curly's finger went on blenching as he pressed the button. Why was she so impressed by it? Far back, as a little girl, she remembered somebody showing her a witchety grub. But that was soft. As was she. Even so, she had squashed the grub. And had a bad dream about it. Oh dear, the liftman was to blame – *Ange*, no other – when they were expected at the Vatatzes'.

Suddenly the door of the cage opened to receive the Golsons. Ange was too detached to appear in any way censorious as he hung on the rope by which he functioned. The Golsons were standing at attention, at what might have been the prescribed distance from a liftman. Curly's calves looked as substantial as one would have expected in a male figure of the better class, but Joan's Papillon by Worth faintly shimmered and fluttered in the draught which entered from the lift-well.

They reached the *rez-de-chaussée* with such a bump that her hands grew hot inside her gloves and she clutched her bag as though she half expected a thief to snatch it. Inside the bag was the present she had hesitated to declare after squashing Curly's suggestion of champagne. It was an antique amethyst brooch, framed, not in diamonds, but a garland of inoffensive brilliants: a charming little piece of jewellery, not made less so by the fact that Mrs Golson did not want it.

Then that bump. The hunchback's hump. *Ange!*

But hadn't they arrived safely? The door of the gilt cage opened. Curly Golson was getting out.

When Joanie told him, 'Darling—I'm going up—back—only for a second. Wait for me in the lounge, won't you?'

Halfway there, he could hardly have done otherwise.

Not only did Ange despise, he must have loathed her while hauling her back to the second floor. He could not understand that so much, almost her continued existence, depended on it.

'*Merci,*' she said. '*Vous êtes très gentil.*'

What she could not have understood was that Ange despised her more for addressing him as no guest ever had at the Grand Hôtel Splendide des Ligures.

When Mrs Golson re-appeared in the lounge she was wearing her tan Melton suit in place of the Worth Papillon. 'Now,' she enquired cajolingly, 'are we ready?'

They went out to where Teakle was waiting to open the Austin's doors.

She realized at once that she must look heavy, dull (perhaps she was) in her tan Melton. The hat sat too close to her heavy brows. She glanced about her nervously, licking her lips, adjusting the veil which bound the straight-brimmed hat to her head and made the whole effect more uncompromising.

Curly was in the driver's seat.

'Oh, do be careful, darling, won't you?'

Did Teakle's steadfast neck despise her as deeply as Ange the hunchback's eyes?

Curly did not answer, and they started off. She rather enjoyed being terrified in their own motor, her husband at the wheel. Lulled by her terrors, she sank back into an upholstered corner, clutching her bag with the amethyst brooch which she might, she hoped, find the courage to offer Madame Vatatzes; it would suit her style perfectly.

As they swept through the grove of under-nourished pines, the stench from the salt-pans prevented Mrs Golson's hopes aspiring much beyond the hatching of sooty needles, through which were revealed those other glimpses of enamelled gold and halcyon.

Very purposeful, he had come out on the front terrace and was calling, 'Eudoxia! Where are you, E.?' wearing the sun hat with the frayed brim, the spokes radiating from the crown, which made him look like an old woman. (E. said it didn't; it suited him.)

Frustrated in his purpose, he returned through the house. Its structure seemed unstable this evening, rattling, groaning, trembling as he passed from front to back: the hovel which only an avaricious *demi-Anglaise* like Madame Llewellyn-Boieldieu would offer tenants poor enough to accept. Poor but not grateful, thank God! He had never been grateful for small mercies in any of his incarnations, not even on becoming what seemed like the last and withering twig of a family tree.

Passing a wall-mirror in the hall he saw reflected in the fluctuating glass, amongst the scales and blotches, this figure in the plaited hat. E. was wrong: it was the face of an old woman and a peasant. Not that the aged don't tend to pass from one sex to the other in some aspects of their appearance. He didn't *feel* that he had undergone a change. E. appeared to appreciate him as much as ever— to love? he sometimes wondered. (If only he could lay hands on that diary. No! There are wounds enough without the diaries; the wax effigies of lovers are stuck with countless pins.)

Angelos Vatatzes steadied himself on a rented console, worm-ridden to the extent that it threatened to crumble. (She would send them a French bill, by God!) This aged revenant in the peasant-woman's hat, stuck with pins down the ages, from Blachernae to Nicaea, and down the map in travelogue to Smyrna and Alexandria. Athens? peugh! that haven of classicists and German *nouveaux riches*.

He remembered in his mother's work-basket a little heart in

crimson velvet bristling with pins. She was not all that good with her needle; she was not all that good. But he had loved to draw his finger through the labyrinth of pins, exploring the textures of the stabbed velvet. He would cower over the crimson heart, anything to postpone the walks along the Prokymea with Miss Walmsley, or Fräulein Felser, or Mademoiselle Le Grand — the governesses who had ruled his life in turn.

The women.

Of all those who had attempted to rule him, empresses, hetairai, his sister Theodora, Eudoxia his colonial 'bride', aunts, governesses, Anna his sainted wife, not so saintly in spite of the candles lit and the raw carrots nibbled at, only one had relieved him of the burden men carry, and that very briefly, long ago.

She was his wet-nurse — a peasant. That perhaps was why he could accept himself as a peasant-woman in a reed hat, and because there is less distance between peasant and emperor than between the Imperial Highness and those who compose the hierarchy.

His memory still showed him Stavroula (the Little Cross) a small woman of blanched cheeks, and enormous globes designed for devouring by the hungry offspring of the rich. (He had loved his milk-brother, however, and had rewarded him later, one Easter while sharing the same bed, by uniting with him in a sea of sperm.)

Stavroula had recurred throughout his youth, offering, always offering: purple figs on a bed of leaves, glasses of cold well-water, food, food, endless food, her face growing smaller, yeast-coloured, welted, in the black kerchief surrounding it, beside the Gulf, and down the coast at Mikhali, its green valleys descending out of Asia powdered with a reddish dust.

He could remember her kissing his hand. Himself always the accepter, in a peasant hat worthy of an emperor.

Tears gushed out as he crossed the kitchen of the villa they were renting from Madame Llewellyn-Boieldieu, and half an eggshell jumped off the table, the surface of which was grooved by use as Stavroula's face had been welted by age and hardship. The shell bounced on the floor which E. had not swept since Joséphine Réboa disturbed them by defecting.

Had E. defected?

Stavroula never would have. That is why he wept for the dead and the past.

He wept for the saints, even the pseudo-ones, the hateful Bogomil — a *Bulgar*.

And reached the back terrace, and shouted, 'Eudoxia! Where to God have you got to?' He hesitated before shrieking, '*Gamo ton olakeron kosmo!* Fuck!' His voice, dying, mumbled, blubbered in a whisper, 'Doxy – for Christ's sake . . .'

In the absence of the one who had abandoned him he ground his head against the terrace table, its marble permanently stained by the early coffee they were in the habit of taking there. He dragged his forehead back and forth, the disenchanted Emperor of Byzantium, Nicaea, Mistra, and all those lands threatened by the Slav, the Turk, the western hordes of schismatic, so-called Christendom – the Barbarians of past and present.

E. did not come. The spirit of Stavroula was not moved to appear. Mamma was at cards in another part of the town, Anna the Soul was no doubt copying aphorisms into a leather-bound notebook, or kissing an archimandrite's clammy white hand. She maintained that the hands of high-ranking monks and priests smelled delicious – of rose-water. It was the only streak of sensuality in Anna. He could not believe in the rose-water; he was sure an archimandrite smelled like any other monk or priest: of flannel vests and frustration, or the throbbing overflow of a dammed-up concupiscence.

Where was E.?

Only today he realized the connection between Anna and E., two scribblers: Anna the copyist; with E., he suspected, it was self-expression or -vindication. No, he did not want to investigate the fruits (too frightening) he was only curious about them. Anna had been religious; he suspected E. was too, but differently. Anna was as Orthodox as a burning candle, E. some kind of life-mystic, poor devil – a potential suicide in other words.

Who was not? unless the vegetables.

He lifted his head from the terrace table. He had promised himself a serene close to the day, one of those perfect evenings on the Coast, with music, conversation, perhaps an *omelette aux fines herbes*, a glass or two of Armagnac, then bed. Instead, blood could be threatening.

'Doxy, where are you? Damn all saints, mystics, literary pretenders . . .'

The only true saint and woman was Stavroula, and for that reason he had kept it more or less secret, from Mamma, Anna, E. Mamma would have laughed at the idea, Anna would not have believed, E. might have, and for that reason, would have been more jealous than any.

His crypto-saint on her knees in her cell-cottage at Mikhali. She tended it, but it wasn't her own, any more than Yanni her giant husband (another slave) his strength dwindling till he ended, a paralysed flitch of bones wrapped in spotless rags, or Babbis the rosy boy who became a congested, resentful clerk.

You kissed Stavroula once on one of the white welts of her old puddingy cheeks and it smelled of the cleanliness which you recognized as earthly evidence of sanctity. (All nonsense of course if all is nothing as it has been decided.)

Again you recognized the smell of sanctity in the purple soil they opened in the graveyard above Mikhali to lower her into. Babbis glaring blubbering the other side of the grave. Resentful of the love you bore his mother? the milk you had deprived him of? more likely the sea of sperm to which you had both contributed while sharing a bed that Easter night. Anyway, he glared and blubbered, this grown boy and portly clerk, while you could not raise a tear for the Dormition of Stavroula and the great abstraction of death. ('Angelos is cold.')

Angelos now crying, his head on a stained table, perhaps crying for himself because close to death. (In those days graveyards, cypresses always on the alert against marauding Turks, belonged by tradition to those who were lowered into their redemptive soil; today all dust, the bones scattered; relatives squabbled over whether they should buy an additional plot — or two — six — of Attic or even foreign soil in which to lay their mortal remains and those of their descendants.)

Somebody knocking, was it? The bell had eroded long ago. Neighbours came round to the back with their offerings of eggs, fruit, a strangled cockerel. Peasants don't knock.

'E.? E.?' He barked his shins against the iron cradle of this hateful marble table.

Above him the French sky held firm, when that above Mikhali, Smyrna, or any of the Imperial staging posts would have split open at his command.

Not far below the terrace where the Imperial Highness was creating such a rumpus, 'Eudoxia Vatatzes' was seated on a rock, bare feet enjoying the texture of stone (and childhood) long arms emerging from these faded, but still lovely, carnation sleeves, to embrace bony knees.

E. had not written up the diary, but here it was, all in the head, in the waning light above the pine-crests, between sea and sky: 'E. Vatatzes' stroking it out of terracotta arms.

'. . . now that I've done the deed, now that I've invited *them*, shall I be brave enough to tell? To commit myself to the Golsons even in a moment of crisis: to Curly's alcoholic breath, cracking seams, Joanie's steamy bosom, her gasps and blunders, the smell of caout-chouc — to dismiss all the mistakes of the past culminating in Marian's driving the tennis ball against the ivy screen in which sparrows are nesting.

Whatever is in store, I must go up. My Angelos is screaming as only a Byzantine emperor can scream.

No, I can never leave him. He is too dependent. Only I am more so. We are welded together, until war, or death, tears us apart.'

He opened the door. *'Qui est là?'*

'Nous sommes les Golsons.'

'Who?'

'Joan and — Curly — Golson.'

He stood looking at them from under that incredible woman's hat, his lower lip protruding and trembling.

Joan Golson, too, was trembling. 'You met my husband. You are Monsieur Vatatzes, aren't you?'

'He is not at home.'

She could hear Curly murmuring behind her, dragging the soles of his stationary boots on the stone paving. In a moment she would be accused.

'But how tiresome of us! Have we come on the wrong day? I'm sure your wife said Thursday.'

'Anna died.'

Joan Golson thought she might burst into tears, when Madame Vatatzes appeared at the end of what must have been a poky hall, but which in the circumstances had taken on the endlessness, the proportions, of a dream perspective, down which this vision was advancing, burnt arms outstretched towards them from long, float-ing, carnation sleeves.

'My dear Mrs Golson, I'm so glad you were able to come.'

The voice seemed to weave, as though through water. Bubbles almost issued from Madame Vatatzes' underwater voice as she delivered the opening line of a role she must have been trying to master up till the last moment, not in a play, more of a two-dimensional masque.

84

Old Vatatzes flung his vast hat on a worm-eaten console. '*Gamo tous olous!*'

'He forgets,' she explained.

He sprayed them with laughter. 'On the contrary, I remember too much.' But seemed to be settling for the inevitable.

Madame Vatatzes resumed her flat, under-rehearsed role of hostess, suggesting, 'Shall we go in here?' Her tone implied there was infinite choice.

Then they were standing in the room where Mrs Golson had seen the Vatatzes on the occasion when she had spied on them. From inside, it looked as poky as the hall, irregular in shape, its floor raked. Or had her own uncertainty brought it about? She wondered as she stood smiling, clutching her bag (it belonged, she realized, not to the Melton velour she was wearing, but the Papillon of her first and perhaps more suitable choice) the bag in which was the little brooch she must decide whether to offer or not. At the moment, in the presence of mad Monsieur Vatatzes, the amethyst brooch seemed too much an exposure of her own secret sentiments, on which his eye would most surely focus with a glittering malevolence. So she grappled the bag to her entrails while tottering on her Pinet heels.

And smiled her most social smile. 'So charming!' Mrs Golson murmured, looking about her at the grubby walls, the battered Provençal furniture, and one or two bibelots of no value in a rented villa. Only the piano had any connection with an experience she might repeat, if those who could gratify her wishes were willing to collaborate by drawing from the warped keys the same skeins of passionate colours and swirl of romantic sentiment.

'Charming! – and so typical!'

'Typical of what?' Monsieur Vatatzes cracked down on her; his nose looked alarming.

'Of those who live here,' Mrs Golson gasped.

If only Curly would back her up, but like most Australian husbands, he never did if one ventured into country considered in any way 'artistic' or 'intellectual'.

Monsieur Vatatzes almost screamed, his spit flying in the faces of his guests. 'We only exist in this filthy hovel! If we live, it is in our minds – the past;' here he turned on Madame Vatatzes, 'though E. rejects the past. Don't you?'

Madame Vatatzes composed her lips into what looked like two

narrow strips of pale rubber. 'Would you care for a glass of *porto?*' she asked the alarmed Golsons.

Her teeth appeared smaller than they normally were, Mrs Golson thought; on the other hand, the feet, she noticed for the first time, were bare, and looking enormous planted in Madame Llewellyn-Boieldieu's shabby carpet.

The Golsons silently agreed, with idiotic smiles and nods, that *porto* would be on the one hand 'delightful', on the other 'the real oil'.

Poor Curly! so far out of his depth, visibly clinging to his clothes as a form of reality in the situation in which they found themselves. Had they been left alone by their hosts just for a moment, she would have nibbled one of his ear-lobes; to Joan Golson there was something delectable about a lobe, like a single oyster on a roundel of bread as opposed to the gross gourmandise of overt sensuality.

But they were not alone. Madame Vatatzes had gone, only too willingly, to fetch the *porto*, and they were left with the old man.

He told them, 'Having company so seldom – and, I must admit, not needing it – one wonders what would amuse the guests.' He looked at them so intently he might at any moment splinter in all directions.

Hands deep in his Harris pockets, Curly found the courage to suggest, 'If you didn't want us, why did you invite us?'

'That, you must ask E.,' Monsieur Vatatzes replied, 'who may now be going for a swim instead of fetching the *porto*. E. is inclined to attempt suicide at all those moments one doesn't care to face.'

'But will probably never succeed if she hasn't brought it off by now,' Mrs Golson contributed, and added, '*I* am the least successful suicide.'

Her husband was amazed. 'Aren't we being morbid?'

'After the Italians, "morbid" is a condition of cheeses,' said Monsieur Vatatzes. 'Human beings are human – *hélas*.' He stood mopping his high forehead on which sweat was glistening.

As she hadn't been invited to sit, Mrs Golson now did so, and her husband followed suit. They might not have been the human beings old Vatatzes insisted did exist, more likely inflated rubber dolls invoked for their hosts to puncture.

Just then Madame Vatatzes returned with a tray, a bottle of *porto*, and four glass thimbles. (Curly used to say, 'Foreigners see to it you don't get drunk at their expense.') On entering the room, one bare foot stubbed itself on the edge of the carpet, and the bottle might have crashed to the floor if Curly hadn't sprung and caught it. (Joanie Golson was so proud of her cricketer husband.)

Madame Vatatzes accepted it all as a matter of course. Indeed, she might not have been present; stooped above the tray, re-arranging the bottle and the glass thimbles, she was as unaware as her bare feet.

Mrs Golson was able to study her afresh, the tendrils escaping from the nape of her neck, the little, almost imperceptible hackles rising from the ridges of her great toes. The finger-joints could have been arthritic, and must have prevented her ever dragging off those antique rings, had she wanted to, but probably she didn't want. The rings of women such as Madame Vatatzes (like Eadie Twyborn) were ingrained and ingrown.

Joan Golson had a sudden brief vision of an enslaved dog or cat rubbing against, licking the beringed hand casually offered for adulation.

She looked at her husband to see whether he had caught her at it.

He hadn't. Curly was more likely preparing for the stroke he had started expecting in recent years. There was a vein in his temple which reminded his wife of that other, horrid one.

She looked away.

'Shouldn't we have something to eat?' Monsieur Vatatzes remembered. 'In for a penny, in for a pound—or is it the pig is in for a poke?'

'Angelos had an English governess,' his wife informed herself as much as those who could not know. 'Wansborough, wasn't it?'

'Walmsley!' He might never forgive her the mistake.

Somewhat to Madame Vatatzes' relief, the Golsons declined food, with incredulous chins and murmurs of 'figures' and 'livers'.

'*But*,' said Mrs Golson, glancing at her husband, 'we were hoping you might treat us to some music.'

'They may not be in the mood, treasure. Nobody is always in the mood.'

That Curly might have developed a sensibility perhaps superior to her own, astonished and annoyed Joanie; it was not to be expected in a man.

'Of course if they don't feel like it. I know one has to feel like it . . .' Then she blushed, looking to the Vatatzes for some manner of corroboration or forgiveness.

Neither of them showed a sign. They had sunk into chairs. Their eyelids looked as solid as stone.

Of them all, only Curly appeared to be enjoying himself, his resentful wife could tell. He had drained his tot of rather nasty wine, and sat revolving the glass thimble between a finger and thumb gigantic by comparison. His calves tensed, he was beating time with the balls of his feet. She hoped he was not about to take the floor.

'Where you've got it over we Australians,' she heard with horror, 'you know how to start early.' He clucked with his tongue in the direction of his empty glass.

'I'd have thought,' she hastened to correct, 'nobody could teach the Australians.'

'What's wrong with the Australians, darling? Except that that's what we happen to be.'

She could not refute it, nor remind him that he would refer to the horrid *porto* as 'rotgut' at some less exotic, more rational hour.

Monsieur Vatatzes had sucked in his lips till his mouth resembled nothing so much as a wrinkle in a sooty lemon, through which was squeezed the sour assertion, 'Other Australians have not come my way – excepting E.'

'What?' Mrs Golson was almost propelled out of her collapsing Provençal chair. 'You're not *born* Australian?'

Curly did not utter, but conveyed his slightly incredulous approval; the Golsons loomed at Madame Vatatzes as though all three had been Christians in a pagan world, that of Madame Vatatzes' husband. He, by contrast, and Orthodoxy, repudiated those who could have been – well, Bogomils, Bulgars – *Barbarians*.

Naturally Eudoxia, torn between opposite camps, was terribly distracted.

At least Mr Golson, regardless of anybody else, poured himself another tot of the very indifferent *porto*. 'To celebrate,' he had the grace to apologize.

While Mrs Golson continued sitting forward on her creaking chair in a state of precarious enthusiasm. 'Do tell!' she coaxed. 'Where are you from? Melbourne?' before venturing breathlessly to hope, 'Sydney perhaps?'

'Oh,' Madame Vatatzes sighed, still not raising her heavy eyelids, 'it was so long ago I can't feel I came from there. Or,' she murmured, 'belong anywhere, for that matter.'

Her husband had opened his eyes and was staring at her with an expression determined to accuse her of any step he might consider false, while she, in her passive stone-bound condition, seemed equally determined not to give him cause, not at the moment anyway. Although impressed by the sight of Monsieur Vatatzes' commanding eyes, Mrs Golson regretted the withdrawal of those other jewelled ones which, now that she had this additional clue, might have enabled her to do her sums on past and present.

It was immensely irritating. She sank back at last, exhausted, exuding in her frustration and her tan velour, the luscious promise, the tantalizing glitter of a *baba au rhum*.

Fortunately for her, Curly at least continued to find his wife luscious. Did Monsieur Vatatzes too, perhaps? For as she sank back into her chair and her brown confection, he rose in his black, his veined hands working like talons, which till now had only dangled limply from his arms and the arms of his chair.

The old cove was wearing round his neck on a broad black ribbon of watered silk, something Curly had already noticed, and dismissed out of loyalty to their sex: a gold emblem in the shape of a two-headed eagle. Could you beat it?

'If it's music they want,' and the Imperial Eagle looked full at E. Boyd Golson rather than at the female of the species, 'hadn't we better give it to them — Doxy?' His teeth seemed to implant ignominy in the one who bore what Mrs Golson presumed was a nickname, an unfortunate one.

Otherwise she was so delighted she drew from her chair all the sounds of threatening collapse. She clutched the handbag which contained the jewel she would almost surely offer eventually to Madame Vatatzes, metaphorically on bended knee.

It was Curly who now withdrew, into a male despair, as the young woman rose and dedicated herself to her husband's wishes and their guests' entertainment. She was delightful of form, moving, swaying, in this bleached-out robe which only a 'bohemian' would be seen dead in, but carrying it off with a style of her own, unlike Joanie (he would never criticize Joan's taste in dress: it was too right and too expensive) but this young erect sheaf, he could see her falling to the reaper's sickle, possibly his own — yes, his own.

He looked at Joanie. She was too entranced by the prospect of culture to cotton on to a man's thoughts, so he eased his crotch, and resigned himself to the tedium he was in for.

Madame Vatatzes had seated herself at her end of the oblong piano-stool. She had arranged everything trailing which needed to be arranged, behind her, thus leaving room for the old boy.

At the same time Joanie Golson was arranging her chin in the hollow of her hand, her beatific smile preparing to be pollinated by the music scattered on it by Madame Vatatzes – less by that nasty old man her husband. Joanie had forgotten her former life, Australia, Eadie Twyborn, and in the present, threats of war. Her receptive soul was yearning to collaborate in giving birth to a promised music.

The silence, Madame Vatatzes, Mrs Golson, even the resistant Mr Golson, all were waiting; when the old Greek stalked towards the piano, in a slight susurration of pin-feathers, and clanking of the gold Imperial emblem.

'Which is it to be, Angelos?' his creature asked.

'Shall we give then *Jeux?*' He laughed, and seated himself beside her on the unyielding stool. 'Yes, *Jeux d'enfants,*' he decided, 'is what I think they ought to get.' You too, his voice seemed to be implying.

So they started out on this prim walk with the governesses, along the Prokymea, or in other cases, round Rushcutters Bay. The bow into which a sash was gathered bobbing against the waterline. Of splintering blue or submerged stocks. And not without its menace of lantana, through which Curly Golson blundered in search of something he could put his hand on. The future scarcely anyone had found. Not Joanie, her freckle-encrusted cleavage bursting with unwritten love letters. The exiled Greek extinguished by his crown, or its substitute the peasant hat, the aura of which he was still wearing, and not the least, the little-boyhood from which he had never disentangled himself.

So they played, they all played, whether actively or not, the *Jeux*, the games Madame Llewellyn-Boieldieu's warped piano keys released. Curly's fingers all thumbs and a blood-blister as he made some attempt at groping after the elusive music. Joanie clasping the amethyst in its several wrappings: of tissue paper, beaded silk, and flesh. More frenetically the two Vatatzes, shoulders bumping as they spun tops, or galloped towards a climax neither they nor Miss Wansborough-Walmsley, Fräulein Felser, or Mademoiselle Le Grand, of dappled necks and crimson nostrils, might ever achieve, rocking and rocking on their stationary rockers.

'Eudoxia,' Angelos Vatatzes shouted, 'your bass is too pedestrian,' and stopped.

Herself seemingly desolated, Eudoxia continued for a few bars in the bass which had offended her husband.

When at last Madame Vatatzes halted, brutal in turn in her abruptness, the governess in black might have brought her ruler down on Doxy's knuckles, the sharp edge on cold morning.

It left the Golsons somewhat confused. For Curly it was simply a case of too much bloody music. Joanie on the other hand bled for her love.

Again they were all sitting at attention, while Teakle, the other side of the wall, somewhere under the olive-tree, was clearing his throat. Mrs Golson heard the subsequent gob hurtle and settle, or so she thought. She saw the amethyst lying at Madame Vatatzes' large feet. Were the hackled toes rejecting her?

They sat until, disregarding all indignities, Eudoxia launched without her husband into deeper seas of music, thrashing out to escape from the weed of human relationships, and he, perhaps recognizing the attempt, joined in with a wild disdain.

The Vatatzes were playing, like many marriages, together and apart, but where their *Jeux d'enfants* had been performed with an angular malice, now the musicians swirled in romantic carnation-tinted circles. Were they perhaps revolving in the waltzes Mrs Golson had heard on that other occasion when she returned to confirm her love? She was sure finally that these were the same waltzes, and breathed so deep she choked on the musty dust rising from bowls of stale pot-pourri and rented carpet, stifled by the moted air where all the poetry of which she had been cheated trembled and expired. Unavoidably, she started coughing behind a knuckle of the hand not engaged with the amethyst.

Mrs Golson was racked by her cough; and not a lozenge in her bag. If only she could have sucked the uncut amethyst, a pebble in her desert of despair, as her wretched cough humped her against recurring themes: her youthful caper with Eadie Twyborn when they crashed that supper dance at the Australia, the circular motion of Daddy's chapped, tremulous hand stroking her cheek, Curly cavorting at the net, all bravura in white flannels, all male, and yes, the smell of a man, which had shocked when first introduced by Doxy Vatatzes, but which now rose naturally enough out of memory and the swell of music.

Whoever the Vatatzes were wooing it was not each other. As their tempo grew more reckless, the piece they were playing was falling apart. She had become the leader in spite of every indication of his musical displeasure. In his narrowed shoulders, shuddering elbows, Mrs Golson sensed a moral disapproval, worse still, a physical crisis. She was reminded of the seizure which had carried off Daddy, and Daddy's only unkind words: *If what they tell me is true, Joanie . . .and what strangers tell is usually true . . . dancing at the Australia with a woman . . . in a corked-on moustache . . . then I've failed to . . .* After which, poor Daddy turned blue. It was one of the many incidents she had never been able to forgive herself.

And this horrid old Greek, what did he know? He had grown so brittle he promised to break on the piano-stool. Would he accuse her from the carpet as Daddy had from amongst the feather pillows which more than likely caused his asthma and cardiac seizure? Joanie could not have borne to be accused again: two murders were too much in the lifetime of an innocent woman whose only vice was a need for tenderness, romantic sunsets, and emotional conceits of a feminine nature.

All of which she had been receiving from the music until the Greek started turning against her.

He sprang up finally. 'I must leave you,' he gasped at his guests.

He looked so livid, Mrs Golson cried out in what she hoped was a compassionate tone, 'Oh dear – there's nothing *wrong*? You're not *ill*, are you?'

Good reliable Curly had risen to support the old fellow if necessary (she had always congratulated herself when Curly, a warden at St James's, carried out the fainted ladies and sat them on the porch during the summer services). Now, in their friends' *salon*, she could have patted his broad back.

But Monsieur Vatatzes assured them he was not in need of assistance or sympathy. 'I am called by nature,' he explained, and walked rather stiffly out of the room.

Madame Vatatzes continued for a short while at the piano as the romantic composition for four hands trailed off into a series of solo improvisations.

Without turning her straight, and for Mrs Golson, still splendid, carnation back, she informed her visitors, 'Angelos is the victim of his bladder. He's practically worn a track, poor darling, tramping to the bathroom in the night.'

She sounded a final treble note and closed the lid of the upright piano.

Curly was preparing to sympathize, but Joanie made sure to quash that. 'I'm so sorry to have put you to all this inconvenience – and upset your husband by coming here.' Much as it pained her to twist the knife, she experienced a sensation of exquisite pleasure from the pain she might have inflicted on the unattainable Madame Vatatzes.

An expression of pain did in fact drift across the sublime face, but from no unkindness on her friend's part, Mrs Golson soon realized; Monsieur Vatatzes was shouting from somewhere deeper in the house, 'Doxy, where are you? Do your visitors mean to spend the night?'

Madame Vatatzes detached herself in a desperately ungainly movement, floundering in her robe, almost but not quite tripping on the hem, as she thumped across the floor on bare feet, making towards her importunate husband.

The Golsons were stranded in a situation each hoped the other might handle.

While from farther out this distinguished boor continued shouting. 'But what possessed you?'

Whatever had was drowned in the gushing of a cistern, the flushing of a lavatory bowl.

'And not to tell me!' Monsieur Vatatzes stormed.

Never would his wife's more murmurous explanations reach the ears of their attentive guests. It was most aggravating.

'You have no consideration – *poteh poteh* – for the feelings of others.'

'Pott-ay pott-ay!' Curly sniggered.

'All this intrigue behind my back! Will you leave me for . . .' the voice was breaking on a high note as it searched for a word sufficiently abrasive '. . . for these *Australians* of yours?'

His wife's reply was wrapped in silence.

'What should we *do*, Curly? Slip away – leave a card perhaps – say nothing – *what?*'

Curly said, 'You're the one who brought it on us, treasure.'

Curly never understood how much she depended on him. Curly, simply, did not understand. Much as she deplored the tedium of sexual intercourse, there were occasions when he might have ravished her, and she would have risen in a shower of grateful hairpins.

The Melton velour was growing so creased in the uncomfortable chair, Mrs Golson finally exploded. 'What do you think they can be up to?'

Curly was hardly responsive. 'Your guess is as good as mine.'

It was Madame Vatatzes who helped decide their line of action by returning to the room after several aeons of silence and waiting, during which Mrs Golson had examined the series of hideous ornaments on display in the rented villa, while ignoring the fact that her own husband was breaking wind. (She would have liked to discuss this habit with Curly, but in all their years of marriage she hadn't.)

Madame Vatatzes smiled. The bony face did have something sublime about it: an expression of fulfilment, in its best moments, and this was one of them Mrs Golson enviously observed.

Smoothing her somewhat dishevelled hair, Madame Vatatzes confided in them, 'He's impossible of course. But there it is – that is Angelos.'

Also smiling, Mrs Golson extended a suede hand. 'It was so charming – and the music.'

They had come out on the front terrace.

'I shall always remember your garden,' Mrs Golson said as they sauntered down between the silver borders, their skirts drawing a perfume from them.

'It was something that happened before we came,' Madame Vatatzes admitted quite humbly.

Mrs Golson turned to her. 'You've added something by being here,' she told the young woman with a gallantry so undisguised Curly might not have been present; though a man would hardly have understood.

Was Madame Vatatzes embarrassed?

In case she was, Mrs Golson hastened to cover her gaffe by dragging a leaf or two from a plant. 'Delicious fragrance,' she pronounced as exquisitely as she could while sniffing at the leaves in her gloved hand. 'What is it?'

'Balm,' Madame Vatatzes replied. 'They say it raises the spirits.'

Mrs Golson did not altogether believe; she suspected her friend had made it up on the spur of the moment, a conceit as delicate as the perfume released from the handful of crushed leaves.

It was an emblazoned evening in which they were standing at the ramshackle gate, Curly cap in hand, wearing the smile he usually adopted for foreigners (because you couldn't accept that the Greek's wife had anything Australian), Joanie adjusting the gossamer to secure her hat for the motor journey, while searching unsuccessfully for some extra-meaningful phrase with which to decorate her leave-taking.

Madame Vatatzes seemed on the verge of making some declaration or appeal as she stood with her hand on the gate, the line of her cheek touched by a last transcendental glow, lips fumbling with elusive words, eyes revealing the same extraordinary mosaic of colour as they had on the occasion of that first meeting, then as self-contained as jewels, now diffused – if not melting. No doubt only an effect produced by evening light. Nor did she find the words she needed to convey that deeper message – which she may never have intended to convey.

So Mrs Golson said, while tying the veil in a bow beneath her chin, 'We shall see you, I hope. *Au revoir*!' and Madame Vatatzes replied, 'Good-bye,' smiling, but at the same time perhaps regretful of what she had left unsaid.

Curly was allowing Teakle to drive them back to St Mayeul and had seated himself beside Joanie. He appeared exhausted by the unusual nature of what they had recently experienced.

But laughed and said, 'You were laying it on a bit thick, weren't you?'

'How?'

'Her adding to the garden by being there!'

She really didn't know how to answer. She had taken it for granted she would be sitting alone on the back seat, refurbishing and adding to her impressions of the afternoon, when here was Curly lifting the veil on her most private sentiments.

She would have liked to let off a firework in his face, but as she did not have one at hand, she replied dully, 'It was meant as a little compliment. One had to praise her, in some way, after the scene her husband made. If he *is* the husband . . .'

'What makes you think he isn't?'

'Nothing,' she snapped.

What made her additionally peevish was realization that the husband's scene had caused her to forget the amethyst brooch she had intended offering Madame Vatatzes. Of course she would not have done so. She would not have found the courage. But might have.

Determined to make good her omission, she set out the following afternoon at the same time as they had driven off on their miscarried formal visit. She did not tell Curly, who was about the town with one of his hotel acquaintances. Nor did she call for Teakle, but hired a cab. Because the vehicle was horse-drawn she finally doubted they would reach the villa much before the hour when they had left it yesterday. She was so distracted she had hardly given thought to her appearance, but had thrown on a drab smocked garment she wore for dusty distances. That she was hatless only vaguely troubled her.

As they drove through the pine-grove, she sidled restlessly on the cracked leather with its smell of hay, and ahead of her the reek of a raw-boned horse, its scours competing with the stench from the salt-pans. At least she had her talisman, the amethyst brooch, clutched in her hand.

She halted the driver at the foot of the hill so that she might approach 'Crimson Cottage' on foot, assemble her thoughts, and perhaps even decide to retreat from the prospect of facing that odious Greek.

She descended from the cab, unassisted of course by the boor she had engaged, and started on her walk. Would the driver imagine, perhaps, that she meant to escape without paying? At one point she turned, and mumbled in her lamentable French, *'Je reviens . . .'* Whether he heard or not as he sat lolling on his seat, he smiled back at one who could only be classified as a *folle Anglaise.*

So she went on, through a quenched radiance, at this hour the sky slate-coloured above interwoven branches, the waves, a heavy periwinkle hemmed with white, dragging back and forth against the shore, her memories of Madame Vatatzes, the glow on a cheekbone, the smile breaking through terracotta, dimmed, if not extinguished.

At the villa the rickety gate stood ajar. A woman in black was stumping, hobbling, snatching at flowers or herbs, gathering for herself a gratuitous bunch. Her movements might have suggested a goat if it hadn't been for the tight bunch which the goat had not devoured.

The goat-woman raised her head as Mrs Golson paused and asked, *'Où est Madame—et Monsieur Vatatzes?'*

The goat-woman arranged her tongue, of a pale mauve shiny with saliva. *'Partis! Partis!* GONE!' she added for one who was beneath contempt, and to emphasize her feelings, swept the horizon with an arm.

'Mais où?'

'Sais pas. Sont partis — le soir? le matin? Personne ne sait — seulement qu'ils sont partis.'

The woman continued snatching at sprigs from the garden. Its martyrdom was Mrs Golson's own, a confusion of perfumes from crushed leaves and released sap intensifying her overwrought state. Added to an intolerable situation, the woman's spit was clearly visible, leaping from her mouth as she spoke; and one of her

96

stockings had lapsed to halfway down the leg revealing a crude bandage through which a stain was seeping.

Mrs Golson could bear the tension no longer. Herself a rival goat, she charged at the gate, almost pushing it down, to arrive in what had been Eudoxia's garden.

The woman in black could not laugh enough, then clenched her teeth as she bound her tight bunch tighter still with some stalks of grass she had torn off.

'*Que sont-ils — vos herbes?*' Now the intruder of all intruders, Mrs Golson heard herself stammer.

The smocked garment she had thrown on for the journey had fallen back, and she realized she was wearing the nightdress in which she had taken her restless afternoon nap.

As though awakened against her will, the woman frowned at her bunched herbs. '*Sont des barbottines. On les met sous les draps pour chasser les puces.*'

Mrs Golson would have to look up '*barbottines*' together with Eudoxia's 'balm,' but her French-English pocket dictionary was not the greatest help and the herb manual somewhere on a shelf in Sydney Australia.

Now, since her friend had left for wherever, there was really no purpose in her staying.

'*Alors,*' she told this female, '*moi aussi, je partirai.*'

But the creature beckoned. '*Venez! Venez!*' The cackle which followed revealed a number of black gaps as well as a span of aggressive gold. '*Faut voir*', she advised, leading the way to the shell of a house around which the sky was darkening.

Curiosity outdoing discretion and even fear, Mrs Golson followed.

The shutters were open, fastened to the outside of the walls, the windows closed, the interior stuffy. In spite of the furniture which she remembered from the day before, the rooms seemed to creak and reverberate like those in a dismantled house.

Her guide led her past mirrors from which Mrs Golson averted her face, and into the kitchen where a door open on the sea and village below, let in an unexpected burst of light, illuminating the Vatatzes' last hours of tenancy: the squalor of unwashed dishes, smeared glasses, coffee grounds, a great over-ripe tomato melting into the papered surface of a dresser shelf.

Mrs Golson would have liked to persuade herself that Madame Vatatzes had been saving up this tomato for its seed. But the thought was bathetic in the guide's presence; the woman in black did not condone improbabilities. From the juice of the putrid tomato, Mrs Golson's glance was drawn to the woman's leg, the musketeer stocking, the stained bandage, on it not so much the signs of watery matter from a running sore, as, Mrs Golson was convinced – pus.

'*Venez! Venez!*' The guide was leading one no longer her confederate but her victim always deeper into the lives of the departed.

The intruders had entered what passed for a bathroom. Choked by the sight of spilt powder, balls of hair, cotton-wool swabs, Mrs Golson put her handkerchief to her lips; she might be developing Daddy's asthma.

'*Voyez! Ils ont oublié ce truc-là!*' the creature shrieked through her gaps, past the bastion of gold.

She poked at an object on a shelf, which as far as Mrs Golson could tell, was an enema of enormous proportions.

The shrieks indulged, the wrath began to pour. '*C'est un vieux salaud – une jeune salope! Ils paieront. Beaucoup! Madame Boieldieu m'a dit.*'

Mrs Golson had retreated into the comparative dusk of the passage.

She dredged up the necessary words and said '*Merci, je m'en vais.*'

But the woman put out a hand. '*Ne voulez pas voir leur chambre à coucher? Ils n'ont fait, vous comprenez, que jouer au piano et baiser . . .*'

'*Non! Non! Non!*' Mrs Golson skirted past the bedroom, through the door of which she caught a glimpse of shadowy, but turbulent sheets; she could not have borne further evidence of the games, perhaps even the stains, of love.

All the way down the hall, out upon the terrace, down the path smelling of tomcat, she was pursued by the woman's diabolical voice as she ran from the flickering images of Angelos and Eudoxia Vatatzes, themselves as diabolical as her own never extinct desires – as she fled towards Curly, honesty, *Australia*.

'*Ils paieront – vous verrez!*' the woman hurled after her.

'*Qui sait?*' Mrs Golson gasped back as she pushed against the collapsing gate, which finally fell.

Who knows what? Herself, certainly, knew nothing, hurrying down the stony hill towards the waiting cab – if it had waited.

But it had. The man was sitting on the high driver's-seat, looking out from inside the tunnel provided by the leather hood. As *la folle Anglaise* hurtled towards him.

*

For no explicable reason, the train was packed on that day. As it drew in at the station they stampeded along its steaming side as part of the lowing inconsolable herd lugging portmanteaux, baskets, parcels, bulging serviettes. Themselves, or rather, their hearts leaping like wild creatures inside the cages of their ribs. To arrive at the doors. To scrape their shins almost to the bone on the iron steps. To scramble panting, dragging, on, on, on board the contemptuous train.

They just succeeded. She forced him up, and after grasping a stanchion, protected him with her strong arm, while a guard, laughing, tried out her buttocks with a hand, pushed the last of the passengers higher, and slammed the door on the lot.

They stood breathing at each other, inhaling the perfumes from the *toilettes*. Even the round smell of shit.

'Well, we are here, E.!' he panted.

More practical, she answered, 'We haven't begun,' and started weaving down the corridor, past the portmanteaux, the baskets, the bulging serviettes, somebody hanging out of a window, a handkerchief held against nausea.

They did squeeze in at last, into one of the wooden boxes, amidst the scowls, the luggage, the children of those already established. They seated themselves in a corner, more closely conjoined than at any moment of their life together, distributing the smiles of the false-humble, in which teeth return to being milk-teeth, cheeks illuminated not so much by the brief innocence as the prolonged guilt of childhood.

After staking their claim they might have looked out of the windows at the view, but on one side the blinds were lowered, admitting no more than a band of flesh-coloured light between hem and sill, on the other a human hedge planted in the corridor presented landscape as a flackering of vines and recurring gashes of red soil. There was also the occasional mountain crest like a heap of unquarried blue-metal.

The old man said to his companion, 'At least we can enjoy the *thought* of wine, but that won't anaesthetize us.'

He laughed in his dry accusatory way. She regretted that, in the haste of departure, after a frenzied night of hallucination and barbed attack, she had forgotten wine and food of any kind, whereas everyone else in the wooden compartment seemed over-provisioned: the crusty bread, the purple bottles they held to their lips, hunks of salami to be sawn at, and rounds of cheese smelling of goat; in one instance, gobbets of truffled *pâté de foie* conveyed by fingers as refined as the bread on which the stuff lay, the flesh dimpling with a diamond or two, the bosom on which the crumbs tumbled as black as the inlay of truffle itself.

The newcomers were lulled at last by motion, the alternate shuffling and hurtling of the train, and the sound of salami skins constantly stirred by the feet of children passing between the rows of knees.

At one point a young mother opened her blouse and offered an enormous breast to her two-year-old, who fastened on it, cheeks working as though he meant to get the whole thing down.

The old man took his companion's hand. 'That is how it was in the beginning, with Stavroula, at Mikhali. So it should be at the end too — in the after life — if we didn't know there isn't any.'

Sight of the suckling child seemed, mercifully, to nourish him. 'Why should you say "at the end"?'

He sighed. 'It can't last for ever. Surely we must arrive soon?'

'Another three-quarters of an hour,' she told him with a simulated authority.

The young woman appeared to be staring at the hands of the peasant opposite, at the encrustations of dirt beneath the broken nails, as thick fingers broke off a corner of crust. She shivered, it could have been from hunger. The widow turned away so as to avoid noticing.

Just then the old fellow flung himself back in his corner, eyes closed, face as yellow as the varnished boards against which it was pinned. He was very frail. The young woman squeezed the handful of bones she was holding. His face was more than ever that of a Byzantine saint, used up in obeisance, less to God than to masochism and fatality.

Or onanism. The widow had taken a pederast *en premières noces,* and survived her experience.

Against her better judgment she was moved by the devotion of the old man's companion, her putting up a hand and touching his forehead. A daughter, perhaps? A mistress would have withdrawn by now. Wives are more matter-of-fact.

Could he be ill? she inquired.

The young woman replied, 'Not ill. He is tired. *Sûrement il n'est que fatigué.*'

But must have found her diagnosis too glib, for immediately she produced a little bottle from her bag, and looked round for a means of administering what the widow knew to be drops, from having nursed and buried two husbands, and one who wasn't.

The widow offered a couple of fingers of Evian. She derived visible consolation from her own charitable act.

After taking the draught, from a glass provided, again, by the widow (which she scoured out with a clean napkin and a generous splurge of the Evian on its being returned to her) the old fellow dozed a little, watched over by his tender companion. If it might not have seemed improper in the circumstances, the widow would have questioned her on their relationship, nationality, place of residence, income, in fact all those details which demonstrate whether an individual is sociably acceptable.

The film of a smile veiled the face of the young woman seated opposite. The peasants gazed while cleaning behind their lips with their tongues. Once or twice the sleeper scratched inside his shirt with gestures the widow condemned as lacking in refinement. The two-year-old wet himself. *C'est écœurant*, the widow considered, *les enfants qui ne sont pas élevés au delà du niveau des bêtes* . . ., while the old man and the strewn salami skin continued breathing.

The widow could not have restrained herself a moment longer from embarking on her questionnaire, if the old man, after tearing so restlessly at his chest that a button flew off the shirt above the waistcoat, had not opened his eyes and sprung out of his corner.

'*Ma — soffoco! Soffoco!*' he shouted.

The blind went flackering out of sight. And he tore the window down.

The other occupants of the compartment were too dazed to protest. They sat blinking at the inrush of light, gulping the currents of air which would surely lay them low in spite of flannel next the skin.

The interloping couple now sat knee to knee, on the edge of the bench, facing each other, beatified by the afternoon light, the draughts of too lusty air pouring through the open window. Or were they reaching into some inner pocket of a relationship where nobody else would have known how to follow? Certainly the peasants, whether French or Gallo-Italian, were only equipped to stare. Nor did the widow's sane mind allow her a clue. She knew only that the foreign couple (spies possibly?) were presenting some kind of sham which she could not fathom. The old man, wearing the ridiculous gilt eagle on a moiré ribbon (something to tell Monique) was no more ill than she—less so, probably, for she had begun to regurgitate the truffled *pâté de foie*.

The train gradually emptied, except for a few Italians trailing towards the frontier. The widow left them for Monaco with formal protestations of goodwill.

They arrived at sunset in a town heavy with dust and a scent of carnations after a day unusually warm for the time of year. Almost as though by arrangement they found a cab. The obstructions and frustrations of the journey were at once erased. Though he did not answer, the driver must have heard of the *pension* the young woman mentioned, for he slashed at his horse and started off in a direction his fare accepted as the only one.

'It does exist then,' the old man agreed. 'I would not have believed it—"My Blue Home"!'

'Any more than "Crimson Cottage"?'

Thrown about on the back seat as the cab climbed a hill out of the embalmed town, they grew hilarious, then settled down. They must not question the nomenclature that panders to the gentility and mysterious origins of those who inhabit the Coast; to dismiss the credibility of 'My Blue Home' and 'Crimson Cottage' might have been to deny the existence of the Nicaean dynasty, the whole structure of Byzantium, including its lynch-pin the Australian hetaira.

'My Blue Home' when it appeared, was a thin edifice overlaid with pinkish stucco and fitted upon a narrow ledge carved out of the mountainside. The woodwork at least was a blistered blue, and the vista a solid azure beneath a powdering of silver cloud. In the circumstances one ignored the criss-cross of lath showing here and there in irregular patches through the stucco, and a show of grey undergarments pegged haphazardly to a clothes-line above the weeds in what had once been a garden. On the other hand, to impress those who might become depressed at signs of squalor, there was a meticulous fresco in the Greek style, of terracotta urns alternating with satyrs and their prey stencilled round the walls between the eaves and lintels of the upper windows.

Leading her charge, the traveller bowed her head and entered.

Like the cab at the station, the proprietress must have been waiting for them. The young woman explained that through unforeseen events she and her husband were arriving *à l'improviste*. There had not been time to telegraph, but she mentioned the name of a lady who had been Madame Sasso's guest and who was a subscriber at Miss Clitheroe's library at St Mayeul. Madame Sasso could not recall her former guest, but knew of course by repute Mademoiselle Clitheroe of the English Tea-room and Library.

Madame Sasso smiled, and explained, 'I spick Eenglish,' to encourage another of the foreigners through whom she made a respectable living.

She was composed of rounded and cylindrical forms, with a vertical arrangement of plump black buttons from the cleavage to the hem of her black dress. After giving the matter thought, she admitted to having a room vacant, which she hoped her guests might occupy until she was in a position to offer something more — *convenable*.

It was a room as narrow as one would have expected in such a narrow house. It was the kind of room from which a maid might have fled without giving notice. To encourage its prospective tenants, Madame Sasso prodded the bed, which gave out somewhat discouraging sounds. The bed matched the room in narrowness, but there was an ample chair covered in a thick green material reminiscent of governesses and schoolrooms.

'Oh yes,' the young woman declared, 'we must have it. We must sleep *somewhere*. My husband has been ill.'

'Not seriously?' Madame Sasso hoped; and would they pay a deposit?

'If we are already here?' the husband pointed out.

'In advance then — if you would prefer it . . .' Madame Sasso smiled.

She tried to make a joke of it, but the wife was of a serious disposition; she opened her bag and brought out two or three notes as token payment.

So they were installed: *Monsieur et Madame Vatatzes — un nom grec*. Madame Sasso was impressed by the old gentleman's distinguished appearance and the beauty of his young — wife.

Left to themselves in their narrow room the travellers spoke in whispers at first. They touched each other often and gently, as though each suspected the other might break, or even vanish.

24th March

Soon after our arrival at this not very savoury *pension* Angelos took to his bed. The awfulness of yesterday's journey was too much for him. A. is prepared to accept this place as an asylum, in which case I do too. I realize by now we can never be separated, not by human

103

intervention (no Golsons!) only of my own free will. There I come up against the big snag. Shall my will ever grow strong and free enough for me to face up to myself? If I wanted that. To leave my one and only lover. I don't. I don't.

He snored the night away in this maid's bed. Myself comfortable enough in the chair until he asked me to come to him. We comforted each other narrowly and fell asleep towards dawn.

Will they hear us? The bed such a musical one, and the house, I'm sure, full of attentive ears.

Dined alone last night as he had no appetite: little separate tables, each with its complement of bottles – pills, spa water, wine eked out from previous meals to be consumed by sour mouthfuls at those to come. Dirty napkins put away in paper envelopes. Overall a smell of thrift and cheap oil.

Most of the guests are English (the *Anglaise* predominating) escaping from bronchitis, rheumatism, taxation, one or two perhaps from scandals. A few faces of mixed race – Levantines? A. would have known, too vocally to be comfortable, if he had been present. Trust A. to spot the *Frangolevantini*.

He ate a splinter of fish, mostly skin, which I took to our room, then he fell asleep again . . .

This morning was an improvement in every respect, though morning usually is. Looking back, my whole childhood is composed of mornings, yet I wasn't happy by any means. The future threatens very early. This growing threat which I'll always associate with unruly masses of purple lantana, and cats lying on hot asphalt as they died from eating too many lizards . . . Or was that a parent's diagnosis?

MOTHER: Don't look, darling. Patches is sick from eating lizards. They somehow poison cats. We'll take her to the vet and he'll make her better.

The vet didn't. I think Eadie hated cats. We were a house of dogs. Father was a cat man, but seldom there – away on circuit, or at the club. Father never wanted his child hanging round, or was in some way afraid. Eadie wanted one constantly.

EADIE: Don't you love me, darling? . . . Then why are you avoiding me?

Eadie's desire to devour – when you could have devoured the stuffy Judge – his man's smell! (This I think more than half explains my relationship with Angelos.)

104

Washed smalls, then walked down into the town. A scent of jonquils, roses — flowers. A yucca flaunting last year's brolly reminded me of home. Always these pointers. In the town the Golsons were out in force — a less showy variety because less affluent than those at St Mayeul. The ladies several years behind in their style, or else in enforced collusion with the past — putting on a brave show however, shaking their plumes, disentangling lorgnettes from lace. Elderly gentlemen in seedy retirement: tweeds in brown or grey, all tending to turn green. With luck their tweeds will see them out. The network of veins in flushed elderly male cheeks . . .

An English church, a squat Gothic in grey stone. Fine avenues at intervals. Outside their version of Miss Clitheroe's Tea-room and Lending Library a group of pelicans and brolgas discuss, not unexpectedly, war. War may be the solution.

Ate a delicious lunch alone on the terrace with my old darling, who had dressed, and persuaded the Sasso to let us enjoy this luxury. Madame S. is impressed by A. They always are till experiencing his rages, his not quite madness, which automatically they interpret as the real thing. First they are insulted, then frightened. May he continue to impress at 'My Blue Home'; morally I am exhausted.

An old servant, Marguerite, arranged a table for us in the patchy shade from an almond tree. Angelos in sentimental mood as we got through our *déjeuner*: a thin, rather greasy soup from last night's fish, *beignets de poisson* (pieces of skin, again from last night's fish, done in batter) something indeterminate as meat. For some reason one did not care. The bay, a breeze shaking alternate light and shade out of the branches of the almond tree, exorcized my thoughts of recent weeks — even Angelos helped.

A. remembers our first meeting when he picked me up on the Canebière. Who picked whom? he her she him, perhaps it was he him . . .

A.: Don't you remember?

E.: I could hardly forget. I can remember the dress I was wearing.

A.: I can't.

E.: You can never remember dresses. To me they mean so much.

A.: [for him, infinitely kind] Your vice. [He was in a stroking mood this morning.] I remember it was raining and we went to that hotel.

E.: Because you were ashamed to take me back to yours. You weren't quite sure what you'd got hold of.

A.: Don't be unkind, E. You can never resist the opportunity to be unkind.

[Marguerite brings the fruit; she has the sly look of a dog who has just disposed of a couple of pounds of fillet beef.]

A.: Do you know, darling, I'm sure we forgot the enema. If we wrote for it they might send it on.

E.: If we wrote for it Madame Boieldieu might make you pay the rest of what we owe.

A.: But I shall miss that enema. It's unlike anything they make today.

The damn enema notwithstanding, lunch on the terrace at 'My Blue Home' was an occasion I feel I shall remember. My old monster would not know it, but I could have eaten him between the courses. How is it the French can get away with pieces of fish skin done in batter? How can A., by looking at me from beneath those horny eyelids, convince me that we are wearing the purple, standing on the steps at Blachernae or Nicaea? more – that I am no longer a fiction but a real human being . . .

Madame Sasso and one of her boarders, a Mrs Corbould, were seated at an accommodating round table in a small *salon* between kitchen offices and public rooms, discussing over their second glass of *poire William* and before laying out the cards, the husbands they had buried, womb complications, and decreasing incomes; it was all too personal to include *les Boches*. As it was around 2 a.m., the other boarders had decamped to their beds with hot-water bottles, tins of imported Bath Olivers, and indigestion, while Marguerite had descended to the lower town with whatever she could scavenge from the evening meal.

Crimson plush and *poire William* were lighting the throats and cheeks of the confidential ladies when this young woman, this Madame Vatatzes burst upon them from the surrounding dark.

'*Mon mari, je crois, est gravement malade,*' she informed Madame Sasso, then remembering that her landlady was a linguist, 'He is having a heart attack.'

Madame Sasso could not have been more shocked. The announcement brought to mind a suicide in Number 17, from which it had taken her reputation several months to recover.

'You are sure, madame? You are not excited?'

Less involved, Mrs Corbould was fascinated by the openwork in the yoke of the nightdress this rather angular, flat-chested young woman had been wearing when her emotions carried her into their presence without additional covering.

'Do not distract yourself, madame. We will see,' Madame Sasso advised, herself trembling.

'But I know!' Madame Vatatzes insisted.

Madame Sasso also insisted, pushing past the young wife to reach the maid's room which the couple were at present occupying. From being English and discreet, Mrs Corbould did not follow, but poured herself another glass, and sat awaiting developments.

Madame Sasso was quick to see. '*Oui, madame, il est bien malade.*'

'Send for a doctor then — can't you?'

'*Marguerite est partie.* I dare not ask the cook. I have no other person.' Madame Sasso parried necessity like an expert, then appeared to remember.

She marched out, her black forms falling into place behind the padded buttons. 'Rouse Mr Genge,' she commanded Mrs Corbould.

Those who knew about such things were aware that Mr Genge, a *pensionnaire* of some years' standing, was in the habit of warming his blue shanks round Madame Sasso's steamy thighs on cold nights when the *propriétaire* was either forgetful or charitable.

Abandoning her *poire William*, Mrs Corbould rose to the occasion.

Madame Sasso returned to the sickroom.

Monsieur Vatatzes was lying, chin raised, his nightshirt open on a wisp of scruffy hair which his wife was stroking with one hand while holding with the other a bundle of yellow bones, not unlike, Madame Sasso observed, the claw of an elderly black cock, the kind which can be served as several courses after careful stewing.

'He is coming, darling,' Madame Vatatzes assured her husband with a tenderness Madame Sasso had not experienced before.

'Who is coming?' he asked. 'Who?'

'The doctor.'

'Oh,' he groaned. 'Only the doctor.'

To do something, Madame Sasso was pouring a glass of tepid water out of a carafe, when she definitely heard, 'I have had from you, dear boy, the only happiness I've ever known.'

Madame Vatatzes turned at once to the landlady. 'Leave us, please. I think it is over.'

Madame Sasso obeyed.

When she had returned to her confidante she could not prevent herself laughing. 'Poor man, he is out of his wits! Last words can often be amusing, as you, madame, will no doubt have found.'

Mrs Corbould found the last words of Monsieur Vatatzes, if not amusing, provocative.

Madame Sasso was pouring yet another glass of *poire William* when the young woman appeared again.

'He is dead,' she said, in what sounded not only a broken, but at the same time, an awakening voice.

Still barefoot, she was wearing a long black cloak over the nightdress with the openwork yoke.

Before the two women could go to her, to initiate her into the formal grief it is usual for widows to indulge in, Madame Vatatzes escaped from them into the night, her gait as long, loping, ungainly, as provocative as Mrs Corbould had found the openwork in a flat nightdress and the elderly Greek's last words.

As soon as she returned from that grotesque encounter with the woman of the suppurating bandage, she slipped off the smocked travelling garment she had been wearing over her nightdress, and after rummaging for a sheet of her best monogrammed letter parchment such as she had used weeks before in starting what became the aborted letter to Eadie Twyborn, sat down to write while her emotions, her dashed hopes, her suspicions and doubts were still seething in her. Yet hesitated before beginning, her glance directed beyond the upheaval of bosom, the delicately manicured fingernails, the plump ineffectual hands, the rings arrayed against the grain of this expensive letter-paper. (Were the rings perhaps vulgar when compared with those of Lady Tewkes – and Eudoxia Vatatzes, despite the fact that one had caught sight of congealed egg lurking in the corner of an agate eye?)

So she held back.

Before writing,

My dear Eadie,
more sober than on a former occasion, as was the comma more humbly inscribed than that other incised, flaunting one.)

She continued sitting awhile to gather courage for the plunge; then:

. . . What I am driven to write you will probably find preposterous, unbalanced, mad, but there comes a point in life where one has to face up to the aspirations, aberrations – failures. I'm sorry if I appear to be diverting to myself matters which concern you before anyone – well, Edward also, to some extent – but men, even fathers, are less concerned with what troubles the sensibility of wives, mistresses, children (of whatever sex). Men are complete to an extent we can never hope to be, as self-contained as those leather armchairs on which they leave their imprint . . .

Here Mrs Golson again hesitated for fear of what she might dredge up from depths she had never yet explored.

. . . Men are kinder than women, if also more clumsily brutal. I have never been whipped by a man as women know how to cut, dispensing pain often of an exquisite kind.

There is this Madame Vatatzes we recently met – and her elderly husband, a Greek if you please! I cannot *blame* Madame Vatatzes for any of the pain she inflicted on me, in fact I believe both she and I might not have accepted this infliction as pain.

She is in any case a radiant creature such as you before anyone, darling, would appreciate. On meeting 'Eudoxia' I could have eloped with her, as you too, Eadie, would have wanted, had you been here. We might have made an *à trois*, as they say! I would have been jealous. I would not really have wanted to share our bed of squalor with anyone else, after escaping from husbands, prudence, the past, into some northern town of damp sheets, iron bedsteads, bug-riddled walls. To lie with this divine creature, breast to breast, mouth to mouth, on the common coverlet, listening to the activity of the street below, flowing by gaslight over the wet cobbles.

There was a moment when I would have made this mistake had I been given half an opportunity. I would have allowed myself to be destroyed not only by a love such as I had never hoped to experience, but by a war which we are told is impending, both in the newspapers, and by what is perhaps the most reliable source in this horrid town, a lady of some authority at the English Tea-room and Library . . .

Mrs Golson paused breathless above her slashed parchment. I am mad, she thought, to pour out as never before on Eadie Twyborn. (Or not mad, perhaps literary without ever suspecting.) Then she continued,

. . . You if anyone, darling, will understand my predicament. I shall always remember how the palms trembled in the winter garden as we toasted our own daring – the amazed faces at that dance as we forced our way amongst the bankers, graziers, barristers, doctors – their *wives* . . . You gave me my first glimpse of the other life and the poetry of rebellion. None of what I hoped for ever began to be fulfilled until a few weeks ago when I met this Eudoxia Vatatzes . . .

Joanie paused again, the perspiration, the downright sweat plumping on the third sheet of parchment.

. . . You will understand — and my misery in finding she has disappeared, with her all hopes of definite evidence for solving a mystery which *concerns you more than anyone else*. I have nothing to prove anything, except those extraordinary eyes reflecting the fears of a small child, seen by night light, years ago.

So there is no reason why I should be writi . . .

Mrs Golson's pen faltered, and the next moment she had seized the sheets containing so much that was deplorable, emotional, naked, and was attempting to tear or worry her shame apart.

She had only to some extent succeeded when she heard, 'What are you up to, treasure?'

She turned, the nightdress slithering off one shoulder; she must have looked — womanly.

'Trying to write to Eadie, darling — the letter I've owed her all this time.'

Showing her the most forgiving smile, he advanced and covered up the naked shoulder, when she could tell he would rather have undressed the other.

'Silly old thing! If we take the *Simla* at the end of the week — as I'm sure you'll have the good sense to agree to — we'll be back as quick as any letter.'

'I expect we shall,' she admitted, fumbling with the bits of paper torn as small as they would ever be torn.

She laughed up at him. And while still holding this confetti of a letter, she accepted with the other hand the one her husband was offering. It had a strength for which she was grateful; she accepted even the hairs on the wrist below the freshly laundered cuff.

(Only to be rid of this 'clever', this 'literary' letter. Eat it? Too constipating. Throw it down the lavatory then. Or would it return to shame her before they left at the end of the week? Scatter it on a walk through the town. Oh, *no*, a trail for Miss Clitheroe to follow and piece together.)

'My nerves are to pot,' she groaned. 'It's this war they never stop talking about.' She held the back of his hand against her cheek. 'How lucky we are to be Australian!' It thrilled her husband's hand to detect this uncharacteristic enthusiasm. 'I shan't be happy till

we're back having breakfast together— in the morning-room— above
dear old Parsley Bay . . .'

PART II

It was his habit to walk the deck before its holy-stoning, while the last wet kisses and the smell of sperm were evaporating. For miles he tramped, up and down and round the corner. He would have liked to think it an exorcism, whereas it was a repetition: he was accompanied by the same, dun-coloured, laden figures returning to the front line; from whatever distance he was still aware of the stench of death. He kept it up hopefully however, all along the choppy periwinkle waves of a Mediterranean on which he was also turning his back, the scents he could recollect, of thyme, pine, carnation and rose, as opposed to the synthetic perfumes of recklessly expectant human beings in the first stages of a long voyage. He liked to think he was reserving himself for something ahead, and that he would emerge at last from the bombardment, not only of a past war, but the past. Unless perhaps, exorcism is a conjuring trick which does not work for those born without the requisites for grace.

At least his clothes were beginning to feel easier on him. He could face faces, the sound of quoits splattering around him, the exaggerated heartiness of returning colonials, and the patronage of the English who were going out to teach them something.

But from most of it he remained aloof, and they wondered why.

They discussed him outside the purser's office, and more brutally, over cocktails in the Smoking Room, investigating the credentials of this possibly regrettable, while desirable young man, this Eddie Twyborn.

Two young women were at it by the rail, one in the authoritarian, English county voice, the other in the loose, but no less assured accent of the established Australian rich. It was an acquaintanceship formed partly out of boredom, partly for mutual protection, somewhere off Crete, on one of the chillier, choppier afternoons of a periwinkle Mediterranean.

'I adore the Med, don't you? It makes me feel I'm abroad at last.'

'I only know it from passing through.'

'Oh well – now – so am I – perhaps for ever.'

'Oh, why?'

'Well, you see, I became engaged to an Australian. That's why I'm going out,' the English girl explained, while looking at a rather small sapphire exposed before her on the ship's rail.

'You won't regret it,' the Australian said without hesitation. 'By the way,' she added, as though offering her immigrant acquaintance a stanchion. 'I'm Margaret Gilchrist. My close friends,' she giggled, 'call me Margs.'

'Oh?' the county one returned. 'Well, I'm Angela Parsons. But answer to Angie.' She too threw in a giggle.

So the relationship was established, as much as anything through confidence in each other's high-lit teeth, of which Angie's were only very slightly buckled.

'I'm so glad we've met,' she said. 'So far it's been a tremendous bore – so under-populated – anyway with men.'

Margs glanced at the small sapphire on the hand grasping the varnished rail. 'What does your fiancé do?'

Angie grew serious. 'He farms,' she said. 'I believe he has,' she manipulated her buckled teeth, 'what is called a sheep station.'

'Oh yes, that's what it's called!' Margs giggled approvingly. 'You're all right there.' But paused. 'Daddy's a doctor – a specialist in diseases of the heart.'

They both looked appropriately grave, steadying themselves on the rail and rocking with the motion of the ship.

Margs told how she had been nursing a bit at the home of her aunt Lady Ifield, in Sussex. ('Not really? I believe Mummy knows her!') Angie had been driving an ambulance, which was how she had met Doug when he was returned wounded from the trenches.

The girls agreed the War had been simply ghastly, though not without its rewarding moments.

'Weren't you ever engaged?' asked Angie.

'Not actually, but almost,' Margs confessed.

'Did you sleep with him?'

'You have to, haven't you? when there's a war on.'

'Exactly! That's what I felt about Doug.'

It was fascinating for the two friends to be thus engrossed in moral issues.

Angela looked round at a husband helping a queasy wife erect a reluctant deck chair. 'Have you ever seen such a collection of pot-bellied men?'

'Every one of them hairy, I'd say.'

'How can you tell?'

'By what's missing on top.'

The two young women shrieked at the waves.

'But hair can be rather fascinating,' Angela said when she had subsided.

Margs looked round. 'There's a smooth one, though — have you come across him? Eddie Twyborn.'

'Oh yes. *Lieutenant* Twyborn.'

'Is he a lieutenant?'

'Was, I'm told. Decorated too.'

Margs looked ready to gobble up, not only the smoothness, but the decoration.

Furtive in their confidences, they both looked round to see the object of them approaching.

He passed by.

He was walking stiffly, his bearing tentative for a man, holding with Gothic hand against his chest the book he had been, or intended, reading. He was certainly not 'pot-bellied', and his well-covered skull, the hair of a cut to suggest an army officer, should have exempted him from accusations of hairiness by those who supported Margs's theory.

It was the face, however, which fascinated, not to say awed, the two observers. It had about it a detachment which could have passed for purity, which each of the girls must have sensed, for Angie said, after he was out of earshot, 'Do you think a man can be naturally pure? I don't mean monks and priests and things — and even those;' to which Margs, struggling with the proposition, replied, 'I'd never thought — but I see what you mean. Oh, yes!'

They looked at each other.

'Did you ever notice his eyes?'

'Of course! His eyes!'

They looked away.

At that moment the sun rent the slate-coloured awning stretched between world and sky, and at once the waves were decked with an evening panoply of gold and hyacinth.

Margs asked, 'Would you sleep with a man now that you're engaged to another?'

'If I did, I'd keep something back for marriage. Marriage is another matter,' Angie nobly replied.

'How right you are! Exactly how I feel!'

Soon afterwards the girls relinquished the rail and went down to dress for dinner.

After taking his clothes off, he lay down on sheets slatted with light, which surrendered their cool all too soon to a sweating body. A couple of days out of Colombo the bunk was as stable as a bed on this motionless sea, its monotony broken only by a random shark's fin; the flying-fish, growing languid, elected to stay below. His own languor did not prevent him forcing himself at his discipline of interrogating La Rochefoucauld, the words tasting musty to a furred tongue, the thought rising like baroque remains in a tropic jungle.

Nos vertus ne sont le plus souvent que des vices déguisés . . .; when according to his own experience the reverse was true.

His book tumbling floorwards, he dozed off, and was soon spanned by the protective wings of this great eagle, who should have been vicious, but wasn't. He could have cried out for the delight they were sharing if he hadn't become otherwise caught up in the stratagems of men, floundering in mud, failing to disentangle himself from the slime and blood of human bowels.

He awoke whimpering, twitching, yelping like a limp puppy.

The steward, a decent little bloke with the scar of an ancient boil visible on a cropped nape, was picking up the fallen book.

'French, eh?' It might have been his batman Pritchett. 'Not dressing up for the fancy ball?'

'Tired of dressing up . . .' Not only in the carnation robe, the pomegranate shawl, but the webbing, the mud leggings, and starting out through the carnival of gunfire and Very lights.

'Go in the altogether, sir,' the pseudo-Pritchett suggested. 'Give 'em an eyeful.'

He laughed down his nose. 'Tired of undressing too.'

'Pritchett' joined in with a snigger. 'Suffering from the old accidie, are we?'

He opened his eyes. 'Could be. What do you know about accidie?'

'Only what a priest told me.' As though released by an invitation the pseudo-Pritchett sat down on the edge of the bunk.

'The priest was suffering from it?'

'Not on yer life! 'E was working it out of 'is bloody system — take it from me — only too successfully.' The steward could not resist slapping the passenger on the thigh.

Oh God, not another! (You didn't mean it exactly like that, when you could have kissed the crater of the extinct boil. Poor bloody Pritchett!)

Recovering himself, the steward had risen and started on a dithering voyage of tidying. 'Only want to encourage you – Lieutenant Twyborn – to join in whatever's offerin'. We're 'ere, aren't we? so why not?'

'Cut out the Lieutenant.'

'But we want to honour yer – in some way.' The poor bastard almost in a state of bubbling tears.

'Thank you.' It sounded so dry, pompous, poopish – insincere, from one who was sincerely grateful. (A situation for La Rochefoucauld.)

'Well, goodnight, sir. Thank you.' There was not quite a click of heels as the batman-steward withdrew.

Turning a cheek against the hot pillow, Eudoxia Twyborn wept inwardly, for the past as well as a formless future.

The Arabian Sea and the Indian Ocean had been slowly cajoling the worst out of shipboard relationships; life was lived in a fever which only Fremantle would reduce. Until then, ex-colonels were ready to engage dangers less explicit than those they had survived; the more adventurous among their no longer seasick wives embarked on recces through the steerage and even into the engine-room. Girls grew breathless from expectation. Youths in sandshoes hovered, trousers hoist above hand-knitted ankles. All of them wanted to express *something*, but didn't. With the result that he in particular never mastered the part they expected him to play.

It was the girl with the creamed sunburn who dared blurt at the one they needed as protagonist for their legend. 'We all know you're Lieutenant Twyborn, so why shouldn't I introduce myself? I'm Angela Parsons of Salisbury, Wilts. Does it sound too American put like that?' Here she giggled and clasped her hands together on the rail. 'I'm going out to my fiancé – Doug Yeomans – who's farming near Brewarrinna.'

It was his turn to expose himself, as she had every right to expect, standing twisting the small sapphire she was wearing on her engagement finger, the desert light flashing on her slightly buckled teeth.

But he could not oblige her.

So she went off into a recitative of gush, 'It's so so so . . . the

DSO . . . we're so so . . . Well, real courage is not for every mortal to achieve.'

By now quite desperate, he replied, 'Courage is often despair running in the right direction.' And stalked off.

The other one, her friend, who tackled him not much later, was the more serious proposition in that she represented extrovert Australia.

'Aren't you one of *those* Twyborns?'

'Which?'

'Well – Edward the Judge.'

'He's my father.'

'And Eadie, Eadie's a friend of Mummy's. Not intimate, but a friend.'

She encouraged the son with a bland smile in a tan which had returned since her stint of nursing at Lady Ifield's Sussex mansion.

'How excited your parents must be to know you're coming.'

'They don't know.'

'Oh? But haven't you written?'

'Not in years.'

There was nothing she could say to that, only reflect her own parents' opinion of Eddie Twyborn's disappearance on the eve of his marriage to nice Marian Dibden, who had done much better for herself in the end with Ken Anstruther the chartered accountant (top of his year).

He saw to it that there was not another encounter until the two acquaintances Margs Gilchrist and Angie Parsons bailed him up by what looked like deliberate accident during the Aden-Colombo run. Planted in the glaring, holy-stoned deck they barred the way. He could feel the sweat trickling down his legs inside crumpled duck.

'Won't the ball be fun?' gushed Miss Parsons. 'What are you going as, Mr Twyborn? Or is it a secret?'

'Going as myself.'

'Oh, no! Oh, Eddie!' Margs protested. 'How *elderly*!'

He could only wince and hope to escape.

They couldn't bear it, and when, as they afterwards agreed, he was looking his most divine.

'I know!' It was Angela's brainwave. 'What if we dress you up as one of ourselves? You'd be a riot!'

Margs could only shriek in agreement.

'Might run you out of business.' He did not mean it to sound as sour as he knew it did, although he could see they hadn't heard it as more than a 'scream'.

He got away soon afterwards.

After finishing his dinner of half a leaden kromesky and a few splinters of frozen pheasant, and detaching himself from the colonial aristocracy (the genuinely kind ladies who would have liked to nurse him back from some obscure sickness he was obviously suffering from, and their more suspicious home-made husbands, creaking and sweating in the dinner jackets enforced on them) he did look in on the ball for a little, and spotted his two friends, the one a hearty improvised sultana, her yashmak stuck to the buckled teeth, the other an athletic pierrette in a costume she must have brought along. The latter's sinewy tanned arms were permanently tensed as though for a volley at tennis. The not inappropriately black pompoms revived the metaphor of an infernal game, which his memory loathed, yet mourned as the occasion of his downfall, the confession of his deficiencies.

He had almost succeeded in putting revelry behind him when he heard sounds of pursuit and, on looking round, saw that Margs Gilchrist had torn free of her partner, a certain ginger colonel going as a baby in pale blue rompers.

'I can't arrive home,' she panted, 'without being able to boast that I danced with the famous Eddie Twyborn.' 'Infamous' might have been the implication, as her nervous, though steely hand dragged him back into the maelstrom of a foxtrot, in which her abandoned ginger baby had continued whirling as solo jetsam.

'Won't you admit there's fun in life?' she hissed at him as they pumphandled through their steps.

'Oh, it's fun all right!' Too hilariously awful funny.

'We all know you've been through hell. But now it's over.'

When it was beginning again, if indeed it had ever stopped.

Margs was determined to prove a point. She had thrust a campaigning vulva as deep as possible into his crotch; her rather flat little breasts were bumping and grinding against his chest; the heat of her wiry body smelled agreeably natural emerging from its mist of talc. He would have liked to feel more than kindly disposed, to have given her the opportunity to think she was making her contribution to post-war therapeutics.

She was grinning up. 'Darling, you may be brave, but a girl's feet aren't the enemy. What about finding something else we could do together?'

He was saved by the ginger baby.

Brandishing its rattle at the end of a hairy arm, it screamed, 'You're hogging the lieutenant, Mummy! Poor Baby, must have a turn.'

The colonel's crotch was almost as possessive as Margie Gilchrist's, and certainly more developed than her breasts.

'Eddie,' the sultana called across the deck, 'save me the waltz. A waltz is what I'm dying for.' To illustrate, she swooned so elaborately that she brought her swaggie partner down.

At that moment the music stopped and Eddie Twyborn escaped from the muscular embrace of ginger arms.

While they were all laughing, stamping, shouting, clapping, he scuttled down the companionway into the smelly-clean bowels of a ship and the asylum of his cabin. When he had bolted his door, taken off his clothes, and shot La Rochefoucauld into a corner, he lay down – expecting what?

All night, it seemed, giggles and explosions, a traffic of clumsy, spongy feet filled the corridor. At intervals a handle was rattled, at others almost wrenched off.

Margie Gilchrist's exploratory vulva, or alternately the colonel's opulent crotch, was forced against his sleep.

Fremantle, 4 mars 1920

Said there would never be another diary, and here it is (like masturbation) in that old *cahier* I found amongst Angelos's belongings – the stationer's imprint A. Diamantis, 26 rue du Commerce, Smyrne (the French touch hovering over every Greek of a certain age and any pretensions).

But Fremantle, the first glimpse, the first whiff of a fate which can never be renounced, is enough to drive the pretensions out of any expatriate Australian.

A party organized for sight-seeing in Perth this morning. It ended up as Angie Parsons, Margs Gilchrist, Colonel 'the Baby' Wilbraham-Edwards, and a widow hurtling back into circulation, Mrs Merv 'call me Dawn' Pilbeam. I gave belly-wobbles as my excuse for not joining; might be a drag on their sport. The party accepted my reasons, while not wholly convinced. They tottered down the gangway on the first stage of their fun-finding, the ladies precarious on their heels, the colonel waving back. All soon quenched. No heat, or is it the glare? more quenching than that of Fremantle.

After letting the party make its getaway, I went down into the town. Rusted railway-lines are strips of red, solidified heat. Wharfies sweating round their hairy navels. I am the stranger of all time, for all such hairy bellies an object of contempt – a Pom, or worse, a suspected wonk. If only one had the courage to stick a finger in the outraged navel and await reactions. Nothing minces so daintily as an awakened male.

Dream streets: the tiny houses in maroon or shit-colour brick. Paint-blisters on brown woodwork. Festoons of iron doilies which suggest melting caramel. Blank, suetty faces of women framed in grubby lace or muslin curtains, as they peer out in search of something to whet their interest. A little pomeranian dog, white coat with patches of pink eczema. An ageing blonde stands holding the dog to her bosom, fat dissolving on her vast arms. A gold armlet eating into a fatty biceps, the neatly folded, obsessively laundered hankie held in place by this dented gold circlet.

Oh, God, but I feel for them, *because I know exactly* – they are what I am, and I am they – interchangeable.

Perhaps I should have gone with the Hoorah Party, fun-finding in Perth. Fremantle is something to be passed over because so painfully personal. No doubt that's why I chose it – the expatriate masochist and crypto-queen.

Drank a schooner in a tiled bar. The acid smell, not quite urine, of draught beer. The 'head' forming as a red hand pulls on the joy-stick. The barmaid's rattling cough accompanied by a blast of morning gin.

An old professional blue-nosed soak, a finger crooked above the slops in his glass, tries to engage the interloper.

o.s.: Owdyer findut, eh? in Fremantle.

ME: All right, I suppose. Yes, all right. [Hopeful laughter]

o.s.: Not all the Poms do. An' I can't see why. [His turtle's neck at work as he swallows the last of the slops.]

ME: I'm not a Pom.

o.s.: Go on! You're not? [He stands looking in need of a reassurance he does not expect to get.] What are yer, then?

ME: [because it's useless to explain.] I'm a kind of mistake trying to correct itself.

Too much for Fremantle. The silence hits me in the small of the back, like the sheet of frosted glass with BAR engraved on a lyre of ferns.

I am in the street. I am the Resurrection and the Dead, or more simply, the eternal deserter in search of asylum. I did not leave Angelos, but might have done so. I did not desert from the army because it would have been too difficult. In such situations you're sucked in deeper, while remaining a deserter at heart.

At a draper's I buy for five shillings a cardigan in grey string. Stagger out again into the glare not knowing why I've made my purchase, except that it might encourage a humility I've never been able to achieve. And there, oh God, is the Greek shop I've been expecting while dreading.

SNACKS DINNERS SODAS SUNDAES
ALL HOURS
PROP: CON ASPERGIS

Will Con the Prop recognize the con?

At the Greek's there is a soft, sticky gloom, the Greek concession to Fremantle's version of Australian brown: an atmosphere made up of frying fat (oil, dripping, or a mixture of both) synthetic 'flavours' mingled with freezing gusts, light filtered through stained glass on to bas reliefs of dusty, brown-gold nymphs. The usual assortment of clotted sauce bottles, cruets and fly-specked 'mee-news'.

I sit and wait at a stained table. For a moment I am tempted to smear my throat and wrists with tomato sauce, snuffle it up through my nostrils, and fall across the table, some kind of Greek sacrifice crossed with an Australian fate – lie there for poor Con to find and misinterpret.

He comes out through the bead curtain, a thickset, short-arsed man, thin on top, but with wisps of damp black hair sprouting from various parts of his body. Thick arms hanging alongside the stained apron. The inevitable wedding ring conspicuously gold on a finger swollen by kitchen rites. For the customer, Con is wearing a golden smile, while Greek eyes wonder whether the Turk has arrived.

E.: What'uv we got for dinner, Con? [The Greek can't know about this hearty self evolved solely for his benefit.]

CON.: Good fress fiss. Tsips. Stike 'n' onions. Stike 'n' eggs. All very spessul.

E.: *Then echeis kephtehthes?*

CON.: No *kephtehthes*. [Tongue held against the palate produces that clicking noise which is the sound of Greek negation.] You spick Grick, eh? [The Greek eyes again suspicious.]

E.: How I speak Greek!

CON.: You not Grick. Where you learn?

E.: In another life. In Byzantium.
[The Greek roars for this mad joke before steering into safer waters.]

CON.: What you teck for dinner?

E.: Knowing the Greek, whatever he decides I must teck.

CON.: [relieved by this lesser madness.] You teck fiss. Fiss is good. [He calls the order through the bead curtain.]

Two boys have come out, one of a superior teen age, and a small inquisitive roly-poly. If the youth is inquisitive too, he has learnt to disguise it. The father, muttering in the background, tells them he has on his hands some kind of foreign, Greek-speaking madman.

CON.: [returning to the foreground.] You titch my boys Grick, sir. Ross and Phil don't wanter learn their own language.
[The older boy prowls in an agony of disgust against the far wall of the café. He would like to dissociate himself from this communicative father.]

CON.: Ross make big progress at 'ighschool. 'E'll study Law.

E.: Poor bugger!

CON.: Eh?

E.: Good on 'im!
[Ross can't take any more. He stalks between the tables and out the shop door, a disdainful Greek imitation of the emu. The father is occupied professionally, but the roly-poly Phil is fascinated by what is new.]

P.: [very softly, as he examines a heap of spilt salt on the surface of the table.] Where you from?

E.: From here.
[The roly-poly's lip, his downcast eyes, are disbelieving.]

P.: You been away for long?

E.: Yes, ages — at the War.

P.: [acquisitively] Got any souvenirs on yer?

E.:   Don't go in for souvenirs. There's reminders enough, if you want them, in your mind.

P.:   No helmuts? Byernets? Didn't you ever kill someone?

E.:   I expect I did.

P.:   Got any medals?

E.:   I lost it.

      [The questions are becoming intolerable, and only beginning. The customer gets up and is preparing to leave.]

P.:   Hey, yer order, mister!

      [For Con is at this moment returning with it, mummified in yellow batter, beside the mound of glistening chips.]

CON.:   You no want yer good fiss dinner? [The incredulous wedding ring on the Greek's stumpy, tufted finger; all the best men are ringed.]

E.:   Oh, I want all right — yes! But somehow always miss the bus . . .

      [Puts down some money and escapes into the outer glare, which blinds at least temporarily.]

'But who will I say?'

'You needn't say anybody, need you? If she's in the garden I'll just go out.'

It was too much for the young parlourmaid. She had reddened all the way up her neck. The points of her cap were quivering for what she had been taught was an offence against accepted behaviour.

'Mrs Twyborn won't like that.' The girl had begun to prickle with tears of anger.

'She was never all that orthodox herself.'

The situation was something the maid's starch was unable to protect her against, so she turned and blundered out in the direction of the servants' quarters.

He was left with this house in which the owners had gone on living without his assistance. He wondered what part he had played in their lives during his absence, perhaps no more than they in his own unwilling memory: a series of painful, washed-out flickers. Unless those who lead what are considered *real* lives see the past as an achieved composite of fragments, like a jig-saw from which only some of the details are missing, or cannot be fitted.

Since encouraging his parents' maid to surrender her responsibility here he was, surrounded by all the details of the classic jigsaw waiting for him to put them together, more alarmingly, to fit himself, the missing piece, into a semblance of real life. He could hear a tap dripping (there had always been a tap dripping in the cloakroom). Hanging from a peg there was the rag hat the Judge used to wear when he went fishing with his mates Judge Kirwan and Mr Mulcahy K.C. Opulence still showed through the texture of scuffed rugs; and on the Romanian mat, the place where Ruffles had pissed was only slightly darkened by time. He hesitated, dazed by the perspective of other rooms, opening through light and memory into a blur of acacia fronds and hibiscus trumpets.

He progressed slowly to the far side of what was referred to as the 'drawing room', with its crumpled chintz, sunken springs ('natural comfort,' Eadie called it), Town Cries, figurines, paperweights, the inherited Dutch chest shedding its marquetry scales, the unnatural photographs of relations, friends, associates, assembled over an indiscriminate lifetime (himself in a white tunic, lace-up boots, simpering from beneath a fringe while holding a sword). Now defenceless (supposedly an adult) standing on the ridge between the French doors, from which he must descend by way of the discoloured marble steps, the corroded, unstable handrail, into Eadie's 'beloved' garden (as her women friends, the Joanie Golsons, referred to it), this morning a chaos of suffocating scents and emotions. He had to face it. Now or never. Must. And did.

And there was Eadie, crouched on her knees with a trowel in her hand, her beam broader in one of those skirts she had invariably worn, a miracle of Scottish weave and an intermingling of dogs' hair clotted with compost or manure. Oblivious as far as you could tell. As were the six or seven little red dogs, scratching, swivelling on their rumps, sniffing, one of them lifting a leg behind Eadie's back on a border of sweet alyssum.

To an outburst of barely synchronized clocks in the house behind, and the little terriers giving tongue, she turned on her haunches, and squinted through the smoke from a wilting cigarette at the intruder in her garden.

Making an uglier face she asked, 'Who are you? Didn't Mildred answer the bell? Who . . .?' then went off into a long whimpering moan, wrinkling up, coughing, gasping.

'Oh!' she cried. 'What you've done to us, Eddie! Whyyy?'

She hung her head, and if the cigarette hadn't slipped from her lips down inside her front, the situation might have grown intolerable, but in the circumstances she had to slap and grab at her blouse, shouting, 'God . . . *damn* . . .' before retrieving the source of her wrath and flinging it into a patch of snail-fretted acanthus.

She clambered to her feet, tottering on legs seized by cramp, dropping the trowel from stiff fingers, again threatened with a landslide of emotion, while the terriers pounced, one of them worrying at a trouser-cuff, sniffing to decide the category to which this unidentified person, possibly no stranger, belonged.

'Shouldn't we embrace?' The gruff warning in her voice at once established her as his mother; and as they advanced upon each other, still the victims of their diffidence, he saw that it was she who was beginning to take the initiative, while he, the passive object of her intentions, was drawn into the labyrinth of wrinkles, cigarette fumes, and more noticeable, a gust of early whiskey.

Wasn't this what he had come for? He closed his eyes and let it happen.

He must have continued standing with them closed, for when it was over she demanded, out of a greed which had not been sated, 'Come on, let me look at your eyes. Your eyes are what I've missed most.'

So he had to open up to the present, to her pair of brown ferrets, and must have repelled them, for she gasped and asked, 'Are you hungry, darling? Arriving so early – and the Customs – the Customs always make one hungry. What about your luggage? Did Mildred take it up to your room? She looks frail, but she's surprisingly tough – only idle.'

'I haven't got it. It's at the hotel.'

'I hope you're not going to make us pay too dearly, Eddie, for being your parents.'

When more than likely Eadie intended he should be the one to pay for a relationship, the mysteries of which might never be solved.

'You don't always know,' he mumbled, 'whether it's as difficult for people to have strangers staying, as it is – well, to stay with strangers.'

They were stranded looking at each other on the spot where drawing room became hall. Anywhere else it might have been unbearable to realize that the son with whom she had wrestled, perhaps even tried to throttle in the agony he had caused while forcing his way out of a womb where he was not wanted in the first place, had become the mirror-figure of herself. At least the doorway from drawing room to hall allowed her to shoot off into the dining room beyond, and avoid further exposure.

Then, with her back to him, she complained, 'My nerves are on end,' and poured herself a resounding whiskey.

Back still turned, she decided, 'Thatcher will fetch your stuff from the hotel. Thatcher's the gardener — no earthly use, except to take the dogs walking. I doubt anyone else would have him if we turned him loose. So Thatcher has become our fate.'

Once more mistress of herself, Thatcher, and most others, she returned from the dining room into the hall, thrust out her hand, and announced through that voracious smile, 'Come and I'll show you your room.'

As though he didn't know it.

'Is the mattress as hard as it used to be?'

But she did not seem to hear as they clumped thumping upstairs, shoulder bumping off shoulder, hands locked in sister-hood.

Delicacy must have overtaken Eadie, for she left him alone in what had been, and evidently still was, his room. Nothing appeared to have been disturbed, neither objects such as books, trophies, a sea-urchin on a window sill, nor the nightmares and unrealizable romances with which the narrow bed was still alive. He prodded it, and felt the same hair mattress on which he had done youthful penance. She had unlatched the shutters, but the glare of sunlight prevented him re-acquainting himself to any extent with the precipice outside, its fuzz of lantana scrub, nasturtiums, and a few precarious pittosporums. Considering that the geography was so little altered, the furniture disposed to receive him back, there was no reason why he should not resume both his rational and unconscious lives, if the unreason with which he was cursed, and worse than that, a rebellious body, would allow him to.

In the meantime he prowled inside the fortress of his room, stepping as softly as he could in case his mother might be listening for his movements, to interpret them. Eadie = Eddie. It was true, but in spite of the war years and the aftermath of peace, he had not yet learnt to accept that he was Eddie Twyborn, the son of Mr

Justice Twyborn — the incalculable factor. He dreaded Edward more than Eadie, who was himself in disguise.

He continued prowling, softer than before, running his finger down the spines, the titles of dustless books: the rejected Profession — *Private Equity*, *Real Property*, *The Law of Contract*, *The Law of Torts*; *The Prisoner of Zenda* and *Robinson Crusoe*; the Kipling birthday presents ('he's such a splendid writer, darling, as you'll appreciate later on'); Swinburne's reeking perfumes, secret orgasms; *The Man in the Iron Mask* — the Bible.

He opened the last, and in it found, in a handwriting gone green with age, the characters cramped by sincerity and doubts:

For Eddie
  on the occasion of his 13th birthday
    from his father
      Edward Twyborn

He might have protested *oh horror horror my own poor father* if there hadn't been a knocking at the door.

It was Mildred and the gardener Thatcher either end of his cabin-trunk.

Mildred panted, 'Where shall we put it, Mr Eddie?'

'On the sofa?'

'Oh, no! Mrs Twyborn would never approve of that. The springs!'

'But there aren't any, and I shan't have to stoop.'

'Shall we leave it here? under the window?' was Mildred's breathless suggestion.

'The rain will come in.' He identified his mother's disapproving voice.

But Mildred and Thatcher were ready to dump the trunk, and did, under the window. The parlourmaid was smelling rather pleasantly of the powder which had given in to her exertions; while Thatcher who took the dogs for walks, and who had adopted silence, probably as an armature against his mistress, stank of what is known as 'honest sweat', or more accurately, dirty socks.

They came and went, bringing in the smaller pieces. Eddie Twyborn, so-called, felt guilty, and prowled worse, with less concern for what might be overheard by Eadie.

As the servants were leaving she did in fact appear, having changed into some sort of haphazard frock, exposing freckled arms and a droughty chasm leading to the breasts which had suckled her child. It was not so much this painful revelation as the face she had tried to disguise by smearing it with crimson and white which made him avert his own.

'Now,' she said, her gaping wound smiling at him from amongst those lesser ones which had healed, 'you must come down and have a drink — and tell me all about everything,' trying to sound like the girl she might never have been.

Did she know he knew? She bowed her head going downstairs in front of the son she might never have had.

When they were seated in the drawing room, each holding as a protective weapon a glass of whiskey as strong as Eadie knew how to pour, and she had lit one of the cheroots he remembered her smoking in the past, only in the tower room alone with the Judge, he asked straight out, 'What became of Ruffles — Mum?'

As though beaten at her own game by the one who should have been 'telling all', she looked at the carpet, and answered, 'Ruffles died.' It left her with a little tic in one cheek.

While like some old mangy, cancerous dog, Angelos Vatatzes was dragging his body out of a corner of the drawing room to lay his head on Eudoxia's knee, asking forgiveness for his devotion.

The apparition drove Eddie Twyborn to concentrate on something which might convey actuality: the waves painted on the Gulf of Smyrna; lizards on burning marble at Nicaea; arabesques swirling out of the Chabrier waltzes at nightfall above Les Sailles.

'Anyway, Ruffles apart,' he said to his mother, 'nothing has changed — here — since I went away. Only the springs have given up.'

Eadie hunched her shoulders and, after plunging her hands into the bowels of her chair as though groping for evidence which might justify his accusation, came out with a high, smoky giggle. 'You're not cruel, darling, I hope. We're not as well off as we were — on a judge's salary.'

'Nobody — that is, none of *us* is ever as well off as we were. It's one of the laws of nature and history.'

He heard her teeth make contact with her glass as she tried to work it out. 'Darling, stop *scratching*!' She smacked one of her little dogs.

Yes, he was being cruel, but only as he was to himself.

Her eyes were appealing to him, asking for some revelation, not quite that perhaps (wasn't she Judge Twyborn's pragmatic wife?) but a factual account of what he had been doing all these years. Had he been taking part in a war, like all young men of decent upbringing?

In case he was going to deny her this simple luxury, she leaned forward, elbow wobbling slightly on a knee, so that whiskey slopped over the lip of her glass. 'Delia died too. Now we've Etty. Her devilled drumsticks are scrumptious. But she bosses me. I can't stand it.'

'She'll probably leave, like Joséphine Réboa.'

'God forbid! I couldn't bear it.' She bit on her cheroot. 'Who was Josephine Whatsername?'

'Somebody who left.'

After that they were at sea.

He thought he felt something crawling somewhere between his crotch and his navel.

Deciding, it seemed, not to let him escape, she leaned farther forward and asked, 'Darling, *were* you in the War?'

'Yes – as it happens – I was.'

'I'm so glad. We would have hoped you were.'

'Who?'

'Well, Daddy . . .'

He would have liked to think that 'Daddy', of all people, would not have condemned him.

'. . . and our friends.'

She was looking at him.

'Who? your friends?'

'Well, darling – everybody.'

She was looking at him more intently still. 'You remember Joanie? Joanie Golson. The *Boyd* Golsons.'

'Vaguely.'

'And Marian Dibden?'

She was sitting forward to take stock. Eadie's therapeutic touch was that of a sledge-hammer.

'When shall I see my father?' he asked.

'Oh,' she withdrew into her chair, 'I was going to ring him, then I didn't because I thought he'd be too upset. I thought when he comes home tonight I'd bring you out into the garden.'

'No.'

'What, then?'

'I'll come out – and just meet him – like that.'

'If it's what you want.' The little dogs skirling at her ankles, she went to pour herself another drink, forgetting his.

Mildred announced. 'Etty says luncheon is ready, madam.'

Eadie Twyborn ducked her head. 'Oh, well, if it's what Etty says . . . I hope it's something delicious for Mr Eddie's return to the fold.'

Mildred snickered, and looked down her powdered front.

There was nothing for it but that mother and son should go into the dining room and continue to 'tell about everything'. Would Eadie of the corked-on moustache flinch if he casually produced the spangled fan and pomegranate shawl, flung them into the conversation? Wait perhaps, till the Judge was wearing his high heels and black silk stockings.

Eadie said, 'I can imagine, Eddie, what you must have suffered – from what one heard of life in the trenches.'

In the lull before the guns opened up again there was only the sound of a dog scratching.

'Did you win any medals?' she asked.

'Only one.'

'I'd adore to see it.'

'I dropped it down a grating in London after I was demobbed.'

'I expect you could get another,' she said, 'if you paid them for it.'

From his window he had watched darkness gathering, a milky sky purpling over, a recent flowering of lights dancing in a thicket as branches were stirred by an evening breeze, all that was left of a ferry now like a child's illuminated pencil-box slid across a smooth black surface in a gap between trees. ('You wanted a pencil-box, didn't you, Ed?' 'Yes, but I thought it'd be a double-decker.' 'Sorry – next time – when you're older.' Later: 'Your father gave it so much thought – such a busy man – you should have sounded more grateful.' Silence. He was not ungrateful. He took the disappointing pencil-box to bed. He hid it under his pillow. He would have defended it from loving hands doing things only for his good, removing angular, uncomfortable, ultimately ridiculous pencil-boxes. He would have been prepared to wound the loving hand as he had when it was laid upon him as a comfort, while he was inhaling the ether. 'They're only going to snip the nasty tonsils, which might otherwise poison your whole system; you won't feel it I promise you, darling.' '*Nhhao*!' the shriek it became in the lint funnel as you were sucked down it, down down, through a scent of pale green fur . . .)

In this evening's silence, nobody, at least for the time being, was suggesting anything for his good. His isolation was not the target for the sounds breaking around it: the chitter of crickets, the twitter from a formation of small migrating birds, a gibber of possums, more human for the demands they were making on one another, the crash of a tram as it rounded a corner in a sputtering of violet sparks.

Shouldn't he *do* something instead of becoming a fixture in this room which had received him back? What rituals were performed before dinner in the house to which he belonged? Did they bathe? Change their clothes? To be on the safe side, he decided not to prepare in any way. Stick to the day's patina of grime and sweat, an additional layer of himself as protection against the moment when he must beard the Judge in the garden.

A figure, he realized, had come down the steps from the drawing room and was hovering amongst the more amorphous masses of shrubs. Impossible to tell whether it were Edward or Eadie. Cigar smoke was no indication of sex. If Edward, would Eadie have warned him of what to expect? Or had she decided to submit him to the same shock as she had undergone, only intensified by darkness, night perfumes, and fragmentation of distant lights? Perhaps you had done wrong to plan the meeting in the dark garden. Face to face in the dim lighting favoured in this house might have been less unnerving, underwater shapes drifting harmlessly around as they took each other's measure. Too bad if a predator appeared. But Eadie had probably been frightened off. She would keep away till the worst was over.

Anyway, he had to go down.

Crossing the drawing room he overheard a voice bullying servants. 'Can we be sure of the soufflé, Etty? You know what a flop the last one was – when Mrs Golson came to lunch . . .' A clattering of crockery. 'By all means take her on your lap, Thatcher. But you did nothing, absolutely nothing, about the cyst between her toes. My poor dear! My darling Biffy! Sentimentality is all very well, but practical attention, Thatcher, is what little dogs respond to.' A cowering silence, almost, you thought you detected, a fearful stench blowing from the kitchen offices.

He forged on. The sound of his own feet covering a jarrah no-man's land between threadbare rugs should not have alarmed an ex-lieutenant (D.S.O.); nor should an ex-Empress (hetaira) of Nicaea, expert in matters of protocol and mayhem, have quailed before a situation involving a minor official even when the official was her father; mere blood relationship never ruled out a bloodbath.

With Eadie in the kitchen, it was unavoidably the Judge smoking his solitary cigar in the quiet of the garden.

Lieutenant Twyborn went over the top, down the marble steps from which brocaded skirts swept dead leaves and caterpillars' droppings.

A shaft of light striking from the house laid bare the long judicial face as well as that of the defendant.

A dry, self-contained man, the Judge was at the culprit's mercy as never on any of his many circuits.

'Why didn't she tell me?' He had to accuse somebody.

The air around them was tremulous.

'I expect she thought it would be less upsetting to let you find out.'

As indeed it had been easier not to forewarn by writing, to leave it to a mingling of skin and veins, the texture of cloth, the tokens on a watch-chain, the spider-moustache which descended and withdrew as on the night when the shutters blew open, never before, never again till now. (Angelos hadn't worn a moustache.)

In the shaft of light the Judge's concern glistened like bone: that this son whom he loved — he did, didn't he? should have perverted justice by his disappearance. Judge Twyborn did not intend to pursue the reason why; it might have been too unreasonable for one who put his faith in reason despite repeated proof that it will not stand up to human behaviour.

To avoid a conclusion he might be forced to draw, this honourable man began asking, 'Did they put soap for you, Eddie, and a towel?'

'Haven't looked, but I expect so.'

'Whatever else is neglected, your room has been taken care of.'

They were stumbling over the earthworks Thatcher's tended lawn had thrown up.

'Are you cold, boy? Your hand is cold.'

'Not unduly.' The hand you were chafing with yours, the molten rivers of veins, would not have allowed it; still, you heard yourself chattering as though with cold.

'Sydney is splendid at night,' the Judge was informing a visitor. 'There's a lot that's undesirable by day, but that can apply, I should think, in any city in the world.'

Fortunately as they reached the steps the techniques of living were taking over.

'Madam says dinner is served, sir. She's afraid of the soufflé.'

Lieutenant Twyborn dropped his host's hand.

Freshly powdered, Mildred stood simpering on the illuminated heights. She had exchanged her daytime starch for organdie frills, frivolous against a more austere background of black.

And Eadie had emerged to reinforce the announcement. 'Yes,' she told them, 'Etty's soufflé is standing up – splendidly. So don't dawdle, Edward, please.'

She smiled at their son. She may have wished to touch him, but something she could not have defined frightened her into resisting the impulse. Perhaps it was his good looks. Handsome men were inclined to intimidate Eadie Twyborn. It would not have dawned on her to credit with looks the man she had married, just as you take for granted some elegant hairbrush acquired long ago, its form less noticeable by the time you've worn the bristles down and realize you ought to do something about what has become a source of aggravation.

As they entered the dining room Judge Twyborn was holding himself so erect he must have been competing with a soldier son. In more normal circumstances, his profession would have assisted him, but the combination of an already mythical war and suddenly recovered fatherhood left him looking overtly respectful.

Eddie saw that the whole elaborate ritual was in store: the mahogany oval laid with worn silver, Waterford glass, in a central epergne white hibiscus preparing to close, while Mildred, straining at her calves against the sideboard, would be catapulted into the kitchen as soon as they were seated, to return with Etty's upstanding soufflé.

Oh God, he could have cried. Instead he bowed his head as for grace, and remembered the fortnight after confirmation when he had expected miracles.

'We don't know, darling, what your tastes are,' Eadie said, 'I mean – in food.'

The Judge sat crumbling bread on the mahogany surface beyond the circumference of a Limerick doily which threatened to stick to his fingers, all doilies to all their fingers, leprous flesh barely distinguishable from webs of lace.

'I mean,' said Eadie, 'whether you're a *gourmet*, or like it plain.'

'Don't you think food depends a lot on time and place?'

Eadie laughed; she would have laughed at anything, even what she hadn't listened to. But Edward Twyborn was looking grave. Eddie hated to feel he might appear a prig to those mournful eyes.

'Do you remember — Father,' the whole scene was so unreal, nothing he might add to it could make it more incongruous, 'you took me with you when a court was sitting at — Bathurst I think it was. We shared an enormous iron bed with a honeycomb coverlet on it.'

'I don't remember,' the Judge said.

'I do.' Or thought you did. Oh yes, you *did*! 'I was so excited I lay awake all night listening to the noises in the pub yard. The moonlight, I remember, was as white as milk. It was hot. I pushed the bedspread off. It lay on the floor against the moonlight.'

'Eddie, you're making it up!' Eadie was out in the cold.

'No, I'm not,' he insisted as he messed up Etty's soufflé. 'Remembering is a kind of disease I suffer from.'

'Hardly a disease,' the Judge muttered through a mouthful. 'Useful, I'd say, if you're to any degree selective.'

'No, a disease,' Eddie Twyborn heard himself persisting. 'I don't know, but suspect that those who can't recall, act more positively than those who are bogged down in memory.'

Eadie announced in a loud voice, 'You can't deny it's a jolly good soufflé.'

'Excellent,' the Judge agreed.

'I remember, on the same trip we had a meal in one of those railway refreshment rooms — so-called. We had corned beef, and watery carrots, and dumplings that bounded from under the knife . . .'

'Oh darling, must we be *morbid*?'

'. . . but it was delicious. Anyway, a delicious memory. Even the brown drone of blowflies, the brown linoleum. Somebody's dumpling shot across the floor.'

Judge Twyborn was staring at his plate, at the soufflé he had massacred.

'I can't believe,' Eadie said. 'Unless you keep a diary. Do you, Eddie?'

'On and off.'

'I've thought about it. But haven't had the courage.' She wiped her mouth, and looked at the mark on the napkin.

Eddie glanced at the father he had wanted to impress and comfort, who was looking as though he had a moron for a son, or worse, some kind of pervert: that honeycomb bedspread, the whole moonlit scene.

While his wife continued wrapped in a state of mind induced by the mark on the napkin.

The Judge leaned across. 'Then I'm not wrong, my dear, in thinking you painted up a bit too vividly for the occasion.'

Eadie exclaimed, 'Oh my God!' and got up to pour herself a whiskey chaser to her wine.

Mildred removed the dishes, and brought on the roast fowl, with bread sauce and sprouts, just as though it were the holidays.

'Are we having the caramel custard with toffee on it?' he asked his mother.

'You're unnatural, Eddie.'

Even before all three were crunching the caramel toffee (Judge Twyborn more circumspectly than the others because of an upper denture) he knew that he should not have come back; he should have kept his existence to himself, or only revealed it to strangers.

Eadie stood up at last. 'This is where I leave the men to the port. I know that's how Edward would like it.' She poured another whiskey chaser to sustain her in her isolation.

She had got herself up in an ancient girlish frock, silver flounces over rose. A tear became visible under one armpit as she scratched her head defensively. She was wearing a Spanish comb in her hair as no Spaniard had ever worn one.

He stood up. He would have liked to say something to his mother, but hadn't learnt the language as do natural linguists and normal sons.

So she extricated herself from what she saw to be a male situation, and was soon cursing Etty, Mildred, Thatcher, between the silences in which she hoped to overhear what was going on in the dining room.

He had failed her. He was going to fail them both, as it is the habit, more often than not, of the children to fail the parents — and vice versa.

He had hardly sat down after Eadie's exit when the Judge began. 'What do you think of doing, Eddie?'

You could hardly answer, Nothing; surely being is enough? looking, smelling, listening, touching.

Instead you said, 'I'm thinking of going into the country. To work.'

In response to a serious aspiration, the Judge became more than ever earnest. 'A practice in a country town – somewhere like Wagga, say – no, Bathurst. I don't approve of nepotism, but could probably persuade Birkett and Blair to take you in. A very reputable firm of solicitors. Blair I know personally. I can't see why you shouldn't aim higher eventually. But feel your way back into the profession you were intended for. I'd die so much happier for seeing you dedicated to the Law.'

The velvet of sentiment and the private bin Edward Twyborn kept in reserve for celebrations introduced a seductive solemnity into their tête-à-tête. Eddie wished he could take himself as seriously as his father required, or that the Judge might have understood the greater seriousness of coming to terms with a largely irrational nature.

'I thought of taking a job, as a labourer more or less – hard physical labour – on the land – and in that way perhaps, getting to know a country I've never belonged to.'

Judge Twyborn's eyes had never looked deeper, more troubled, as though some private obsession of his own were on the point of being discovered.

In fact his son barely noticed; he was too surprised at the improbable idea which had come to him the moment before. Its morality must have appeared admirable, if stark, to the one in whom he was confiding. His more innocent confidant would not have seen it as Eddie Twyborn escaping from himself into a landscape.

Oh yes, it was an idea he would more than consider; he could not wait to put it into action; he was already surrounded by the train smell, frosty air, his oilskin rolled, heavy boots grating on the gravel of a country siding. (Would those who came across him notice that the boots were recently bought and that his hands looked as ineffectual as they might prove to be?)

But the landscape would respond, the brown, scurfy ridges, fat valleys opening out of them to disclose a green upholstery, the ascetic forms of dead trees, messages decipherable at last on living trunks.

'I'd never thought of anything like that – for you, Ed,' Judge Twyborn admitted glumly; the port no doubt made it sound the sadder. 'That the son of a professional man like myself . . . Oh well, why not?' He laughed rather disconsolately. 'The Law – or medicine, or any other profession, shouldn't be allowed to become a religion. Lots of reputable young men have made a go of it on the land. We can get someone to take you on – not as a labourer. When members of our class are involved,' the Judge approached it gingerly, 'they call it *jackerooing.*'

An easier way? Eddie suspected it was, and not without a touch of nepotism, when he had aspired to be a 'hand'.

'I'll speak to Greg Lushington. I see him on and off at the Club.'

What had been a solemn occasion became the more solemn for an excess of port and an excessive unreality.

When the door was flung open. 'I can't bear it any longer. The girls have pissed. Aren't you men ready for your coffee?'

She had stuck the Spanish comb at an even more improbable angle. She had started blinking and expostulating.

'I'm worried about Biffy's cyst. All my little dogs die of cancer. Soon I shall be left alone – without the strength for rearing puppies.'

Cheeks pale by now, her mouth gaped open like a target in a fair.

Surprisingly, Judge Twyborn aimed. 'You'll never be left alone, my dear. There'll be a host of surviving fleas – and probably a paralysed husband.'

On and off the parents had hopes of displaying their son to those they considered their friends: Edward's fellow judges, barristers, doctors, architects, sometimes a leavening of graziers. ('You'll find country people speak a different language,' Eadie told him, 'but they're warm-hearted, well-meaning'; adding in the course of her introductory remarks, which were intended as persuasion, 'Some have greater pretensions. Ethel Tucker, for example, is reading Proust, if you can believe, down in the Riverina.')

She would start sighing, almost mewing, before announcing, 'We're having a few close friends to a little *drinks* party. We'd so love it if you'd look in.'

He staved it off. 'I don't feel I'm ready. The languages alone.' She sat looking at him incredulously. .

'Though Ethel and I might become mates if we don't rush it.'

'Oh, Ethel's no great shakes. Take it from me. We were at

school together. Ethel was practically illiterate. I had to write her love-letters for her.'

'Was the marriage a success?'

'Marriage doesn't necessarily come of the love-letters,' she mused.

She looked at him. 'You're not ashamed of us, are you, Eddie?'

Unable to explain the reason for his diffidence, he could only murmur, 'Two such honourable characters . . . Why should I be?'

She blushed. 'I'm not all that honourable. And you sound as legal as your father while pretending not to be.'

Exposure in its most painful form was for some reason delayed till later than he had expected. 'If you don't want to meet anybody else, I must bring you together with my old friend Joanie.'

'Joanie?'

'Golson — Sewell that was.'

'Hardly remember. Suppose I do — just; I was quite small.'

'But later, surely. You can't have been away all the time at boarding school. She remembers you and is dying to meet you.'

He gave no indication of accepting or refusing.

'She'll be coming to afternoon tea tomorrow. I do hope you'll make the effort, darling.'

After that she took her dogs into the garden and gave them a good flea-powdering in preparation for Mrs Golson's visit.

The day of the visit turned out heavy: morning yawned through a green-gold late autumn haze; hibiscus pollen clung to the shoulder blundering against those brooding trumpets; the air you breathed felt coated with fur; and under the rose bushes which Mrs Golson must skirt that afternoon, a crop of giant, speckled toadstools had shot from the compost overnight.

At breakfast (Eadie presiding over a battery of shapely but dented Georgian silver, in a steam of strong Darjeeling) the Judge informed them, 'I ran into Lushington, lunching yesterday at the Club.' Before revealing the outcome of their meeting, he paused to convey a liberal forkful of kedgeree past the spidery moustache. 'He says,' said the Judge while masticating conscientiously, 'he'll take you on at a — nominal — wage. Like many of the rich,' here the Judge defended himself by hunching his shoulders and clamping down on the kedgeree, 'Greg Lushington is stingy. Oh, he doesn't *mean* to be. He understands it as thrift — which is how he came by what he's got. Thrift is something we poor professional coots are unable to indulge in. We can only aim at retiring early, to cosset investments.' He let out an enormous sigh, and continued munching, stray grains of rice trembling on the tips of the more detached hairs in his moustache.

'Sometimes I wonder, darling, whether you are emulating Gladstone.'

'How?'

'All this — mastication.'

He ignored it, while continuing to munch.

'Lushington would see you, Eddie. But returned last night to his property.'

'Most of the time half-sloshed,' said Eadie.

'How do you know?'

'I can tell,' she said, 'by instinct.'

Silence fell on a debris of haddock bones and rejected rice. Eadie was entering the desert which lies between the breakfast cuppa and the first snifter.

'Lushington says that, as a jackeroo, you'll share a cottage with the manager — which, I take it, is meant as compensation for the nominal wage you'll be receiving.'

'Fair enough,' Eddie Twyborn heard himself; morning apathy had dulled the glint in his brave idea.

All three Twyborns sank their chins and sipped their strong Darjeeling.

Eddie felt the sweat trickling down his temples.

When he had done all there is to do at that hour he went out and roamed. He took a tram to the city and bought some pencils for which he had no immediate use. Later in the morning he caught sight of the Judge sniffing at cigars in a tobacconist's; later still, his mother buying a card of buttons in a store. So that all three, for the time being, were employed.

He might have evaporated completely towards the time for afternoon tea, if what Eadie would have called his 'morbid streak' had allowed him to resist a glimpse of Joanie Golson. So he hung around the periphery.

The doorbell rang and Mildred in her frills ran to answer.

A breeze had broken out in the garden, stirring the perfumes, the pollens. The harbour had become a sheet of corrugated zinc. Mildred was using a hankie.

'Well, Mildred, how nice to see you. Are you keeping well?'

A grateful sogginess issuing out of the hankie.

'Are *they* all well?'

The felted distances were the more intriguing for remaining invisible; he, the would-be voyeur, preferred to train his mind's eye on the person formed by Mrs Golson's voice.

Eadie, entering from the garden, slipped where marble verged on jarrah.

Joanie must have caught her.

'Thank you, darling. Such a stand-by. You're my *rock*!'

'I'd have thought Edward . . .'

'Edward is my judgment.'

A high breathiness in Joanie. 'But rocks suggest bulk, don't they? When I've been at such pains to reduce.'

'Oh, you have, of course you have! You're looking positively flimsy, Joanie – in your blue – that panama so light it's ready to fly out the window.'

'One never knows how to take you, Eadie.' Mrs Golson sounded peeved.

'Take me? No one has attempted that in years.' Eadie Twyborn, too, was breathy, but in the bass, subsiding, it seemed into the sofa's non-existent springs.

Mrs Golson must have subsided shortly after, her impact more audible. 'Anyway, *he* is here. Cheer up, Eadie! Am I going to have a glimpse of him!'

'Who can tell?'

Mildred bearing tea-things was competing with a gardenful of birds.

'It remains to be seen,' Eadie continued cryptically, to keep it from the servants.

'Nowhere else,' Mrs Golson vouchsafed, 'does one find such delicious bread-and-butter rolls.'

'Etty learned them from the nuns.'

As Mildred had withdrawn, the two ladies went into a giggle.

'Oh yes,' Mrs Golson gasped, 'we can learn a lot from the nuns, I'm sure.'

After that they must have fallen to counting the crumbs or searching their thoughts, until Eadie embarked on the pedigree of somebody who had married someone.

'Did you know,' Joanie interrupted, 'that Marian is expecting another?'

'Yes, Marian's expecting another.'

'Does she know that Eddie is back?'

'Who can say? I'm too discreet to ask. But the world is full of indiscretion.'

A southerly had risen to trouble the garden; it was bashing the helpless hibiscus trumpets. From where he was stationed, round the corner in the study, he could look out and see flesh already bruised, shredded. Soon he must declare himself, face other damage at the tea-table, for all anybody knew, perhaps even create worse.

So he held back.

'You know, Eadie, when we were away that time in France, before the War, there were several occasions when I was about to write you a letter.'

'That was when you were neglecting me.'

'It would be difficult to say, Eadie, who was neglecting who.'

Half a French door was slammed shut by the mounting gale. Nobody rose to attend to it.

'Was there something specific you had to write about? Or only that you still loved me — and were too cruel to reassure.'

'Of course I still loved — I do still love you! Of all people, I think I'm the one who understands you.'

'To understand a person can make her most unlovable.'

'Oh, darling, you do know how to stick the knife in!'

'Then why did you want to write, and didn't?'

'I didn't because I had no concrete evidence.'

'Of what, Joan? Only Edward can be as tiresome.'

'Well, you see, I met this very beautiful, very charming young woman — a Madame Vatatzes — married to an elderly, mad Greek.'

'Ah, now we're coming to it! You had an affair with this very charming, beautiful young woman. You comforted her in her husband's madness.'

'You're the one who's mad! I've never been unfaithful to you, darling.'

'Will you give me your hand on it?'

'It's far too buttery — and far too hot — but if you must.'

Round the corner in the study Eddie Twyborn was enveloped in this same buttery silence of schoolgirl pacts and womanly frustration. Could he escape the dénouement of then and now?

'If you didn't have the affair, what else was there to confess, in this letter you didn't write?'

'It would sound too silly. I couldn't tell! There's nothing to back it up. Only that she had such extraordinary eyes.'

'She won you over. She seduced you, Joanie.'

'Nothing of the sort.'

'In your thoughts at least.'

The silence was palpitating.

'I don't think you're being honest with me, Joan.'

'I am, I tell you. You're unfair. Well, nobody's completely honest in every corner of her mind. Are you, Eadie?'

Eadie did not answer.

Joanie said, 'I don't believe Eddie's going to appear.'

'You could be right.'

'You frightened him off.'

'How?'

'By wanting to possess him.'

'Isn't he my child?'

The storm broke in the drawing room as against the gale outside in the garden.

'You do, you know!' Joanie Golson was riding both inner storm and outer gale. 'Everybody!' she seemed to exult.

'Oh, people are cruel! One only asks for trust – certainty . . .' There was a terrible glug-glugging, an infernal bath water escaping. 'That's why one keeps dogs, I suppose.'

'Oh, darling, don't! Nobody else knows how to hurt.'

'Only Eddie. Eddie's an expert.'

'You can depend on me, Eadie darling. Didn't you say I was your rock?'

Shattered by now, he must slip away, regardless of the consequences. The shadow in other people's lives oppressed him as much as the shadow in his own – the unpossessed.

He glanced back from the hall and there in the depths of the drawing-room mirror was this inchoate mass of flesh gobbling desperately at flesh. Was he the cause of their Laocoon's breaking up? Nobody could have told, because at this point Eadie kicked the tea-table, the remains of the nuns' bread-and-butter rolls, the uncut jam sandwich, the Georgian family silver lovingly acquired at auction – all crashing.

'Oh God, Joanie, they'll hear! Do help me pick it up. They'll see. Mildred's so sharp – I'd give her the sack – if I thought I'd get anybody else.'

He stole away – the word for thieves and ghosts. The bottoms erected between himself and the shambles neither observed nor accused, as hands scrabbled to repair a situation for which he, perhaps, was totally responsible.

As the waitresses, plump or sinewy, wove and interwove in their uniform black with white flashes, the head waiter, that giant currawong, a sheaf of menus tucked into a wing, swirling and descending, in nobody's pay yet open to persuasion, and woe to the heads he might crunch off as a reward for unworldliness (Mr Effans, no other), those seated at Sunday luncheon in this most reputable Sydney hotel should have felt assured, and for the most part were, the napkins so thick and nappy, the excessive cutlery so solid and elaborately incised; you could play a chord or two if you chose on either side of your brown Windsor soup.

In fact Eddie Twyborn did. But the Chabrier did not swirl to the same extent as the head waiter, whose gyrations were constantly bouncing the tips of his tails off the convexity of his splendid calves.

Eadie grumbled. 'I don't know why you brought us, Edward. We could have lunched much more happily at home. Instead the servants – Etty and Thatcher anyway; it's Mildred's afternoon off – will be eating their heads off at your expense and blaming me for being their mistress.'

'I brought us, my dear,' said the Judge, trying out the surface of his brown Windsor, 'for the sake of old times, and to give our son a little treat.' Here Judge Twyborn might have been blowing on his soup or laughing up his sleeve.

'Old times . . .' Eadie mumbled; then, as though stung by memories, she cried, 'I think I was born before my time!' and hit the rim of her plate with her spoon.

'Sshhh!' It was the Judge.

'How do you see it, Eddie darling?'

Eddie was, wrongly, seated between them. The Judge should have been the centre-piece.

Dragged out of focus, and scalding his palate, Eddie said, 'I like to think, Mother, we're all of us timeless.'

She began whimpering at her untouched soup.

It could have become embarrassing if a lady had not borne down on them in a braided costume of another age, leaving after an early luncheon; she might have referred to it as 'dinner'.

She said, 'It's such a joy to see you, Mrs Twyborn – Judge,' smirking at the son of whom she had heard, 'one of our most distinguished families, re-united.' Nodding her little postillion hat, she showed them her teeth, in one of which the nerve had died.

'The War might have destroyed us, but didn't,' the lady told them.

'So kind,' Eadie murmured, and bowed her head above the untouched soup.

Eddie asked, 'Who is she?'

'Red Cross or something like that, I think. I met her when we were knitting for you, darling.' The nerves had not died in Eadie's teeth, but nicotine had coated them; everybody had been through it.

The slaves removed the plates and produced others. There was the roast beef with its ruffle of yellow fat, and Yorkshire pudding baked in the shape of a tight bun.

'Everything in order, Judge?' asked Mr Effans, who had not yet received recognition for his favours.

'Everything. Why not?' the Judge demanded, laughing.

In deference to an old hand, the head waiter smiled and withdrew.

Eadie was again bent on disapproval. 'Now that is a woman I can't take to.'

After advancing some way into the dining room, the object of her aversion had seated herself on the opposite side. If she was aware of the disapproval Mrs Judge Twyborn was aiming at her, she gave no indication of it.

The two women sat not exactly looking at each other.

'Who?' asked the Judge, glancing out like some noble beast interrupted in his grazing.

'Marcia Lushington,' Eadie hissed.

'She didn't go back with Greg,' their son remarked, to take an interest in a world which was shortly to include himself.

Eadie said, 'I think they suit themselves. But stay together for convenience. I suppose we shouldn't hold it against them.' She petered out in a rackety cough.

The Judge was slopping around in the shallows of gravied pumpkin and beans.

Mrs Lushington blew two streams of smoke down her nostrils, which must have irritated Mrs Twyborn almost beyond control, for she ground out her cigarette, not in the ashtray provided, but in her practically untouched beef.

The Judge laid his knife and fork together in the puddles of gravy, the sludge of greens, as humbly as he might have in any railway refreshment- or country tea-room while on circuit.

From admiring his father's velvet muzzle, Eddie fell to observing Mrs Lushington.

Her dress proclaimed her a rich dowdy, or fashionable slattern. If the monkey fur straggling down from a Venetian tricorne gave her head the look of a hanging basket in a fernery, the suit she wore was buttoned and belted in a loosely regimental style, an effect contradicted in turn by several ropes of pearls which she slung about while studying the menu.

Marcia reminded Eddie somewhat of a raw scallop, or heap of them, the smudged, ivory flesh, the lips of a pale coral. Undaunted by her surroundings, her tongue suddenly flickered out and drew in a straggle of monkey fur, which she sucked for a second or two before rejecting. As she continued studying the menu, torturing the enormous pearls, glancing up from time to time at nobody and everybody, the faintly coral lips worked against her teeth, as though she had already eaten, and was trying to free them from fragments of something unpleasant.

Eadie couldn't bear her apple pie. 'I don't know why you insisted, darling, when you know I don't care for sweets.'

The Judge, who enjoyed his pud, was masticating gently, and ignoring.

Eddie asked his mother, 'What have you got against Mrs Lushington?' His schoolboy treat was making him feel magnanimous.

'Nothing — actually — nothing,' Eadie admitted. 'Except that she's a common piece — who came off a cow farm at Tilba — and caught old Greg Lushington — and led him by the nose ever since.'

'Come on, Eadie, aren't you unfair?' the Judge intervened. 'Greg may have wanted to be led.'

'It's no less deplorable — from whichever side.' After making this virtuous pronouncement Eadie lowered her eyes.

Just then Mrs Lushington blew two fiercer blasts from her nostrils, and without ordering, rose from the mock-Chippendale, and began to leave the dining room, her slouch as contemptuous as it was fashionable.

'Good on 'er!' Mrs Justice Twyborn remarked.

Her son was left with his own image in the glass on the opposite

148

wall. He was surprised to find himself look as convincing as he did, and wondered whether this had been Marcia's impression too. Probably not. For the reflection was already fluctuating, in the satin shoals, the watery waves of the mottled glass, as well as in his own mind. He was faced, as always, with an impersonation of reality.

All night, it seemed to him, he heard the twitter of birds migrating. In the luminous dark and his half-sleep he saw their eyes outlined with white pencil, as Eudoxia had touched up hers with black.

As Marcia Lushington had, what's more.

Marcia was lying, buttocks upturned, an abandoned china doll.

Eddie could not bring himself to respond to the breakfast bell, but waited for his parents to disperse. Then he went into the kitchen where Etty and Mildred were scurrying in bleached-out blue and Thatcher was smoking a vile pipe.

The girls chittered, 'Oh, Mr Eddie!' and Etty dished up strips of a leathery omelette.

The spittle seethed in the bowl of Thatcher's pipe. 'It's yer last day, eh?'

'What makes you say that?'

'Well, isn't it?' the gardener persisted.

He could not have denied what his parents might have.

He continued sitting over this late and fragmentary breakfast, but realized he was embarrassing the servants: the cook and maid taken up with their work, the gardener too, after his fashion.

Later in the morning, on packing his shamefully new clothes, the few indispensable possessions, the tube of toothpaste he had ruptured with his heel, he went down to face his mother.

Eadie Twyborn was seated on the flight of marble steps leading from the drawing room into the garden. On her tweed lap she was holding a beatific subject, one of her matted terriers. She was combing round his genitals, obviously causing him anguish of a kind, but whoever it was grinned and submitted.

Eadie said without looking up, 'That is one I lost – and have recaptured.'

Her son ventured, 'Not a flea, surely?'

'Why not? We're all swarming, aren't we?' Her occupation was making her drowsy. 'If not with fleas, thoughts – desires . . . Sometimes I think your father's the only one who isn't afflicted.'

She grimaced at the shadowless Australian light, and back at the flea she was crushing between blenching nails.

'That,' she said with some satisfaction, 'is the creamiest flea I've ever squashed. I often wonder about their sex. Is the little agile one the male – the creamy monster his mate? Or perhaps age, not sex, is responsible for the physical difference.'

She must have helped herself to a snifter earlier than on most mornings.

When he let himself out of the house that evening he wondered whether Eadie realized. Probably not. He would have liked to run into the Judge on the pavement; he would have half-liked Edward to go with him to the station, but his father must have been about the town on some honourable business of his own.

As the train glided alongside the platform in that sickening stench of departure Eddie looked out the window, still hoping the one face might materialize, the drooping moustache, the loosely furled umbrella, and that his father would leap aboard as a more athletic youth might, or Eudoxia Vatatzes, cramming Angelos into a packed corridor.

But no one appeared at the end of the long damp perspective, and Eddie Twyborn withdrew his head. The guard would think him peculiar enough without the 'concrete evidence' of watering eyes.

He had in his pocket a letter of instructions. In the course of the night he read it several times, while the supply of greenish drinking water jumped and shuddered in a bottle secured by a metal circlet and bracket at the same level as the upper berth, and the commercial gent snored on his back in the bunk below.

'Bogong',
New South Wales,
25th April 1920

Dear Eddie,

Thank you for yours of the 19th inst. referring to your journey south on the suggested date.

Ask the guard to stop the train the following morning and put you down at Fossickers Flat, where my manager Don Prowse will meet you with a vehicle, and convey you and your traps to 'Bogong'.

I must warn you that life on the land is not all violets (and these days far from profitable) but your dad tells me you are set on giving it a go. I for my part look forward to making the acquaintance of my good friend Edwd. Twyborn's son. I know that my wife, if she was here, would join me in bidding you welcome, but she is at present paying a little visit to shops and friends in Sydney.

Yrs cordially,
Gregory K. Lushington

'This is it!' the guard shouted. 'Fossickers Flat.'

'Is it? Oh. Yes. It is.'

The only passenger for the Flat, he had come bundling, tumbling out, fumbling with his case and valise, barking a knuckle on a door fitting. Then the run along the gritty platform to make some show of helping the guard drag his trunk down from the van.

'Looks like you're 'ere for an extended visit!' The man was laying out a minimum of joviality on one whose Christian name he would not be staying long enough to learn and use.

Already he was flagging the train on its way.

Out of conscience, or some store of fundamental kindness, he thought to call, 'so long, Jack!' to the poor bastard left behind on the siding as himself swung aboard.

So Eddie Twyborn was stranded in this landscape, the well-read letter of instructions and welcome cooling in his cold hand.

The landscape too, was cold, and huge, undulating in white waves towards distant mountains of ink blue. Rocks, not strewn, but arranged in groups of formal sculpture suggesting prehistoric rites, prevented monotony taking over the bleached foothills. These were almost treeless. Distracted eyes in search of cover would have had to content themselves with one or two patches of dingy scrub, the most luxuriant of which straggled alongside the railway siding known as Fossickers Flat.

Eddie Twyborn found refuge at last, less in the trees themselves, than in the sounds of life in their branches: the *tsst tsst* of invisible small birds, wrens possibly, as he remembered them from his childhood, and here caught glimpses finally, not of the flashy cock, but the humbler, yet more elegant hen. The hen wren's industry drew him back, out of the abstractions propounded by the hillscape and glazed air, into the everyday embroidery of life, the minutiae to which Eudoxia Vatatzes had clung as insurance against the domes of Byzantine deception. (Did poor Eadie in her Sydney garden find the same satisfaction in combing for insect-life round her terriers' genitals?)

Consoled by the sound and movements of the wrens as they skirred among the scrubby branches, Eddie Twyborn was not at first aware that a car of sorts, trailing a heavy wake of dust, was lurching down a road as white as the hills from which it had been carved. It was the dust he noticed first, for distance and the concerted wrens obliterated sound. Only in the foreground did the Ford start chugging with any purpose, clattering towards its apparent goal.

Of dislocated joints and flapping hood, it ground to a standstill below the siding. A door was torn open and slammed shut before the driver came round and showed himself. He was of middle age, a reddish man in clothes which seemed to inconvenience him judging by the contortions to which he was subjecting his shoulders, while easing his crotch, and flinging evident cramps off a pair of well-developed calves. In spite of the rights he enjoyed as a native, he might have felt that the stranger stationed above him on the platform had him at a disadvantage. For he took up a stance, legs apart, hands on hips, as he stared upward. What may have been intended as a smile of welcome was turned by his disadvantage and the position of the sun into a ginger-stubbled glare.

' 'Ow are we, eh?' he drooled in conventional tone. 'You beat me to it!'

Insufficiently rehearsed, the amateur mumbled and smiled back.

'Never know with the fuckun Woolambi Mail. It comes or it don't. Today it came.' The professional laughed, and exercised his musclebound shoulders more violently than ever to restore them to working order.

Nobody thought of starting an exchange of names, taking it for granted there could be no other than the manager and the jackeroo, Don Prowse and Eddie Twyborn.

Without delay the ginger one mounted the ramp and there began a ritual male tussle to possess the baggage. It was over too soon. As he hoisted the trunk on a shoulder it must have gratified Prowse to detect and dismiss decadence, while Eddie following with case and valise wondered where civilization ended, and still more, where it began.

The manager kept up a muttering as he lashed the trunk to a rusted rack, his activities accompanied by the glaring smile directed nowhere in particular. The backs of the hands at work with such authority were scabbed in places and tufted with orange hair. Eddie felt ashamed of his own unblemished, unskilled hands, and planned to keep them a secret for as long as he could. He hid them in his trouser pockets, where they started jingling his key-ring, his change. (What to do with hands had always been a major problem.)

'All set.' Not quite a statement, nor wholly an interjection, Prowse jerked it out from behind his Adam's apple.

The intimidated Eddie Twyborn climbed in on the passenger's side. Prowse began doing things to the car with immense and impressive dexterity, which did not prevent it bucking and sidling, threatening to throw them out before they left the starting post.

'What's he like?' Eddie asked in an untimely effort to establish himself.

'What's – who?'

'Old Lushington.'

'Greg's all right,' the manager shouted through a thrashing of gears.

They were cavorting by now, over the stones, towards a cleft in the bleached hills.

'Soft old sod, but all right,' Gregory Lushington's manager intoned. 'Not here all that much. Bugger's always *globe* trotting. Been to bloody *Patagonia*. Done the China coast. Climbed the Himalayas – well, some of the easy bits.' Prowse snorted slightly. 'Wanted to see the rhodradendrons.'

It lulled the passenger to hear about his boss's travels. It removed him to some extent from the driver's side and what he suspected the latter's judgment to be. He did not feel he could count on Prowse's liking him; yet there was a tingling attraction on his own side, generated, if he would admit, by those hands lying heavy on the wheel.

Suddenly the manager turned to him and said, 'In the War, weren't yer, Eddie?' It sounded almost an accusation.

'I was – yes. I was.' He couldn't apologize enough on sensing it was what Prowse would have wanted.

153

'Well, I wasn't. I was doing what they considered a necessary job. I would 'uv, of course. I talked it over with old Greg. Greg's had it easy all his life. Hasn't come in for anything – war or otherwise. Full of money like a tick with blood. Marcia thought I oughter go. That's 'is wife. She's away in Sydney. Back any day now. It's easy for a woman, isn't it? to decide what a man oughter do in a war. Some women need a man dead before they can appreciate 'im.'

His glance hectic (he had a lip sore breaking out), Prowse was looking to his passenger for corroboration.

'Perhaps you're right,' Eddie replied, reconstructing the beige Marcia framed in straggles of monkey fur.

The manager calmed down. They were climbing, dipping, swerving, skidding in a sticky hollow; they were facing the direction from which they had come.

'Fuck that!' said Don Prowse, and laughed his throatiest from behind the Adam's apple.

Eddie Twyborn smiled a lulled smile. His fate was in someone else's hands.

They reached a signpost pointing along a main road. They even ran a short distance over the road's luxurious surface before turning off again into the country of rudiments and stones.

While still on the metal Prowse explained, 'This is the way to Woolambi. Where the good times are – six pubs, four stores, the picture-show. Get a screw too, if you're interested in that.'

They continued driving.

'There's a root or two closer home if you get to know. I always say there's roots for the lookin' – anywhere.'

Again the driver glanced at his passenger for approbation.

'That's so,' Eddie answered, and wondered to what extent his companion was convinced.

'This is it,' the manager announced.

Even if his guide hadn't told, everything signalled arrival. The act of getting down to open gates, even the rustiest, the more resistant, the most perversely chained, gave the stranger a sense of belonging somewhere. A mob of sheep scampering in initial fright was persuaded to turn, halt, and observe those who were possibly not the intruders of its first impression. The phalanx of sheep stood firm, some stamping, coughing, every one of them archaic inside a carapace of what could have passed for stone wool, down to a tinge of parasite moss suffusing its general dinginess.

Winter was well on the way at 'Bogong'. It showed in the staring, wind-ruffled coats of half a dozen horses in the next paddock. Wheeling and pig-rooting, the near brumbies halted only when almost on top of the car, their bright expressions from under wispy forelocks prepared to enjoy such entertainment as human beings had to offer. Here too there was a glint of moss in quizzical muzzles and, possibly by reflection, in fetlocks rising out of a short-pile carpet of a virulent green.

Presently a string of sheds, together with a huddle of cottages, their paintwork faded to a pale ochre, showed up amongst the white tussock on a river bank.

Two stockmen were riding at a distance, slouching, bumping with accomplished ease one behind the other on razor-backed nags whose slatternly tails almost swept the ground. Weather had cured the riders to a colour where they could have passed for Red Indians. They ignored the manager, as he them, more from convention, you felt, than from actual animosity.

Soon there was a bridge of loosely bolted planks buckling beneath the leaping car. Never had river waters looked glassier, more detached in their activity. Eddie Twyborn shivered and breathed deep for the encounter. Then they were across, above them in the middle distance a long low homestead, its windows dark and unrevealing behind a low-slung veranda, beneath a fairly low-pitched, red-painted roof, in corrugated iron. The homestead had a somewhat prim air, that of a retiring spinster of no pretensions beyond her breeding.

The car did not make for the homestead, but for a cottage closer to the river and surrounded by the expected complement of sheds, yards, iron water-tanks, and what must be the dunny. Hawthorns were crowding in upon another deep veranda, providing a break-wind, if also probably a break-light for the rooms inside.

Don Prowse turned on a sourly beatific smile for one who might have been the bride of a shotgun marriage instead of an unwanted offsider wished on to him by his employer. 'Snugger than it looks, and at the week-end you can bugger off to Woolambi if it suits.'

Eddie Twyborn felt the complete misfit in Don Prowse's aggressively masculine world; whereas a relationship was waiting to develop between himself, the huggermugger buildings, even a bitter landscape. If the river appeared at first sight hostile, it was through the transience of its coursing waters to one who longed for the reality of permanence.

He was made clumsy and unreal by the manager's continued remarks, by his attempts at friendliness, by the man's insistence on shouldering the cabin-trunk again, on grabbing hold of all the baggage if he could get possession of it – in doing the man's work in fact. It was humiliating.

It might have become worse, creating a puppet tittuping helplessly through slush and puddles, if a woman hadn't appeared, neither young, nor all that old, at any rate her hair still black, her cheeks as tanned and ravaged by the climate as those of the 'Red Indian' stockmen loping on their lean horses.

'Mrs Tyrrell,' Prowse grunted by way of introduction under the stress of shouldering the trunk and carrying the suitcase.

Mrs Tyrrell mumbled through a smile, licking her thin, natural lips. She revealed two brown, upper fangs with nothing but her tongue to fill the gap. She was dressed all in black, whether from grief or for practical reasons, it was not possible to tell. She simpered a lot, and hugged a bobbled crochet shawl round narrow shoulders. In the lower regions, what had once been a laundered apron had failed to protect her practical black from a storm of flour.

Anyway, Eddie Twyborn had hopes of this Mrs Tyrrell, her bright black eyes already alight with confidences and an offer of sleazy kindliness.

'Bet you're hungry, mister,' she said. 'Fix yer some breakfast. Bet Mr Prowse won't say no to a second breakfast. 'E's a good doer.'

At the same time she started a struggle for the valise with which the young man had been left. He clung on desperately, as though possession of it were his only means of self-assertion.

'Independent, are we?' Mrs Tyrrell cackled through her gap, a detachment of mongrel hens joining in as they shot across the slush from under her feet.

'Never thought about it – frankly,' he gasped.

Such strangeness strangely expressed must have dried up her repartee, for she fell silent, one hand on the disputed valise. He could feel Mrs Tyrrell's skin slithering against his own, hard and greasy at the same time, the broad golden wedding-band turned by age to the colour of brass.

So they staggered on, and into the house, allies, it could have been, against the manager's overtly masculine back.

'This do?' the latter asked.

He released the trunk, which crumped on the boards and shook the whole structure of the room.

'Yes, it's fine!' said Eddie Twyborn out of a deathly sinking.

He stood with his hands on his hips as he had seen men do, and smiled, while the others read his thoughts, no doubt correctly: Don Prowse grinning through the ginger stubble, Mrs Tyrrell bird-eyed beneath a row of little jet black hair-rosettes.

If they would only withdraw, the room might become his, just as the imagination can clothe a skeleton with flesh, even kindle a spirit in it. They did leave him to it finally: the stretcher with the army blankets, shelves curtained by a straight length of faded cretonne, a frayed mat on the dusty boards, on the chest an enamel candle-stick, its broken candle aslant over gobbets of stale wax, on the wall a deal-framed glass to mirror his jaunty disarray.

He was alone at least – 'independent' as Mrs Tyrrell might have described it.

He could hear her in the kitchen. He could smell the mutton chops she was charring, the cabbage-and-potato she was 'frying up'.

'A good-lookun young cove, Peggy,' he heard Don Prowse's voice.

Then her cackle, tailing off into a sigh, and something about 'a mother', and 'women is only pack 'orses', through the stench, the spitting of fat.

Should he go out to them?

After their delayed breakfast, his second in the manager's case, of chops and veg followed by wedges of yellow sponge and dobs of enormous floury scone, Don advised, 'Better settle in, Ed. We'll talk things over later.' He showed his teeth in an educated smile, while Mrs Tyrrell stood watching from beneath her hair-rosettes, lips parted to reveal the cavern behind her gap.

'Gotter unpack,' she murmured.

While the jackeroo did just that the cook came in and draped herself over a deckchair as faded as the cretonne curtain masking the shelves in the room which was becoming Eddie Twyborn's.

Mrs Tyrrell said, sighing, scratching an armpit under the black, bobbled shawl, 'You gotter take what comes, I've always said. Man or woman. Prowse wouldn't understand that. You would,' she added.

'Why would I?'

'Because you're yer mother's son,' she said, peering at him and licking her lips.

'How do you know?'

'Well,' she said, 'I'm the mother of seventeen Tyrrells — a football team of boys — but the girls is what counts.'

'I'm a boy,' said Eddie Twyborn.

'We know you are,' Mrs Tyrrell agreed, munching on her mauve gums. 'The boys!' she munched. 'Bet your mum would've been glad of a girl.'

'I don't think so. She would have preferred to be barren, I think.'

'Go on! There's no mother wouldn't 'uv chose ter be a mother. Not even our poor Else, with that bloody Kevun pokin' the hell out of 'er. Gets what 'e wants, then 'e beats 'er up. We 'ave 'im put in, but the damage is done. The kiddies are worth it, Else says. Arr, the women!'

Peggy Tyrrell sucked her gap passionately.

'Marcia — Mrs Lushington — give a beautiful quilted dressin'-gown after Kev put the fifth in Elsie's oven. Arr, Mrs Lushington's good — a lovely woman.'

Mrs Tyrrell was writhing in the faded chair, which must have done the P. & O. run under Lushington auspices. 'Both my girls,' she said, eyeing the tube of toothpaste he had ruptured with his heel in Edgecliff, 'both was married with their own teeth still in place. Only lost 'em afterwards. Thing about teeth,' she said, 'you don't 'ave to clean 'em if you 'aven't got 'em.'

'You don't,' he agreed.

She had begun eyeing the underpants he was bringing out.

'Wouldn'tcher like somethun to eat? Prowse is gone with the men 'n won't be back to lunch.'

'Which men?'

'Well — Matt 'n Denny — the men!'

Presumably the 'Red Indians'.

He didn't hanker after lunch; he only wanted Peggy Tyrrell to leave him alone. Which presently she did, sighing and burping. Glancing round, he caught sight of her through the doorway, moving plates of sponge and plates of scones around the kitchen table as though playing a game of draughts with herself.

She was what is called a 'trick', and he knew that he would be glad of her.

After arranging his possessions, all of them objects which might remain dispensable, he left the house to which he had been consigned, and walked along the river bank. He half-expected Peggy Tyrrell to follow. When she didn't he looked back, and sure enough, there she was, hesitating on the edge of the dry-rotted veranda, in a gap between hawthorns, tightening the bobbled shawl around her shoulders. He turned away and hurried on, persuading himself he was not guilty of betraying a relationship so recently formed.

But he felt guilty, and gashed a glaringly new boot in tripping over a rock.

Would he ever succeed in making credible to others the new moleskins and elastic sides? At least people were more ready to accept material façade than glimpses of spiritual nakedness, cover this up with whatever you will, pomegranate shawl and spangled fan, or moleskins and elastic sides. Joan Golson had accepted a whole vacillating illusion, romantically clothed and in its wrong mind. But on entering the world of Don Prowse and the Lushingtons he suspected he would find the natives watching for lapses in behaviour. All the more necessary to cultivate his alliance with Mrs Tyrrell: women whose wombs have been kicked to pieces by a football team of sons, and who have married off daughters still in possession of their natural teeth should be more inclined to sympathize with the anomalies of life.

He forged farther along the river, stumbling over tussock, stimulated by rushing water, repelled by the patches of virulent green which recurred in this coldly feverish landscape, then turned in towards what he sensed to be forbidden ground, the land surrounding the Lushington homestead.

Far from betraying the lives of its owners to strangers, denuded trees and shrubs showed up the stranger in his trespass. Would Greg Lushington descend, or was he out with the manager and his 'men', super-managing his barren slopes? There was no sign that anyone inhabited the house; not that this is ever indication. You could hear in the distance a barking of dogs as they jerked at their chains and fretted the iron and woodwork of kennels.

At the foot of the wintry Lushington garden, where thorns of

naked Chinese pear caught hold of the intruder's sleeves and
shoulders and sycamore seed was drizzled down the nape of his
neck, there was a basalt wall surrounding three headstones. Eddie
Twyborn was on the point of pushing open the elaborately
designed, iron gate, a rich folly if ever there was one, to give more
attention to the graves and their inscriptions, but became
distracted by the sound of the loose planks of the 'Bogong' bridge
shuffled together by the passage of a car.

It was a black, mud-spattered Packard, slowly driven, but with
a possessive confidence, towards the house. The trespasser ducked
behind the skeleton trees as though caught out in the spangles
and embroidered pomegranates of the European drag he liked to
think he had abandoned.

He walked back quickly the way he had come. The brown
waters of the river reflected the thoughts of one who was unwise
enough to unmask them on its bank. The river froze him. He
could not imagine what he was doing at 'Bogong' — or anywhere,
for that matter.

Mrs Tyrrell was standing waiting, he was relieved to see, on
the edge of the dry-rotted veranda.

'Marcia come back,' she told him. 'She'll 'uv brought me
somethink. Marcia brings the loveliest gifts.'

'She must be all right then?' He tried it out in the manager's
voice.

Mrs Tyrrell sucked her gap before answering. 'She's right
enough. Nobody's ever *all* right. 'Aven't you found that out,
love?' She ended up in a cackle, in which he joined, while
avoiding contact with a callused hand.

The cottage was full of dusk, smoke, and a smell of roasting
mutton.

'Better take a squint at me shoulder,' Mrs Tyrrell immediately
announced.

Satisfied, she slammed the oven shut again.

'Arr, dear, the winters,' she sighed, 'they make a person cry!'
then, more cheerfully inspired, ' 'Ere, you little bugger, why
don'tcher make yerself useful and light the bloody lamp? Prowse'll
be back any minute an' say we're not dermestercated.'

While he fumbled with and lit the lamp, she busied herself
investigating a cabbage for slugs. 'I'll like 'avin' you around,' she
told him; 'you an' me 'ull get on like one thing.' She sighed
again, disposing of a colony of slugs. 'It's the girls I miss out 'ere.

Never the boys. Not that you isn't a boy,' she realized. 'But different. A woman can speak out 'er thoughts.'

He should not have felt consoled, but was, to be thus accepted by Peggy Tyrrell. The flowering lamp he set between them on the oilcloth made a little island of conspiracy for the woman's blazing face and the pale ghost of what people took to be Eddie Twyborn.

Presently they heard a truck, boots, a slammed fly-screen door. Eddie would have chosen to delay the manager's presence, but it was soon with them in the dining-kitchen, not least the stench of his recent exertions.

Don Prowse was overpoweringly cheerful. 'Quite domesticated, aren't we?' His hands sounded like sandpaper.

When he had gone to throw water at his torso and rid himself to some extent of the stench, Peggy Tyrrell winked at her ally.

'Dermestercation! What did I tell yer? Can't get over 'ow 'is wife walked out on 'im. You'll 'ear all that when 'e's warmed up.'

He returned, the hair above his forehead glittering in a watered, orange slick. He produced a bottle from the lower regions of a hobbledy dresser and poured himself a handsome tot.

'Learned the lay of the land, have we?' Always smiling, his teeth were his own, and good. 'That's the dunny, if the old woman didn't tell yer,' he pointed with his pipe through a smoked-up window. 'It's a two-seater – for company.'

Eddie Twyborn said, 'I've never done it in company, and perhaps I couldn't.'

The manager grunted. 'Perhaps you could in a place like this. A judge's son could get ground down like anybody else.'

Eddie Twyborn might have agreed.

Perhaps Don Prowse realized. ' 'Ere,' he said, 'you'd better have one for the first night. Everybody finds 'e depends on 'is grog in these parts. When you get yerself a bottle, you can write yer name on it, and I'll write mine on mine.'

They drank their whiskey in company. Eddie was glad of this employment for his hands, and it made him feel more masculine.

'Didn't he say anything?' he asked.

'Who said what?'

'Greg. Didn't he ask to see me, perhaps? He's my father's friend.'

'Greg's a slow old bastard. Never know what 'e's thinking. 'E'll ask all in good time – whoever yer father is.'

They knocked back the whiskey, and the old woman produced a blackened shoulder out of the oven.

'Greg's off again — round the world,' Prowse informed them while carving. 'He likes the travel life. And why not? If you can afford it.'

Prowse must have been very well paid not to have sounded vindictive.

'Is Marcia going too?' asked Eddie.

'How — Marcia? What do you know about Marce?'

'Nothing. But she's back. I saw her driving the Packard up the road.'

Prowse hacked the black mutton and Peggy Tyrrell relieved the cabbage of a boiled slug.

'No,' said Prowse, 'Marcia's not going with Greg. She sort of belongs more to "Bogong" — not that you'd think it at first sight.' The carvers slithered into the gravy. 'Marcia's of the land — if you know what I mean. Greg only inherited it.'

They sat down and began their meal. Everyone, it seemed, even the newcomer, was involved in a primitive ritual, no grace, but plenty of tomato sauce.

Just as Eddie had sighted yet another slug, the telephone almost tore itself from the wall, and the manager leaped at it.

'Yes, sir . . . Yes . . . Yes, Mr Lushington. Yes . . . In the morning . . . Eddie was asking whether . . . Yes . . .'

When he had returned to his creaking chair Don Prowse somewhat unnecessarily informed them, 'That was the boss. 'E'll see yer in the morning, Eddie. Wants to take a look at the wethers on Bald Hill.'

They made further play with their mutton.

'I told you,' said Prowse, spitting out some gristle, 'Greg is slow, but wouldn't forget — least of all 'is friend's son.' A second shred of gristle followed the first.

Mrs Tyrrell produced the spotted dick.

After their meal, as he smoked his pipe and drank another whiskey or three, the manager grumbled, 'It's the winters that get you down on the Monaro. If you could escape the worst of it — drive up north and thaw out on the coast for a coupler months — like the moneyed bastards do — or Europe.' A tear of frustration, alcohol, or retrospect had appeared surprisingly in a corner of one of Prowse's eyes. 'The winters were what the wife couldn't stand. She walked out on me — I'd better tell you

162

before others do. It was the cold. Well, good luck to 'er! She was never much use to a man. It's the kid I miss. Haven't seen 'er since they went.'

Mrs Tyrrell had continued sitting in a corner, yawning, and holding her forearms. Old tales left her untouched. She might have been a gnarled, half-burnt tree stump.

If Prowse's confidences touched Eddie, it could have been in the light of his own contemplated defections from Angelos Vatatzes. He could smell the night trains he had never caught towards a hypothetical freedom somewhere beyond the Côte Morte. In the front bedroom of this creaking house the departed Mrs Prowse, all pallor and resentment, might have been awaiting her orang-outang on the iron bedstead with the brass knobs.

If he had been a woman in body as well as psyche, Eddie might have put out a tentative hand and touched an orange paw.

On realizing that it would have been for his own comfort rather than the sufferer's, he shivered and suggested, 'Think I ought to be turning in.'

'You've got something there, Eddie.' It was again hearty, banal, masculine; never more masculine than when they went outside together, backs at the oblique, pissing on the frost.

'Christ!' chattered Prowse. 'Freeze the balls off yer, wouldn't it?'

The newcomer had begun to feel that perhaps he was more inured to cold from life in the trenches, not to say exposure during a female existence.

Or he could have been numbed by exhaustion and the situation he found himself in. As he fell asleep under the army blankets and the threadbare bedside mat, Peggy Tyrrell could be heard through the wall mumbling a drowsy rosary. Then there was the slamming of the screen door as Prowse went outside again. It occurred to Eddie that the manager had only just relieved himself, but could be — who cared? — moved to sit alone one side of the two-seater dunny, chattering with cold, black mutton, and retrospect.

'Looks like you slept in.'

He roused himself to see Prowse standing in the doorway.

'Didn't wake yer the first morning. Lushington's not an early riser. He'll come down when 'e feels like it. So take yer time, Ed. Peggy'll have yer breakfast ready if you let 'er know you've done yer fly up.'

The manager's splendid teeth grinned before his manliness withdrew.

Thin white sunlight was glittering coldly on gritty boards. Eddie Twyborn revolved and wove himself deeper into the cocoon of army blanket. He was conscious of too supple arms, the tendrils of armpits, the manager's image fading from the crude doorway.

He got up presently, and while forcing with trembling fingers metal buttons through holes a size too small for them, called out, 'Hey — Mrs Tyrrell — what about breakfast?' in a voice he hoped the manager might have approved.

'. . . when you want ut . . .' her toothless cavern reverberated through what sounded like a cascade of thick crockery.

Outside in the frost there was a shambling of hooves, champing of chaff-scented bits, and a more intense perfume from dung recently dropped on frozen ruts.

He looked out and saw the Men rolling cigarettes under the eaves of a thawing roof. They were waiting for the manager, or more formidable, the owner of the acres to which they were enslaved.

Eddie was finally presentable enough to face his ally Mrs Tyrrell. He wondered whether he should clean his teeth with paste from the ruptured tube, but didn't. He went out smelling of sleep and the hairy blankets he had slept in.

No doubt taught by her football team of sons that this is a man's world, Mrs Tyrrell didn't turn a hair. She tossed several charred chops and a mountain of fried-up cabbage and potato on to the plate waiting for him.

'Marcia didn't bring me a gift.'

'How do you know?'

'Mr Edmonds come down with the meat and veggies.'

'Perhaps she did, and he hasn't found out.'

'Everyone knows everythin' at "Bogong". Little enough happens — without Lushingtons come or go.'

With one hand, she sat stirring her pink tea, with the other slightly titivating the tiara of greasy little hair-rosettes which framed her forehead.

'Well, that's Marcia for yer,' she munched, and added, 'it's 'umankind.'

'I'd have brought you a present,' said Eddie, somewhat hypocritical above his chops, 'but didn't know about you.'

164

'Of course you didn't, love!' she giggled. 'And anyways, you learn not to expect too much.'

'I've never expected too much,' he murmured, and knew it was a lie, his lips thick with mutton fat and what would probably remain unfulfilled longing.

He went outside presently, his hopes of fulfilment higher in that they were humbler. After stalking through clumps of horehound, he seated himself on one half of the two-seater dunny, among the faded smells of wood-ash, lime, hen-shit, and old yellowed newsprint. Lulled by suspension in time and surrender to natural functions, he felt comforted at last, chafed his goose-flesh thighs, wiped himself on a recipe for pumpkin scones, and prepared to receive the morning's orders.

The stockmen comprised a father and son, Jim and Denny. They remained silent when faced with a new arrival, not to say jackeroo, but egged on by the manager, extended hard hands in a gesture of cold welcome. Jim the father was leaner, more ravaged, more taciturn by nature, perhaps more aware, though not all that older than Denny his son, who had obviously shot too early from his father's loins probably as the result of an excruciating Monaro winter. Denny at least smiled, out of witlessness it seemed, as much as good will. His head was afflicted with the shakes. His eyes squinted from behind tin-rimmed spectacles, one wing mended with a length of greasy string. He was carrying a black stockwhip which, from moment to moment, he flicked, at a solitary blade of anaemic grass, or at one of his own cringing curs, as though proud of this symbol of his office in the 'Bogong' hierarchy.

Discouraged by their owners, Eddie squatted to convert the dogs, two narrow-headed mongrels distantly related to the deerhound, and a little faded kelpie bitch. One deerhound snapped, and each continued looking blank from behind lolling tongue and yellow fangs, but the little kelpie whined, and was on the way to prostrating herself, torn between convention and desire for affection. Tail between her legs, she compromised by daring to rest her paws on Jim the father's knee, and was knocked back by the knee for her pains.

'Gid down, yer bloody bitch!'

The corrected bitch slunk away, while Eddie was made to realize that it wasn't done to touch dogs.

'What's her name?' he asked with caution.

165

'Dunno that she's got a name. She's just a dawg, ain't she?' her owner replied, and spat out a shred of tobacco.

Denny the son nearly laughed his head off. 'My dawgs 'uv got names,' he claimed. 'This is Cis and that's Captain.'

Jim the father turned away in disgust, but the dogs themselves seemed to join in Denny's simple mirth, grinning, golloping, and snapping at the air.

Eddie might have felt unhappier if his attention hadn't been diverted. Prowse re-appeared leading a horse of the same strain as those the stockmen had tethered to a rail, except that the mount which was to be his looked shaggier, wilder-eyed amongst his forelock, and from every angle worse put together. His colour might have been described as creamy, but smeared with Peggy Tyrrell's frying pan.

'This is yours, Eddie,' said Prowse. 'He's no great shakes to look at. But quiet. We call 'im the Blue Mule.'

Even Jim saw fit to laugh. It was the laughter of experience over ignorance and city ways. He spat again, and smoothed the moustache hanging like two black bootlaces either side of his invisible lips.

At this moment there was a great gnashing and barking of dogs, sidling and fretting of wild-eyed horses, as a pack of little foxterriers shot round the corner of the shed where the ill-assorted company was assembled. The Blue Mule snorted and kicked when the leader of the terrier pack flung himself on the kelpie bitch in an attempt at rape.

Jim the father cracked his whip and caught the terrier in the balls just as the master of the pack arrived.

'Now, now, Jim!' complained the one who was the boss judging by the manager's subservience. 'Shouldn't be such a bastard, should you?'

Another one in spectacles, the boss didn't leave off smiling. Whereas Denny the stockman's glasses were framed in inferior metal, Mr Lushington's were gold-rimmed, their lenses so large and round his expression would have benefited by their shape had he been less benign than his manner suggested.

As the terrier was yelping for his slashed balls the manager tried to joke it off. 'Looks like Jim didn't get it from the missus last night. Eh, Mr Lushington? What 'ud you say?'

Mr Lushington only smiled. He was an elderly pear-shaped gentleman, seated on a chestnut taffy-tailed hack of considerable girth, which gleamed, as did his rider's leggings, from constant attention by those who serve the rich. Across the pommel of his saddle, he carried, neatly rolled, an oilskin to protect him from the worst caprices of the weather. While at his heels, or those of the resplendent chestnut, skipped on wooden legs the terrier pack at various stages of growth and decay.

Prowse must have thought it time he impressed those under him with the confidential nature of his relationship with the boss, for he approached as close as the latter's stirrup-iron allowed, and informed him in a lowered tone of voice, 'This is Eddie – the cove we had the letter about. I expect you'll like to have a word with 'im.'

The manager, the two stockmen, the jackeroo himself, all were looking to the owner to dissolve the state of impotence to which his position had reduced them. But Mr Lushington implied only obliquely, by a drawn-out whinnying sigh, that he had absorbed his manager's information. Still smiling from behind his gold-rimmed spectacles, he sat looking, not at the young man recommended to his patronage, but at the chain of distant hills.

'The Judge's son,' Eddie Twyborn thought he heard before the grazier turned his chestnut and, preceded by the terrier pack, made for the paddocks, the respectful manager and two stockmen leaping at their saddles, the jackeroo almost rupturing himself as he landed on a pommel, on the razor-back of his awkwardly articulated nag.

As a boy on holiday in the country Eddie sat ponies no better and no worse than others, but had lost his dignity astraddle the beast known as the Blue Mule. He took up a position at the rear of the Lushington cavalcade, thumping with his heels at unresponsive ribs.

The party crossed the jingling bridge, hooves spanking over loosely-linked planks, and headed out along the flat. An anus opened and disgorged, a vulva split and gushed. Only the ostracized Eddie Twyborn at the tail end was to any extent aware of such events. Greg Lushington and Don Prowse were turned in their saddles towards each other, exchanging esoteric information, the one wearing his normal protective smile, while the other had pinned on the bland badge of unashamed sycophancy. Between the head and the rear of the column rode the apathetic stockmen, blue-serge shoulder blades resigned to the action of their brumbies' razor-cruppered, harsh-coated rumps.

Eddie's nose began to run, his eyes to smart from the wind, and a little from humiliation. All he had experienced of life left him, not that it would have been of much use, reduced as he was to ignorant boyhood in remotest Patagonia. There was surely some dormant instinct he could summon up in self-defence. After all, he had been decorated, officially for valour, though actually for a desperate instinct which had carried him across no-man's-land in what they considered the desired direction. Now, in a man's world as opposed to no-man's-land, with a litter of rational, unrevealing clues replacing the irrational signposts of nightmare, he found himself at a loss. In his boyhood he had shown a slight talent for wood-carving (a kookaburra on a cigar-box lid) and for tying some of the fancier knots. With another boy he had modelled a crusaders' castle in plasticine; they had won a prize. These were all he could produce out of the waste-bin of memory to pit against the esoterica of Gregory Lushington and Don Prowse; even less open to human advances the two stockmen, whose silence and primitive forms suggested links with chthonic forces.

So Eddie Twyborn thumped desperately with his heels at the shaggy barrel of the Blue Mule, who refused to share his rider's urge to keep up with the cavalcade, perhaps accepting disdain as the passport to a peaceful existence; while the rider was forced to admit that he had to shine, regardless of geography, climate, or whichever sexual role he was playing.

As he continued thumping automatically at his wholly unresponsive mount, loss of faith in himself was replaced by an affinity with the landscape surrounding him. It happened very gradually, in spite of a sadistic wind, the sour grass, deformed trees, rocks crouching like great animals petrified by time. A black wagtail swivelling on a grey-green fence-post might have been confusing an intruder had he not been directing one who knew the password. The red road winding through the lucerne flat into the scurfy interior seemed to originate in memory, along with the wood-carving, boy-scout knots, and plasticine castle. For all the contingent's knowledgeable remarks on wool, scours, fluke and bluestone as they mounted the contours of Bald Hill, the scene's subtler depths were reserved for the outcast-initiate.

He allowed his horse to convey him at last as the latter would have wished. The two of them furled in the gusty swaths of an autumn gale, snatched at by meagre, isolated trees, warned by the cawing of watchful crows, the animal seemed to maintain a logical distance between themselves and what is considered normality.

Whenever the cavalcade halted the laggards drew abreast to the tune of renewed outbursts of instruction from the boss and 'yes yes Mr Lushington' from his acquiescent manager, 'bluestone the creeks termorrer,' bluestone being the apparent panacea. In the keen air it glittered for Eddie-Eudoxia like a Byzantine jewel.

The stockmen had ridden off to muster the mob of Bald Hill wethers, the chief objective of this somewhat desultory expedition. Like a cluster of parasites infesting a hide of almost identical colour, the dirty fleeces of the sheep could be seen in slight motion in a cleft on the stony hillside.

Embracing the panorama with a Napoleonic gesture, the grazier announced, presumably for his protégé, 'Wonderful sheep country. You wouldn't find better on the Hunter, though the fellers up there don't care to admit it.'

Eddie did not know what to do beyond grunt back in manly fashion. His boss seemed appeased.

By now the shouts of the stockmen had startled the mob of sheep, and the frantic exertions of the little faded kelpie were keeping them bunched as she drove them in the right direction.

On arrival, the sheep propped, milled in tight formation, then fanning out, stood coughing and staring, some of them stamping. Awaiting further orders from her tyrant, the kelpie flattened herself on the stones.

'A wormy-lookin' lot,' their owner grumbled. 'Need a good drenchin'. Drench 'em, Prowse.'

Though the manager may have felt his employer was intent this morning on thinking up jobs to impress a newcomer, he agreed that the sheep looked wormy and ought to be drenched; wasn't it his mission in life to tell Mr Lushington what he wanted to hear?

The latter had lost interest in his sheep. He was leading his entourage in another direction, when Denny's mongrel deerhounds put up a rabbit. They gave chase. The leader snapped. Between them they tore their squealing prey to bits, and devoured it down to the last inch of opalescent entrail and bloodied fur.

Mr Lushington had slowed down his chestnut until on a level with his jackeroo's nag. 'Bit boring for you,' he said somewhat surprisingly, 'until you learn what it's all about.' He dug with his whip-handle at the Blue Mule's withers. 'Perhaps you never will. Perhaps you aren't for it.'

Eddie suspected Gregory Lushington was endowed with more perception than he realized, but mumbled back, 'It's what I'm here for,' and was immediately depressed by the lack of logic in his remark.

The logic of those with whom he had been brought together was as simple and direct as the glimpses of illogic in the landscape around them were subtly diffused. But Mr Lushington's next remark made it hard to decide where he, or indeed, anybody stood. Turning his full gaze on his new acquisition as he had not up till now, he told him, 'In Sweden they boil a piece of fish skin in the coffee. It's supposed to bring out the flavour.'

'And does it?'

'Opinions vary,' Mr Lushington said.

He continued staring full face at his protégé from behind the gold-framed spectacles with a solemnity the younger man could only return.

Till simultaneously each burst out laughing.

It was too much for the manager. He had lost control of his star puppets. He began to scowl. There was a smell of class in the air.

Greg Lushington had turned his back on the present. 'Your dad used to come down here. Do a bit of fishin'. When we were younger . . .' From his fixed stare and muted tone of voice, old Lushington was re-living it visually. 'A good looker in those days. Still is – the Judge. And you've inherited the looks – if I may say so without turning a young man's head.'

It was positively a courtship. The manager would have felt more disgusted if at that moment Captain and Cis had not put up another couple of rabbits, which took refuge in a nearby warren.

Returning to the present Mr Lushington grumbled, 'Eaten out by rabbits. Dig 'em out, Prowse. That's something for the winter months. Break Eddie's back, I expect. But that's the way to break 'em in.' Again he dug his stockwhip at the Blue Mule's smudged withers.

'Yes, Mr Lushington,' Prowse agreed. 'We'll get young Eddie

on to that.' At the same time he gripped his mare's belly so hard with his spurs that the poor beast let out a fart and curvetted sideways.

Mr Lushington grinned.

'Did you know my mother?' Eddie asked in the absence of other inspiration.

'Your mother? No.'

'I thought you might have met her.'

'No,' he said very firmly. 'Never.'

They rode a little.

'My wife's met her,' he said, 'I think. Yes, I'm pretty sure Marcia knows Eadie Twyborn.' They rode some more. 'There's a lot of a woman's life a man doesn't know about. I mean,' he hastened to add, 'all those lunches – and afternoon teas – and the letters they write one another – and the telephone conversations. We wouldn't *want* to know, would we?'

Eddie agreed because it was expected of him. Actually he would have liked to know some more about Marcia Lushington of the beige eyelids and fringe of monkey fur. But realized he must keep her separate from Greg. Perhaps later on he would cross-question the manager.

Prowse was looking grimmer and grimmer. 'Talking of lunches, Mr Lushington – what about a bite of tucker ourselves?' he mentioned, and laughed.

The boss did not reject the suggestion, nor did he satisfy the man he employed by accepting it outright.

They had descended from the slopes and were riding amongst the white tussock and briar patches which fringed the river before the emerald lucerne stands took over farther down.

On reaching an overhang of sheltering rock Mr Lushington asked, 'This suit you, Don?'

It was the first time Eddie had heard the boss call the manager by his first name. He wondered when you did and when you didn't; perhaps it was allowed when you knocked off for lunch.

'Fine, Mr Lushington. A pretty decent windbreak.' Though he did not attempt to return the familiarity, Prowse had jumped down, and was rubbing his hands together with boyish and at the same time passionate informality.

Sliding off the willingly passive Blue Mule, it was Eddie Twyborn who felt old, stiff, and formal.

Mr Lushington dismounted with considerable professional

dignity. On his feet he looked more than ever pear-shaped, even toadlike, without losing his aura of authority and wealth.

The stockmen flung into automatic action and in the Twentieth Century did the sort of thing that has always been expected of serfs: snapping twigs, kindling fire, filling quart-pots, setting these to boil. The democratic spirit of Australia prevailed only after congealed chops were produced from saddle-pouches and the quarts had boiled: men and boss sank their teeth into fatty chops, trying to outdo one another in a display of ugliness and appetite.

Mrs Tyrrell had supplied Eddie with chops, but he could not have joined in the tea ceremony if Greg Lushington had not eased his own blackened quart in the direction of his friend's son.

Blinded by smoke and steam, scalded by the tea in which he sank his mouth, Eddie lowered his eyelids to convey his appreci-ation of a ritual.

Judging by his smile and the expression refracted by the spectacles, Mr Lushington was delighted, but Don Prowse swallowed what could have been a lump of gristle. He began to cough, and frown his orange frown.

'Get you a quart, Ed — first trip to Woolambi.'

Towards the end of the meal he offered Eddie a sip from his. The tea was by then cooler, if not less bitter. He was able to take several gulps. The manager sat nursing his knees, looking along the river as though to dissociate himself from his own gesture.

'Moth! Bloody moth!' Denny the son of Jim began shouting, golloping, beating ineffectually with a torn-off gum-switch at a creature which had fluttered out from the lee of their rock shelter. 'Make good bait if you can catch the bitches.'

'Set down, Denny,' his father advised.

Denny obeyed, though Captain and Cis continued snapping awhile at the air which had contained the departed moth.

Mr Lushington said, 'That's one of the bogong moths. There's a season of the year when they gather in the mountains — a regular moth corroboree. The blacks used to go up, and feast on them, and grow fat.'

Their lips and cheeks glistening, the whites looked replete and drowsy, if not with moths, with mutton chops. Only Eddie Twyborn felt nauseated. To stave off his queasiness he almost broke silence disgracefully by returning to the subject of Marcia, but swallowed the impulse along with his sensation of nausea.

172

The party staggered up. They packed their tackle. Except for tooth-picking, the work day seemed over. Well, the evenings set in early at 'Bogong'. The inky shadows were already gathering along the river flat and in the mountain clefts.

The party rode off in the direction of evening fires.

Rounding the shoulder of a hill where briars had taken over, Mr Lushington said, 'Root out the briars, Prowse. That's somethun else for the winter months. Get this boy to help yer. That's what 'e's here for. Experience.'

The boss left them the other side of the loose-jointed bridge, followed by his terrier pack.

'See you, Eddie,' he called back; then with somewhat diffident daring, 'You'll have to come up and meet my wife — who knows your mum.'

Eddie felt too tired as they rode towards their own quarters, but must draw Prowse on Marcia, unless Peggy Tyrrell made that unnecessary.

'How're you doin', Ed?' Their knees bumped; it might have been deliberately and with a forced heartiness on the manager's part. 'You look fucked out!' He laughed, but not unkindly, or it may have been cajoled out of him by his mare's fondling the bit with her tongue in anticipation of a feed of oats.

Any evening Eddie Twyborn looked and felt fucked out. It was what he was there for, wasn't it? He did, however, wonder, picking at the raw blisters on his hands. He derived a morbid pleasure from letting the water out of the blisters, farting after boiled cabbage, or mashed swede with the lumps still in it, listening to Prowse tell how Kath walked out taking Kim with her.

'Kim's the kid, is she? Why did you call her Kim, Don?'

'Why not? It's a name, isn't it?'

There was nothing to reply to that.

'Any'ow,' Prowse said, 'I think it was Kath's choice.' He seemed satisfied that Eddie had given him the opportunity to blame his wife for something else.

'What about Marcia? What's she like?'

'Another woman.' He poured himself another whiskey; he had grown surly.

Mrs Tyrrell was more forthcoming, if only slightly so, on an evening when Prowse said he had to go up to the homestead to a conference with Lushington and the accountant who was down from Sydney.

'Marcia?' Mrs Tyrrell hid a yawn behind her hand. 'She was from Tilba way. That makes 'er foreign to some, but I was allus broad-minded where foreigners is concerned. Anyways, she did well for 'erself catching Lushington. Cupboards full of lovely gowns. An' furs put away in calico bags. Mrs Edmonds, 'oo 'elps, showed me the furs when she 'ad 'em out to air. Couldn't let Marce go to the ball smellun of mothballs.'

'Are we ever going to set eyes on Marce?'

'Sure thing,' Mrs Tyrrell munched. 'She offen rides round the paddocks with Greg and Prowse. Or Prowse alone — it don't worry. You can't say she's not a good sort, though some run 'er down — say she's a stuck-up nobody from Tilba. They say — well, I'm not gunner repeat. Those are the ones she don't wanter know. You can't know everybody, can yer? Even I know that.' She sighed and resettled herself.

'Yes, you'll see Marce. When you're wealthy you've got time to put in. Arr, it's hard on the women — the wealthy ones along with the others. You can't expect 'em to spend all their time readin' the libr'y books or shakun the mothballs out of their furs.' Peggy Tyrrell's eyes were at their brightest, their blackest. 'Lushington wanted a son. I reckon they must'uv give up after the third go. They're all there,' she said, 'in the graveyard down below the house. Arr, dear,' she sighed, 'it's the funerals I miss out 'ere. Never missed a funeral in town. Knew everybody like me own 'and. They allus invited me ter do the layun out.'

She went to bed after that. The following day would be Sunday, and though reared a Catholic, she was looking forward to the Protestant service. Every third Sunday the Reverend Hannaford came out from Woolambi. On Sundays Peggy Tyrrell wore four extra teeth between her fangs. The teeth spent the week greening in a tumbler of water on her bedroom sill.

He was coming to terms with his body. He had begun to live in accordance with appearances. His hands no longer broke out in blisters; his arms, if not muscular, were at least lithe and sinewy. Sometimes on a calm day, by snatches of winter sunlight, while straining fences, digging out rabbits, or following Prowse's tractor to loop a chain round a clump of briars, he might take off his shirt, and the men would watch, not respectfully, but without showing too much disapproval: Prowse in his smelly overalls, Jim and Denny in their khaki shirts buttoned up to the throat, their frayed serge jackets discarded only at the height of summer; or old Lushington might ride by, apparently for the sole purpose of sharing with his friend the Judge's son some joke which wasn't. At first irritated by the old man's partiality for an ignorant novice, the men finished by accepting a relationship based on education or class.

Prowse possibly didn't. It was difficult to fit the manager into any social category. He was as liable to lapse into educated speech as Greg Lushington would talk uneducated to his men.

Prowse said, 'I used to read before I married Kath. Ever read any Peacock, Eddie? Or Meredith? There's a writer for you!'

'No. My education was neglected. My father intended me for the Law.' It wounded him to wound the Judge, and not so unintentionally.

'Well, you missed something if you never read *Headlong Hall* or *The Ordeal of Richard Feverell*. Though it's all gingerbread of course. I gave it up when I married and life became serious. Kath thought reading novels a waste of time – they weren't real. She was for magazines. She kidded herself she knew the people she'd seen once or twice on the social pages. She could talk about their homes, their clothes – their divorces, by the hour. It was her religion like.'

Prowse poured himself another drink. 'My old man warned me against getting bogged down in any sort of myth. Dad was an Anglican parson who lost his faith, then went broke on a place where Mexican thistle had taken over.'

The parson father and the bookworm son were such unlikely apparitions that Eddie wished he had the courage to conjure up Eudoxia in the same weatherboard room.

Prowse swallowed an ugly mouthful. 'Went out into the paddock one night and shot 'imself through the mouth – amongst the bloody thistle.'

Eddie began to feel an affection for poor bloody Prowse, which didn't accord with his own intentions, and which probably would have earned him one on the jaw from that scabby fist.

'You *men*!' Peggy Tyrrell had come in from some outer darkness. 'Yarn yer 'eads off if yez gets 'alf a chance – and accuse we women at the same time!'

*

175

Eddie Twyborn was cantering home. It was a tranquil evening beneath a pale green sky soon to darken. Curlews could be heard calling in the tussock with an abstract melancholy which was curiously comforting. In bays scalloped from the river bank, cushions of white scum had collected, bobbing against the vigorous flow of brown water. A trout rose, and plopped back.

He was content, with evening, with the scent of frost, his own smell, the stench of leather on a sweat-sodden horse.

He had even developed a kind of affection for this gelded monstrosity the Blue Mule, dipping, swivelling, dislocating, then re-uniting in its various components beneath his thighs. When the animal snorted and shied. The tangled mane was cutting into the rider's fingers. Before he started falling. A sawdust puppet dragged. Trampled amongst sparks from the road. Under this feverish green sky, curlew calls, cushions of bobbing grey-white scum, the gobbets of a horse's vegetable dung, flow of blood, of water, of blood. Of the burst puppet. Fading into the green white. Drowned in crimson . . .

The brakes were applied so violently, the chassis shuddered, the headlamps danced.

'Hi! Ed, boy? Ed?' It was Prowse's voice, boots approaching stiffly over frosted ruts.

The figure lying on the edge of the road began stirring. Eddie Twyborn, realizing that he was still himself, grew conscious of the pains shooting through his ribs, legs, head. He must have been concussed by the fall. None of him was manageable, anyway by his own efforts but oh God, he was still here, if he wanted to be; he was not yet sure. He would have liked to eat an ice, a sorbet delicately flavoured with cantaloup, morello, or pistachio.

Don Prowse was mumbling grunting panting as he encouraged dragged finally lifted. 'Lucky I was out in the yard when the bloody horse got back.'

'Poor old Mule. Nobody's fault.'

Their passage to the little runabout Prowse drove about the place, to work, was excruciating to say the least. Accomplished in the end, Eudoxia, deposed empress or current hetaira, would have liked to thank, or in some way reward, the sweaty brute who had carried her halfway across the Bithynian plain. She might even have allowed him to ravish her in one long painful orgasm.

Instead, after being lumped on the tray of the vibrating Ford runabout, beside a coil of fencing wire, several spanners, a jack, and a spare can of petrol, Eddie Twyborn fainted.

They discussed whether to transfer the patient to the Woolambi cottage hospital.

'No, no,' he protested, already belonging to a dun-coloured, draughty, weatherboard room, which light entered only when wind agitated the hawthorns outside; he had begun to associate light with the motion of his head against the pillow and hawthorn spikes scratching at glass.

'*No!*' he repeated.

'Not if anythink ain't broke. Not if the poor bugger don't want it,' Mrs Tyrrell insisted. 'I've taken on worse 'n this. Nursed a family of seventeen, and a 'usband in the last stages of cancer.'

He had a sudden vision of a withered dug flexed for action.

Dr Yip agreed.

Prowse had explained before the doctor's arrival, 'Doc's got a touch of the Chow, Eddie, but a good bloke for all that.'

The patient responded to an exotic eye, to the wind-burnt hands with under-cushions in crumpled pink. The doctor decided there was, in fact, nothing broken, perhaps out of deference to the sick man's passionate wish not to be moved.

They all took turns at mauling him, particularly his forehead: it had become their dearest possession, talisman against thwarted love. He closed his eyes and let them get on with it.

He overheard Peggy Tyrrell and Prowse, whose strength had been enlisted in lifting the body, quarrelling over a hard stool in a bedpan sent down from the homestead.

'You can't tell *me* . . .' Peggy hissed.

'I'm not trying to!' Don's voice was trembling with rage.

You awoke on another occasion, and again it was a hand polishing the talisman of a forehead.

It was the hand of old Lushington himself.

Seated on a slat chair beside the iron stretcher he was got up in his usual pigskin leggings, the same cord riding breeches, and the straight-set cap in heather-mixture tweed which he had not thought of removing for his visit to a sickbed. From the angle at which he was sitting, the spectacles looked blank, like the headlamps of a car gone out for day.

'Only came down to have a look,' he remarked on whipping his hand away from the forehead. 'You don't want to exert yourself. Don't feel you have to talk, Eddie. Half of what we say isn't worthwhile, anyway.' He heaved against the fragile, slatted chair. 'That's what I tell the wife, and she won't agree. Most women are terrible nags.'

Eddie closed his eyes. 'I thought you were leaving – sir – for Europe.'

'Yes – but not yet – but later.'

Gregory Lushington had brought as offerings two irregular oranges, a wizened apple, and a brown banana. 'It's the best we can do locally.'

He also fished out a couple of letters. 'The mail. I'll leave you to peruse it. And hope to see you about soon. Marcia – my wife – joins me.'

When the visitor had gone Eddie continued holding the letters between the bones of his unconvincing fingers, breathing gently, eyes still closed. He must read his letters, but not just then.

The next morning he was strong enough to make the effort. His fingers trembled, however. The first envelope when broached fell clattering amongst the eggshells and the crusts of bread.

Dearest Eddie,

They rang to tell us. Needless to say I was *horrified* – but relieved to hear you had survived this alarming accident. Ethel Tucker's husband George was killed outright, only recently, by landing on his head.

To get you back and then almost to have lost you! I don't know why I deserve such retribution, though no doubt your law-trained father could find a reason for it. Perhaps it is because I should never have been a wife or mother. Who knows? I am surely not as bad as some who get away with worse.

I would come to 'Bogong', but you – and Mrs Lushington – might not approve. I think I know my place at last.

Bless you, my darling boy!

Your

Mum

PS. Biffy is ailing – very miserable – a heavy infestation of tapeworm – and, I suspect, a cancerous growth – I shall be devastated if I lose her – nobody can understand, but there it is.

Eadie T.

The letter joined the eggshells as he opened the second envelope, addressed in his father's formal hand.

My dear boy,

This is bad news, though not as bad as it might have been. At least you are in good hands. Greg Lushington will see to it that all which ought to be done is done.

I thought of taking the train down. Then it occurred to me it might embarrass you. I know how you value your independence and dislike any display of emotion.

With best wishes for a speedy recovery,

Your affect.

Father

He drowsed a little after finishing the letter, pondering over the impressions one makes on others, in this case so perversely contradictory he suspected the Judge to be shielding himself from experiences he did not wish to undergo. For a moment he and Eddie were again adrift in a moonlit sea, on a honeycomb bedspread, the yard sounds of a country pub rising through an open window. The dreamer would not have regretted drowning in love with Judge Twyborn.

Instead he was returning closer to life every day, to the clash of metal and men's voices, horses' hooves and dogs barking, the shambling and squelching of cows filing down a hillside towards their milking.

The bails stood between the homestead and the cottage. Mr Edmonds was in charge of the dairy, and several other provinces: he curry-combed the Lushington hacks; he polished their car with a secret unguent; he coaxed forked carrots and staggy cabbage out of the frozen 'Bogong' earth; and twice a week cut a sheep's throat after a desperate wrestling match. He was a small, mild, buttoned-up man, like a wood carving painted predominantly red and black. His wife helped about the homestead and was Mrs Tyrrell's chief informant on what was going on 'up there'. There was a cook too (Mrs Quimby and Mrs Tyrrell had long since broken off relations) and Dot Norton the rabbiter's daughter whose duties were unspecified.

'Dot's what you'd expect from a rabbiter,' Mrs Tyrrell considered.

'What's wrong with a rabbiter?'

'A rabbiter — from them I've knowed — could never ever associate with nothun better than bally rabbuts.'

Dick Norton the rabbiter was certainly a runtish rabbit of a man, never seen but mounted on one of the strain of 'Bogong' nags, an outsize army trenchcoat trailing almost on the ground, and a pack of incestuous mongrels running at his horse's heels.

'But his daughter — what's wrong with the rabbiter's daughter?'

'I've got nothun against Dot,' Mrs Tyrrell protested; then in virtuous volte-face, 'I'm not accusin' 'er of nothun, poor cow. It's not 'er fault. I'll take 'er side in any showdown. Mrs Lushington 'ull think of somethun. Marcia's on Dot's side.'

Marcia as *dea ex machina*. His strength returning, he hankered less for acquaintanceship with one who was too much a legend for his present life to accommodate. She had remained inhumanly remote while his flesh-and-blood friends and allies had quarrelled over the contents of his bedpan and the techniques of lifting him on and off. Though hadn't Marcia at least contributed the pan? Or so he had been told.

Mrs Tyrrell informed him, 'Now that you've got yer strength back, love, I'm takin' the opportunity of drivin' inter town this week-end. Prowse is off to see some girl and 'as offered me a lift. Which I've accepted. I don't doubt you can do for yerself. You're not one of the *helpless* males — I can see by the way you use a needle. Anyways, I'll bake cake enough ter see yer through, an' all you'll 'ave ter do is shove the blessed shoulder in the h'oven.'

He was almost too anxious to see them go. Morning and evening, using a stick, he was able by now to hobble along the river bank. More than ever his surroundings yielded quiet subtleties: a combing of cloud, a hare starting up from its nest in the tussock, a flotilla of geese rounding a bend in the river. The silly sheep, recovering from initial shock, resumed their grazing, perhaps recognizing a kindred spirit.

He hobbled and clumped and hobbled, or sat when his leg gave out.

On one occasion in the days preceding Mrs Tyrrell's week-end he came across a miserable stunted female, of lashless, red-rimmed eyes, and nostrils pinched so close together the gristle could barely have allowed the passage of air. Seated on a rock beside the river she averted her face from his approach, holding her head at a discouraging angle.

He knew at once, but had to ask, 'And who are you?'

'I'm Dot,' she replied unwillingly. 'Dot Norton. I help at the house. You're Mr Twyborn,' she said. 'They was talkin' about you.'

'What were they saying?'

'Oh, I dunno — yer leg,' she gulped and sniffed, 'yer dad. They're talkin' about askin' you up.'

'People don't always do what they talk about doing.'

'That's somethun you don't need to tell me!' said Dot Norton.

She started re-arranging her dress over the early months of a pregnancy. She was the kind of runt whose last phase would be huge. He decided he'd better not look at her.

'Look at these geese,' he said. 'Have they gone wild, or are they still domesticated?'

'Eh?'

'Do they belong at the homestead?'

'Not as you'd say,' said Dot Norton. 'They're not exactly wild neether. They're old,' she said. 'They lay soft eggs and nothun ever comes out.'

She turned on him a look which expressed envy of the luck of elderly geese.

'I wish I was barren,' she said very earnestly.

'If you were, you mightn't.'

He did sincerely believe it for that instant: to be rent between birth and death was the luxury of normal women.

It was obvious they had discussed life too deeply, for Dot grew prim.

'I better be goin'. Scrape the bloody parsnips,' she said, 'or Mrs Quimby 'ull rouse on me.'

She stood up, pulling down a crumpled woollen dress over her increasing baby.

'Don't worry, Eddie,' she told him. 'Mrs Lushington means to invite yer — and soon.'

He hobbled back to the cottage.

'Where've you been, you little bastard?' Mrs Tyrrell asked.

'Along the river.'

'It's too late for invalids along the river. An' Mrs Edmonds come lookun for yer with this.'

She produced one of the coarse tumblers with which the cottage was provided, and in one of which her Sunday teeth spent the rest of the week. But aslant this particular glass reclined a single, white, wintry rose, possibly the last rose ever, its invalid complexion infused with a delicate transcendent green.

Against the tumbler Mrs Tyrrell rather coyly propped an oblong parchment envelope which in no way went with her own blackened hand and the huggermugger little dining-kitchen in which they were standing.

As he tore through the envelope, he saw she was watching, but overtaken by recklessness he could not care, nor for what she might read on his face as he read.

Dear Eddie,

You may wonder why I haven't been in touch before. It could be from laziness — or diffidence — I'm really quite a shy person. But now that we're over whatever it was, Greg and I would love you to come to a meal this Saturday night, when we understand you will be on your own. About 7, shall we say?

Sincerely

Marcia Lushington

This last of our roses is a token of I don't know what. There is nothing else I can offer. Do, please, forgive my earlier omissions.

He left the kitchen without offering to share the contents of his letter, and Peggy Tyrrell must have felt she ought to respect his decision.

No doubt it was his silence which provoked her superiority as the time approached for her departure to town. Long before the driver showed up, she jumped into the passenger's seat, clutching an irregular brown-paper parcel, sucking her green, week-end teeth, lolled in the high-standing Ford and looked out with an expression which suggested 'if you have your mysteries, I can have mine' from under a great black hat, constructed rather than made, out of stiff, dusty ribbon. Except for the battered brick-red face she was a vision of total black. It was her normal going-out dress, though on this occasion she was looking forward to a funeral of some importance. If the late mayor happened to have been both a Protestant and a swindler, Peggy Tyrrell was never known to let moral scruples stand between herself and her favourite form of entertainment. 'Besides', as she was fond of saying, 'if you're born with morals yerself, it's up ter you to forgive the poor bugger 'oo wasn't' — a precept she didn't always obey.

Now while Mrs Tyrrell sat waiting, serenely, if mysteriously, in the car, Eddie, lying on his bed beneath the vantage window, could hear the manager endlessly buffing his town boots. The preparations for this expedition were unusually elaborate. In the intervals between the roaring, the pounding, the explosions of the chip-heater, which shook the unstable cottage's whole structure, there was the sound of a razor painfully dragged through a three-day stubble. Then the thrashing and splashing of water, the thumping and grazing of large limbs coming to terms with a narrow metal tub.

Prowse showed up unexpectedly before putting on his shirt.

'If you ever feel like it, Ed,' he announced from the doorway, 'there's plenty of hot little sorts in town. Let me know and I'll fix up something for yer.'

Eddie thanked his would-be procurer, who had advanced some way into the room.

Prowse was at his most ostentatiously virile, in faded moleskins and heavy, conspicuously polished boots, a generous golden fell wreathed round the nipples of the male breasts. He stood looking down at the passive figure before him on the bed. The thick arms looked strangely powerless, and the smile which accompanied his invitation to lust, directionless, and finally evasive.

Eddie let Prowse withdraw without helping him by remark or glance. In fact, he turned his face, and was staring at the side wall from under half-lowered lids. He felt as powerless and evasive as Prowse had looked. If he had spoken he might not have been able to control his breathing.

'See you tomorrow night then,' the manager called as he slammed the fly-proof door and thundered over the veranda.

The car was heard driving off.

Alone in the house, Eddie was possessed by a sensation of freedom from the need to control his more obsessive desires. Contingency was no longer a threat. On his visit to the Lushingtons, one of whom he hardly knew, the other not at all, he would have every opportunity for impressing strangers with the self which, he felt sure, was in process of being born, and which was the reason he had chosen a manner of life on the whole distasteful to him.

Till the image of Dot Norton was inserted into his mind to start his conviction wobbling. The tearful undersized girl nursing her pregnancy by the river, unhappy in her possession — but possessed. Her figure fading into the vision of brute arms, nipples wreathed in a fuzz of gold. Into Marcia Lushington's nostrils breathing cigarette smoke from under a fringe of monkey fur.

He got up as quickly as his lameness allowed, re-read the letter of invitation, looked in the glass at the reflection of his personally unappealing face. The rest of the afternoon he spent imitating Prowse's preparations for the week-end orgy at Woolambi, except that he devoted all of ten minutes to filing and buffing his nails, an occupation in which Don would never have indulged. Or would he? The surprises other people can spring are all the more surprising for being unimaginable.

Don. Only rarely had he addressed Prowse by his first name, and it entered his thoughts just as rarely. It had the same brashness, brassiness of tone, as the man himself, not without appeal. *Marcia* on the other hand conveyed the opulent ripple of soft, creamy flesh, the penetrating scent of an exotic flower unrelated to the delicate accents of the greenish-white winterbound rose.

As the hour for their dinner approached he lit the hurricane lamp. He considered whether to take his stick, which by now he scarcely needed for physical support, then decided on it, more in the nature of a theatrical prop. He was wearing a suit made for him in London after he had been demobbed. Looking at the reflection in the glass he had begun to convince himself of an existence which most others seemed to take for granted.

He could not be sure whether Prowse did, just as he would probably never believe wholly in his own positive attributes — if what is masculine is also necessarily positive.

As often happens in the approach to an Australian country house, it was difficult to decide where to breach the Lushington homestead. There were verandas, porches, lights, snatches of piano music, whinging dogs, skittering cats, archways armed with rose-thorns, a drift of kitchen smells, but never any real indication of how to enter. Australian country architecture is in some sense a material extension of the contradictory beings who have evolved its elaborate informality, as well as a warning to those who do not belong inside the labyrinth.

After blundering around awhile he was finally admitted by the fresh-faced Mrs Edmonds, wife of the groom-cum-dairyman-cum-gardener. Herself who aired Mrs Lushington's furs, and who had brought the invalid white rosebud down to the cottage.

She said, 'They're expecting you, sir, in the droring room.' She was too shy or too untrained to go farther than indicate the direction in which the room lay.

He might have blundered some more if it hadn't been for light visible in a doorway at the end of the passage and a few groping piano chords of musical comedy origin. The piano act, he suspected, was staged by Mrs Lushington to lure him in.

In fact it was her husband brooding over the piano.

'Vamping a bit,' old Lushington explained with a bashful smile. 'It helps pass the time.'

Leaving the piano, he advanced and asked, 'What's your poison, Eddie?' as though he might rely on alcohol to dissolve human restraints.

Lushington himself, still wearing leggings and cord breeches below a balding velvet smoking-jacket, was already comfortably oiled. 'You're well, are you?' he asked. 'You look well.'

Eddie was prevented answering either of his host's questions by the entrance of a little yapping Maltese terrier with a delicious sliver of a pink tongue who proceeded to skip around, blinded by his own eyebrows, excited by his own frivolity.

The guest spilled a finger of what smelled like practically neat whiskey as the dog's mistress appeared.

'We haven't met,' Mrs Lushington said, 'but I know you, of course, from the Hotel Australia.'

'How the Australia?' her husband asked in some surprise.

'On an occasion when I decided not to lunch there,' she answered. 'It all looked too *bloody* – like some awful club, full of the people one spends one's life avoiding. Too much *flour* in everything – and a smell of *horse*radish.'

Mr Lushington looked perplexed. 'But we've always enjoyed the old Australia. You run into so many of your mates. And you, Marce, have never found anything wrong with the food.'

But Mrs Lushington was holding out. She raised her chin, and smiled. Like Peggy Tyrrell she enjoyed her mysteries, while being more than half prepared to share them with one who was not quite a stranger, but almost.

'Stop it, Beppi!' she advised the Maltese, who was chivvying the fur with which she was hemmed.

'Darling,' she asked her husband, 'are you going to pour me a drink?'

As Greg Lushington was too deeply immersed in the mystery of his wife's betrayal of the Hotel Australia, she advanced and did it for herself with a most professional squirt from a siphon covered with wire-netting.

Marcia was wearing a long coat of vivid oriental patchings over her discreet black, less discreetly sable-hemmed, skirt. It was in the upper regions that discretion ended completely, in an insertion of flesh-coloured, or to match Marcia, beige lace which strayed waistwards in whorls and leaves. Her daring must have deserted her in dressing, for she had stuck an artificial flower in the cleavage of lace or flesh, a species of oriental poppy artistically crushed, its fleshtones tinged with departing flame.

'Do sit,' she invited their guest, 'if you can see somewhere comfortable. Other people's furniture, like their coffee, is inclined to be unbearable.'

The Lushingtons' drawing-room furniture was a mixed lot: armchairs and sofa in the chintzy English tradition, with a few pieces of what looked like authentic Chippendale, and rubbing shoulders with them, humbler colonial relations in cedar, crudely carved by some early settler, or more likely, his assigned slave.

There was also the grand piano at which Mr Lushington had been discovered vamping, on it a Spode tureen filled with an arrangement of dead hydrangeas, autumn leaves, and pussy willow, in front of it, framed importantly in gold, a portrait-photograph of a younger Marcia, one hand resting possessively on what must have been the same piano, draped at the time with a Spanish shawl.

Noticing their jackeroo's interest in pianos, Mrs Lushington asked, 'Do you play?'

'I used to,' he said, 'badly, I was told, but my enthusiasm made me acceptable.'

'Greg is the musical one,' nor did Mrs Lushington resent it. 'He'll thump quite happily by the hour. I tried as a child, but my chilblains didn't encourage me to practise. I think a piano's necessary, though — as part of a room, to stand things on.'

Her husband, who had flopped down in a rickety cedar grandmother chair, continued bemused by her recent remark, or else it was his most recent whiskey. 'I can't think what makes you say that about the old Australia.'

'Oh, darling, leave it! It's only that one isn't the same person every hour of the week.'

She was prepared to laugh for her own conceit, when her little dog, jumping from the sofa to her lap, darted his tongue between her opening lips, and incipient mirth was replaced by barely controlled annoyance.

'I like to think I've been the same person,' Mr Lushington said, 'every hour of my life.'

After smacking her naughty dog, Mrs Lushington was again disposed for laughter.

'I know you do,' she said. 'That's what makes you adorable.' Getting up, she went behind his chair and, bending over, kissed him on the crown of his bald head. 'Don't you think he's rather sweet?' she asked.

Eddie was relieved to gather that her question was rhetorical. His own affection for the old man was too delicate to bear exposure.

For all her affectation of lightness and mirth, Marcia Lushington revealed glimpses of a more sombre temperament. Where her black, rather coarse, glistening eyebrows almost met, there were flickering hints that black frowns were the order of her day. Unlike so many other women, she had not yet cut off her hair, which was arranged with some skill and tortoiseshell combs in a chignon above the nape of her neck. Though substantially built, height and flowing lines helped her to get away with it; full lips were only faintly painted the colour of scallop-coral, beneath a too heavy Caucasian moustache; overall, the raw-scallop tones would have made her flesh look unduly naked if it had not received the benefit of powder. Her regrettable feature would have been her teeth if they hadn't looked so durable: they were strong, but too widely spaced, and in the moments of her assured mirth, bubbles would appear in the gaps.

Her eyes were fine and dark – none of your blistering Anglo-Saxon blue.

During the evening Eddie remembered what Prowse had said about Marcia's being 'more of the land'. He might not have agreed had he not experienced the vast undulating Monaro, and if, on the way to dinner, he had not brushed against an old natural-wool cardigan hanging from a hook under a hat in stained, dead-green velour. These very personal belongings had the smell of tussock and greasy fleece, which gusts from Marcia's Chanel temporarily overpowered.

In the mock-Tudor dining room, mint sauce took over from

Chanel. Greg Lushington stood at the sideboard carving the leg like a surgeon under hypnosis.

There was no nonsense about the Lushingtons' feeding habits.

'Do you approve, darling?' he asked. 'The gravy isn't too floured, is it?'

'Shut up, Greg!' she returned. 'It was a mood, that's all.'

Mrs Edmonds who was waiting on them smiled for what she did not understand, while through a hatch there was the suggestion of a suetty face (Mrs Quimby? relations with whom Peggy Tyrrell had severed) and the pinched, rabbity features of Dot Norton the rabbiter's daughter above a wet floral apron.

The Lushingtons started eating their way through the slices of mutton, the roasted potatoes, the baked pumpkin, the wads of bicarbonated cabbage. They obviously enjoyed the feudal glory in which they lived.

'Is Prowse your friend?' suddenly Mrs Lushington saw fit to ask the jackeroo.

'We haven't quarrelled,' Eddie answered cautiously.

'Why should they? Poor Don!' Mr Lushington murmured.

'A quick-tempered, a passionate man,' retorted Mrs Lushington, fitting a little of everything on her fork.

They were being watched more intently than ever, Eddie realized, by Mrs Edmonds against the sideboard, and the rather more animal eyes through the hatch.

'Poor Don – his wife left him,' Mr Lushington continued.

Marcia replied, 'We all know that – even Eddie, I imagine, by now. Her leaving was to everyone's advantage, surely?'

Greg Lushington had spilt some gravy on his already spotted smoking-jacket. He sat rubbing at the place with a napkin.

'They were wrong for each other,' he murmured, as though nobody else ever had been. 'She hated him.'

'He hated her.'

'I think he was hoping the little girl might bring them together.' The litany unfurled, more, you felt, for the Lushingtons' benefit than their guest's.

After a while they fell silent, mashing at a shambles of potato and gravy. Mrs Edmonds replenished the glasses with Burgundy of an impeccable French vintage.

On the walls of the mock-Tudor dining room there were several photographs of Greg holding stud rams by the horns, vaguely smiling in the direction of the camera, and one of

Marcia astride a show hack, his arched neck almost wholly swathed in ribbons. From beneath the brim of what might have been the dead-green velour at the beginning of its career, she was looking moody in spite of her success. (It surprised Eddie; for Australian women were usually photographed grinning from ear to ear.)

There was a baked pudding with strawberry jam and clotted cream. From his nursery days he seemed to remember it as Queen of Puddings.

'Don't you adore food?' Marcia asked through a mouthful, and only just prevented a trickle of cream from escaping. (A woman of importance, she was allowed sloppy table manners.)

It was obvious that her husband loved, her servants admired her, Mrs Tyrrell enjoyed her patronage, and Prowse considered her a 'good sort'. It was he, Eddie, who must be wrong in having doubts, while drawn to her as part of an exercise in self-vindication.

It was perhaps how her husband was drawn to undertake those journeys, in Patagonia, down the China Coast, through the foothills of the Himalayas, of which he told at length over coffee and liqueurs afterwards in the drawing room. His wife, who must have heard it many times, yawned an accompaniment to his narrative. The guest listened intermittently.

'. . . in Russia they serve tea in glasses. They hold the sugar in their mouths, you know . . .'

Russian sugar, Swedish fishskin: these were the incidentals which intrigued dear Greg Lushington. While Eddie found himself fascinated by the Oriental poppy in crumpled silk, ever more insufficiently arranged in Marcia's beige cleavage. She seemed to realize. She kept glancing down, giving the petals a tweak to spread them. The brilliant coat had slipped sideways off one shoulder. She shivered, and righted it. Greater nakedness might have come more naturally to her, but not in midwinter in the Monaro.

Greg Lushington was straying somewhere along the Nevsky Prospect; he closed down after draining his brandy.

Remembering one of his mother's conventions, Eddie murmured, 'Delicious coffee' of the watery stuff they were drinking; then, louder, 'Any fishskin, sir, to bring out the flavour?'

But Greg Lushington's rosy jowls had subsided on his velvet lapels.

Marcia sighed. 'That old Swedish fishskin!'

Seated beside the fire, irritably agitating an ankle beneath her broad sable hem, she bent and picked up her sleeping Maltese dog, to comfort one who was in no need of comforting.

She said, 'You must find it all very boring.'

'Why should it be?' he asked.

It was her turn not to know the answer.

'I could lend you books,' she said, 'if I knew your tastes.'

'I haven't felt any inclination to read since coming to "Bogong".'

'Then we've properly seduced you!' Her wry smile was directed at the collapsing fire.

As the only conscious male present, perhaps he should put on another log, for Greg had let out the faint sizzle of a snore, followed by a short, querulous fart.

Marcia immediately raised her voice. 'Don't you think you ought to go to bed, darling? We know you're tired. Eddie will forgive you.'

The old boy rose, tottering like an enormous cherubic baby, and said after sliding his hand down one of his protégé's shoulder blades, 'Anyway I think I'll – take a little nap. See you later, everyone.'

After that there was an opening and closing of doors, a lavatory flushed, and a final closing.

Marcia said, 'He's taken a great fancy to you. Greg badly wanted a son. I failed him. But he doesn't hold it against me. He's a good man in all his instincts. That's what makes it more dreadful.'

'Why should it?' His teeth were chattering.

'If a man is truly good, he rises above hurt. We're the ones who are hurt.'

She sat watching her own tossed ankle. 'What do you think of Prowse?' she asked.

'I haven't thought about him enough.' He wondered whether she would know he was lying.

'No,' she said. 'Prowse is a human animal. No more. But the poor brute has suffered.'

Marcia too, was shivering, hugging herself more closely inside her Oriental coat.

He bent down and began clumsily stacking logs on the fire.

'Rather extravagant!' she twittered.

The fresh logs spat and crackled.

Marcia was leaning forward in the direction of the renewed flames. 'Do you know about the bogong moth?'

He did of course, but was not allowed to resist the reprise she was launching into, '. . . up into the mountains at a certain time of year, to eat this moth. It's said to taste rich and nutty . . .'

Hunched above the crumpled poppy in her beige cleavage, she had parted her lips on the strong teeth, in the gaps between which the downy sacs of moths might have been disgorging their nutty cream.

Marcia herself at that moment was not unlike a great downy moth irrationally involved in an obscene but delicious cannibalistic rite; in which she must involve some other being for his initiation or destruction.

She said, in a very intimate voice, for they were both crouched over the fire, 'No one has been able to explain to me why you came here. There's something too fine about you for this kind of life.'

He was balanced again on the razor-edge of motives, between truth and lies. 'I wanted to live simply for a while. To think things out. Yes, to think.'

She said sourly, 'You've come to the very worst place! It numbs thought, or pinches it out. We've hardly one between us.'

'There's the country.'

'Oh, yes, there's the country!' She threw back her thick, creamy throat, and closed her eyes, and smiled with the expression of fulfilment which explained what Prowse had said of her. 'The country itself is what makes it possible — even at its worst, its bitterest. But one needs more that that, surely?' She opened her eyes and looked at him. 'Wouldn't you agree, Eddie Twyborn?'

How false was Marcia Lushington of the grand piano for standing things on, the Spode tureen, the French Burgundy, and mock-Tudor dining room? He couldn't very well decide for being something of a fake himself.

'I think,' she said, and now she was probably dead-level honest, 'you may have something I've always wanted. That fineness I mentioned.'

'What about your husband? A good man. Isn't that something better than whatever this "fineness" may be?'

She bared her wide-spaced teeth in what was a mirthless smile, and he found himself responding to it, while repelled. 'Oh yes, we know all that! The good — the virtuous — they're what we admire — depend on to shore us up against our own shortcomings — with loving affection.'

She fell silent after that, and looked down along his wrist, his thigh.

'The other,' she said, 'needn't be lust, need it?'

Half burnt half chilled beside the leaping fire, he discovered himself, to his amazement and only transitory repugnance, lusting after Marcia's female forms.

They stood up simultaneously. If they had hoped to escape by withdrawing from the heat of the fire, the diminishing circles of warmth inside the room brought them closer together.

Her body was a revelation of strength in softness.

'What about Greg?' It was his conscience letting out a last gasp.

'He won't wake this side of daylight.' She sounded ominously certain.

She led him through a frozen house from which the servants had already dispersed, either to its fringes or its outhouses. They bumped against each other, slightly and at first silently, then in more vigorous, noisy collusion, the little Maltese terrier staggering sleepily behind them, trailing the plume of his tail.

When the sky had started greening she switched on the lamp to verify the time. They were by then a shambles of sheet and flesh, the Maltese dog exposing in his sleep a pink belly and tufted pizzle.

Switching back to green darkness she said, 'I was right, Eddie.'

'About what?' Considering his own respect for the old man her husband, he was not too willing to allow Marcia Lushington the benefit of knowing her own mind.

'The fineness.'

'Oh, *stuff*!'

He started extricating himself from what he had begun to see as a trap, a sticky one at that.

'Perhaps I'm wrong after all,' she murmured and heaved. 'Perhaps all men are the same. The same crudeness. Blaming you for what they've had.'

'It isn't that,' he said. 'You wouldn't understand. Or would be too shocked if I tried to explain.'

She was hesitating in the dark.

'Why? We didn't do anything perverse, did we? I can't bear perversion of any kind.'

Bumping and shivering, he started putting on his clothes. Once the Maltese terrier whimpered.

'Eddie?' Again she switched on the light. 'Men can be so brutal. And you are not. That's why I'm attracted to you. I don't believe you'd ever hurt me by refusing what I have to offer.'

Heaped amongst the blankets, the crisscrossed sheets, and punch-drunk pillows, her mound of quaking female flesh appeared on the verge of sculpturing itself into the classic monument to woman's betrayal by callous man. What he looked like, half-dressed in underpants, shirt-tails, and socks with holes in the heels, it gave him gooseflesh to imagine.

'Even if you haven't quite the delicacy I'd hoped for, perhaps we could comfort each other,' she blurted through naked lips, 'in lots of undemanding ways.'

He buckled his belt, which to some extent increased his masculine assurance, but it was not to his masculine self that Marcia was making her appeal. He was won over by a voice wooing him back into childhood, the pervasive warmth of a no longer sexual, but protective body, cajoling him into morning embraces in a bed disarrayed by a male, reviving memories of toast, chilblains, rising bread, scented plums, cats curled on sheets of mountain violets, hibiscus trumpets furling into sticky phalluses in Sydney gardens, his mother whom he should have loved but didn't, the girl Marian he should have married but from whom he had escaped, from the ivied prison of a tennis-court, leaving her to bear the children who were her right and fate, the seed of some socially acceptable, decent, boring man.

He was drawn back to Marcia by the bright colours of retrospect, the more sombre tones of remorse. He lowered his face into the tumult of her breasts.

'There,' she murmured, comforting, 'I knew! My darling! My darling!'

She was ready to accept him back into her body; she would have liked to imprison him in her womb, and he might have been prepared to go along with it if they hadn't heard the rushing of a cistern in the distance.

'I better go,' he mumbled.

'Oh, no! It's only his bladder. I know his form. Poor old

darling! You don't live with someone half a lifetime without getting wise to every movement of the clockwork.'

The little dog whinged, and dug a deeper nest in the blankets in which to finish his normal sleep.

'Eddie?'

He resisted her warmth reaching out through the dark to repossess him. He withdrew into the outer cold, not through any access of virtue, rather from disgust for his use of Lushington's wife in an attempt to establish his own masculine identity. Marcia apart, or even Marcia considered, women were probably honester than men, unless the latter were sustained by an innocent strength such as Greg Lushington and Judge Twyborn enjoyed.

As Eddie let himself out into the night the images of Eadie his mother and Joan Golson joined forces with that of Marcia Lushington, who had, incredibly, become his *mistress*! The trio of women might have been shot sky high on the trampoline of feminine deceit if it hadn't been for the emergence of Eudoxia Vatatzes at Eddie Twyborn's side.

Eddie went stumbling down the hill through the increasing green of the false dawn, the light from an outhouse window, and the scented breath of ruminating cows. In his own experience, in whichever sexual role he had been playing, self-searching had never led more than briefly to self-acceptance. He suspected that salvation most likely lay in the natural phenomena surrounding those unable to rise to the spiritual heights of a religious faith: in his present situation the shabby hills, their contours practically breathing as the light embraced them, stars fulfilled by their logical dowsing, the river never so supple as at daybreak, as dappled as the trout it camouflaged, the whole ambience finally united by the harsh but healing epiphany of cockcrow.

Scattering a convocation of rabbits, he went in through the hedge of winter-blasted hawthorns, into the mean cottage in which physical exhaustion persuaded him it was his good fortune to be living. He lay down smiling, and slept, under the dusty army blankets, in the grey room.

That noon, while enjoying the luxury of a solitary Sunday frowst, after the minimum of cold mutton with mustard pickle, and the dwindling warmth of a brew of tea, he heard a sound of hooves and the metal of a horse's bridle. He looked out and saw, not his mistress of last night, but Mrs Lushington his employer's wife tethering her hack to the rail outside the feed room.

It was startling in these circumstances and at this hour of day. He heard himself muttering. He took up the pot to pour another cup of tea, by now tepid and repulsive, but found himself instead draining the pot to its dregs through the spout.

Fortified, if ashamed, he went out to the encounter with this stranger already knocking at the door.

'I hope I'm not intruding,' she began what sounded a prepared speech. 'Usually on Sunday, after lunch, I go for a ride, otherwise Ham gets out of hand. As I was passing this way I thought I'd look in – see how they're treating you – whether they've made you comfortable.'

She smiled out of unadorned lips, unnatural only in dealing with a rehearsed recitative.

He brought her in, or rather, she brought herself.

She said, 'It's a horrid little house if you look at it squarely.'

'I've grown attached to it.' He might begin resenting Marcia.

'At least in your case it's only temporary.'

Her conscience salved, she started stalking through the house as though she didn't own it and hadn't been there before; perhaps she hadn't. For Sunday afternoon and the land which was hers, she was shabbily dressed, in the old dead-green velour and stretched cardigan in natural wool, with riding pants which, in spite of exclusive tailoring, did not show her at her best. As she went she peered into rooms, dilating and contracting her nostrils in the manager's doorway while glancing with a frown at the photographs of Kath and Kim, murmuring on reaching the cook's bedroom, 'Poor Peggy Tyrrell – rough as bags, but such a dear,' turning her back on Eddie Twyborn's unmade bed.

When they reached the dining-kitchen she started rapping on the oilcloth, which made the crumbs on its surface tremble and her engagement finger flash.

'I ought to apologize,' she said, teeth champing on the words the other side of those bland lips, 'for anything that happened. It was my fault. Oh, I know you'd think it was, Eddie, even if I didn't admit it. Because you're a man.'

She paused as though giving him a chance to exonerate her.

'I shouldn't have thought of blaming you,' he said. 'It was a moment of shared lust. It surprised me that I enjoyed it. But I did.'

Marcia looked most surprised. She suppressed a little gasp. Her eyes were glowing. 'Well,' she said, 'it isn't the sort of thing a man usually says to his mistress. I knew I was right. You're different, Eddie. You have a quality I've always hoped for – and never found – in a man.'

'To me it's only conscience – for having fucked the wife of a man I respect.'

'Oh, darling,' she breathed, all the masculinity gone out of the tailored riding breeches, the imperiousness out of her engagement finger, 'don't put it like that! I adore my husband. That's something else.'

She was reduced to cajoling sighs, and whimpers she might have learnt from her Maltese terrier, and whiffs of the perfume she had been wearing the night before, which he now realized was predominantly hyacinth, and that hyacinth is haunted by the ghosts of wood-smoke and warm ash.

She might, they might both have wanted it again, wood-smoke and ash and all, on the army blankets of his unmade bed. She had brushed against him, the full breasts, the fleshy lips. He was about to respond when repugnance took over.

She said, 'You're right, darling,' and re-settled the green velour.

Then they were walking back along the passage, from which rooms opened in accordance with the accepted pattern, from suburbia to the Dead Heart. Their feet went *trott trott* over the linoleum lozenges.

Her voice cut in. 'Have you noticed how the exceptional person almost never turns up in the beginning?'

'But Greg – the husband you love – the man I'm fond of?'

'Yes,' she moaned, 'I love him.'

They had reached the fly-proof door. He must let her out before they established whose dishonesty was the greater.

'What about this Sunday ride you were on about – to work the oats out of your horse?'

'Well,' she said, 'yes. Do you want to come for a breath of air? You look pale – Eddie. Then we'll go back to tea with Greg.'

She gave him a rather wan smile. The flesh seemed to have slipped from her cheekbones, the eyes more enormous and liquid than ever: she had assumed that invalid expression he had noticed in those who suffer from guilt, or who hope to effect a complete conversion.

Again he felt physically drawn to her. He could have fucked her on the fallen hawthorn leaves amongst the rabbit pellets.

She must have felt they were preparing a desecration, for she coughed and said, 'Mrs Quimby makes the loveliest pikelets. We always have them for Sunday tea. Greg insists on them.'

While he went to saddle his horse, she was fiddling with hers, stroking his neck, adjusting the girth, generally seducing Hamlet her overfed bay.

'Why,' she called when he re-appeared, 'the *Blue Mule*!'

He laughed back. 'I've become attached to him too.'

'Oh, but that's typical! We must find you something — something more appropriate.'

'How "typical"?' he asked.

'Of Prowse.'

'But why?'

She had lapsed into a mystery of silence and the wood-smoke of stale hyacinth perfume, which a brash wind set about exorcizing.

They were heading in the direction she had chosen, or which, perhaps, had been chosen for them. His dislocated nag had difficulty in keeping up with her splendidly paced bay gelding. Hamlet gave the impression of responding to his rider's wishes without surrendering his independence. Ears pricked, neck arched, his eyes surveyed the landscape from under sculptured lids. From time to time he snorted through veined nostrils, either in surprise, or out of contempt.

The Blue Mule galumphed slightly to the rear or, if his rider succeeded in coaxing him level with their companions by dint of heel-kicks, bumped Hamlet's flank. Occasionally there was a clash of stirrup-irons and grazing of boot against boot. Some of their progress was humiliating for Eddie Twyborn, some of it comforting: like keeping up with Mummy.

It made him laugh at one point, breaking in on Marcia's thoughtfulness. She had fallen silent as though brooding over the acres which, seemingly, she loved, or perhaps dissecting her questionable adultery of the night before.

'What is it?' She laughed back less in mirth than from sociability.

'I believe you know my mother,' he said.

She began by a series of little murmurs implying denial. 'Yes and no,' she admitted at last. 'We've met. I'm *acquainted* with Eadie Twyborn, but you couldn't say we *know* each other.'

'Where,' he asked, 'does acquaintanceship end and knowing begin?'

Their horses carried them forward as Marcia considered in silence and frowns how she might answer that great social question.

'Do we know each other?' he asked.

She bit an unpainted lip. 'You have a streak of cruelty!' But had to laugh finally. 'I hope we know each other – and shall deepen our friendship.' She reached out and stroked the back of his hand. 'I need you.'

But he persisted; it must have been the 'cruel streak', 'You don't answer my question: where acquaintanceship ends and friendship begins, and why my mother remained the wrong side of the barrier.'

Marcia frowned one of those frowns which blackened the skin between her eyebrows. She must have dug her spurs into Hamlet, for he started cavorting and she had to rein him back. Only when she had brought him round on a curve, almost nose to nose with that abnormality the Blue Mule, was she prepared or forced to answer.

'Well,' she said, 'as you've asked for it, I'll tell you what I think of Eadie Twyborn. She's a frowzy old drunken Lesbian – who once made a pass at me,' she said.

'Shouldn't you feel flattered? Any pass is better than none.'

'Ugh!' she regurgitated. 'Not between women. And that nice man – the Judge.'

She rode ahead aloof and virtuous, until the Blue Mule chugged abreast again.

'Of course there are some women,' she said. 'Take Joan Golson – Eadie's friend – everybody knows about that. You couldn't hold it against Joan – not altogether – because she's in most ways – so – so *normal*. You must have met the Boyd Golsons although you were away so many years.'

Eddie muttered that he was acquainted, but did not know them. Marcia may not have heard; she had fallen into a trance, from which she issued in the tone of voice they adopt for money and pedigrees.

'. . . frightfully rich in all directions . . . Joan was Joanie Sewell of Sewell's Felt. Ghastly if you come to think, but substantial. And Curly — Golson's Emporium. Curly's the bore of bores, but another substantial investment. So there you are.'

'A normal conjunction.'

'But darling,' she screamed against the wind while seizing his wrist, 'leaving Joan Golson aside — and Eadie — it was you who brought your mother up — I just don't care to associate with abnormality.' After a little pause she continued, 'Some women are *inveterate.*' He wondered where she had learnt it. 'They adore to have queer men around. They find it amusing. A sort of court fool. I couldn't bear to touch one.'

'You must have touched a few,' he suggested, 'a few of your women friends' fools — if only in shaking hands.'

She said, 'Oh well — as a social formality one has to — don't you understand? Fortunately,' she added, 'most of them go away to Europe. They're too ashamed.'

The riders rode.

The winter sun was forcibly withdrawn behind a sliver of nacreous cloud. The hills undulated in time with the horses' gait, or at least with Hamlet's. Eddie's disastrous mount only created a tumult, as though they were stumbling over molehills or excavated rabbit warrens.

Marcia remarked, 'Nobody understands or loves this part of the world as I do. Not even Greg who was born here. None of them.'

He saw no reason for questioning the sincerity of what she had said.

'I believe Don understands how you feel,' he told her.

'*Don!*' She bared her wide-spaced teeth as she had at the moment when telling about the bogong moths and he had visualized her devouring them. 'What has Prowse been saying? That crude and repulsive man.'

'Only that you love the country.'

'Oh.'

She subsided after that.

They had completed a circuit, he realized, and were returning towards the homestead and the clutter of cottages and sheds which comprised the heart of the Lushington property of 'Bogong'. The paddocks were a grey-green like Marcia Lushington's old velour. They rode past eruptions of wiry briar, graced by notes of tingling scarlet and a flickering of wings or incipient leaves. Invisible birds were calling through the cold air along the river, the wraiths of curlew or plover; he could not have told; Marcia would have.

Suddenly she began chanting, at no one so much as the landscape spread out before them, 'A foreigner came here once – one of those complacent Hunter Valley squatters – and said – behind my back of course – that "Bogong" is sterile country. Would you dismiss it as that having lived here?'

'Hardly barren. You'd be out of business if you were,' he tried to console.

'Oh,' she coughed, or spat, 'you're talking like a man now! *Business* – super-phosphate – *cross*breeding!'

She turned in her saddle and wrenched his hand from the pommel where it was resting.

She said, 'Darling, you know what I mean.'

He did, but he couldn't do anything for her.

They rode on hand in hand till they reached the outskirts of the Lushington garden and the walled graveyard he had found on the occasion of a walk.

The drew in their horses outside the elaborate gate, or perhaps Hamlet knew where to halt.

'Did somebody – did *Prowse*,' Marcia asked, 'tell you about this too?'

'He told me only that Greg had wanted a son.'

'All men do, I expect,' she said, 'to vindicate themselves.'

'I think I'd prefer a daughter.'

'But you're more sensitive, Eddie,' she blurted, 'whatever you may do or say to destroy my opinion of you.'

Briskets pressed to the wall, the resting horses forced him to read the inscriptions on the headstones inside:

GREGORY LUSHINGTON
born 28 May 1912
died 5 August 1912

GREGORY LUSHINGTON
born 5 May 1914
died 6 January 1915

GREGORY DONALD PROWSE LUSHINGTON
born 17 May 1917
died 19 November 1918

The riders did not linger.

'Why "Donald Prowse" if you despise him?' he asked as they rode away.

'Oh – it was after Kath walked out. Greg wanted to do something for him. I did too, for that matter. We thought it might help to make him our child's godfather. The child died,' she ended. 'He died.'

They rode on, the horses bowing their heads, so it seemed, though of course they were returning to home, fodder, and idleness.

After unsaddling their horses at the stables, they walked towards the house, where they saw Mr Lushington had come out and was waiting for them, the lenses of his spectacles discs of gold.

Adopting a tone of jovial annoyance, he told them, 'I'd begun to worry.'

'Why? That I'd fallen off?' asked his wife chidingly.

'No. That the pikelets would go soggy, and Mrs Quimby give notice.'

'We'll eat them soggy or not,' Mrs Lushington declared. 'As far as I'm concerned, pikelets are a means of conveying melted butter to the mouth.'

She gave her companion a melting smile at the same time as her husband brushed up against his son *manqué*.

'Did you have a good ride?' Mr Lushington asked Eddie.

'Yes,' she answered for him. 'And talk. So much better than stewing in the house over old stud books and agricultural pamphlets.'

'Oh,' said Mr Lushington, 'what did you talk about?'

'Things,' Mrs Lushington replied. 'Life, I suppose. But not in any intellectual way. So you needn't worry.'

He hiccuped once or twice and stumbled on the steps they were mounting.

'If you'd like to know, I didn't stew over old stud books or agricultural stuff.'

'What did you do then?' his wife asked with an aloofness which suggested she was listening intently as she took off her stretchy cardigan and faded velour.

'I wrote a poem,' Mr Lushington confessed.

'Those!' she sighed, tizzing up her hair, and when they had emerged into stronger light, 'You've got it over?'

He said he had – 'more or less.'

They were all three staggering slightly.

'What was it about?' Mrs Lushington asked, now that it was out in front of one who was, in most essentials, a stranger.

Thus cornered, Greg Lushington bleated, not unlike one of his own stud rams, 'I expect it's about love — that's where everything seems to lead — in some form or other. Unfulfilled love.'

His wife hurried the party as quickly as she could towards a room referred to as the Library, where she knew the deliquescent pikelets would be found, and which housed the encyclopaedia, the dictionary, and her ration of novels from a lending library in Sydney. Anything else in the way of books, anything suggestive of Greg's vice, must have been hidden from neighbourhood eyes in some unfrequented attic.

The Lushingtons brightened at the prospect of pikelets and tea, and Beppi joined them from the kitchen regions where he must have scoured a pan already.

They distributed themselves in what was another neo-Tudor room: dark panels, stone fireplace, with a suite of leather furniture straining at its buttons where it wasn't sagging on its springs.

Marcia poured tea into Staffordshire cups skating uneasily in their saucers. Some of the service had been riveted. She heaped their plates with pikelets. Little embroidered napkins had been provided, which was just as well, for the Lushingtons were soon in a somewhat buttery condition.

He too, in their company, was transported back to nurseryland, to Mummy and 'your father', which was what the Lushingtons wanted, except that for a moment Marcia's pikelet must have turned to flesh, and Greg's mouthful to a difficult word in one of the disgraceful poems.

Greg wiped his fingers on one of the embroidered napkins; as fingers they were rather too delicate, and in their efforts to demonstrate their practical worth, one of them had gone missing; a thumb wore its purple nail like a medal; yet the palms, showing pink, were those of a rich and idle man, who mumbled through the last of his mouthful of pikelet, 'The word should have been "placebo" ' before dabbing at a trickle of butter.

'Oh God,' Marcia complained, 'I wonder what you'll come out with next.'

Wiping his fingers and turning to Eddie, Greg Lushington began telling, '. . . when I was a boy foxes used to kill the turkeys. We never heard a sound. But sometimes a terrier — we always kept a pack of them – would bring in a dead fox. All done most silently. Once, I remember, an old dog – Patch – almost blind with cataract – brought in a turkey gobbler's head instead. I had a governess, Miss Delbridge, who fancied herself at the piano. She was playing a Chopin mazurka at the time. As she was pedalling her soul away, Patch laid the turkey's head at her feet. A kind of love offering – or that's how I saw it.'

'A love offering!' Marcia exclaimed. 'How could a little boy have known?'

'By instinct of course – like dogs. I bet Eddie would have known.' Mr Lushington paused, thoughtfully exploring the corners of his mouth. 'Old men know more perhaps, but never grow as wise as they hope.'

The fire leaped in the stone hearth, then relapsed into a drowsier tempo; it should have been a comfort to those seated round it.

'Oh dear, all this is horrid – morbid. I wasn't expecting anything like it – with my pikelets – after our ride.'

Beppi must have interpreted her disapproval as an invitation. He started barking, and from lying on the sofa, jumped upon his mistress's lap, put his front paws on her bosom and started licking her glossy lips.

Mrs Lushington laughed. 'Disgusting little dog!' she shrieked, and pushed him down, but immediately snatched him back, and gave him a kiss on his wet blackberry of a nose.

'Hydatids, Marcia . . .' her husband warned.

Which she ignored. 'I adore you,' she told her dog, 'as you ought to know.'

Greg started groaning up out of his chair, not without a faint fart or two. 'I'm going to leave you,' he announced. 'There's something, I realize, I ought to alter in the last line.'

He was obviously obsessed by words, when Eddie had thought his obsessions lay almost anywhere else: sheep, worms, the sons he hadn't got.

He reproached Marcia for not having told him about the poems.

'Why should I have told?' She pouted. 'If you tell too much in the beginning there's nothing left for later on. That's why so many marriages break up.'

'Why are you against poetry?' he asked.

'I'm not. Everyone else is. So I don't make a point of flaunting it in their faces. It might put them off us. Actually, I always leave a book of verse on the stool in the visitors' lav. Nothing too long. Narrative poems,' she turned appealing eyes on him, 'are no go in a cold climate.'

Contrary to reason, his mistress was warming him again. He went and propped a knee on the sofa beside her, where a whiff of last night's perfume and a smell of cleanly dog rose up around him. At the moment he was perhaps drawn to Greg's unexpected dedication to poetry as much as to his wife's voluptuous charms. He was even disturbed by a ripple of grudging affection for his own mother. For it occurred to him that the unexpected in Eadie Twyborn was similar to that which linked the Lushingtons. He would have liked to share his discovery of their common trait, but remembering Marcia's antipathy, he confined himself to fingering her cleavage where a blob of butter, fallen from a pikelet, had hardened into what could have passed for one of Eadie's antique brooches.

'Darling,' Marcia sighed, looking up, 'not on Sunday, and while Greg is tidying a poem.'

So he realized that he was dismissed, and had better lump it, together with the Mule, down to the cottage. What surprised him more than anything was his desire to possess Marcia again, and in spite of the dangers inherent in the act.

With this thought, he pressed a kiss into her mouth, and was received into some buttery depths before firm rejection.

No less firmly he stormed inside the deserted cottage, his masculine self flinching neither at chill nor dark. He lit a lamp, and as the flame steadied, his 'love' for Marcia became more credible; his affection for the human creatures with whom he shared this hovel grew. How Eudoxia might have reacted, whether she would have approved of, improved on, or cynically dismissed his sentiments, he did not stop to consider, but flung out to the yard, and after assembling logs and kindling, stoked the kitchen stove, and lit fires in the cook's room and the manager's. Peggy Tyrrell's looked more desolate for the empty tumbler on the window-sill, its water swaying as he moved around. As he knelt at the manager's hearth he shrank slightly, from sensing the stare of Don Prowse's thin wife aimed between his shoulder blades.

After he had got the fire going, he turned round, determined to outstare Kath. Not succeeding, he decided to go one better: he threw himself on the loosely articulated iron bedstead with the brass knobs. It heaved and expostulated obscenely. Through some collaboration between glass and firelight, Kath appeared to blink and withdraw — and were those two elongated tears? That is how icons behave, as he knew from Angelos Vatatzes, and how miracles are recorded. If Kath was scarcely Don's miracle, her photograph was his nearest approach to iconography.

At what precise moment the party returned from town, Eddie Twyborn could not be sure. It was after dark and the fire was failing. He must have fallen asleep on Don's bed under Kath's ousted stare. Fingers dug into the honeycomb spread at the Woolpack (or was it the Wheatsheaf?) he had been watching the wooden partners gyrate to Miss Delbridge's mazurka: Edward and Eadie, Marcia and Greg. He was powerless to choose; Eddie, it seemed, had always been chosen, whirled out into the figures of the dance, whether by Marian, Angelos, Marcia, Mrs E. Boyd Joanie Golson; even his afflicted parents had attempted an unconscious twirl or two. Would he never dare assert himself? He was becoming aware of Don's torso at the bedside: nipples surrounded by whorls of rosy fuzz opening out into flat expanses of ginger bristle. Don smiling; closely associated fox's teeth in contrast to Marcia's blunt, open-spaced portcullis poised to crush unwary bogong moths.

He jumped up. He could hear Prowse backing the Ford into the corrugated shell referred to as 'shed' rather then 'garage'. He could hear Mrs Tyrrell scuttling across early-frozen puddles to reach her kitchen.

Under Kath's timeless stare he began hastily straightening and tautening the honeycomb bedspread. Threw a knot of wood on the fire. Went out to face whatever dreary post-mortem.

'Arr, dear, it was a lovely funeral,' Mrs Tyrrell announced from amongst the glimmers, the flickers of the kitchen. 'Before I come out 'ere,' she said, 'to earn a crust, they relied on me to lay out the dead, but Mayor Craxton was such a bugger, I wouldn' uv wanted ter stop up any 'ole in 'is body. I'm tellun yer — 'e was real crook.' She was peeling off her black kid gloves, and had brought back a brown-paper parcel, smaller, if as irregular, as the one she had gone away with. 'Yes,' she said, 'but I gotter admit, it was the loveliest funeral I was ever at.'

After professionally raking the stove, and leaving for her room to remove her week-end teeth, she returned hatless and in her apron. 'Thank yer, love. I would 'uv thought as only a woman would 'uv lit fires for another. I knew you was different, Eddie dear.'

Prowse would be a different matter again, who now came stamping into the house, the fly-screen falling back into place, door slamming. The cottage shuddered. So did Eddie, who had faced worse and been decorated for it. He went out into the passage and stood too erect in the manager's doorway.

'How was it?' he asked.

'It was all right — and it wasn't — as you'd expect where women's concerned.' Prowse was bending over the bed smoothing the honeycomb spread.

Had he noticed signs of disturbance? the imprint of a body? Or was it an automatic gesture? Impossible to tell.

'I admire your good sense, Ed, not to let yerself imagine you're in need of a bloody woman. If it wasn't one thing, then it was the other. She was wearing the rags, or another had to get 'erself up for the mayor's fuckun funeral. There was one expected 'er old man to be out that night at the Lodge, but you never know with the Masons, sometimes they finish early. Les did. Must 'uv been out of bloody spite.'

Only then, the manager faced the jackeroo. The lines in his face were deeper than before he went away, his shoulders slumped. He was pretty surly, and already far gone in grog.

'Fetch me the bottle, Ed,' he ordered, after plumping down on the honeycomb bedspread. 'It's in there — or oughter be — beside the po — with me name on it.'

Eddie fetched out the whiskey, the level of which did not encourage hospitality.

'I'll treat you to one,' Don offered.

Eddie accepted, and fetched a tooth-glass, suspecting that his host would prefer the bottle.

'So I settled for the town bike,' he told, 'and more than likely brought back the clap.'

He turned on a clanking, tin-can laughter, but subsided soon after, and sat looking up at his sober familiar. He could have been asking forgiveness, his expression an early-morning one, tingling with a day's growth. How deep his sudden innocence went you might only have found out by touch, a temptation Eddie Twyborn resisted.

Prowse twitched, and shrugged off what a subordinate could

have interpreted as weakness. 'What about you, Ed? How did you go about the week-end?'

'I didn't go about it. Can't say there's much to report. Had a meal with the Lushingtons,' he admitted.

'Well, that was that,' said Don, shuffling his feet on the bedside mat. 'We know about supper with the Lushingtons. Old Greg's a decent cove.' Don continued sitting, and between swigs from the almost empty bottle, resumed stroking the honeycomb bedspread.

Suddenly he looked up and spat. 'Christ, that shit — that — Kath!' and keeled over on the bed.

The last of the whiskey would have trickled from the bottle if Eddie hadn't seized and returned it to the po cupboard. He eased the legs on to the bed. The highlights of yesterday's polishing had quite gone out of the manager's boots. The tweed jacket might have been exposed to rain, its sleeves wrinkled well above the wrists, and straining at the armpits and biceps. As it would have involved a major operation, or love rite, to do any more for Don Prowse, Eddie extinguished the lamp and left him.

Mrs Tyrrell was slicing cold mutton; she warmed it up in floury gravy, with a handful of capers to pander to the tastes of any possible gourmet.

'You had supper last night,' she said, 'with Marce and Greg. That was nice.' How 'nice' he wondered on hearing how well informed she was on various other matters. 'Greg's leavin' for England Toosdee.' Eddie experienced a twinge for his own undeserved ignorance: not to have been informed by his patrons after so much loving patronage; to be kept in the dark by his mistress, his employer's wife, was less galling than the deceitful behaviour of his adoptive father the crypto-poet.

Wounds were no deterrent to Mrs Tyrrell, who must have been slashed to shreds in her time, what with the climate and a family of seventeen. 'They say,' she said, 'as Dot's gunner marry Denny Allen. Mrs Lushington 'erself arranged it. The poor bloody imbecile Denny — but Dot couldn' expeck better. Mrs Lushington done right, I reckon, for all concerned. Otherwise Dot 'ull pup along the river bank, for all 'er father 'ull do about it — or 'erself catch the bagman 'oo come sellun the separator parts — 'oo she says is the father — 'oo isn't, as everybody knows.'

'How do they know?' Eddie insisted.

'They know,' she said. 'Because.'

She brought out a plate on which were arranged some wedges of cake of an unnatural yellow.

'You ain't been 'ere long enough,' she said. 'But everybody knows. Mrs Lushington was right. An' Denny 'ull be as pleased as punch when they put a baby in 'is arms. 'E won't notice 'e got it without any of the effort.'

As they sat consuming stale cake and considering life's cross purposes, Eddie felt at last that he belonged.

'I'll go to bed, Peggy,' he announced. 'I'm tired.' Indeed, his eyelids were behaving like iron shutters over which the owner, apparently himself, was losing control.

'You could be,' said Mrs Tyrrell, observing him too intently.

'I'm surprised Greg left without a word,' he told his employer's wife.

'That's Greg,' Marcia said. 'Without his unexpectedness he might have become unbearable. And you, Eddie, shouldn't be upset by his absence.'

They were seated on the leather sofa in the neo-Tudor library. She laid a hand between his thighs: But her availability did her a disservice: today his mistress left him cold.

'I'm not *upset*,' he insisted. 'Only he's someone you grow fond of. And I thought he might have mentioned his going away.'

Marcia laughed. She got up. It was again Saturday, and Prowse and Mrs Tyrrell had driven into town.

'Greg,' she said, 'is one of those kind, simple men, who insinuate themselves, and leave you flat without realizing what they've done. Which is why women take lovers – the not so kind, not so simple – like you, Eddie – who know how to hurt deliciously.'

'How?' He was astonished that he could have hurt anybody as practised as Marcia Lushington. He considered himself far more hurt by Greg Lushington's silent defection.

'I thought you were my lover,' she told him, 'and that on occasions like this, we could lose ourselves in each other.'

From ramping up and down against the lozenges of neo-Tudor glass, she came and sat down again beside him and started nibbling his nearside lobe.

'Darling?' she breathed into the ear, to encourage him and satisfy her hopes.

'But I never set out to lose myself. Finding myself is more to the point.'

Marcia laughed bitterly. 'I hadn't thought of myself as a test-tube!'

Contemplating her own reflection in a glass framed in the fumed-oak overmantel, she told him a while later, 'You destroy me, Eddie. But how agreeably!'

Mrs Edmonds came in, ever so discreet. 'Mrs Quimby is wondering, madam, if Mr Twyborn will be staying to supper.'

'I expect so,' Mrs Lushington answered. 'Yes, of course. He's on his own.'

'No,' he said. 'I'd better not. I've letters to answer. If I don't get down to it, I never will. And I ought to write to my mother.'

Mrs Edmonds at least appeared convinced by a situation Mrs Lushington could only accept with decent resignation. She looked down her front and re-arranged it.

'You're right, Eddie,' she agreed. 'You shouldn't neglect your mother.'

After eating a ration of cold mutton alone in the cottage, he began regretting his decision not to let himself enjoy Marcia's cooked meal, her down pillows, the warmth of her body. Was he a masochist as a man? He didn't think so. He would have been had he loved her; he wanted to love, and might still, somewhere in the geography of flesh, come across the wherewithal for kindling its spirit. Up till now he was only enjoying the perks of love and the re-discovered womb.

He did, however, get out his writing-pad to justify his decision. Was the pad another masochistic touch? It was one he had bought from a Syrian hawker who came round from time to time. Marcia not unnaturally would have despised the ruled paper from his cheap pad. Even the slatternly recipient of his duty letter had a taste for expensive writing-paper, with watermarks and monograms; if Eadie had forsworn her grandfather's coat of arms it was due to an inherent bashfulness.

So it seemed to him, as he sat poised above his ostentatiously modest pad, by the light of the kerosene lamp, that he was the only dishonest one.

'Bogong',
Sunday

In his state of drift, at the mercy of 'Bogong', the Lushingtons, the climate, and other influences, some of them inadmissible except to himself, the date eluded him.

He wrote

Dear Mother,

too bleak, too upright, and waited for what comes shooting out, finally, like milk, or sperm . . .

. . . should have written an age ago, and you'll wonder why I haven't. Physical exhaustion no doubt, Monaro cold, spasmodic depression. But don't jump to the conclusion that I regret having come here. If nothing else, my body is hardening. I'm learning much that is practical in its own context, otherwise irrelevant. I can hear you laughing, and to some degree I share your amusement. I wish I had inherited more of my father's legal blood and rational approach to the seriousness of life. But there we are — Eadie!

What I'd like to correct, Mother, is your impression of Marcia Lushington. She's not what I'd call a *bad* woman, or not much worse than most of us, if our components could be seen squirming under the microscope. The bacilli of my own nature might appear related. Aren't you perhaps blaming her for showing up your own faults? That is how most blame is doled out. I shouldn't be accusing you of this if I didn't know how alike we are. It should have brought us closer together, but never has. If I'm more lenient to Marcia it may be because I have none of her blood in my veins, while given to the same sensuality, lust, deceits. If these traits seem more evident in Marcia, it's because she's had greater cause to develop them. In a graveyard beside the house three short-lived children are buried. Greg wanted them there. He wanted a son. At least one of the dead children is not his, I suspect for no good reason beyond that of knowing my own capacity for deceit to be the equal of Marcia's. Since I have never conceived or begotten a child, there is less concrete evidence in my case, only the shadows of deceit which flicker through the undergrowth of a life which has not been without its shady patches.

Marcia is respected by her servants, the neighbourhood, and obviously loves the land she owns. She is loved and respected (I believe) by her husband, an amiable, virtuous character, whose simplicity disguises intuitions of which he seems only half-aware. He has just gone off to Europe, for what purpose I haven't been told. If Marcia knows, she doesn't show. She is prepared to indulge his motives, perhaps because they suit her purposes. From my own experience, I'm inclined to think that Greg's frequent disappearances are part of a desire to lose – or find himself, which perhaps one never succeeds in doing.

I shall leave you here, dear Mother, hoping I haven't written anything too distasteful.

Love,
Ed.

When he had finished, he sat looking at the word which promises so much, yet never illuminates to the extent that one hopes it will. He was tempted to climb back up the hill and creep into Marcia's great warm womb of a bed. When more than likely she would not have had him since his rejection of her earlier that evening.

Instead he got between the army blankets, on his own narrow stretcher, and dreamed an astonishing dream in which Marcia played no part. He awoke in the Sunday dawn and burrowed deeper into the blankets, trying to mend his broken dream. Of course he did not succeed, and was left with the gritty resentment of those who are dispossessed by waking.

Whatever else fragmented and eluded, the themes of conscious life flowed into a common stream, of endlessness rather than infinity: the takeover of day from night, summer from winter, the diet of mutton, slug-riddled cabbage and grey potato, Peggy Tyrrell's recitative of births, deaths, and lotteries, Prowse's morose narrative of Kath's defection. Eddie could have touched Kath, rounded out like a waxwork, her belongings crammed into a pair of Globeite cases, the kiddy trailing by its celluloid arm a doll in a tartan frock. Kath had barely left before she started leaving again, her sour-milk complexion emphasized against the sooty mesh of the fly-proof door. Don had half a mind to go out at night into the paddock and suck on the muzzle of a gun, like his dad, to put an end to it all.

Eddie pointed out, 'You couldn't do it, with Greg away, and Marcia up there on her own.'

'Marcia's not all that helpless.'

'But depends on you.'

Don smiled a sceptical ginger smile. 'Help me off with me boots, Ed.' He had finished the last of the current bottle, his name pencilled in copybook hand below the maker's. 'Don't know what I'd do without yer.'

After the final assisted contortion out of singlet and pants into pyjamas, the manager subsided on his bed, at the summit of which the brass balls had been jingling an accompaniment.

It was correspondence which alleviated the prolonged phase between winter and summer at 'Bogong', and those Saturday nights when, Don and Peggy away in town, Eddie climbed the hill and shared what Marcia described as 'the scrumptious meal Mrs Quimby has prepared for you, darling – she'd have fobbed me off with a poached egg.'

Marcia would ask sharply, 'What have you heard from my husband, Eddie?'

Eddie would tell of the highly coloured post-card he had just received, with its snatches of information on Roman churches, race meetings in England and Ireland, or the train journey from Bergen to Christiania.

'But surely he's written to you?' he asked.

'Naturally he's written to me. At some length.' She sighed. 'He sent me a poem about a glacier.'

'Then I can't think why you're anxious to know what he wrote on a post-card to an acquaintance.'

'Aren't I at liberty to wonder what he writes to others?'

'I'd like to read one of his poems.'

By then the table had been cleared, the servants gone to their quarters, and Marcia and he withdrawn to the warmth of her bed and their united bodies.

'The one about the glacier,' he added, kissing her between breasts which had begun to heave and protest.

'It's far too private,' she told him. 'I mean,' she said, 'you only show your poem to those you want to see it – unless, of course, you throw it wide open to the public.'

Round him she had wrapped importunate thighs.

'Rather like a cunt,' he suggested as he strained to return the passion expected of him.

'Oh,' she moaned, 'I find this sort of thing – so hateful – in you – and know you'll – never – love me.'

After reaching their climax, and while still coupled, she tore her mouth apart from his, her head thrown sideways on the pillow.

'Like somebody I got to hate.'

'Like who?'

'Somebody I was fool enough to sleep with. Somebody I thought might love me. Who turned out to be a man like any other.'

'Not Greg, surely?'

'Oh, leave Greg out of it! He's the husband I love and respect. I don't have to sleep with Greg to love him.'

She had switched on the lamp. She got up in some agitation, and after flying in several directions at once, all distraught buttocks and breasts, put on a gown, and sat herself at the dressing table, feeling her cheeks, her throat, as though for damage.

While Eddie continued lying in the bed, drowsily combing at his armpits. 'Perhaps we shouldn't have started by fucking. Then we might have learnt to love each other.'

'How I hate that degrading word!'

'I was only using what they use.'

She had taken up a pot, and was creaming her face, slapping at it. 'I don't mind whether I never see you again.' She went on slapping.

Soon after, he got up and began dressing. When he had finished, he kissed her on the side of the neck. 'Poor Marcia! I hope you'll find the love you need.'

'I don't *need* love,' she whimpered.

'The fucking, then.'

'Go!' she shouted. 'And don't come near me. If Greg were here . . .' she tailed off. 'I'll write to Greg and tell him he ought . . .' but again her voice and the impulse expired.

So he went. He might have packed his bag that night and asked Don to drive him to the train on Monday, but could not feel he was intended to break away from 'Bogong' yet. Marcia's shoulders, as he took his leave, had only half-decided to shed him. He did not want it, nor, he liked to think, did others for whom he had discovered an affection. Peggy Tyrrell, for instance. If he had cuckolded Greg Lushington, his fondness and respect for that decent man were intact. As for Don Prowse, what would he do without somebody to pull his boots off?

Dearest,

I love your far too rare letters, but found this latest one surprising. You *are* of course just that, or you wouldn't have disappeared as you did before the War, without explanation (even since, there has been no attempt to explain, and your father and I are left nursing unhappy guesses) then shooting off to bury yourself at 'Bogong', to lead what amounts to a *labourer's* life.

I know that Edward has the highest opinion of that boring old Greg, which you, apparently, now share. Perhaps he is someone who appeals to men. I accept that. Men are what one can only *accept*. What I cannot stomach is Marcia Lushington from any viewpoint – who you are *pitchforking* at me as though you were having an affair with her. Darling, are you? But don't tell me, I couldn't bear to know.

Incidentally, the Golsons – my sweet Joanie who for some reason you avoid, and Curly, another of the male bores – share your passion for the Lushingtons. They have visited several times at 'Bogong'. Curly goes trout fishing with Greg, with Marcia too (apparently she casts no mean fly). Joanie rests with a good book. As far as I am concerned, it would have to be an extra good read, down on the farm with the Lushingtons.

Marian has had her fourth. No trouble – any of them. If only you had married nice healthy Marian, it would have made such a difference to all our lives. I'm sure I should have been a changed woman – the whole family lunching together at the Royal Sydney on Sundays. I believe grandchildren would have liked me.

But I'm not accusing you, Eddie dear. Nothing ever happens as it might. So let us forgive each other.

Your poor old
Mother

PS. The third cyst between Biffy's toes has, I'm glad to report, ripened and burst, but alas, she's preparing a season.

PPS. Your father is on circuit in the north-west – I don't doubt enjoying himself exceedingly.

PPPS. Don't think I begrudge Daddy those country duties which mean so much to him.

While sifting flour for a batch of scones, Mrs Tyrrell announced, 'They've fixed a date for Dot Norton's weddun.' Raised breast high, the sifter trailed a veil. 'Arr, it 'ull be lovely!' She assumed the expression that some women wear for a bride. 'Mrs Lushington 'ull see to it that Dot has a proper outfit – and everythink the baby 'ull need.'

'But did they trace the man who came selling the separator parts?'

'Nao!' Peggy hawked, and abandoned her dainty fingertip technique working the butter into the flour.

'But if he was the father?'

'The father ain't what matters. It's the ring. No girl wants the loaf in 'er oven to turn into a bastard on 'er 'ands.' She slopped the milk; she kneaded her dough so passionately the basin almost flew off the oilcloth on to the lino.

'Besides,' said Mrs Tyrrell when things were again under control, 'It wasn't the separator man.'

'How do you know?'

'If yez been around long enough, you know.'

'Then who's the official father?'

'The who?'

'The one that's gunner be registered,' he nagged.

'Arr,' she paused. 'Denny,' she said. 'I told yer, didn't I?'

'But he's a half-wit.'

'No worse than a lot of others. There's padded rooms in a lot of the Woolambi homes.'

'Won't he mind fathering another man's child?'

''E'll 'ave a woman ter bake for 'im, an' boil 'is mutton. That's what's practical, ain't ut?' Her gums showed him she was growing resentful as she marshalled her scones on her baking sheet.

'Sounds extraordinary to me. Shocking.'

'Anyways, it's what Mrs Lushington arranged.'

'Knowing the father?'

'Everybody knows the father. But I'm not sayun. If you wanter know more, better ask Marce.'

'It's none of my business.'

'When you've been on at me the last 'arf hour?' She shoved the baking sheet in the oven and slammed the door. 'That's what's wrong with edgercated people – argue, argue – waste yer time in argument.'

She laughed rather bitterly, and flounced out, but returned soon after, the wrinkles in her cheeks veiled in what looked like the flour with which she had dusted her recent batch of scones.

'I'll tell yer, Eddie,' she announced, 'but confidential.' She started munching on her gums. 'No! I'm not gunner!' she exploded. 'Even though 'e's a rabbiter, Dickie Norton's a decent bloke – and I reckon a widower must feel the cold down there along the bloody flat.'

Spring did take over at last, if spasmodically, days of brilliant, slashing light alternating with a return to leaden rain squalls; the nights still crackled as he stood shivering, pissing from the veranda's edge on to frosted grass.

By day a visible green had crept along the grey shoulders of the hills, but the tussock remained bleached and sterile throughout the flat. Birds seemed to soar higher, to sing more shrilly, solitary wagtails to swivel more expectantly on the strand between the barbs of a wire fence, peewits tumbled through the air in pairs, briar clumps greening over were filled with the twitter of small, serious bird-couples.

The river flowed through the spring scene, at times with a mineral glitter, at others with a supple, animal life, each aspect probably more apparent to stranger than to native. In fact it seemed to Eddie Twyborn that, with the exception of Marcia Lushington, who was actually 'from down Tilba way', the native-born remained unaware of the landscape surrounding them, except as a source of economic returns and a fate they must accept, or in the case of Denny Allen, a river from which, by some stroke of imbecile genius, he could land a trout after one flick with a dry fly; he might even have succeeded with a naked hook.

Denny would stand amongst the tussocks flicking at the rippled water, itself as brown and speckled as a trout, despoiling the river time and again.

'What are you going to do with so many?'

'Take 'em 'ome to the missus.' He smiled his most imbecile smile from behind his steel-rimmed spectacles and grooved, greenish teeth.

'Dot mightn't thank you for bringing such a lot. Gutting trout!'

'Mrs Allen don't gut no trout. Guttun's my job,' he said proudly.

Scrawny, sawney, his woollen singlet buttoned up to where the hair broke out in a frill below his plucked-cockerel's throat, the greasy waistcoat never discarded whatever the temperature or time of day, Denny Allen was a happy man Eddie Twyborn often found himself envying.

On one of the more benign mornings of this reluctant Monaro spring Eddie and Denny were digging out a warren not far from the river bank.

'How's the baby?' Eddie asked.

'Got the colic.'

'What do you do for it?'

'Dunno.' Denny grunted, and dug deep into red earth. 'Mrs Allen knows. She give it some kinda water.' He slashed deeper with the shovel, fetching up from a nest below tufts of fur and wads of withered grass. 'She knows – the mother!' His exertions made him salivate, and the saliva was carried by the wind in a long, transparent loop.

Eddie dug. His hands no longer blistered. The skin had hardened. A man's hands. His whole life had been so preposterous, to think of it made him laugh.

Denny followed suit, for the joke he had not been asked to share. He never seemed resentful of a status forced on him by lack of wits. Perhaps his intuitions as stockman, fisherman, and rifle shot, raised him in his own estimation to a level which compensated.

They dug away.

Denny started slobbering. ' 'Ere she is – the bloody mother!' he shouted.

He flung out a shovelful of bleeding fur which his matted hounds slavered and gobbled.

'An' 'ere's the kickers!' Denny shovelled out the litter, which followed the doe down the gullets of the ravenous dogs.

'It's fun, ain't it? you gotter admit, Eddie!' Fulfilled, Denny sat panting, laughing, on the edge of the trench, rejoicing in his skills, waiting to return to the wife who had been made an honest woman and the child who was officially his.

On such an enamelled morning Eddie, whose own contentment was never more than transient, as capricious as a Monaro spring, felt less disgusted than envious of his simple friend. Happiness was perhaps the reward of those who cultivate illusion, or who, like Denny Allen, have it thrust upon them by some tutelary being, and then are granted sufficient innocent grace to sustain it.

As it was about the middle of the day and the warren by now destroyed, the pair of rabbit murderers prepared to take their lunch break. Denny had got together one of his miraculous fires out of a handful of dead grass and another of twigs, and the two quart pots were already steaming and singing, when Eddie noticed a horseman descending the hill behind them.

'Mind if I join you blokes?' It was the manager returning from some unspecified employment, or simply from riding round exercising his self-importance.

He and Denny were soon monotonously intoning the exchange of comments on weather and wool, fluke and worms, lucerne and sorghum. Eddie wished he could join in, but did not think he would ever master the liturgy. A certain repugnance or perversity in the face of their ritual solemnity would always prevent him.

He remained seated inside the palisade of his own thoughts and the surrounding landscape. It may not have been sexual ambivalence after all which prevented him identifying himself with other men; his true self responded more deeply to those natural phenomena which were becoming his greatest source of solace.

Prowse and Denny were still at it, while knocking the ash off the ends of their loosely packed cigarettes, as he finished his cold chop and the last yellow crumb of Peggy Tyrrell's cake. He got up and wandered contentedly enough a little way along the river, when suddenly the warmth, the light, the glistening flow of brown water, moved him to take off his clothes. He lay awhile, exposing his vertebrae to the sun, almost dozing, his genitals pricked by dead grass.

Roused by the approach of his companions' voices, he was driven by confusion, if not shame, to plunge into the river below him. The effect was electrifying, the water so cold the breath was almost beaten out of his lungs, his only thought to survive in the suddenly malignant current when he was by no means an indifferent swimmer.

As he swam he glanced up, gasping, blinking from under a wet fringe, at Prowse and Denny seated on their horses, staring down, the horses snorting, Denny embarking on a frightened giggle, Prowse frowning or glaring, lips drawn back in a smile which conveyed both scorn and unwilling admiration.

'Better watch out, Ed. If you flash yer arse about like that, someone might jump in and bugger yer.' The message was made to sound as brutal and contemptuous as possible. 'What about you, Denny? Are yer game?'

Denny's giggles were cut short. 'Not on yer life! Not gunner bugger nobody. Might catch a chill.' His hand went up to his already buttoned woollen singlet. 'Missus 'ud rouse if I went 'ome crook. She's got enough with a baby on 'er 'ands.'

Prowse withdrew his non-smile and the two horsemen sauntered on their way, leaving their companion to follow if he had any sense left in him.

Eddie climbed out by handfuls of tussock and footholds of rock. From feeling like a helpless drifting frog at the mercy of the current, he was again a naked stumbling man, the ribbons of a burning wind lashing and sawing at his shoulders. In his isolation he was free and whole, but only momentarily. He saw not so much the healing landscape as the images of Marcia and Prowse alternating in the dancing light. He tried to extinguish them by putting on his shirt, but they continued flickering, beige to burnt orange inside the dark tunnel of shirt.

When he was again decent, he rode after those who had contributed to his humiliation and who might think fit to remind him of it. Probably not Denny: he was too simple, and must himself have been humiliated in other forgettable circumstances. Prowse, in his position of authority and inviolable masculinity, might be less willing to let a victim off the hook.

As it happened they gave no sign of recognition when the delinquent caught up with them. The three rode together in silence broken by horses' wind and the jingling and chafing of harness. Denny yawned noisily, a horse's yawn which exposed his broad green teeth. Very erect, Prowse simply glared back at the glare from under the brim of a stained felt hat, every bristle of his stubble tipped with gold.

The morning after, Prowse called out to Eddie who was saddling the Blue Mule for work, and told him rather sulkily while looking in the opposite direction, 'You'll find a filly over in the yard. You're supposed to have her as a replacement for that bastard you've been riding up to date.' He spat, and added, 'A *black* filly.' And walked away towards the little runabout he drove around the place on busier occasions.

The filly was an elegant beast of evident breeding. When Eddie fetched her down to the harness room, he called out to Prowse, who was having trouble starting his truck, 'Who should I thank for this luxury?'

Cranking hard at his unresponsive vehicle, the manager who fancied himself as a mechanic was growing steadily crankier. 'Why – Lushington of course,' he grunted back. 'Isn't he the owner?'

'But Greg's away.'

'I had a post-card asking me to find you a decent mount.'

'Well, thanks, Don. Where *is* Greg?'

'Eh?' The truck farted once or twice and started, almost knocking its driver down. '*Switzerland*!' he shouted. 'Greg's in Geneva.'

Eddie was in laughing mood. 'Was it a *pretty* post-card?' he called.

Prowse was so incensed, either by the effeminate word, or his own indignity, that he jumped inside the truck and drove off without answering.

When Eddie had saddled the delicate creature his new horse, and she stood snorting back at him, all forelock and rolling eye, Mrs Tyrrell came out to congratulate and admire.

'Arr, she's lovely, ain't she? A real treat! A little darlun!' she gushed like some lady of a higher class, and unfolding her arms from under the black bobbled shawl, stroked the glistening neck and even planted a kiss above the beast's tremulous muzzle.

Eddie was suppressing his own delight, to reveal in private to the object of it. 'Wonder what we ought to call her? We'll have to think of a name, Peggy.'

'Coalie,' she announced without second thought. 'Coalie's 'er name.'

'How do you know?'

'That's what Marcia said it is.'

'What's Marcia to do with her? It's Mr Lushington's horse. Isn't he the owner of "Bogong"?' he reminded a lesser servant with a primness he immediately deplored.

'That may be,' Mrs Tyrrell agreed dreamily. 'But I'd say Mrs Lushington bought the horse. Marcia's a great one for gifts. You should 'uv seen the bassinet she give Dot and Denny for that poor squeaker of theirs.'

Eddie mounted his 'gift' and headed for a boundary fence Prowse had told him off to repair. The filly went cautiously at first, then with increasing pleasure in her own paces, and only random snorts as they left the settlement behind. Several times she shied, and once almost scraped him off against a sapling when a rabbit scut startled her. But horse and rider were becoming acquainted, accepting each other.

'Coalie!' When he had been flirting with the shameful idea of calling her 'Ouida'. Would Prowse have known enough? Who had at one stage confessed to Meredith.

But Coalie — and *Marcia*!

He was standing on the brow of a hill without his shirt, the black filly tethered close by. He had finished straining a difficult length of fence where it plunged into a gully, and was rucked over rocks, and damaged by driftwood and floodwater, when his employer's wife rode up.

'What a coincidence,' she remarked, 'to meet on what is – if not my favourite – almost my favourite ride.'

Faced with the extent of her idleness, he must have looked as surly as the manager. He was also, somewhat ironically, embarrassed by her finding him without his shirt, but her brief glance showed no sign of proprietorship.

He put on the shirt and stood stuffing the ends into his pants. During this operation she even looked away, her face expressing disinterest rather than modesty.

'I've always liked it up here,' she said. 'It's different from the rest of the place – rough, but sheltered. It's good for having a howl in if you feel like one.'

'Do you often feel like having a howl?'

'Not often. But sometimes. Like anybody, I expect.'

He went to untether the black filly.

'Do you like your new horse?' she asked.

He was surprised at her use of the generic word; he would have expected her to be more specific, like a horsy man revelling in horsy terms. But she seemed as detached as her own bay gelding, arching his neck only tentatively, his nostrils suspicious of an unfamiliar female.

'She's a nice little thing,' Eddie admitted with equal restraint. 'It was good of Greg to think of me – in Switzerland.'

'Actually,' she said, 'he's in Canada – on his way home – if he isn't sidetracked to Ecuador.'

'But thought of me, none the less.'

She did not answer immediately, but as they descended the steep incline, swaying in the saddles as their horses propped and felt for a foothold amongst the rocks, Marcia suggested, 'It might have been Don's idea. I believe the grouchy old monster has your welfare at heart.' Then she uttered a short flat laugh. 'In fact, I'd say he's quite fond of you.'

Marcia sounded, or was trying to sound, as indifferent as when she had shown him that his naked torso was of no interest to her.

Eddie said, 'I don't think I understand Prowse,' and pricked up his ears for Marcia's reactions.

She did not react. Perhaps they were not deceiving each other; it was becoming boring.

They emerged from the scrub into a pocket of pasture at the

foot of the hill where ewes were lambing. Some of the mothers hurried their offspring away, others continued ruminating, unwilling to disturb the wriggly lamb bunting at an udder. One ewe stood transfixed, but only for a moment, torn between the instincts for self-preservation and motherhood, then resumed licking at the gelatinous envelope containing a lamb recently dropped. The parcel on the grass responded to her continued rasping: the lamb began breathing, rising, tottering into the first stages of its life.

'There!' Marcia herself breathed, and led them at a tangent to avoid disturbing the lambing ewes.

This woman of a certain age, in her velour of a dedicated dowdiness, and stretched, even ravelled old cardigan, looked curiously innocent. She had little connection with Marcia Lushington his mistress of thrashing thighs and voracious mouth. While the body remained heavy enough, the spirit which possessed it seemed to have regained a purity of youth.

Whether he sensed the transformation, the opulent gelding on which she was mounted was carrying his rider with a prim, spinsterly respect. And the new black filly had thrown off any vestige of unbroken folly and was stepping out, thrusting her neck into the wind with a show of conscientious, almost ostentatious, maidenly sobriety.

Marcia broke the silence. 'What are you going to call her?' she asked.

'I'm told her name is "Coalie".'

'Oh God, *that*! Nobody belongs to their given name. Or some of us don't, I like to think.'

She fell to giggling, and he joined in. They were soon bumping against each other, uncontrollably, unreasonably, like schoolgirls who have shed the boys during an interval at a dance.

Till they came upon a second mob of lambing ewes; when Marcia sobered up. 'Let's go this way,' she breathed, 'so as not to frighten the poor wretches.'

She took him by the wrist to guide him. Again she was a mature woman, but one in whom purity had never been disturbed by lust. She was the mother who had buried three children in the graveyard at 'Bogong', and who could not have conceived the third in the circumstances her pseudo-lover Eddie Twyborn had suspected.

Consequently Eddie loved her for the moment with a pure,

unadulterated joy. He lowered his eyelids against the glare, and finally closed them. He could have nuzzled the breasts he visualized inside the old ravelled cardigan.

Marcia must have led him purposely on the opposite side from the Lushington graveyard. On reaching a stand of aged pear trees below the house, she turned to him and said, 'You know, Eddie, how I appreciate you, don't you? What I'm trying to tell you,' she said, 'is how much we – all of us – love you – whether you realize it or not.'

The suppleness had gone out of her voice, the flesh fallen from her cheekbones, the chalky ridges of which had something of the agelessness of the hills surrounding them.

He might have continued staring at this other Mrs Lushington if their horses had not begun to sidle.

Whereupon Marcia rustled up a handful of reins from the pommel of her saddle. 'I'm so glad I came across you where I did. Wasn't it a lovely ride back?' She lowered her eyes, and there was nothing dishonest in her modesty. 'I don't think Prowse could hold it against me for taking you away from your work.'

If they hadn't been within view of the house, he would have kissed Marcia Lushington for a tremor in her right cheek.

Anyway, she had turned her horse. Jaunty with the knowledge that a feed of oats waited for him, Hamlet was bearing his rider off, this middle-aged woman practised in adulterous rites.

Summer was upon them, a sun the fiercer for being so long watered down, waves curling white on hectic seas of barley grass. After hanging his blankets on the line to air he found them crawling with the minute threads of yellow maggots.

'Arr!' Peggy Tyrrell laughed. 'It's only the blowies. If it wasn't for the good old blowie you wouldn't know for sure that summer was with us. Give yer blankets 'ere, love, and I'll fix 'em for yer.'

She carried them off, and returned them decontaminated, if reeking of kerosene.

He found himself slouching stupefied in the saddle as he rode round the paddocks, squinting through his lashes to keep out the flies, his skin cured to the tone and texture of any of the local stockmen. To a stranger he might have passed by now for a local. Often his companions forgot he was not one of them and asked his opinion, which they seemed to accept. But he did not believe he would ever learn to fool himself, as apparently he could deceive others, and as so many others deceived themselves.

Prowse, for one.

On an occasion when Mrs Tyrrell's monologue had driven each of them early to his room, the manager called through the thin wall, 'Why don't you come in, Ed, and have a yarn? Not very sociable, are yer?' The voice was still accusing when his offsider appeared in the doorway.

'You couldn't call either of us sociable, walking out on poor old Peggy.'

'Arr, Christ! Peggy's all right. But women finish by givin' yer the gripes.'

'The girls in town?'

They were seated opposite each other, pyjamas limp, rank with summer.

'Girls!' Prowse grunted. 'There's a time and place for anything.' His need for sociability forced the manager to pour his guest a drink. 'That one — Valda — that I told you about — I might even marry if the wife 'ud give me a divorce. But Kath's the sour type that hangs on to what she considers 'er rights after she's bloody shown she doesn't want 'em.'

He knocked back his drink, scratching at his chest through the gap in his pyjama coat.

He brought out an album. 'These 'ull make yer laugh!' he promised, while appearing far from mirthful himself. 'Old photos.'

He began turning the khaki pages on yellowed to greyer, more recent snapshots, in most cases meticulously mounted, with captions in white ink.

A few loose snaps slid out in the beginning. He gathered them up, but not before Eddie had identified the thin woman from the enlargement on the wall.

'That's Kath,' Prowse muttered unnecessarily before leafing on through the album.

'Here's Valda,' he indicated more enthusiastically with a blue thumbnail Eddie could remember receiving a hit from a hammer.

A plump smiling girl in a hat, Valda was shown holding a racquet as she stood pressed against the tennis net.

'Take it from me, Valda's the good oil!' Prowse bumped his guest's pyjamaed knee with his.

They forged on. There were the blank spaces from which Kath

must have been dismounted, only in half-hearted revenge for the enlarged Kath still ruled his room.

'That's poor little Kim,' said Prowse.

She looked a disapproving child, with more of her mother in her than her father. The moment after she had been snapped, her upper teeth would more than likely have clamped on her lower lip as she wondered whether she had done right in exposing herself to a camera.

Prowse turned and turned.

'That's me brother.' He sighed. 'He was killed in action.'

'Me brother' was a Light Horseman, too bronzed, too lithe, too beplumed, too much of a good thing, with death already in his light eyes.

Prowse turned the page too quickly.

After the brother, the group was something of a relief: of average, clumsy, lumpy blokes.

'Those were some mates of mine – who enlisted. It was taken just before they embarked.

Eddie was examining the mates, when Don flicked the page.

'Don't think, Eddie, I wouldn't 'uv enlisted. I know you were in the War. They told me about yer decoration. I would 'uv. But Greg pointed out I was doing a necessary job. And Marce;' as Eddie had heard several times before.

The coarse fingers were torturing the pasteboard edges of the khaki snapshot album.

Eddie Twyborn felt like blubbing as he hadn't since he came across his first corpse.

'So you see?' The host poured them another drink.

Prowse turned the pages of the album.

'Who's this?' Although you knew.

'That's Mum.'

She had an aggressive jaw and was wearing an A.I.F. brooch pinned across the V of a print frock.

'She never got over Bert's death. Well, you can understand.' Don sounded as though he were making excuses for his own earlier excesses.

'And this?'

'Mum when she was younger.'

Mum was holding a frocked moppet with abundant curls. Rather a pugnacious, scowling child. A miniature of herself in fact. Mum's scowls were girlish then.

225

'But the kid?'

Don's thumb rasped against the edge of the page. 'That's bloody me! That's how she kept me! That's what they do to yer when you're helpless,' he bellowed. 'The women!'

His knees were bumping against his guest's, through the thin sweaty poplin of summer pyjamas.

Eddie said, 'I've got to get some sleep, Don, or I shan't be up in the morning.'

'Anyway,' the manager said, 'we had a yarn. And that's something I didn't think yer capable of.'

'How?'

Without answering, Prowse bowed his head; he was pretty far gone by now. Several snaps of Kath fell out of the album.

Eddie wondered whether he should pick them up, but didn't.

He stood for a moment looking down on the bowed head, at a balding patch on top of it, that of an orange, tonsured monk.

He wondered how the man would have reacted had he bent and touched the patch of skin. He was tempted to do it. Drained of his masculine strength and native brutality, Prowse was reduced to a harmless, rather pathetic ape. Eddie's heart was thumping, but he managed to restrain his inclination. It was too incredible, to himself, and might have shocked one who was perhaps not drunk enough.

Instead he put his arms under the armpits and began easing Prowse on to the bed as he had done many times before.

'Thanks, Ed — you're the good oil . . .' he thought he heard as the heavy arms slithered briefly over his ribs.

Then the head lolled back on the pillow, the smile withdrawing from fox's teeth into a glare of bronze stubble.

Prowse slept, and Eddie turned down the lamp, till the familiar smell of untrimmed wick filled the darkened room.

At night the dark grew suffocating in the felted rooms of the creaking cottage. The cries of the sleepers tormented him: Peggy Tyrrell for her rheumatics and her daughters, Don Prowse for God knew what — the war he hadn't enlisted for, his dead brother, the failure of his marriage, Valda in her hat offering the good oil through the net.

On a certain night Eddie could no longer endure the manager's mutterings, his farts, the metallic jingling of a bed the other side of a thin wall. He got up, thinking to spend the rest of the night by the cool of the river, but had hardly got the screen-door open when the voice intercepted him.

'Where yer goin', Ed?'

'Down to the river. I'll stretch out there on a blanket. It's too bloody hot inside.'

Prowse laughed. 'I'd join yer,' he said, 'if the mozzies wouldn't get us.'

Eddie persisted, but found the mozzies did get him.

'What did I tell yer?' Prowse murmured.

Prowse would go outside to have a pee and, braving mosquitoes, stay there longer than making water warranted, perhaps in company with his glowering mum, Kath gnashing on the terms of separation, the brother's Light Horse plumes blowing in the false dawn. Eddie heard the bugle. He heard the screen-door mosquitoing as Don returned. A heavy, orange bungling. Stained poplin hitched to contain the load which women despise, and desire.

On one occasion Eddie was dreaming of the thin, green-skinned child. *I'm Kim who are you? I'm nobody. You must be someone everybody's somebody. You're right there Kim I'm my father and mother's son and daughter* . . . She looked as distrustful as the snap with its white-ink caption let into the khaki page of the album. Her lip so disapproving. The two of them a couple of prigs: a chlorotic child and a governess with aspirations to lust. Then she said *Ed I love you* in her father's voice. She put out a pale claw. They were grappling each other in a common desire related to childhood and despair. Before her mother broke in through the disapproving rustle of a screen-door.

He woke after that. It was the actual dawn after the false. He could hear the sound of Don's belt, the buckle hitting the bedstead. Mrs Tyrrell was raking the ashes in the stove. She sighed and burped. There was a smell of burning newspaper and sticks. A cock crowed, pitting his fire against the cool of dawn.

'What do you say if I drive us there?' Prowse had become this eager child, rocking on the balls of his feet beside the shining black Packard Mr Edmonds had been working over earlier in the afternoon.

'There, but not back,' Mrs Lushington stipulated in the kind of voice Mum Prowse might have used on her frocked and ringletted boy. 'I'll drive back.' She was very firm in her decision, her frown hidden by a flesh bandeau powdered with small metallic beads which collaborated with the evening light to flash what could have been messages in code.

Although her edict was strong enough to have sprung from a dogmatic male, Marcia Lushington had never looked more feminine to Eddie Twyborn, her rather too large, powdered breasts barely controlled by flesh charmeuse. Almost always neutral, this evening she emitted flashes of green from swathes of that same tone as the seas of young barley grass which stormed through 'Bogong' in the spring.

She was obviously flattered by his looking at her, and as she thought, quite rightly, appreciating her appearance. She touched his hand as they entered the black Packard, where the manager, in a suit which had grown too tight for him, had already seated himself like an attendant husband.

Marcia muttered, 'I'd better sit beside old Don — restrain him if he's had a couple for the road.'

Don most likely hadn't heard; he was too engrossed in examining the controls awaiting his touch, delighted by the prospect of driving the Lushington Packard on even an inconsiderable journey.

Eddie got behind. Marcia looked round and smiled from below the flesh bandeau, its metal beads sifting a radiance, of the theatre rather than the spirit, out of the hard, natural light.

Don pronounced very gravely, 'This is something like it,' juggling with gears as they finished with the slope below the house and straightened out across the stony stretch before the bridge. 'Oh God,' he mumbled, and again, 'Jesus Christ — it's good to be driving a real car!'

Marcia was sitting straight-backed. Eddie suspected she had been brought up on religion: a Methodist from Tilba. Greg could only have been C of E, Marcia Methodist — or Baptist? though she'd picked up a wrinkle or two from the Romans.

He was still undecided on the denomination from which Marcia Lushington had lapsed, when he glanced out, and there was Mrs Tyrrell beside the loosely articulated bridge, her gums parted, her sticks of arms raised from out of the bobbled shawl.

'Good on yez!' Peggy called in a burst of Saturday evening despair, perhaps remembering the funerals she had missed, the corpses she hadn't been invited to lay out, since accepting to finish her pensioned life working for the Lushingtons of 'Bogong'.

They waved back, trailing the perfumes of brilliantine and bath salts, they waved at that crucified cow, poor Peggy, beside the bucking bridge. They could afford to be magnanimous as they drove off to the party to which they had been invited.

Marcia had walked down to tell Eddie. 'It's the Winterbothams.' She stood looking at the toes of her shoes; how the stones had scuffed them. 'Next Saturday evening. Everybody's dying to meet you.'

'Why — what do they know?'

Marcia snorted, and continued looking at her martyred shoes. 'Well, you're here, aren't you? With us. And you're your father's son.'

'And what about my mother?'

'Oh, yes, yes! Of course your mother. We know about *mothers*!' She crimped her brows.

Then she added, 'They probably also want to decide whether you're my lover.'

So now they were driving to the Winterbothams' party.

In yet another footnote Marcia had thought to explain. 'We'll have to take poor old Don along, otherwise he might turn against us — or commit suicide, or something.'

So here was old Don driving them to the Winterbothams. Of 'Belair'.

It was a house of greater pretensions than the Lushingtons' discreetly ramshackle affair, more of an Edwardian city mansion, in ox-blood brick with tan ironwork, all illuminated for the party, if self-advertisement weren't perhaps the rule. Music was already bursting out, or anyway saxophones and drums were tuning up. The arriving guests were made aware that 'Last Night on the Back Porch' and 'Marquita' were in the band's repertoire.

Don Prowse swirled his passengers round the oval rose-bed, and brought the black Packard to a standstill. His marriage may have failed, but he was a perfectionist in his handling of a car.

'Well,' sighed Marcia, 'this is it.' She might have regretted their coming.

Later in the evening, as the French champagne frothed over, and at least one of the guests had dropped his Pavlova on the parquet, Don explained to Eddie, 'Old Greg could write a cheque and buy out Winterbothams any time they asked for it.'

There was no asking for it tonight. Winterbothams appeared on top of the wave, Harold, a tall, cadaverous man whose scabby hands had earned all that they had got hold of, from cedar panelling and Sèvres urns, to his wife's Paquin model and his own uneasy dinner jacket.

He welcomed the Lushingtons' acquisition by putting an arm round his shoulders and exposing equally uneasy teeth in a ferocious china smile. 'Heard about you, Eddie. What can we get you to drink?' Like Greg Lushington, Harold Winterbotham seemed to think that by rushing a stranger behind the veil of alcohol his own uncertainty would glare less in the stranger's eyes.

The greatest diffident of all, Eddie Twyborn saw through their play too clearly. If he could have shown them the defenceless grub inside what they took to be flawless armour, they might have established some kind of bumbling relation-ship. But he could not. Instead, he and Harold fell back on alcohol and the momentous question of what Eddie should have to drink.

One look, and Bid Winterbotham swept Marcia Lushington behind the scenes, into the undressing room of confidences, but Marcia almost immediately brought herself back. She stood patting her hair, glancing in and out of the Winterbotham mirrors and between the bars of the hired music. It seemed as though she knew it all, and Bid offering the savoury boats to Eddie Twyborn in preference to the 'Belair' regulars.

Marcia patted her hair the harder for the regulars: Mrs Temperley who was Somebody's Cousin, the doctor and his wife (only the profession held them together), the junior partner of Crewe and Caulfield, the Dicks of 'Pevensey', the Braddons of 'Saltash', Robbie Boyle a Papal count. Standing centre on the Winterbotham Aubusson, Marcia might have been holding a post-mortem on a doubtful prawn from her savoury boat.

She looked to Don Prowse for relief, but occupied in helping himself at the buffet, he did not give it. She looked to the Winterbothams' so-called Romney *Conversation Piece*, but again received no support. She turned her back, always humming, always patting her heavy chignon.

Geoff Scott, who had tried several times, but never succeeded in making her, approached as though preparing to try again. She gave him her banana-split smile. Always patting her back hair. Always keeping an eye on this jackeroo of theirs.

As hostess, Bid Winterbotham had led her guest somewhat

apart from the others, ostensibly to mother him and make him feel at home. They were seated on the Queen Anne settee, its high back to the room, its front to the *Conversation Piece*, for which the Winterbothams let it be known they had paid a fortune.

(Later in the evening, between dances, Marcia was at pains to make good an omission on her part. 'I should have told you, darling – Bid is what they call nervy. She can't sit with a man on a sofa without starting to toy with his fly. Everybody knows about it. They forgive her because she's such a good sort.')

Indeed, the regulars had watched with sympathetic interest as Bid and the popular jackeroo sat on the straight-backed settee making conversation in front of the *Conversation Piece*. They knew by her hunched shoulders and his blenching cheeks that the operation must have begun.

'I adore everything old,' Bid was telling the young man, her long, nervy fingers flying in time with her monologue, 'antiques – paintings – you've probably heard about our Romney.' She did not wait to hear he hadn't. 'The Art Gallery wants to steal it from us – before Harold *gives* it to them.' She looked perfunctorily at their work of art while explaining. 'It's the Lady Etterick of Etterick with her family. We're somehow descended – on my side, that is – but go farther back than the Ettericks – to Mary Queen of Scots, and away beyond.'

She had a long thin tongue, which curved at the tip as though preparing to dart from her ancestral past into present possibilities. 'I adore lace – *old* lace,' she confessed, and her flickering eyelids flung a whole web of it in her victim's face. 'One of my great-aunts was famous for her tatting, in Maitland where I was born.' Bid Winterbotham's long nervy fingers flew like her great-aunt's tatting shuttle, in and out the air, between tweaking at a fly-button.

Eddie might have stirred more uneasily if Marcia hadn't leant over the back of the settee and asked, 'How are we going, Bid?'

Bid answered, 'Famously,' and raised her throat like a shag caught swallowing another's fish.

The two women agreed to share their mirth at least, Eddie the fish glancing up into Marcia's laughing, powdered cleavage.

The Winterbotham party, the Winterbotham friends, in particular the Papal count of roving eye, made him love his patroness. He loved old Don, who had brought him another glass of champagne, or what was left of it after its frothing over on the way.

'You're all right, Eddie. You know I like yer.'

The object of the manager's approval looked sideways at the orange paw planted on his shoulder. How he should deal with the paw, he had no idea. He had never made a positive decision, unless to escape from the tennis-court and marriage with Marian Dibden, and his dash across no-man's-land to assault the enemy lines, though in each instance, it could be argued, the decision had been made for him by some incalculable power, just as on a lower plane, his fucking Mrs Lushington had been initiated not by himself but by Marcia.

After the second encore for 'Marquita' Marcia and he were sitting it out, forking up some supper from the Winterbotham Sèvres.

'I keep on forgetting to tell you,' Marcia was munching her way through the last of her Russian salad, 'I've got some friends coming who'd adore to meet you.'

'Too much adoration,' Eddie protested, 'in the Monaro,' and disposed of his plate on an ormolu console.

'Can't you allow for a manner of speaking?' Marcia took his hand and laid it amongst a detritus of beetroot which had settled in her charmeuse lap.

He said, 'I could allow for anything,' and nibbled with genuine appetite at his mistress's neck.

She glanced round before continuing, but nobody had seen, except perhaps the Papal count, and at the far end of the room, a girl so awkward and unobtrusive as to be of little consequence in Mrs Lushington's estimation.

'These friends,' Marcia returned to the topic his indiscretion had interrupted, 'they haven't exactly met you – or may have long ago – it isn't clear. They know your parents. Joanie Golson, who I love – Curly the husband's a bore, it can't be helped – but Joanie's an old friend of your mother's.'

He could have been wrong, but Marcia had grown quizzical, he felt. She had never looked so much a raw scallop – with guile concealed in its fleshiness.

'Why do you shy away, darling?'

He was relieved of the necessity of answering by the girl he had noticed at the far end of the room. She was weaving her way through the guests, and if Marcia and he were not her goal, she was headed vaguely in their direction. She made an unprepossessing impression, in a drab frock carelessly worn, thick black hair uncombed, if not positively matted.

'That's Helen — the daughter,' Marcia casually answered his enquiry. 'Poor thing, she's most unhappy,' though Mrs Lushington, it sounded, was not prepared, or did not know how, to deal with such unhappiness.

The girl cast a shadow in otherwise shadowless surroundings under a Venetian chandelier.

Marcia sighed, and swept the beetroot off her lap. 'At least she has her weaving. I expect that does something for her.'

'I hope to God it does, because if it doesn't, nothing else will.'

At once he regretted his boozy non-sympathy. Across the short distance which was all that now separated them, the girl was staring at him. She had a harelip, he began to realize, so badly sewn the teeth behind it were sneering at him, and yet it was not a sneer: it was suppressing a cry as she climbed upward, out of the pit of her own monstrosity, to convey some message, or perhaps only asking for help — even offering it to one in whom she recognized signs of monstrosity or hopelessness.

But he was neither helpless not hopeless, was he? He looked to Marcia for confirmation, but she was gathering up her party luggage, and glancing round to locate her manager before leaving.

At the same moment the Winterbotham parents erupted on them, almost as though to shield this desirable young man from the daughter they could not begin to explain. Bid's mouth had lost its symmetry, her fingers any calculated direction, their sticks threshing at the air like the spokes of a skinned umbrella, while Harold's more knobbly, human fingers tried to control them.

'But he's gorgeous, Marce — gorgeous — and all this time you've been hiding him!'

Marcia announced, cold and flat, 'It's time I drove my contingent home, if we can manage the manager.'

At this point the Papal count was engaging Don.

Harold told Eddie, 'Better come back some *morning*. We're better in the mornings. I'll show you the stud beef.'

The guest looked back once through the gush of eternal affection avowed by the Winterbotham parents and friends, himself and Marcia lugging Don more or less by his armpits, and there was Helen, standing as though in the spiral of a willy-nilly.

Another moment and their breath might have united, her teeth clashing with his through the wounded lip.

As it was, she stood grinning through her affliction at what he saw she recognized as his.

The band was lurching into yet another reprise of 'Marquita' as Mrs Lushington revved up the black Packard. 'My *men*,' he heard Marcia shout at the hosts of 'Belair', but the reference was lost in the general hubbub.

Then they were driving down the moonlit clefts, between the stereoscopic buttocks of hills, amongst the lacy tatting of antique trees. If the trees looked less substantial, once or twice his cheek, his closed eyelids, were stung as though by strands of wire. He opened his eyes to see a fox, its red eyes glaring at him from the bed of a dry creek, before it turned and skittered away on spindly legs into the scrub.

In the same way the Winterbotham rout skittered from his mind. His head bumping, as they drove between the white, recurring hills.

Waking from a doze, he asked, 'What became of the shawl? The Spanish shawl in the photograph. On the piano.'

Marcia snorted her disbelief. 'Fancy noticing that shawl! And remembering it tonight.'

What he remembered more vividly was Helen Winterbotham's non-smile, as sculptural as the natural details through which they were driving. The Spanish shawl no more than flickered like the tail end of the Winterbotham rout, the Winterbotham friends, Bid's nervy fingers.

'Actually,' Marcia said, 'the shawl flew out of the car somewhere on the way back from a Winterbotham party. Greg was ropeable,' she giggled. 'He'd paid quite a lot of money for it. In Seville.'

She guided the Packard round a curve.

'Actually,' she said, 'he couldn't complain as much as he might have. Because he had been with us to the party. It was fancy dress,' she confessed, and with a naked shoulder warded off any disapproval on her lover's part.

'What did you go as?'

'Carmen.' It fell like a stone into the river bend they were crossing.

'For a time,' she explained on recovering herself, 'Bid and Harold were all for fancy dress. They had the most extravagant costumes made for them by The Buttonhole.' Marcia's voice had

234

assumed the humble tones of the disguised rich. 'Bid as Queen Elizabeth – the Primrose Pompadour – God knows what. Harold I forget – but something to match.'

'Did you find anyone to match your Carmen?'

Half-turned towards the back seat, she entered on a suppressed shriek. 'Don was my Don José.'

Don must have been sleeping.

'And Greg – if he was of the party?'

'Greg insisted on going as himself.'

Marcia drove more painstakingly.

'Of course you won't approve, Eddie. The young are too wise.'

'I can't feel I'm young. I've got an old man hiding inside me. Always been there.'

Marcia did not at once comment, but finally came out with it. 'I wonder whether you'll find a young man in the old man you're going to become. It would give your life balance, and be a kind of justice, wouldn't it?'

He might have enjoyed that more if he hadn't felt moved to ask, 'What did Helen Winterbotham go as?'

'Nothing. She shut herself in her room. She wouldn't come out.'

'Too wise again.'

'Or too brutal!' Marcia gave her most brutal laugh. 'The young love to hurt.'

They were driving over the loose bridge at 'Bogong'. They were arriving. Don Prowse was deposited.

'Shall I come with you, Marce?' asked Eddie.

'No, darling.' She flung off his dutiful kiss. 'You don't want to, and I can't bear sozzled men.'

She looked back, however, after re-starting the car. 'Don't forget the Golsons. They'll adore to see you.'

Mrs Tyrrell had an announcement to make; her voice refined to what she probably considered gentility, it reproduced the tone of a provincial newspaper's gossip column which, in her own state of illiteracy, she could never have read, but with which her daughters and her cronies must surely have made her familiar. 'Madam is expecting 'er friends Mr and Mrs E. Boyd Golson, arrivin' Thursdee on a short visit. Wealthier, I'm told, than Lushingtons themselves. Mrs Edmonds says there'll be a big shivoo Saturdee night, after the guests 'uv rested from their drive. Mrs Edmonds couldn't say for sure, but would take a bet that Mr Twyborn and Mr Prowse has received an invite to the homestead.' After which, Mrs Tyrrell lapsed. 'That Mrs Quimby don't know whether she's comin' or goin'. She's lost the nozzles to 'er pipin' outfit. All I can say is, good luck to 'er.'

On the Thursday evening, while unsaddling the black filly and mixing her feed, Eddie watched a car approaching across the flat. The Golsons were driving a maroon Minerva. As the planks of the 'Bogong' bridge alternately rattled and thundered, he saw a thicker, balder Curly at the wheel, and Joanie wearing lipstick, jowls, and dark glasses. She had bound her head for the journey, and perhaps country abandonment, in a chiffon scarf. Curly had congealed; he was looking straight ahead; Joan glanced about nervously with the dry bemused expression of one who has been reading a road map with only intermittent accuracy for the last few hours.

He felt for them, for all those who had survived the game, and Angelos, no longer there, whom he had truly loved, though to be honest, had often only just restrained himself from axing, just as Angelos had not been able to resist drawing the knife. Now more than any of them perhaps, he pitied the E. Boyd Golsons entering Lushington territory with the air of those who have lost their way on dusty roads and road maps held upside down.

He divorced himself from his sweaty mare and went inside.

'Don,' he called with an aggressiveness unnatural to him, 'aren't I due for some leave? What about letting me off for the next few days? I've been thinking of riding across the mountains, down to the Murray.'

Don came out from his room grinning his ginger grin. 'It's all right by me, Eddie. But what 'ull Marcia have to say?'

'Why Marcia? You're the manager, aren't you?'

'She's pretty possessive if she takes a fancy.' Don couldn't turn off the grin in the stubble which would have to wait till Saturday. 'Well,' he said, 'I expect it's up to you in the long run – if you want to take the leave that's due. And what odds any bloody Golsons?' His teeth snapped shut on his conclusion.

Eddie and Don stood looking at each other from opposite ends of the brown passage.

'See, Eddie? *I* won't hold anything against yer.'

There was a whispering of dry-rotten woodwork, a dull protest from warped lino, the scratching, almost like spirit-writing, of hawthorn spines on glass. Prowse didn't approach any closer, but steamed outward, it seemed.

Eddie presumed he could take his leave at any moment and that Don was prepared to face Marcia's wrath. Eddie and Don understood each other in the brown, dry-rotted passage, while Peggy Tyrrell seared the mutton in a cavern beyond concern.

He set off the following day as Marcia, Joan, and Curly were hitting golf balls on the mini-course below the house. They were wearing the clothes, their limbs assuming the attitudes, of the Philistine upper class. Behind a hearty façade, they appeared somewhat lethargic as they put in time till lunch. (The Golsons would not have admitted to boredom because country life is virtuous.)

At that distance no one's attention was drawn to the insignificant figure of a horseman, and he was soon well along the road which stretched through the white tussock, skirted the emerald upholstery of a lucerne pasture, and wound finally into the hills.

He had taken with him in his saddle-bags enough salt tucker to tide him over if night caught him between townships. He did on several occasions camp out, more by choice than through necessity, the heat of day giving place to agreeable tremors of mountain cool as he lay in his blanket on the rough grass, head propped against his saddle's sweaty padding. He could not remember ever having felt happier. At the same time he wondered whether he could really exist without the sources of unhappiness. Half-dozing, half-waking to the tune of his horse's regular cropping, and in his half-sleep what sounded like a pricking of early frost or needling by stars, he knew that his body and his mind craved the everlasting torments.

He found himself dreaming, or thinking, of Don Prowse seated in sweaty pyjamas, the snapshot album open on his lap, revealing snaps of Eddie Twyborn as he had most surely never looked in innocence or wantonness, and one of Eudoxia Vatatzes in pomegranate shawl, the spangled fan outspread to screen her breasts. *Looks a regular cock-tease, eh?* Don again, standing at the end of the brown lino passage, the light from the doorway behind him opening like a giant camera-lens. Eddie Twyborn put up a hand to ward off the photographer. Who, more purposeful, was standing at the bedside, red nipples as unblinking as foxes' eyes in the surrounding fuzz of orange fur.

He was more amused than ashamed of his dream – or thoughts, if they were. He got up to re-tether his horse. She whinnied to see him, and he stroked her muzzle. Theirs was an honest relationship.

On one such occasion he dreamed of someone, he could not at first be certain, this snapshot dream was something of a double exposure, till finally he saw he was sitting beside Helen of the Harelip. They were seated on the brink of a rock pool, its water so clear and motionless they dared not breathe for fear they might ruffle its surface into some ugly and disturbing pattern. Whether the emotions they shared were joyful, it was difficult if not impossible to tell, only that they were united by an understanding as remote from sexuality as the crystal water in the rock basin below.

During his ride it occurred to him that he did not dream of Marcia; he only thought about her, and then coldly, briefly, on the longer, burning stretches of road.

When he had been away a week, Eddie returned to 'Bogong'. Peggy Tyrrell ran down to the bridge, her bobbled shawl spread like a crow's wings in flight, her thin black arms flailing at the evening. 'Mrs Lushington just about threw a fit, Mrs Edmonds says. She's been lookun for yer. She's been onter Tumbarumba – Toomut – half the Monarer. Better make yerself good with 'er, love, or you're a gonner.'

And Prowse came out on the veranda. 'Nearly got me the sack, you bugger. I told you Marce had taken a fancy.'

'What about the Golsons?'

Prowse looked down at the meniscus of a slanted whiskey. 'They drove off,' he sighed, 'in the bloody Minerva. There was nobody to make a fourth at bridge.'

After the prodigal had bathed, the manager came into his room. 'We did miss yer,' Prowse said. 'We wondered what 'ud happened to yer – down on the Murray.' Eddie felt the finger, apparently checking on vertebrae. 'Could 'uv got murdered or somethun . . .'

Mrs Tyrrell came in, but retreated on noticing nakedness. 'Come on, you men,' she shouted. 'There's a shoulder of mutton and baked pumpkun for tea.'

Before obeying her summons, Prowse advised, 'I tell you, Ed, make it up with Marcia, and make it quick.'

Eddie decided to wait, which was what Marcia herself must have decided.

*

Denny and Eddie had been moving the wethers from Bald Hill down to the woolshed for crutching the following day. The men's faces were pale with dust, each a different kind of clown.

'Ever done any crutchun, Ed?' Denny sniggered. 'Break yer bloody back – snippun the dags off a sheep's arse. Just you wait. You'll be sore enough termorrer evenun.'

'Have to get Peggy to rub my back.'

'Wouldn't like Peggy. Too bony.' He hesitated thoughtfully. 'Missus is bony. But Dot wouldn't rub, I reckon, even if you asked 'er to.'

Dot's husband sounded more resigned than sad.

'You never know if you haven't asked. You never know of any body what they'll come at till you've tried it on.'

'You reckon?'

Eddie had developed an affection for his simple mate, which he believed was reciprocated. They were brought closer by the evening light, and on Eddie's side, the melancholy knowledge that the chasms created by language and class must always keep them apart.

When they had yarded the silly wethers (what was worse, in the presence of sheep Eddie always ended by convincing himself of the silliness of his own existence and human behaviour in general) his mate suggested with furtive pride – Denny did in fact glance over his shoulder, 'Why don'tcher stop off at our place, Ed, an' drink a beer?'

'I mightn't be welcome. Your missus'll be getting the tea. Or changing a nappy. Or washing one.'

'Dot's all right. She don't wash too many nappies. She 'angs the same one out ter dry. Dot's not as bad as they make out.'

So Eddie couldn't let Denny down, the couple of clowns slouching in their saddles as the newcomer had seen the natives on his approach to 'Bogong' that first day, only that the native skin was now toned down from bacon to beige.

Despite acclimatization and acceptance, he experienced a faint tremor of discovery approaching the Allens' huggermugger shack, Cortes, as it were, playing on both sides of the fence. But Denny did not notice, which made his mate, whether Cortes or First Clown, the more regretful of his isolation.

Dot came out. She was looking smaller, sharper than on the occasion of their first meeting, during her pregnancy. Tearful then for a moral lapse, she had grown fierce in defence of its fruit.

Like the rickety shack she had acquired with marriage, her legitimized child was a property.

Denny quailed somewhat, but found courage to ask, ' 'Ow is she?'

' 'Ad the colic all evenin'. She's sleepin' now.'

The mother might never have seen Eddie before. Dot Allen had probably dismissed him to the limbo of foreigners and amateurs.

'Thought you was gunner be late,' she told her husband, 'when I've almost got yer tea ready.'

'Well, I'm not late, am I? An' tea's not ready.' His burst of logic was unassailable. 'You know Eddie, Dot. I've asked 'im back to drink a beer with us.'

'Not with me, you haven't. Haven't the time for swillin' beer.' The shack shuddered as she swept inside.

Denny brought a bottle that had been hanging by its neck at the end of a rope inside the iron water-tank. He ventured into the kitchen and returned with a couple of chipped and stained enamel mugs.

'No time!' Dot shouted from within.

The beer was warmer than one would have hoped, and its head rising, slopped over into wasted pools.

Dot called, 'Hope you men aren't gunner get drunk an' wake 'er up.'

'Not enough ter get drunk on.'

'I've known you do pretty well on a little.'

Encapsulated in evening light, the two friends sat looking out across the plain. From the shack drifted the eternal smells of boiling mutton and burnt cabbage.

'Don't wanter wake the baby,' the mother shouted between bursts of hardware.

The baby had begun, indeed, to cry.

Dot came out. She was carrying a plate, on it a used paper doily she must have scrounged from a great house, and on the doily, some fingers of yellow cheese of varying thickness and length.

'They say,' she said, 'If you eat somethin' fatty . . .'

She returned inside. The baby was by now in tongue to split the shack's buckled boards.

'There!' the mother shouted. 'You've waked 'er! I knew you would. Bringin' back mates. You don't 'ave no consideration, Denny.' She choked on that.

Denny was smiling, lips a glutinous mauve, the sunset glinting on spectacles mended with string as grimy-greasy as the wool on a sheep's back.

'Wot's wrong with my choo-choo?' he called back. 'My little choo-choo!'

He went inside, and returned with the screaming, congested infant.

Denny sat on the edge of the veranda dandling a tantrum. 'Choo choo choo!' At one point his love dribbled down from the violet lips in a slender thread of saliva, while the baby thrashed around, revealing that her nappy was out to dry.

She was a sharp-featured child, as sharp as her mother, but the little scalp already showed a drift of golden down.

Dot had emerged preparing some fresh outburst, only to find the baby laughing up, parrying the last traces of saliva, her tender, gummy smile related at the other end of time to Peggy Tyrrell's toughened grin.

Dot stood looking down on Denny, on the black, cockerel's feathers plastered by sweat to a balding skull. 'He's good with the baby,' she conceded. 'Denny's good,' she murmured.

Her person might have trailed after her voice, withdrawing into everyday life from a moment of revelation which was almost inadmissible, if there hadn't been an intrusion, an active violation of grace.

Eddie was the first to notice the approach of Dick Norton the rabbiter, mounted on his skeletal nag, the rabble of his mongrel pack at heel.

Dot was not long after in spotting her dad. 'You keep off!' she shrieked. 'We only want peace in this place. Fuck off, dirty old man!'

Though into high summer, the rabbiter was dressed in a cardy the colour of split peas and a cap with ear-flaps in fake fur.

'I'm yer father, ain't I?'

'Yeah, Dadda, we know!'

'I'd of thought everyone knew about everythink. You're no saint yourself, Dot.'

'We try, don't we?' Dot screeched. 'Anyways, from time to time. An' we've got Mr Twyborn 'ere — on wot was a social visit till you showed up.'

Purple in the face, the baby had been handed back by Denny to the mother.

He had risen, very dignified, his head trembling, with its wisps of damp black cockerel's feathers. 'Yes,' he golloped, 'you fuck orf — fuckun old Dick!' the spittle flying in all directions.

He whipped inside the shack, returned with a gun, and fired a couple of shots at what was by now practically darkness.

There arose a yelping of dogs, the whinge of a spurred horse. ' 'Oo'd want a social visit with a bunch of bastards like youse?'

The baby shrieked worse than ever. Again Denny let off the gun.

There were sounds of retreat. If it hadn't been for the baby's screams, silence would have descended on a landscape reduced to formlessness except where the last embers smouldered on a distant ridge.

'There! There!' the mother coaxed in a burnt-out voice.

'Choo choo choo?' Denny giggled, still exhilarated by his masterful initiative.

Dot sighed. 'What will Mr Twyborn think?'

She didn't stop to consider for long. The Allens were going inside to their overdue meal of boiled mutton and cabbage, or breast.

As Eddie Twyborn untethered his horse and rode away, he wondered whether he wasn't leaving the best of all possible worlds.

Peggy Tyrrell was waiting for Eddie. 'You've upset 'im,' she said.

'Upset who?'

'Prowse,' she said. 'I never seen 'im so upset. Couldn' eat 'is tea. Went to bed. Thought you must 'uv been throwed again. Or went for a swim and drownded.'

'It's not all that late. I stopped off for a beer with Denny.'

'But you was expected. Mr Prowse is the manager, and responsible for those under 'im.'

Mrs Tyrrell sounded unusually prim. She was on Prowse's side all right, perhaps with some axe of her own to grind, or perhaps it was only self-righteousness raising its head.

He ate his stuffed mutton flap and would have gone to bed while she scraped the dishes if he hadn't heard a sighing, a groaning, a jingling of the bedstead, from the manager's darkened room.

He paused in the doorway before entering his own. 'What's wrong, Don? Not sick, are you?'

There was a prolonged silence meant to impress. 'There's nothing *wrong* — Eddie. We were only wonderin' about you — those who have yer interests at heart.' A pause, a cough, then the sharp hissing. 'Cripes, I got a pain in me guts!'

'What about a tot of bi-carb if I bring it?'

'Thanks, Ed, it can't be indigestion. Didn't eat me tea. Didn't feel up to stuffed *flaps.*' Again a groan, and jingling of the bed. 'I never talk about it, but Dad's old man died of cancer, Eddie.'

Eddie said, 'See you in the morning, Don.'

'Don't think I'm fishing for sympathy,' the manager called after him. 'But I can't say we weren't worrying about yer.'

As he undressed he could hear a listening. He could almost hear sandy eyelashes thrashing the silences, then after he had put out his lamp, Prowse rising through a jingle before going out to pee off the veranda. He could hear him listening, barefoot on the brown lino, after returning.

When sleep fell on Eddie Twyborn, a penful of wethers milling round him, Marcia was possibly there. Yes. Though in what capacity he could not remember when he awoke to a pale sky and dwindling stars the morning of the crutching.

In the next room the manager must have been lying on his back, while in the kitchen Mother Tyrrell was raking the stove and calling on Our Lady to rid her of her aches.

It was a long day at the shed. At noon Jim the Father brought in a mob of ewes when yesterday's wethers were barely accounted for.

' 'Ow's yer back doin', Ed?' Denny Allen called to his mate.

The manager came and went, more often absent than present, though when there, he would muck in with the men in short ostentatious bursts, impressively muscular in a singlet. 'Better to get it over — even if it buggers us,' he advised his team.

Prowse chose the cleaner sheep, Eddie noticed, himself drawn, it appeared, to the daggier ones. It was an aspect of his own condition he had always known about, but it amused him to recognize it afresh while snipping at the dags of shit, laying bare the urine-sodden wrinkles with their spoil of seething maggots, round a sheep's arse.

At one stage he found he had picked a ewe who must have detached herself from her own mob and joined the wethers. Before becoming fully aware of the difference in sex of the sheep he was handling, he had cut off the tip of the vulva. Nobody noticed his clumsiness or distress. As the day lengthened and the men grew tired, the blood flowed copiously from under the most professional hand. Lacerated beasts were sometimes dismissed with kicks and curses.

At least the sound of snipping soothed, and the smell of tar rising from wounded, blown crotches. Some of the sheep raised their muzzles, baring their teeth in ecstasy or agony at the treatment they were receiving.

From squirming on the greasy slats, they regained a precarious balance as Eddie Twyborn straightened a fastidious masochist's back. He must have been grinning like a skull. His blisters had burst and become raw patches from manipulating the hand-shears.

Denny laughed. ' 'Ow you doin', Ed feller?'

During one of his appearances Prowse laid a hot, appraising hand on the novice's back. 'Eddie 'ud make a professional shearer if he only knew it.'

Towards mid-afternoon the manager decided he did not want the wethers returned to Bald Hill. He told off Eddie to drive them to a rested paddock at some distance, while Jim and Denny, and he in theory, finished crutching the ewes.

'Can't write home and say I'm a slave-driver,' he told the jackeroo, who was by then too dazed to think of an answer.

It was some relief to be off on his own, his back broken, his blistered hands listless on the reins. Released from their recent ordeal, the wethers trotted meekly enough, their heads working as though by strings concealed in their papier mâché armour. In her automatic movements, the mare too, seemed relieved, jingling the metal on her bridle, lowering her head to snort at the dust, prodding stragglers with her muzzle.

An animal acquiescence had descended on all those involved in the migration through the coppery glare of late afternoon, in which, on the other hand, trees were shedding a less passive drizzle of silver light.

They reached the distant paddock, its fence in such poor repair he saw himself returning in a few days to that other back-breaking operation of digging post-holes, tamping down the stones round renewed posts, and straining vindictive wire. In his present exhaustion he accepted the state of affairs with a degree of cynical resignation, slammed and chained the netted gate, and headed for home.

His horse had carried him perhaps a mile when he was overcome by drowsiness. He dismounted, and after tethering the mare to one of her front fetlocks, lay down beneath a tree, on the pricking grass, amongst the lengthening shadows. He did not sleep, but fell into that state between waking and sleeping in which he usually came closest to being his actual self.

This evening he started remembering or re-living an occasion, it was a Sunday afternoon, when he had felt the urge to see his fortuitous mistress. Never in his life had he felt so aggressive, so masculine, or so impelled by the desire to fuck this coarsely feminine woman. He deliberately thought of it as *fucking*, and spoke the word on his way up the hill between the cottage and the homestead. As he walked he was looking down at his coarse, labourer's boots which he was in the habit of treating with rendered-down mutton fat. The boots matched his intention, just as no other word would have fitted the acts he performed with Marcia, nothing of love, in spite of her protestations. Except on another, more accidental occasion when they had ridden together through the paddocks, sidestepping the imperfect expressions of perfection.

Each incident had taken place so long ago, if not in time, in experience, Eddie Twyborn could only watch them in detachment as he lay dozing or re-living beneath his tree, the face of Greg Lushington, that amiable absentee, re-forming amongst the branches. However intangible, Greg's presence made his own behaviour the coarser, the more shocking.

The house when he reached it on this Sunday afternoon had about it an air of desertion. A cat raised its head from where it was lying in a patch of winter sunlight. A wiry strand of climbing rose was rubbing deeper the scar it had worn on a corner of painted brickwork.

As he wandered round, considering his plan of attack, chains rattled against kennels, mingling with abortive barks and faint moans of affection for one who had ceased to be a total stranger. He entered by the kitchen door. The servants were gone, either to town or their own quarters. The only life in the living rooms was a stirring of almost extinct coals (on tables, copies of the London *Tatler* and library books from Sydney which amounted to Marcia's intellectual life).

He looked inside her bedroom more cautiously, for fear of disturbing a migraine or a monthly.

Silence and the absence of its owner played on the frustration growing in him.

He flung himself on the bed, of the same oyster- or scallop-tones as those of Marcia his mistress (incredible word). There was Marcia's familiar scent, not so much a synthetic perfume as that of her body. He lay punching at the down pillows, prising out of crumpled satin handfuls of opulent flesh, until present impotence and an undertow of memory forced him off the bed to rummage through the clothes hanging in the wardrobes.

Starting in frustration and anger, he was cajoled, pricked, and finally seduced by the empty garments, the soft and slithery, the harsh and grainy, the almost live-animal, which he held in his arms. He fumbled with his own crude moleskins, the bargain shirt from the Chinaman's store. The laces of his wrinkled boots, stinking of rancid mutton fat, lashed at him as he got them off. He stood shivering in what now passed for his actual body, muscular instead of sinuous, hairier than formerly, less subtle but more experienced.

He needed no guidance in entering the labyrinth of gold thread and sable, the sombre, yet glowing, brocaded tribute to one of Marcia's less neutral selves. And still was not satisfied by the image Marcia's glass presented.

He stormed at the dressing-table, roughing up his hair, dabbling with the beige puff in armpits from which the heavy brocaded sleeves fell back, outstaring himself feverishly, then working on the mouth till it glistened like the pale, coral trap of some great tremulous sea anemone.

He fell back on Marcia's bed.

And the footsteps began advancing with a male assurance which had been his own till recently. Eudoxia Vatatzes lay palpitating, if contradictorily erect, awaiting the ravishment of male thighs.

The movement of her heart had taken over from all other manifestations as the door was pushed farther ajar, and the head intruded. It was Greg Lushington, sightless behind his spectacles. Neither the glare from Norwegian glaciers, nor the heady air of Himalayas or Andes could have blinded him, for he was still rooted in his own country of pale, nut-flavoured moths.

'I just wanted to tell you, Marce, that the word was wrong – in the poem, I mean. What I thought of as "placebo", you remember? ought to have been "purulence".'

Then he smiled, and immediately withdrew, not wanting to disturb his wife's rest.

And Eudoxia Vatatzes threw off her borrowed clothes, as Eddie Twyborn broke up the scene he was re-living in the gathering shadows, returning from the boundary paddock after a day's crutching.

He untethered his mare from her own fetlock and returned to the settlement known as 'Bogong', where Peggy Tyrrell, inside the illuminated kitchen, was engaged in the evening ritual of maltreating food into the semblance of a meal. Tonight there was a smell of onions – and was it beef on the boil instead of mutton? Some days earlier Jim Allen had destroyed a cow, her leg broken by a fall down a gully.

This luxury of cooking smells united with the stench of his own body, greasy wool, and tar from the anointing of sheeps' wounds and fly-blown wrinkles, while inside the shed, as he mixed his horse a feed, the sweet scents of chaff and oats mingled with the no less intoxicating, if baser stenches he had brought with him.

In the darkness beyond the feed-room proper, in the depths of the shed where a soft mountain of chaff was stored, a landslide had been started by a cat pursuing a rat. There was a deathly squeal as the cat pounced and worried its prey, growling at the human intruder.

From her stall the mare was whinnying at him impatiently. She glared and snorted, stamping on the brickwork with small, elegant, shod hooves. Her greed as he poured the oats and chaff whetted his own appetite for sodden onions and stringy cow passing as beef. (He would have liked to believe his own disguises more convincing. Well, it had been proved that they were.)

Leaving his ravenous horse to her feed he heard the iron door pushed farther open on grudging hinges. Against a sky paling into darkness it could only have been Prowse's bulk advancing unsteadily into the sweet must of the shed's enveloping gloom.

'What is it, Don? What've I done wrong this time?'

The form came shambling on. 'Wrong?' A familiar blast of whiskied breath was introduced into the gentler scents of the stable and the dusty draught from chaff set in motion by the huntress cat.

'Yes. I'd like to know. I never seem to do the right thing by you.' It wasn't quite honest.

'Nothing wrong, I suppose – Eddie – in being true to yerself.'

Prowse's bulk had reached the point where they were bumping against each other in the darkness.

Eddie realized that, up against this laborious drunk, he was simulating drunkenness.

'And what's myself?' he dared.

There was a pause, and the sounds of overheated, crackling iron and slithering chaff.

Till Prowse was prepared to come out with it. 'I reckon I recognized you, Eddie, the day you jumped in – into the river – and started flashing yer tail at us. I reckon I recognized a fuckun queen.'

All the while Don Prowse was pushing his bulk up against Eddie Twyborn's more slender offering.

'See?'

'If that's what you saw . . .' Eddie knew that his voice, like his body, was trembling.

Prowse suddenly grew enraged. He, too, had started trembling in a massive way, smelling of sodden red hair almost stronger than the whiskey breath, shouting, pushing his opponent around and about with chest and thighs, spinning him face down in the chaff.

'A queen! A queen! A fuckun queen!' Sobbing as though it was his wife Kath walking out on him.

Prowse was tearing at all that had ever offended him in life, at the same time exposing all that he had never confessed, unless in the snapshot album.

His victim's face was buried always deeper, breathless, in the loose chaff as Don Prowse entered the past through the present.

Eddie Twyborn was breathing chaff, sobbing back, not for the indignity to which he was being subjected, but finally for his acceptance of it.

When Prowse had had his way they lay coupled, breathing in some kind of harmony.

Till the male animal withdrew, muttering what could have been, 'You asked for it – you fuckun asked . . .'

And got himself out of the shed.

The victim lay awhile, wholly exhausted by the switch to this other role. Then stood up, chaff trickling down skin wherever it did not stick inside rucked-up shirt and torn pants — the disguise which didn't disguise.

Complete darkness had fallen outside, except where Peggy Tyrrell's sibyl, in the illuminated window across the yard, was rising through the steam from the suet pudding she was easing out of its cloth. She glanced up once into the outer darkness, her sibyl's eyes contracting, before resuming the ritual of her suet pud.

In the days which followed, they went about doing what had to be done. They used only the words required. They depended on the objects surrounding them, grateful for the furniture of daily life.

The manager announced with the solemnity of an alderman, 'We can expect Mr Lushington back in the near future.' Reduced by several tones, his voice sounded furred up.

After giving morning orders to Jim, Denny, and the jackeroo, he added importantly, 'Get on with it then. I've got to go up to the house to do some accounting in Mr Lushington's office.'

Mr Prowse shaved regularly now. The texture of the burnished skin fascinated Eddie Twyborn.

Don would lower his eyes on finding himself scrutinized.

His clothes were more formal. He was, in fact, the manager, who almost never mucked in as he had on the day when the men were crutching.

The jackeroo became more formal too, asking at tea for information on cross-breeding, wool sales, and crops.

Mrs Tyrrell gravely served the pudding, and sat afterwards, hands folded in her apron, like Our Lady of Stains.

Marcia alone had no part in the play which was being enacted. Though he looked for her from a distance, Eddie failed to catch sight of the black Packard, the bay gelding or the solitary figure hitting a golf ball on the mini-course below the house.

One night after the manager had gone up to do some more accounting, he thought he heard her voice, not that which issued from the thick, thyroidal throat of the sensual woman who had dragged him into her bed, but of the tentative girl who had ridden with him the day they had met by accident in a far paddock.

He went out preparing to investigate.

For no good reason beyond infallible instinct Mrs Tyrrell called,

'Mrs Lushington, Mrs Edmonds says, is suffering from a heavy cold.'

And he called back, 'I hope Mrs Edmonds hasn't brought it down with her. It wouldn't be fair if you were laid up so soon after your ma's visit.'

Herself fairly mature, Peggy had an ancient mother, Ma Corkill, who had been out to 'Bogong' recently to investigate her daughter's situation.

Mrs Corkill, the she-ancient of she-ancients, did not aspire to hats as did her daughter, but wore her hair in the semblance of a hat, a creation such as insects weave out of leaves and twigs, and dead grass, its structure containing a suppressed hum, which erupts in a sizzle of red-hot needles if anyone is unwise enough to poke it. (Neither mother nor daughter approved of hair-washing: 'it don't do nothun for yer health, dear;' and in fact, as Peggy Tyrrell confessed, neither had ever washed hers.)

Unlike her daughter, who was still in possession of the fangs to which she hitched her Sunday teeth, the old lady was completely toothless. Her vocabulary was sparse but serviceable, particularly after she had taken a dose from a medicine bottle she carried in an apron pocket, or seated with Peggy on the double dunny, or holding a post-mortem in the daughter's bed after the lamp had been blown out. As the smell of extinguished wick ascended, the women's voices would entwine in a duet embellished by roulades and trills worthy of a more rococo age.

Ma Corkill's visit to 'Bogong' had its climax in her flinging a kettle of boiling water at her daughter halfway through the third day. She was collected by a Tyrrell grandson, almost as mature as his mother it seemed, as he sat in his convulsive Ford, under the brim of a green-grey Sewell felt, the neckband of his shirt gathered together by a glass ruby in a brass claw.

'What can yer do,' Mrs Tyrrell asked, 'if it's yer own mother?'

Nobody had the answer to that; least of all Eddie Twyborn, who had never found the answer to himself.

Least of all on his way up the hill to face Marcia's displeasure for his neglect and his avoidance of her friends the Golsons, or perhaps on overcoming that displeasure, to prove to himself that she was still his mistress. It was most important that he should decide how much of his life was serious and how much farce.

Though late enough, there were signs of life, sounds of

conversation. No car parked in the drive. Marcia might have persuaded a servant to stay behind and receive her confidences, or perhaps, he began to fear, Prowse had come up for some of that office work by which he boosted his self-importance.

Eddie passed the office window. In a deserted room a single light bulb under a white porcelain shade was engaged in a battering match with walls enamelled an electric blue.

The voices were coming from that vast and hideous mock-Tudor library. The windows and glass doors had been thrown open to summer. He halted in the darkness on reaching the narrow carpet of light laid across the tiles from doorway to garden.

'You're all very well when you need a bloke,' Prowse was grumbling.

Marcia laughed what was recognizably a bored laugh. 'We might as well admit there's a practical side to every human relationship.'

'But no one's ever used me as you have.'

'I'd have thought I was useful to you – at a certain stage – when your wife couldn't stand any more.'

'Yes, but I thought you had some feeling for me.'

'Yes, I did have. But feeling doesn't always last. Like tastes. When I was a little girl I couldn't eat too much Yorkshire pudding. Then, suddenly, I couldn't touch another mouthful.'

'But you called one of the kids after Prowse.'

'Oh yes, I know. That was Greg. He was sorry for you. He wanted to do you a kindness, Don.'

'And what did you do for Greg? The kid was ours, wasn't he?'

'Who knows? Oh God, don't let's start going over it again!'

She had begun walking about. There was the sound of struck matches, then the smell of the Abdulla cigarette which Marcia smoked.

'Lost yer taste for Yorkshire pud, but you might develop it again. Like you've started coming at the other.'

There was half a sigh, half a snort from Marcia. 'If you must put it that way . . .'

'You were the one that put it.'

Marcia appeared in the doorway, the necklaces of Venus eating into her heavy throat, the smoke blown from her nostrils indicative of extreme irritation.

Eddie saw that he hated Marcia.

'Don't let's argue!' she insisted from beside the drooping, gold-tipped cigarette.

'Then let's have it out the other way. That's what you'd call practical, isn't it?'

'How?' She raised her head imperiously.

'You know I do it good.'

She stood looking out into the dark. 'You make it sound so gross.'

He had come up behind; the thick orange forearms appeared round her waist. 'That's what you're all about, Marcia. What you want. And what we do so well together.'

'Oh,' she whimpered, 'there's more than that!'

'Funny you only recently found out.'

'Lives change.'

'Funny it happened after Twyborn came. You're not on with Eddie, are you, Marce?'

'What a thing to imagine!' She had broken free and turned back into the enormous room. 'We have a fine relationship – Eddie and I. His friendship is something I value immensely. He gives me so much more than any of the other boring clods in the district.'

'Me included.'

'Oh, *darling*, I didn't mean to be rude! You're someone I value differently. You're part of our lives. Greg and I do appreciate you, Don.'

'Useful – practical – profitable. Like a ram or a stud bull.'

At this point there took place a considerable trampling of the moth-eaten Afghan carpet as she tried to sidestep his accusations and her stud followed her round the room.

'This Eddie Twyborn you have the fine relationship with – you don't know what you've got on yer hands. Well, I'll tell yer. He's nothun more than a bloody queen.'

There was rather a long pause. 'I haven't any evidence of it,' Marcia Lushington replied as last. 'Have you?'

'I can put two and two together.' He must still have been pounding about; the windows were rattling. 'If there's anything I can't stand it's a queen.'

'Because he's sensitive,' she said, 'you draw wrong conclusions.'

'So sensitive he let you down. And now you want the bull again.'

Silence was spreading in widening circles through the mock-

Tudor library. The listener visualized numbers of the *Bystander* and *Tatler* in disarray on occasional tables, and the goose-fleshed covers of Marcia's subscribed novels from Dymocks' and Angus and Robertson. He saw the great fireplace with logs awaiting next winter, and in an ashtray the butt of a gold-tipped Abdulla, its thread of incense uniting with the languor of summer.

Then someone or other was groaning, churning up the heavy silence, a mouth rejecting a mouth from its depths, a body dragging itself away from another equally elastic.

She said, 'You're right – up to a point,' and laughed one of her thicker laughs.

Which must have been devoured instantly.

When she came up for breath she said, 'All right, Don – we do understand each other. But you'll never understand Eddie Twyborn.'

If Prowse didn't reply, it was because she was leading him out of the room, into a distance she and Eddie had explored together on freezing Monaro nights, now this steamier, more bestial version of what the novice had tried to see as a pilgrimage.

Eddie hated Marcia Lushington more than he hated Don Prowse. He might have progressed along the wall through outer darkness to overhear more, if his humiliation hadn't already developed to its utmost: the humiliation of jealousy, more of Marcia than Don.

He returned to a dark cottage where Peggy Tyrrell seemed to be dreaming a sibyl's dreams.

After taking off his clothes, he lay down on his narrow stretcher and began automatically masturbating.

The following day was a Saturday, and Prowse had driven into town, to pubs and other less salubrious pastures, taking with him Mrs Tyrrell, who was looking forward to a scene with her mother and a funeral scheduled for the afternoon.

Towards four o'clock, after shaving and bathing, Eddie went up the hill to the house. He found Marcia alone on the veranda, reclining on an old bleached cane chaise. On her outstretched thighs, one of her library books, which more than likely she hadn't been reading, was lying spine upward. She was dressed in a worn grey flannel skirt and a blouse unbuttoned to the opulent cleavage, sleeves turned back to expose the elbows and the blue veins on the reverse side. Her arms were hanging listlessly for the brief but intense Monaro heat. Her face expressed a disenchantment, whether real or cultivated, radiating from a nose made thicker, soggier, by the heavy cold Mrs Tyrrell had reported.

'Can I be dreaming?' she said at last, cutting into the remark with a grudging smile, and coughing thickly to enlist her cold.

'No,' he said, 'I think we're real enough,' and laughed.

He sat down on an upright chair, another member of the suite in dilapidated, bleached cane.

Whereas he had planned to be cruel, biting, dramatic, he felt sympathetic towards her: it must have been those red, swollen eyelids, or else his bath had cooled him off. His clothes sat so lightly on him, he might in other circumstances have felt the urge to take them off, to stretch alongside her, no longer a lover, but some lean and ingratiating breed of hairless dog, licking her wrists, expecting an exchange of caresses.

'Why did you treat me like that? And as far as I can see, all because of the poor Golsons. Now, why?' She hectored mildly.

'I'm not prepared to go into that.' He sounded tense; his light mood was leaving him.

'You've made me very unhappy,' she told him, 'Eddie, dearest – for no good reason that I can imagine. When I most need your – company – your confidence, you treat me as though I'm in some way diseased.'

'They tell me Greg is expected back at any moment. That will be fine for you, Marcia.'

She almost suppressed a frown. 'Dear old Greg! Not everyone appreciates him, but I think, Eddie, you do – you and your father.'

There was a silence in which the cane furniture showed signs of disintegrating.

Marcia said, 'I must go and make us some tea.'

'Don't bother.'

'But it's what we do at four o'clock. Don't expect a lot of food, though. Mrs Quimby's mumping over something or other, probably preparing to give notice.'

The fact that he, too, was more than probably going to leave made him melancholy, sitting on the Lushingtons' veranda with the river flat spread before him, the brown river meandering through bleached tussock, the sensuous forms of naked hills on either side: a landscape which had engaged his feelings in a brief and unlikely love affair he was about to end.

If all love affairs are not, perhaps, unlikely. Only the meat of marriage convinces, if you are made for it, and open to conviction.

A hornet was somewhere ceaselessly working on its citadel, and under the eaves hung a swallow's nest temporarily abandoned by its tenant, in each case evidence of the continuity which convinces animals better than it does human beings, unless they are human vegetables.

Marcia returned carrying a tray as though it were the sort of act she wasn't used to performing. Her shoulders drooped, her bare arms looked defenceless, even pathetic. Perhaps she expected him, as a lover, or simply as a man, to jump up and help her with the tray.

But he didn't: he was too distant, and at the same time too absorbed in everything happening around him, the fidgeting sound of the hornet, on the faded plain the brown river, static now, swift in memory, over the veranda tiles Marcia's shuffle in a pair of scuffed, once elegant, crocodile shoes.

She arranged the tray on a table, yet another member of the weathered cane family.

A generous wedge was missing from the jam sandwich, its pink icing buttoned down and slightly stained by a wreath of crystallized violets. Though a cake for a country occasion, the recalcitrant Mrs Quimby had failed to pipe a message on it.

Marcia let off a misplaced giggle. 'There we are, darling!' She would have liked to appear girlish, but suspected at once that he would not allow her.

He sat, chin lowered, staring ahead. He saw himself, alas, as a farouche schoolboy refusing to let Mum have him on. Poor Marce didn't know about it, while he had the unfair advantage, at any rate since last night, of knowing almost everything.

She poured the tea, of a delicacy which must have been wasted on the district, and which they would have discussed afterwards: that hogwash of Marcia Lushington's.

Along with the barbarians, Eddie was not appreciative enough. The pink festive cake was stale. The cruel scene he had rehearsed would have to be enacted eventually.

'There you are,' she said very humbly as she tried a fragment of the cake, 'I warned you.'

'But did you?' His cup slithered like stone on the saucer, his chair grated on the tiled veranda.

While Marcia Lushington sat holding her teacup in both hands, to prevent a trembling from showing, and to let the steam take the blame for her watering eyes.

She protested, 'I don't understand. I thought you loved me.'

In his case, it was the crumbs of the stale cake which were trembling; he brushed them off with a disapproving, and as he saw it, suddenly old-maidish hand.

'I was fond of you,' he admitted; and then not too honestly, 'because affection was what I thought you wanted;' less honest still, 'I couldn't love you for respecting poor old Greg.'

She sat up jerkily on the edge of the grating chaise.

'There you've caught me out, Eddie. You've caught us both. Because,' and now it was her turn to look out along the bleached plain, 'I find I'm pregnant.'

The hornet was worrying the silence worse than ever, a fiery copper wire piercing but never aborting a situation the enormity of which could only be human.

Eddie began to laugh. It made Marcia look more becolded.

'However cynical you may like to be thought, I'm glad the child will be yours: Greg is fond of you,' she said, 'and it may be the son he and I have failed to get.'

'It might be another failure – like the one you had with Prowse.'

He thought the silence would never end: a balloon swelling and swelling, but never bursting, in spite of the hornet's efforts, in the late light of a summer afternoon.

When Marcia said, 'I don't know what you mean.'

'I was going by the names on the graves – as well as more positive evidence.'

She leaned forward, her chin broader for being propped on the heel of a hand. 'It could be Greg's – just – from before he went away. But you were what I wanted.'

'Or Prowse?'

She ignored it. He got up soon after. She was still staring at the breached cake, its yellow more unnatural, its pink more lurid in the evening light.

'I think you're cruel by nature,' she said.

He didn't answer: he was arranging his belt, because his manly shirt was coming out.

'Now I believe you're what I was told you are.'

He didn't bother to expose any of them worse than they were already exposed.

The landscape which might have healed was withdrawing into dusk; it was the landscape he had loved, peopled with those the magic-lantern projects without their knowing, like Greg Lushington the Crypto-poet, Mr Justice Twyborn the Bumbling Father, Peggy Tyrrell of the Football Team. Even, perhaps, Don Prowse the Brute Male.

Only Marcia was excluded, looking out through her becolded mask at Eadie's son. No one but Eadie, another woman, could have dealt her this cruel blow. Eadie was the judge, and women have more of justice in them.

Eddie blubbered to himself going down the hill, not for Marcia, but Angelos, legs sticking out straight and stiff on a maid's bed in that *pension* before the frontier. Men are frailer than women. Don Prowse, for all his meaty male authority, was not much more than a ping-pong ball knocked back and forth in a sinewy female set. Most sinewy of all, an aggressive anima walled up inside her tower of flesh.

Till accused by the child in Marcia's womb, Eddie Twyborn cut short the ping-pong game, returning to his actual surroundings and candidacy for fatherhood.

He awoke to hear the car manoeuvred under cover, the crackle of paper as parcels were undone in the kitchen, a man's curse when a wing was grazed on a corner of corrugated iron, a woman's sighs and invocations as the depths of her body, and even more, her spiritual tatters, caused her pain.

The walls of his normally putty-coloured room were spattered with light from the manoeuvred car, translucent patches, with iridescent threads superimposed as he rubbed his eyeballs to rid them of an itch and hurry them into awareness of what was happening. He reached down to cover up his nakedness, but fell back upon the stretcher where he had been dozing: it was too hot, it was too hot. He couldn't bother. The blanket too hairy. Since coming to 'Bogong' he had dispensed with sheets, out of masochism or delusions of masculinity.

The petals of light flowering on the walls were suddenly wiped out by darkness.

Silence was broken by the creaking of a fly-proof door, a

257

renewed outburst of female sighs, male boots hurled against the wall of a fragile weatherboard house.

Any frail male could only cower and try to assemble an acceptable identity, any female, because tougher, more fibrous, consolidate her position inside the cloak of darkness.

Though Peggy did creep along the passage to hiss, 'I oughter warn yer, love, 'e's 'ad a fair few. Don't let yerself get drawn in. 'E's cantankerous ternight.'

After Prowse had martyrized the skirting-board with his boots, and let out a round fart or two, and the housekeeper had shut her door, silence again descended where the rats hadn't taken over, the rabbits and the hawthorns — night in fact, but not yet dreams.

'Eddie?'

It was Don Prowse in the doorway: a heavy body bungling, stomping, chafing, a voice reaching out after what it hoped might be conciliation. If the thought hadn't been so grotesque, Prowse was less cantankerous than what he probably considered seductive.

'Ed.' No query, it was pure statement in search of a solid presence.

The body continued advancing, stubbing its toes here and there, groaning, gasping. A rite of sorts had started taking place in the shuddering dark of this dry-rotted room.

'. . . you got me worried, boy. I never did anything like it before. Don't know what came over me. I been thinkin' about it — what you must think . . .'

The penitent must have had a fair idea of his bearings, either from instinct or from a glimmer of light the hawthorns allowed through their locked branches, for he reached a point where he crashed on the stretcher alongside its occupant.

Prowse was crying, expostulating, and apparently stark naked. Eddie's own fastidious nakedness became aware of prickling hair, tingling with moisture like a rain forest, at the same time the smell exuded by sodden human fur. He was surrounded by, almost dunked in, these practically liquid exhalations.

What was both alarming and gratifying, he knew that he was being won over, not by the orange brute so much as poor old Prowse of the snapshots with meticulous white-ink captions, the husband of Kath, and by the spirit of Angelos Vatatzes, whose cold eyelids and rigid feet still haunted memory.

It was too much for Eddie Twyborn to endure. He was rocking

this hairy body in his arms, to envelop suffering in some semblance of love, to resuscitate two human beings from drowning.

Prowse managed to extricate himself. He rolled over.

'Go on,' he moaned, 'Ed!' and bit the pillow.

Eddie Twyborn's feminine compassion which had moved him to tenderness for a pitiable man was shocked into what was less lust than a desire for male revenge. He plunged deep into this passive yet quaking carcase offered up as a sacrifice. He bit into the damp nape of a taut neck. Hair sprouting from the shoulders, he twisted by merciless handfuls as he dragged his body back and forth, lacerated by his own vengeance.

Prowse was crying, 'Oh God! Oh Christ!' before a final whimper which was also his ravisher's sigh.

They fell apart finally.

Eddie said, 'Go on, Don. That's what it's about, that's what you wanted.'

He couldn't deny it, except, 'I hope you won't hold it against me, Eddie.'

'Go on, get out!'

Prowse heaved, protested, curled himself into the shape of a prawn against a form which, having vindicated itself, refused to respond. Prowse's sighs of entreaty, his redundancies of love, were surprisingly like Marcia's.

'If that's what you say — and feel.'

'All I want to say is, I'll catch the train tomorrow evening at Fossickers, and would like you to run me over, Don. Otherwise, if you'd rather, I'll hire a car from town.'

After a short whimpering silence, 'If that's what you've decided, I'll run yer there.'

A damp paw put out on a renewed voyage of exploration. Eddie Twyborn rejected it, in spite of the scabs on the obverse side, the dry cracks, and the freckles he remembered.

'Go on, Don — get!' It sounded unconvincingly male.

The manager heaved, the stretcher creaked. Prowse was diving in the direction of the doorway. He must have bumped his head or some other part of his anatomy on something more solid than darkness.

He cried out, 'Oh Jesus! Oh fuck!' before slewing round the corner into the passage, slithering several yards on the lino, and falling into his own room.

*

Mrs Tyrrell was tearful. 'I dunno wot's took you, Eddie. I thought you was more dependable. Most men aren't dependable. Rowley weren't — though 'e was me husband, an' dead since. The boys aren't — they got their wives. Only the girls. Well, that's 'ow it is. I thought you was different — like me daughters, but different.'

Eddie was at first embarrassed, then moved to feel her weather-cured face, together with a smear of tears, ground against his cheek. At the same time he became enveloped in the bobbled shawl, in whiffs of kero, eaudy Cologne, and the overall stench of mutton fat.

A brown-paper parcel was thrust at him. 'A few bloody sandwiches fer the journey. There's mustard in 'em ter make 'em more tasty.'

In the corrugated shed the manager was revving up the Ford, the afternoon light as remorseless as the fossicking hens.

Eddie Twyborn could only say, 'We'll write, Peggy,' regretting that it sounded so upper class.

' 'Oo'll write? You, if I'm lucky. But 'oo's gunner read it to me? 'Oo that I can trust — at "Bogong" — or anywheres — fer that matter?'

He got himself out, together with the greasy parcel, the suitcase and valise with which he had arrived, lighter for his boots and work clothes which he was leaving for Denny. The too ostentatious cabin trunk was already strapped to the rack.

The manager drove doggedly, his heavy hands bumped by the wheel. Eddie dared not look at the hands, let alone the face, which smelled overpoweringly of shaving soap.

In a paddock through which they were passing, sulphur-crested cockatoos were screeching as they tore down stooks of oats.

'Bloody cockies! You can't win,' Prowse mumbled; he sounded fairly acceptant for the moment.

'Greg'll be back,' he announced farther on, as though pleased to think his responsibility for marauding cockatoos, and anything else, might be ended by the owner's return. 'Nothing lasts for ever, eh?'

He glanced sideways, no doubt hoping for his passenger to corroborate, or even suggest that past events are expungeable if you put your will to it.

Eddie did not return the glance for fear of finding a mirror to his own thoughts. Instead, he glanced down and encountered the wristwatch. A utilitarian affair, sitting rather high on the hairy wrist, the watch was attached to a sweat-eaten strap, narrow to the point of daintiness. He had barely noticed this watch before. Now it wrung him. Had he been a child instead of this pseudo-man-cum-crypto-woman, he might have put out a finger and touched it, to the consolation of both of them.

In the light of shared desire, it was some consolation to himself to remember a moment in which he had embraced, not so much a lustful male, as a human being exposed in its frailty and tenderness.

This, of course, was no consolation to Don Prowse. Who knew. But only the half of it.

They drove bumping through the paddocks, and as on arrival, so on departure, brumby horses wheeled and approached, eyeing them through wild forelocks, sheep milled and halted and stamped, wooden masks conveying that expression of disbelief for the same two intruders, who had got to know each other in the meantime, so much better, or so much worse.

They drove, and arrived at Fossickers Flat.

Prowse looked at the wristwatch and grumbled, 'Don't know why you got us here so early.'

And Eddie replied, 'I arrive everywhere too early, or too late. It's my worst vice.' He laughed, but Prowse's expression could have been taken for thoughtful.

After unloading the luggage they stood about together on the siding.

'Look, Don, you don't have to hang about.'

But Don did: mouthing, swallowing words to which the thick lips failed to give birth.

'Should 'uv rung to reserve a sleeper. But you caught me on the hop, Ed.'

'Probably no sleepers left. Not at the last moment. Anyhow, I don't expect I'll sleep.'

Was it too perilous an admission? They crunched up and down the siding, beneath the painted sign FOSSICKERS FLAT. A rudimentary shelter might have offered asylum to a parcel, never to escaping prisoners or queered lovers. In the scrub across the track, the zither notes of small birds seemed to be conveying bird facts which evaded expression in human terms.

'We'll all miss you, Eddie.'

'Oh, go on, Don! Don't be a cunt – for God's sake go!'

GO!

Legs apart, shoulders hunched, the bare hills behind him, the man looked every bit a puzzled, panting, red ox.

But as time ticked away on the crude wristwatch, it was Eddie Twyborn awaiting the pole-axe.

'All right, Ed. All *right*!' Again the manager, Mr Prowse had matters in hand. 'You got yer bags. You'll get yer ticket on the train. I'll shove off.'

As he did.

Eddie turned his back on the diminishing trail of dust, and the Mail arrived eventually, the guard descending to jolly the ascending passenger.

'Not offn we get one at Fossickers, sir.'

After the two had heaved up the baggage, he flagged the engine.

Eddie Twyborn sat in the corner of his empty compartment and was rushed away, past the skeleton trees, the hill with its cairn of lichened rocks, faces hungry for events outside a shack at a level crossing. A bronzed, exhausted, country evening gave way to night, which had the smell of soot.

The brown-paper parcel had fallen off the seat on to the floor. He ought to pick it up.

He was too passive, it seemed. Jolted onward, through Bungendore and the rest, he closed his eyes. But did not sleep. Sleep might always be denied him, except in the form of dreams, or nightmares.

Sydney
5 October 1929

Dear, dear Mrs Lushington,

It was so kind of you to write to me and send the snap of your little boy. I do feel for you, deeply – a claim which no doubt you'll interpret as hypocrisy, grief being such a personal matter we must bear on our own; others can sympathize while only superficially understanding.

I keep returning to the picture of this little boy so dear to you, and so cruelly taken when his life seemed assured. I believe he has the stamp of both of you, in equal parts. Not that I know either of you, *really* – Mr Lushington only on abysmal formal occasions when mere women are admitted to a gentleman's club; you even less, in spite of an unacceptable encounter best forgotten, and the time you appeared for Sunday luncheon in the dining room of the Hotel Australia, and scanned the menu, and blew smoke at us from under monkey fur, and left, for some reason, contemptuously. I am not criticizing, dear Mrs Lushington, what at that stage would have been my own attitude. I think I was only resentful of the behaviour of one I might have liked to know.

If I can claim to know your husband slightly, it is from those pompous functions in the men's club; better since you sent me your little boy's picture, for I went at once to Edward's snapshot album, and there came across those ridiculous touching glimpses of men at play while taking themselves seriously: drinking schooners of beer leaning on the bar of a country pub, smirking over the tennis net as they clumsily protect the girls who have been their partners, never so exposed as when posturing in thighboots and all that mackintoshery beside some mountain stream with the trout they have ravished from it. (I know I'd stand accused in any court, but don't think, Mrs Lushington, that I don't love my judge.)

If my impressions of your husband are inclined to fade, and my impression of yourself remains distinct, it is because that snap taken by my mind's eye as you and the Twyborns sat in the dining room of the Hotel Australia shortly after my son's return is as clear as the moment itself. That is how I see you and as I recognize you again in the snap you sent me – unmistakably your features – and those of Mr Lushington.

I believe I can detect in your letter hopes that we might meet and found a relationship on the sadness and disappointment we both know about. Let me assure you, Mrs Lushington, that much as I sympathize with you, and grieve for you *as far as one can*, it would be a vast mistake.

What I would like to convey to you is that losing a child in death is so much better than losing a grown – what shall I say? *reasoning* child, to life. As happened to me for the second time. And to my darling Edward, of course. Though I think men must – they can only feel it *less*, for not experiencing it in their depths – dragged bloody from their own entrails.

Oh I mustn't go on like this. You ask what news I have of Eddie. I can only answer NOTHING. As the first time, so the second. He is swallowed up. Whether in death or life, it is the same. We should not have aspired to possess a human being. Your memories, I think, are more cherishable because more tender. He did not know enough, mine knew too much of what there is to know.

Thank you, Marcia, for the letter, and the snap, and for sharing your despair, which I expect time will help us quench in the humdrum.

Eadie Twyborn

PS. Let me put on record that, much as I disapproved of the monkey fur, I would have loved to wear it, and envied the one who did.

PART III

With the exception of the cook, a floating member of the household, and usually young, lusty, insensitive, none of the occupants of Ninety-One any longer enjoyed the luxury of sleep. In Nanny's case it scarcely mattered: senility was her solace, so, at least, her former charges had decided for her. Maud and Kitty were the ones who suffered, but how much worse insomnia might have been without the deplorable trafficking opposite.

At first they had been prepared to pit their prudery, their virtue, against the goings-on at Eighty-Four. Kitty's virtue in her younger days hadn't been much more than a theory which members of her class professed in order to divert censure, and an admirable arrangement it was, till with age and reduced circumstances she suddenly found herself set cold in the aspic of fact. As far as anybody knew, Maud the elder, flat and plain from the beginning, had never had the chance to test her virtue, and nobody, not even Kitty, would have been indiscreet enough to probe. Now she was safe, as indeed was Kitty, though less willing to resign herself to safety. Only relatives reviving a sense of duty called on the two sisters, the Ladies Maud Bellasis and Kitty Binns, for Kitty had acquired a dubious husband, at whose disappearance she had been brave or proud enough not to revert to the family name.

All this was ancient history, to which the ladies actually belonged while liking to see themselves as 'modern'. Even Maud was given to smearing a trace of lipstick over the cracks in pale, rather tremulous lips, while Kitty went the whole hog, and blossomed like a tuberous begonia. If she no longer enjoyed sleep, and teeth made eating a difficulty, she could toy with the thought of shocking. But whom? Most of the shockable were dead. Unless, under their lipstick, Kitty and Maud themselves, who were intermittently shocked by what Kitty visualized, and the timorous Maud only dared suspect was going on at Eighty-Four.

As what was happening, however discreetly, in the house opposite became unmistakable, the sisters had considered protesting, going to the police, taking their Member a petition from a neighbourhood roused by disgust for overt immorality. But could the neighbourhood, Beckwith Street in particular, be roused? Colonel Bewlay might even be patronizing the house in question, his wife too short-sighted or too simple to know; the Creeses were too common, the Feverels too much abroad, the shopkeepers at the end of the street sufficiently business-minded to welcome the woman's advent — her drink orders alone.

So the noble sisters lapsed in their intention to resist corruption and parade their virtue, and the house opposite became good for a giggle over their own drinks. For Kitty had dived headlong into the cocktail age, while Maud sipped a nervous sherry on occasions when nephews and nieces remembered the old girls in Beckwith Street.

'We'll just have to be broadminded.'

'But do you *see* anything, Aunt Maud?' asked a tickled nephew.

'Oh no, we don't *see*. But we're inclined to hear in the small hours. Last night I definitely heard screams.'

'I didn't — but perhaps there were,' Kitty reluctantly admitted.

'Definitely,' Maud insisted, slopping her sherry.

'Poor girl!' It was Esmé Babington, who later entered an Anglican order.

'Well, I think it was a woman, but it might have been a man,' Maud considered.

'I hope a man,' Kitty sounded most vehement, 'a husband,' she added in the bass.

After an oblique fashion the sisters began shedding their opposition to the establishment across the street. Perhaps they were too old to resist, or so old that they derived a voluptuous pleasure in associating themselves with imagined rituals of a sexual nature.

Exonerated by senility, Nanny told her former charges, 'One of Mrs Trist's girls gave me a sweetie on my way back from the grocer's. It was lovely. Done up in gold. It was full of drink. Do you think I'm drunk?'

'No, darling. Only old. Though as we grow older, drink does have its way with us.'

'I think they're nice,' said Nanny, 'Mrs Trist's girls — and Mrs Trist.'

'Mrs Trist can be most charming — whatever else.'

'Yes, yes, charming — charming,' Maud echoed Kitty's verdict.

'That doesn't mean we must *condone*,' warned Kitty, 'in any sense, what most people would consider reprehensible.'

But condone they did: Kitty of the floral chiffons and tuberous begonia mouth, Maud's tremulous, paler lips, and lavender voile with its flickering white polka dot.

What persuaded the ladies to condone was, more than anything, Gravenor's patronage. Not that they saw much of their favourite nephew. Taken up as he was by living, they would not have expected to. But he sent them a case of champagne at Christmas and on their birthdays, and occasionally took them for a drive. More than this they would not have expected of Roderick: he was too busy shooting birds, landing salmon, yachting, motoring, escaping from the toils of mothers who wished him to marry their daughters, and fluctuating more generally between watering places, the Stock Exchange, and the House of Lords. From time to time, if they were lucky enough, they caught sight of their favourite, if elusive nephew arriving at or leaving the house which played the most considerable part in their withering, insomniac lives.

She appeared, usually at unorthodox hours, speeding her guests (exclusively male), her bracelets refracting the street lighting. More often than not she would re-appear at dawn, the jewels shed, her garments soberly, almost anonymously, reflective. If on her return by more blatant light the Bellasis girls were looking out from their separate bedrooms, as they mostly were, she took to waving a long arm, and smiling out of a chalky face, for she had shed her make-up along with the jewels.

What she could be doing at that hour they often discussed: not banking the takings, it was far too early; walking for her health more likely, or listening to the birds, heavenly even in a post-War London.

Like London itself, Maud and Kitty in their reduced circumstances were distinctly post-War, without realizing to what extent they were also pre-. Perhaps Mrs Trist realized, looking as she did like a Norn, in her long sweeping colourless garments of the false dawn, as opposed to the hectic colours and lamplit jewels of earlier.

Mrs *Eadith* Trist.

It was Evadne who came up with what one could hardly refer to as the woman's 'Christian' name, together with the unsolicited detail that you spelt it with an 'a'. Evadne was one of the long line of incompetent cooks death duties had forced on them: Evadne

269

the most incompetent of all, because so knowledgeable, a crypto-novelist the sisters suspected from her habit of shutting herself in her bedroom and rattling away on a typewriter while potatoes melted and veal scallops shrank to slivers of wood.

The Bellasis girls still had not broken down enough of their inbuilt discretion to ask the cook what she was up to on the typewriter, when the wretch left, perhaps having got what she wanted. But there was an occasion shortly before, when the sisters had caught sight of their cook coming out of the house opposite, and Kitty could not resist asking, while Maud stood breathing over her shoulder, 'What was it like inside, Evadne?' And Evadne had replied, 'Lush!' her rather goitrous eyes shining, the moist lips in natural puce hanging open in what was halfway between a smile and the savouring of an experience.

The sisters were too mortified. In discussing with Maud their cook's expression, Kitty described it as 'obscene'. They were relieved when she left and they could settle down in peace to poaching their own eggs and burning their omelettes before the next incompetent arrived. While thanks to Evadne, their imagination flowered more luxuriantly, in marble halls where odalisques reclined on satin cushions in gold and rose, and gentlemen with familiar faces, cousins and nephews, their favourite Gravenor, even their father the late duke, unbuttoned their formal black.

It was preposterous, monstrous, but delicious, neither Maud nor Kitty would have confessed.

Instead they settled down to the humdrum of living, hardly life, in which they no longer had a part, except as extras stationed at a window, waiting for the real actors to appear. In the absence of these there was the passage of clouds above narrow red houses, and earthbound plane-trees exchanging dead hands for live members in clapping green.

Whatever the climatic or seasonal diversions, the sisters continued to observe the activities at Eighty-Four, perhaps a little less avidly for coping with Nanny's incontinence, a leaking roof, tuck-pointing which needed renewing, and drains which nobody would come to unblock. Sometimes after midnight each sister would admit that she was ageing, but only to herself, as she counted the ticking of a secret — the word they had been brought up not to mention — turning and turning on the turgescence of a sour stomach.

Unlike Maud, who scarcely ever dreamed, or if she did, was spared remembering, Kitty once found herself taking part in a dream involving a clamorous plane-tree, its foliage replaced by the faces of girls, as flat and formal as those on a pack of cards, till fleshing out, jostling, leaping, tumbling, Kitty among them, strewing the roots of the tree with a turmoil of quaking buttocks and sticky bellies.

She preferred the hour when dawn takes over from darkness. Ada could be relied on to deal with any fag-ends of trade, and allow her to indulge her passion for strolling unnoticed through streets to which the colours were returning, the life beginning to trickle back. Her route was almost always the same, down Beckwith Street to the river, along the Embankment, and over the bridge to Battersea. Best of all, she loved her stroll through the deserted park (thanks to the keys which patronage had provided her with). Hair damp, a naked face somewhat haggard in a light turning from oyster to mauve.

Mauve was her colour when in full panoply. While following a timeless fashion, she dressed with extravagant thought. Strangers stared, barbarians commented aloud, and small boys hooted at her in the street, but those who knew her, patrons and those she patronized, ended by accepting with sentimental affection the more baroque aspects of her self-indulgence: the encrustations of amethysts and diamonds, the swanning plumes, her make-up poetic as opposed to fashionable or naturalistic.

But at the hour between the false dawn and the real, the moment when past and future converge, she was as much herself as a human being can afford to be: lips stripped, though not without a vestige of enamel in the deeper of the vertical clefts; in the shadows created by a too pronounced jawbone traces of the mauve powder in which she veiled herself at other times. For the more normal perspectives of life she could not lay it on too thick: on high occasions she went so far as to stick a *grain de beauté* on her left cheekbone, a punctuation mark in the novelette she enjoyed living as much as the one Evadne Schumacher, the cook-novelist at the house across the street, was obsessed to write. Perhaps it was Evadne who had conceived the additional conceit of the violet cachou Eadith took to chewing when got up in her purple drag.

She came to terms with reality between the two dawns in the deserted park. Somewhere between the fragrant scent of fresh cowpats and the reek of human excrement. Between cold roses, their perfume still to be aroused by sunlight, and the great blast of overheated scrub. The damp hem of her unfashionable dress dragged behind her as she left the park and crossed the other bridge.

In Beckwith Street she might wave an arm in a last romantic gesture at the scarified faces of the noble ladies at Ninety-One before disappearing through the red-brick façade of Eighty-Four, the house she owned thanks to her patron, into the atmosphere of spent cigarettes, stale cigar, dried semen (and again, human shit).

Girls were grumbling, moaning, snoring, while a last client knotted his tie and prepared to face respectability. If he were among those she favoured, she might fry him a dish of bacon and eggs to speed him on his way. At that hour the smell of frying bacon came as nostalgic as lost youth. So Mrs Trist considered, in her dawn dishabille, in what some people referred to as her whore-house.

She had started in a small way, almost without realizing, while healing her own wounds in the maisonette in Hendrey Street. She was too disgusted with herself, and human beings in general, ever to want to dabble in sex again, let alone aspire to that great ambivalence, love. She could only contemplate it as an abstraction, an algebra. She was very lonely; for a time her only friends were trades-people and servants, who offered her a comforting reality.

She had a job with a fashionable West End florist. They respected her, though she provided them, she understood, with the kind of cynical joke the English, or anyway sophisticated Londoners, enjoy. She was also something of a mystery, which they didn't enquire into because of her efficiency, and in her peculiar way, the woman had a distinction which warned them off. Customers depended on Mrs Trist for advice, and ignoring her somewhat bizarre appearance, recognized her taste. Even the more sophisticated and cynical respond to the pressure of a strong hand.

Of the other assistants, Annabel might have appealed more, Eadith thought, but they could not take her seriously: she was too pretty, too scatty, too much the professional amateur. She had abandoned the solid architecture of her noble origins, running out hatless into the labyrinth of lapsed values. Inside the labyrinth, of course, she was not bereft of her own kind: they met and lost one another in the search, playing at hide-and-seek in Harrods, falling drunk in gutters, shooting one another in some amusing mews, developing abscesses from jabbing themselves too often through their stockings. No, it was not the Honourable Annabel that her own kind, far less the rigid, hatted ranks from which she had defected, felt they were able to rely on; it was the rather odd Mrs Trist, of the pronounced jawline, as she appeared above the artificially bedewed banks of lilacs and lilies, and exquisitely unnatural long-stemmed rosebuds, her searching, bedazzling eyes the climax of the mystery which so intrigued those she impressed. No one, finally, would have cared to investigate her peculiarities or origins for fear of dispelling a myth they wished to cultivate. (Not that some didn't indulge in a tentative stab over the brown-bread ices at Gribble's.)

Annabel confided in her. They became friends. It was a case of *faute de mieux* on either side. Mrs Trist enjoyed the girl's wide-eyed, loose-mouthed prettiness, her clear, tea-rose skin, the whole effect belonging to those banks of artificial-real flowers at the florist where they were both employed. Annabel was drawn to the older woman's composure, her strength, the severe line of the pronounced jaw.

On one occasion Annabel confessed over the martini Eadith had just mixed, 'If there were anything of the Lesbian in me – which there isn't, quite definitely – I expect I'd want to sleep with you.'

Eadith said, though perhaps with a shade less conviction, she thought there was nothing of the Lesbian lurking in herself.

'My trouble is,' Annabel gulped almost the whole of her martini, 'I need men – a constant supply – and how to get it I don't know – short of going on the streets – and that's so sordid, isn't it? You might find yourself accosting your relations on a dark night.'

Eadith suggested, 'Couldn't you handpick a few by daylight and book them for later?'

That too, Annabel thought, kicking at the toe of one of Eadith's shoes, might bring complications with it. Considering where she lived. Unless she took a room, which would be an expense – unless she charged.

'And then, Eadith, shouldn't I be a whore, darling?'

'I expect you would.'

The two women laughed their way deeper into the situation which was preparing.

Eadith poured another martini.

Annabel thought, 'Perhaps you could let me a room, darling. We might go into business together.'

Eadith said, 'I don't think I want to become a whore. Once, perhaps. Not any longer.'

Annabel gulped a second martini. 'At least you could let me the room. Look after me, so to speak. I'll pay you a percentage. We'll make it a business arrangement.' Annabel threw back her head, exposed her slender throat, and laughed. 'That bloody florist's!' Her flower-mouth looked downright ugly.

'It won't be very pretty, you know.'

'Oh — yes!' Annabel stamped her glass on the table beside her with such force she broke the stem. 'I know, I know!'

That neither of them knew, Eadith Trist only realized after they were into the business venture.

Not that Annabel's handpicked men didn't pay a handsome dividend. While Eadith continued working for the florist, Annabel gave up her job: she was too tired, or too indolent; after the night's activities she had to sleep in.

Eadith had not yet begun to see herself as a bawd, because Annabel, her sole investment, was so independent. Sometimes after Eadith had brought in her grapefruit and coffee before leaving for the florist's, Annabel would cast off her sloth and start loading her mouth with lipstick. 'I must get myself some sex,' she announced, snapped her suspenders, and set out for Victoria Station.

After a time, Eadith decided to engage Bobbie, a healthy girl originally from Derbyshire who was now unhappy working in a post-office. Bobbie suffered from B.O. and had to have a few facts explained, but attracted certain men, some of them highly connected.

Annabel's connections were among the highest, those relations she had been afraid of accosting in the dark. (It was through Annabel that Eadith Trist met Gravenor, some degree of distant cousin, and discovered that she too was related, if not through blood, in spirit.)

The two girls Annabel and Bobbie found each other sympathetic. Eadith might come in from work and discover them seated in her armchairs chewing at apples. Annabel lusted after Cox's Orange. She would grow quite childish shaking her apple to hear whether the pips rattled, to be able to identify her favourite.

Annabel looked petulant and trivial, whereas Bobbie suggested a cottage apple, not the Cox's Orange Pippin, but a windfall of some larger variety. One of her breasts was blemished: it hung lower than the other, but did not detract from her charms, it seemed.

Brought back by Annabel, Gravenor preferred the blemished Bobbie.

He told Eadith, 'Sleeping with even a distant cousin is a little bit incestuous.'

Gravenor was a reddish, anyway a sandy, man. Mrs Trist decided in the beginning that she was not physically attracted to him; she mustn't be, and in any case, she still had in her nostrils the equivocal smell of orange fur.

This was how she became established as a bawd. There was soon a third girl called Mercedes, a Jewess from Macao, whom Lord Gravenor also fancied.

Not long after the advent of Mercedes, who lived out and came in at night to collect a client, there was a plague of mice in the flat, in the whole house as Eadith found out from the other tenants, with whom she had succeeded in remaining on amiable terms.

In her kitchen, little more than a cupboard, there were mice hanging from the shelves; she found their droppings scattered like the spillings from a packet of tea. One morning early she awoke to feel a dead mouse in her pyjamas. She had evidently crushed it by jamming her legs together in her sleep.

The time had come to send for the mouse-catcher.

He was a pallid, but stockily built young man, with a smell of socks. As he moved about the flat distributing his baits, little squares of bread soaked in some lethal liquid, she found herself following him for a reason she could not have made sound rational: she was fascinated by a whorl of hair just above the nape of his neck.

'Soon clean the little bastards up. Poor little buggers!' he kept repeating.

It pleased her that he did not modify his speech in her presence, and at the same time she wondered at it. What was it that made people have confidence in her when she had so little in herself?

Over a cup of tea, which he accepted in preference to coffee, he talked a bit about himself. He was a Geordie, from outside Newcastle. As a young lad he had gone to sea in the merchant navy, but nearly bloody well killed himself by falling down a hold.

They fell silent after the episode of near death. He sat staring at her, his legs stretched out in front of him, feet encased in heavy shoes. His confidences and their de-mousing operation had brought them close. His expression suggested he would not have been surprised, in fact he might have welcomed it, had she expected something of him.

She had stopped him going into Annabel's room. 'There's a friend in there. She works on a night shift. She's asleep. She wouldn't thank me if I let you wake her.'

'That's just where the little buggers might have their hideout — behind the skirting. If you'd let me lay me baits we'd nab the lot that much quicker.'

She wouldn't allow it. She even laid her hand on his arm to emphasize her disapproval.

As they sat over their tea he told her he was qualified to exterminate all kinds of pests: rats, cockroaches, bugs, beetles in the woodwork. He gave her his firm's card.

He said somewhat surprisingly, 'A lady like you won't have heard of crab lice. I caught the crabs when I was with me ship and we put in at Port Said.'

Taken unawares, she all but confessed she had caught crabs while in Paris on leave from the trenches.

'They're the tenacious buggers,' he said.

His pallid north-country skin was pricked out in black. She found herself becoming bored.

'Did your wife knit you those socks?' she faintly asked from behind her cigarette smoke.'

'No,' he said, 'me mum.'

He told her he was not married, but going steady with a decent girl.

They lapsed again, while his grey eyes continued staring at her, the smell drifting from the large stitch of the grey woollen socks.

'Are you foreign?' he asked.

So it was only that.

'I suppose you might call it foreign,' she said, and did not choose to elaborate.

It was curious that she should be more attracted to the mouse-catcher than to Annabel's relation Lord Gravenor — though she could have loved the latter, she believed, if she allowed herself to fall from the trapeze into the trampoline of love.

She did not intend to, however, while waiting for Gravenor's appearances, then flexing her nostrils, smiling too much, playing with her rings, lighting too many cigarettes.

He reminded her of the creeks running through her Australian childhood, clear water flowing over sand, pebbles, skeleton leaves, a rusty tin, the possible discovery of a fortune in zircons. Then again, he had rusty, chapped joints and knuckles, in spite of noble English lineage. There were times when he chilled her, others when, without touching, he chafed her into life, like sandpaper on callused skin. Unlike other men she had known, he always smelled delicious, usually of French Fern expensively bought in Jermyn Street.

There was a period when he stopped patronizing them. She could think of no explanation for it. Increasingly petulant and usually sloshed by lunchtime, Annabel had an idea her cousin was somewhere in the South of France.

Eadith, who had given up her job with the florist to manage her troupe, still only consisting of Annabel the defected Honourable, Bobbie the blemished cottage apple, and Mercedes the Macao Jewess, suddenly found her mouse-free flat impossibly full. She must expand, but how and where? To her mortification she was too passive to decide.

At this point Gravenor returned, his absence unexplained, nor was there any reason why he should account for his movements to Eadith Trist of all people.

He came to the flat one afternoon while the girls were out, either shopping in their desultory fashion for things they didn't need, or drooling at a cinema, in Annabel's case literally exploring the darkness at the same time.

Eadith told Gravenor, 'I must get out of here. I've had enough of this appalling huggermugger life in a flat.'

'I've always wondered why you do what you do.'

'As I wonder why a man like you should want to take advantage of what we offer.'

'Men are different.'

'Not so different as they'd like to think.'

They sat looking at each other.

Gravenor said, 'It's curious we've never slept together.'

'I expect, instinctively, we didn't want to spoil something better.'

'According to tradition it needn't be like that.'

'But most likely would — a noble lord and a common bawd.'

They continued observing each other, the lines on their faces straining and widening like the circles on water.

'It isn't natural,' he said before they burst out laughing.

'Who's to decide,' she replied, 'what is natural and what isn't? The most touching marriage I've known was that between an imbecile and an incestuous strumpet.'

'Then wouldn't ours stand a chance? Or at least, a trial?'

'You're talking nonsense!' She got up angrily and started stamping round the narrow room in front of its extinct gas fire. 'What I wanted to say when we shot off at a tangent was that I'd like your help in establishing myself in a large house, for purposes the world considers immoral, but which can be aesthetic — oh yes, *and* immoral, we know — but no more so than morality can often be. Better to burn than to suppurate.'

He too, had stood up, wanting to brush, to touch, to console her. She avoided his attempts and, soon after, Mercedes and Bobbie came in with the fruits of their shopping, and Annabel with the man she had picked up at the Bioscope.

The man said, 'When I sat down to enjoy *Captains Courageous* I didn't expect to have a bird in hand when the lights went up. This dame's insatiable. And I've got to be at Upper Norwood by seven.'

Gravenor and Eadith stood looking at each other with unexpressed pleasure, smoking Turkish, their elbows resting on the narrow ledge which had replaced the mantelpiece in this improved flat while the others got on with their various activities. Bobbie had bought a jumper she wasn't at all sure about; nursing an incipient toothache which made her look like a white camellia turned yellow at the edges, Mercedes hung around on the off chance that she might be needed.

Presently Eadith had to leave her guest to attend to a client frantic to catch his bus, and an Honourable whore in a tantrum.

Gravenor left her to it.

But he helped her establish herself in the house in Chelsea, where Mrs Trist became an institution, a cult, even with many who considered themselves far above anything like that. Among them, officially respectable women. Even Lord Gravenor's sister. But that was later.

Eighty-Four was ideally situated in an obscure street not wholly residential. The small businesses and post-office at one end made

Mrs Trist's venture seem less an assault on gentility. Most of the houses were run down, some to the verge of seediness. A few had been converted into bedsitters, where beginners and the defeated cooked little meals on gas-rings and wondered whether they had another shilling for the meter. On the whole the householders, even those still in undisputed possession of their property, had seen better days, in theory at least: officers retired from the services, amongst them Anglo-Indians, aspiring or unsuccessful actors, a writer whose play of years before had been forgotten by all but those with total theatrical recall, a detritus of minor nobility, and recently arrived Colonials who hoped in time to master the accent and pass as English.

In most cases large, the houses were in brick of a glaring red, of a style still submerged in that limbo which exists between architectural fashions. Nobody entered Beckwith Street unless they belonged or had business there, or were passing through from a fairly spacious, but also unfashionable square, to reach the Embankment beyond. Although their relationship was only a tangential one, Beckwith was not unconscious of the river as a source of life. On gloomy days, brick which might have been reduced to a sullen ruby, seemed to respond to the glimmer off water. On brighter occasions the street acquired dash from the clatter and importance of traffic as it surged at right angles, parallel to the silent river. Some of the inhabitants preened themselves on the fame of the Great who had lived along the Walk. Others, less impressed by a plaque, hoped that by living in the neighbourhood they might be permeated by a spirit of place.

All but the most cynical or materialistic were appalled, anyway in the beginning, by what was happening at Eighty-Four. If later they became acceptant, Beckwith was the kind of London street which is permanently on the relapse. Empty milk bottles once put out seemed to stand indefinitely, unless falling like hollow skittles in the night. On sunny mornings there were skeins of cats entangled on the short tessellated walk between pavement and front doors. In houses where the vanishing race of servants was still to be found, whether the sad put-upon variety, or those who are doing an enormous favour before twisting the knife by giving notice, either sort would rise out of the areas, and from behind iron bars glance up and down the street as though in search of something they might never find – unless at Eighty-Four.

There the painters were in, the decorators, the long rolls of carpet discarding their factory fluff, vans of expensive new or antique furniture looking as though it might never belong to anybody.

Some of the disgruntled maids had caught sight of HER. Wearing dark glasses. Shielding herself with a sunshade on days when there wasn't that much sun. She was an American, a South African millionairess whose fortune came from diamonds, a lady from Golders Green setting up a stylish knocking-shop she didn't ought to be allowed to. Somebody must be behind her.

Only in the latter detail was the neighbourhood voice speaking the truth. Mrs Trist remained fortunate in those who were protecting her, who cajoled the police, and introduced on a paying basis Cabinet Ministers, visiting Balkan royalty, even scions of the British monarchy encouraged to 'get it out of their systems' before they were presented to the public as models of propriety.

Gravenor's aunts, Lady Maud and Lady Kitty, who dropped to the state of affairs early on, ended by not batting, in the one case a pure, in the other a more raffish, freckled eyelid. What they were spared was the knowledge that another more distant connection had been actively employed by the Trist woman. It might have disturbed them too deeply, not so much the active employment as the fact that Annabel Stansfield had fallen under a train before the move to Beckwith Street.

The girl's death shocked Mrs Trist, as though it were the first event in her life for which she could be held, however indirectly, responsible. Angelos Vatatzes had been old at the time of his death, and the flight from Les Sailles forced on them by Joan Golson's feverish interest in Eudoxia. Again, in the Monaro (if you overlooked boredom and climate) those in whom passion was aroused were more accountable than Eddie Twyborn, its passive object. (What you do to your parents, the living deaths you may cause, Mrs Trist fleetingly considered, are their own fault for having so carelessly had you.) But poor Annabel, though a born harlot and mid-morning alcoholic, might have been Eadith's own crime, as she now saw it: the herbaceous face, the fragile but lustful body, crushed by a train — at Clapham Junction.

Yes, Mrs Trist was devastated, to the extent of rummaging for black and hiring a car to drive her to the crematorium. The driver, a decent little fellow, asked her whether she was Australian.

Closeness to death made the details of personal history seem irrelevant, so she evaded his enquiry, whether sympathetic or inquisitive, while noticing that one of her black gloves had a hole in the index finger, that her skirt was too short for bony knees, and that her shins needed attending to. Her feet she had tucked out of sight.

Caught in the traffic somewhere to the north she found herself thinking about Hell, her own more than Annabel Stansfield's or anybody else's. Because your own hell is what Hell always boils down to. Her own was upholstered well enough, by Heal, and several more exclusive firms, but how well was it going to wear?

Passing through Regent's Park, driven by this small, decent man, she wondered where the rot sets in. She was glad of her dark glasses. She had started scratching surreptitiously at various parts of her anatomy, feeling for invisible lumps, behind the upright driver's back.

They reached the crematorium, where Annabel's remains were consumed to the satisfaction and mild relief of a handful of relatives, and friends from earlier on — and the visible distress of a stranger seated by the door, in dark glasses, and furs in spite of a warm day.

At Eighty-Four the alterations were going ahead: builders, tilers, floor-sanders, glaziers, each trade apparently unconscious of the damage it was doing the others while pursuing its own. Still running the establishment in Hendrey Street with the help of Bobbie and Mercedes, Eadith Trist in her few hours of rest wondered whether she would ever succeed in paying for her folly. Leave alone her moral account, there was this material mansion which had taken possession of her, and which her taste was converting from a drab and musty barrack into a sequence of tantalizing glimpses, perspectives opening through beckoning mirrors to seduce a society determined on its own downfall. If it had not been so determined, the puritan in her might have felt more guilty. She might have taken fright if Gravenor appearing at her elbow had not suggested at intervals that he and his friends would pay for what was no more than the transformation of an ugly and unfashionable house into a thing of beauty.

So she accepted her own corruption along with everything else and started casting the play she had been engaged to direct by a management above or below Gravenor and his exalted friends.

She realized that her poor whores, Bobbie from Derbyshire lolloping inside her blouses, Mercedes the lean Macao Jewess, even the flowerlike, defunct Annabel, were the rankest amateurs: a first essay in theatre. She set her sights on more subtle aids to depravity, such as would delight Gravenor's friends, and as she had to admit, Gravenor himself.

But on nights when overtaken by remorse, after she had moved in, though before the house was finished or staffed, she might stamp along the Embankment, face to the darkening river, its steel mirrors reflecting the underbelly of truth, unlike the domestic looking-glass which reveals the worst with cheerfully objective candour. Honestly, she couldn't think why she had taken the direction she had. Or she could; one always can — but can't. She would have liked to see the house razed. On the other hand she wouldn't like. It was her work of art: its reflections, its melting colours, the more material kitchen quarters, the less and more material girls she was bringing together, each skilled in one or other of the modes of human depravity.

Her whores. She would expect them to obey what she saw as almost a conventual rule. If she had been artist or mystic enough, she would have inspired her troupe, or order, to chasten with boredom and self-examination those whose lust they indulged. As she was chastened by her own unrealizable desires. As she tramped the Embankment, her hand skimming the parapet between herself and the river, she was touching Gravenor's squamous skin: the ignoble lord, her would-be and rejected lover, who might have wrecked the structure of life by overstepping the limits set by fantasy.

She turned back and reached her half-finished house, which was smelling of sawdust, paint, new carpets, and a pork chop Ada had been frying for her. The chop was served on a kitchen plate, a kidney still prettily attached, and accompanied by onion rings and apple quarters. She sat down to it without even shedding her cape, in her greed her jewelled hands clattering against whatever she touched, Ada hovering in close attendance.

While she was living in Hendrey Street Ada had come to her as cleaner: a squat, dour woman from the North, which part of it Eadith could never remember, if she had ever known. Unwilling to share the details of her own life, she did not expect others to offer autobiographies, unless it was their vice to expose themselves. Ada might have been a gloomy companion, black hair scraped back from the forehead, thick, glistening eyebrows, high cheek-bones and a heavy mouth, which suggested Slav origins, or the face of Verlaine. What saved her from being a menace were her bursts of electrifying laughter for some private joke, usually unfunny when it was coaxed out of her, and a sweet, illuminating smile for those in whom she had put her trust. That somebody had betrayed her trust seemed probable. It was what drew her closer to her mistress. In time Eadith grew to believe that Ada might die for her. It was a sad thought for one who had made up her mind that she herself would die by an act of God and not from the wounds of human love.

Ada (Potter was her other name) would be dressed in self-knitted silk jumpers while surrounded by her brooms, her mops, and buckets of grey water. She had lived somewhere Kennington way; even that wasn't pinpointed. In Beckwith Street, promoted to a higher rank, she was got up in browns, or black, with white eyeletted or lace collars, a conventual habit if it hadn't been for a cameo of nymphs and satyrs Mrs Trist ordained her deputy should wear at her throat. Ada grew sterner with authority, her smile the sweeter when it re-appeared on the heavy face. Eadith began to include Ada in the list of those she had loved: Angelos Vatatzes, Edward Twyborn, Peggy Tyrrell (grudgingly, the frightful Prowse), the cold, squamous Gravenor. She wondered how she could show her love apart from leaving this servant a jewel. Love can never be conveyed except by the wrong gestures. So poor Ada of the sweet smile, too hairy no doubt in the context of her womanhood, would never know.

The flowers for her hothouse Mrs Trist took time to acquire, intending them to be as exquisite, as diverse, as unexpected as satiated man might desire. Seeming to sense they would look out of place, Bobbie and Mercedes faded away without rancour before the Hendrey Street flat changed tenants, while aesthetic standards saved Mrs Trist from the extremes of conscience. An artist must guard against the tendency to sentimental indulgence, an abbess resist threats to a vocational ideal. The inspired bawd has in her a little of each.

(Only when giving way to her inner nature after a few brandies, masticating with the ugly greed which a gob of chewing-gum induces, seated at a dressing-table opposite a probably fake rococo mirror in the small but splendid room referred to by the innocent or generous as 'Madam's boodwah', she could have cried, in fact she did let out a yelp or two, for the actuality she had been grasping at all her life without ever coming to terms with it. On reaching one of the lower levels of her dilemma, she would fart at her own reflection in the glass, and after pressing the flavourless gum into a crevice of rococo plaster, fall on the bed, ruffling her body-hair, heaving and sobbing, and if favoured by images and orgasm, perhaps drop off for an hour or two.)

Her girls, the lubricious sisters composing the order of which she was head, only saw her in perfect command. She liked to have them cluster round her: her ranks of mimulus, and leopard lilies, and pale orchids on resilient stems.

There was a black orchid from Sierra Leone.

There was an unexpected, contrasting tuft of pink oxalis, from Leamington. A schoolteacher still in her spectacles. Mrs Trist insisted on the spectacles.

All her spring flowers, her vernal nuns, appeared scrupulously sprayed. She aimed at cultivating in them that effect between the tremulous and the static which the flowers in an expensive florist's window derive from artificial dew. Their clothes she chose herself, and she made it a rule that clients should not see their prospects naked in the public rooms; nakedness, she felt, discourages desire, though many would have dismissed her view as morbid idiosyncrasy.

Sometimes in the late afternoon her girls might assemble without their gorgeous habits in what had been the withdrawing room, which extended the whole of the first-floor front, and expose themselves to the pigeon-tones of light slanting down the street from the river, their nipples and the soles of their feet emblazoned with rose and gold, a suggestion of ashen mauve adrift in the clefts between breasts and thighs.

It might be the rosy spiral of a navel at the apex of an embossed belly, or elephant-creases in upturned buttocks, or the sculptured ebony fetish from the hills above Freetown, which most delighted Madam when she came in at a slack hour to consort with the roly-poly of girls, clustered on divans and overflowing on to the pile of the still untrampled Heal's carpet. Herself always fully clothed, she sat amongst them, caressing tender flesh with her tongue, dabbling her fingertips, almost making music as she combed youthful skin with her brittle crimson talons.

'God, madam, you'll wear out the stock before the shop opens!' Helga groaned; a frail blonde, she was in actual life the lover of Jule, the Sierra Leone negress.

Mrs Trist laughed and moved to the couch where Elsie the ex-teacher was reclining, sharp pink nipples tantalizing in the light sifted through beige net, trickles of light settling in moist, prickling crotch.

Elsie hoisted an elbow. 'If you don't let me alone, Eadith, I might bite off the first cock I catch sight of. And no one but Madam to blame.'

Mrs Trist withdrew her lips from a Mount of Venus in oxalis pink.

She sat up and said, 'Let's see what we've got for tea. Better get up our strength, girls, before the lions prowl in, looking for the jungle.'

The girls jumped up, giggling, squeaking, flopping, exchanging slaps and kisses, and got into old comfortable shifts, most of these the worse for rouge, liquid powder, and other signs of their trade, before trooping down to the kitchen to see what Mrs Parsons had for them. It might be faggot-and-peas, or chitterlings, or bangers and mash, followed by the strong Indian tea most of them could not have done without. Elsie enjoyed a glass of ginger beer, and Melpo brewed her own coffee in a *mbriki*. ('That *prick* of yours, Melp! The sound of the word gives me the shudders at five o'clock of an afternoon.')

All mucking in together at the long, scoured, kitchen table. All the clatter and yammer of a platoon of whores. Lashing their tongues round a mouthful of good, solid fare. Then reckoning with their stomachs, their thoughts, in the steam from strong tea, or over an eggshell of muddy Greek coffee.

Mrs Trist herself often joined in, plumes trailing through chitterlings as a long sinewy arm reached out across the communal table for another boiled potato. Her mouth gone to pot. Her over-strong chin piled with mauve to purple shadow.

When satisfied, they sat around in their comfy gowns and sleazy kimonos picking their teeth with their nails, scratching breast, armpit, or crotch in the practical manner a girl's anatomy demands. Assuming little faint airs of ladies they had known or thought themselves to be. Those more convinced of their own superior origins farting and burping to apologize for what their colleagues could not boast.

Till the doorbell might sound, when the whole order tingled to its nerves' ends and the Mother Superior became the Sergeant-Major.

'Go on, youse! Shoot!' she shouted. 'The lot of yer!'

And they all shot, in their bedraggled, bedrizzled, comfortable garments. To become the creatures of caprice and fantasy the evening might demand. The sulky amongst them more hesitant: those who had seen a penis too many preparing to give notice like any over-worked maid, who couldn't carry up another tray or black another grate, or on a higher level, wall-jumping nuns who imagined an outside world in which love was less abstract and choice free.

They filed out to their dressing rooms, or cells, and were soon patting and smearing themselves, or asking forgiveness and guidance of Our Lady (not forgetting the Panayia).

At this hour Mrs Trist was superb, at her most forbidding, stalking through the public rooms in her bracelets, plumping a cushion, to the vast irritation of the noble sisters opposite drawing brocade over net which had ceased to be opaque, filling japanned or Fabergé boxes with cigarettes, rose- mauve- or gold-tipped, their perfumes mingling with the smell from stale tobacco-crumbs left inside, ordering Ada, Ida and Vi to fetch the dishes of salted almonds, oily olives, sheathed pistachios which blunt Anglo-Saxon fingers avoided entirely, or on being caught out, heeled under velvet fringes of sofa or divan, or in the case of more reticent or passive clients, waiting for expert nails to split the phallus-shaped pistachio and pop it, if not an oily olive, into a complacently fleshed, or thin and chapped, though equally greedy, male mouth.

These were the preliminaries. Only a girl or two at first shuffling amongst the empty nutshells. Bored. Mrs Trist in attendance, encouraging participation and choice. Frowning on any individual who did not appreciate the favour he was being done in her superior house, and anyone who threatened to pass out too soon. For those who met with her approval, for his looks, or for having paid somebody else's unpaid bill, she was likely to cook a dish of kidneys and onion rings at dawn, before going out for her walk through a deserted park.

To get the stale air, cigarette smoke, kidney fumes out of her hair.

To receive the kiss of morning, the more acceptable for being

286

so delicate and abstract compared with the sweaty, abrasive, rib-cracking embraces of venal men.

Herself was able to avoid those; no one would have dared, not even Gravenor her patron.

He was driving her to look at a famous garden thrown open to the public for some charitable purpose. It would have pleased him better to take her on a normal occasion and force the owners (family again) to receive his companion, the proprietress of a fashionable brothel, if she hadn't preferred anonymity outside her professional sphere.

'I still wonder why you got yourself into such an ugly business,' he told her while driving down a Sussex lane.

'But it's not all ugly. You of all men should know that. Some of my girls are superb, some of my jewels are collectors' pieces.' She laughed her laugh, dry enough for a dilettante to appreciate; as he obviously did. 'Besides, I didn't get myself into it. I was nudged at first, then pushed, the way one is. Certainly I could have resisted but oh well, I didn't. We go along with the times, don't we? If that's the way the current is flowing, most of us are carried.'

Rocked by the car between stuffy hedgerows, the grass verges full of cow-parsley and hay fever, they were growing indolent.

A little farther on he put out a hand, and took the hand nearest him. Yet a little farther, on sensing danger, she withdrew.

'I'd say you take full advantage of all my house has to offer. And helped found it, for God's sake.'

'For God's sake, the reason I keep coming back is for you – not any of your boring whores. Risking every bone in my body with some thrashing negress, exposing my parts to an angular Midlands schoolteacher. If you won't let me fuck you, darling, what I enjoy is the supper, or best of all, breakfast when you cook it for me.'

They rocked, and laughed.

'It's as simple as that. Or could be,' he said.

In any of its permutations her life had never been simple. Would she have enjoyed it more if it had? She thought she wouldn't, then that she would. And again, not; she did not covet the confidence, the 'strength', the daguerreotype principles of even the most admirable one-track male, nor, on the other hand, those mammary, vaginal, ovarian complications, the menopausal hells of a sex pledged to honour and obey. Yet she would have loved to receive this dry-cool man Gravenor inside her, to leave her mark on his skin for acquaintances to discuss and deplore, as though teeth-marks and bruises preclude love and respect. She could have loved and respected Gravenor in spite of his flaws, which she understood for their being to a great extent her own. She envied those in a position to love without reservation of any kind. Probably there were few such loves. At the heart of most marriages, even spiritual attachments, lurks the whore-nun or the nun-whore.

'What is it?' he asked.

'Nothing.'

Arrived at the stately home, they drove between heraldic gateposts, and were soon immaculately sauntering through historic gardens, admiring the azaleas, losing themselves in the yew maze. The alpines were exquisite that year.

She was proud of her parade of girls. On better nights the ritual developed a refulgent swank. Not only in the public rooms, but in the private consummation of the client's lust.

A craftsman had fitted a concealed eye to each cell of this elaborate comb of which she was the animating principle. She would not have disclosed to anybody the existence of what was in a sense a humiliating toy, least of all to Gravenor, whom she must continue to admire, but who, as voyeur, would have been reduced in her estimation. She could not have explained how a common peep-hole becomes an omniscient eye, how it illuminated for her the secret hopes and frustrations struggling to escape through the brutality, the thrust and recoil, the acts of self-immolation, the vicious spinsterly refinements which shape the depravity of men – her own included. She would have liked to believe that, even if it did not purify, lust might burn itself out, and at the same time cauterize that infected part of the self which, from her own experience, persists like the core of a permanent boil.

She was devoted to her more dedicated girls, and decorated with her jewels those most likely to act out her gospel. The nucleus of her order lived in. Then there were the novices, on call. They were unreliable on the whole; they even got married and quietly distributed themselves through outer suburbs and provincial cities, where they upheld virtue against those they suspected of backsliding. Mrs Trist couldn't blame them, but distinguished between amateurs and those in whom she recognized a vocation.

Whatever their rank, they all got together in the kitchen, sitting over bacon-rind and the sludge of congealing egg as they discussed the night's activities, rehearsing a gimmick for the next session, wondering what unnecessary goods to splurge their earnings on, the more silent, she could tell from confidences made on private occasions, mentally adding to the balance of pretty substantial savings accounts. Some of them were supporting aged parents, a husband, or a sponging lover. A certain girl handed over most of her money to a church.

Lydia was one of Mrs Trist's most beautiful and accomplished whores. She had hoped to become a concert pianist, and worked hard enough at the piano at the convent where she was educated. In spite of the enthusiasm of the nun who was her teacher, and the prospect of going to Paris to study with a famous virtuoso, she realized her music was less a vocation than the desire to dazzle.

'Oh, and I was lazy too, Mrs Trist. The everlasting practice!'

'I'd have thought that being a whore was as demanding in its way – and everlasting.'

'Yes, but you just let it happen.'

'From what I hear, the men who have had you are impressed by your great virtuosity. That must be more than just letting it happen.'

'Oh no, it's the same as virtuosity in music – when there's just that – nothing more than the desire to astonish – no heart or compulsion.'

Lydia sighed and looked at her watch. 'I'll be late,' she said, 'if I don't get a move on.' Every morning she went to early mass, and evenings to confession. Some of Lydia's clients, her boss suspected, had left their cassocks behind them.

'I feel fucked out, Mrs Trist,' Lydia confessed, driving the lipstick down on her mouth, clothing her lips decently before receiving the sacrament. 'I'm thinking of giving the game away.'

'I wonder anybody so religious ever thought of taking it on.' The whore-mistress sounded prim.

'If it gives pleasure . . .' Lydia smoothed her lips with her lips.

Staring at herself in the glass she had never looked so lustrous; the white parting in the blue-black hair, the delicate nostrils, and bland mouth. Her confessor could only have found Lydia's sins forgivable.

'But any day I could give it away.'

'What would you do instead?'

'I'd really like to fall asleep and wake in Heaven.'

Mrs Trist could not quiz the girl on her conception of Heaven because Lydia would have been late for mass.

The bawd went to her own room and fell asleep so deep that, on waking, she could not remember where she had been.

Lydia didn't return from mass. Days later her body was found in a North London canal. Her confessor was arrested for her murder.

Bridie was another Catholic, but a lapse. She had blue eyes, black-fringed, in a white, Irish skin. She was strongly built, with broad shoulders. There were some who suspected her of being a pretty man in disguise. Mrs Trist knew otherwise, even before she had positive proof of the Irish whore's womanhood.

Bridie had brown hair so thick and curly it had that matted look. In fact, 'There are men,' she confessed, 'who accuse me of housin' lice in me curls. Sure, I tell 'em, bein' Irish-born, I've had experience of the nits, but their creepun and crawlun would never let me entertain 'em permanent like.'

Though Mrs Trist saw to it that the girl was as beautifully presented as the others, Bridie was the perfect slut in her room. On the first occasion when Eadith found a litter of prawn shells on a Bokhara rug, along with balls of combed-out hair, and in one corner a sanitary pad, she had to protest.

'There are some clients,' the girl began excusing herself, 'who enjoy a bit of natural clutter. And if the prawns 'uv gone off, so much the better — the men feel at home.'

Admittedly Bridie had a rather more esoteric clientele; she specialized in whips and chains. ('If I draw the line, madam,' she said at the first interview, 'it's when it comes to the shit-eaters.')

The bawd would have liked to think the expression a metaphor, but from her experience of life she knew that shit means shit.

She engaged Bridie for her good humour, her intrinsic beauty, and what she sensed to be a gift for dealing with the perverse in human beings without condescending to the afflicted or martyring herself.

She dressed the girl in a timeless style, not unlike the one she affected to disguise her own peculiarities: long, trailing, romantic skirts which at that period could have looked ludicrous if a woman were unable to carry them off. Eadith did, through her authority, and the mystery surrounding her. Bridie was a different matter. Her shoulders and bosom were allowed to reveal their magnificence. But the trailing skirt acted as a curtain which, as the performance got under way, was raised by fits and starts to excite her audience.

Bridie had a club foot. 'Some gentlemen,' she laughed in her slow, good-natured way, lowering the thick black fringes on the blue of her eyes, 'some of 'em come in their pants at the sight of me surgical boot.'

Mrs Trist recoiled momentarily from her own power to pander to the worst in human nature. In the beginning, while still inexperienced, she had had her doubts about what she was doing, but as time itself seemed to pander, and from scattered inklings, to be preparing some kind of cataclysm, she allowed her power to overpower.

Most of those who patronized her outwardly discreet house were to some extent lusting to be consumed. In the age in which they were living it had become the equivalent of consummation. She was never more aware of it than when passing Bridie's closed door in policing the premises for which she was responsible, she heard men's knees grinding prawn shells deeper into her Bokhara rug, the thinning knees of minor civil servants, and on one occasion the more opulent pin-stripes of a Home Secretary.

If at times her moral self condemned the rites she had initiated, she realized that the sensualist in her would always raise a frustrated head. Her torments were only a muted version of the more theatrical shriek overheard on one occasion by a noble lady across the street.

Ada came to Madam. 'There's a feller downstairs. I wouldn't see him if I were you.' Net ballooning at the window opened on its catch of river light.

'Better to face it,' Mrs Trist decided.

'This,' hissed Ada, 'could be one of the big-time cops.'

'I'll see him, Ada. If you'll tell him.'

Freckled by the past, wrinkled by encroaching age, her hands trembled: you can disguise them temporarily in a mail of rings, trailing sleeves, eventually gloves.

She went down to what was referred to as the 'office', a small disordered sitting room, across the hall, filled with letters waiting to be answered, receipted bills, autographed photographs of the famous and infamous who professed to love her, and easy chairs in which cats loved to sleep.

He was seated, a domed, rather hairless head rising above the padding of the chair. She frowned to see his feet propped on a velour pouffe on which the girls sat to tell their grievances. When the sound of her clothes prompted her caller to stand up, he was of medium size, stocky build, cobby-calved, thighs too intense; they might have been those of a former rugger three-quarter.

He greeted her with a smile of sorts.

'What can I do for you?' She smiled back after a fashion.

He said, 'I've got an hour or two to put in, and would like to be entertained. I'm told you can arrange it for me.'

'It depends on your interests.' One side of her smile had stuck, as smiles will catch on a gold tooth, though she hadn't one in her head.

'A girl' was what he wanted; he might have expected his order to be wheeled in on a trolley.

She took him up to the reception room on the first floor, and rang for Ada to send in Elsie the Leamington teacher, Edwina a recent acquisition fresh from her finishing in Switzerland, and, as a gamble, Bridie from Cork, Ireland. The girls looked bleary and disgruntled in the morning light. (Edwina might easily give notice and retire to Belgravia.) There was a blue vein almost palpitating in the customer's left temple. Elsie from Leamington did not please, Edwina might not have been there, but Bridie seemed to score.

They went along together to her room. Holding their breath, Mrs Trist and Ada dared congratulate each other; when after a few seconds they heard what sounded like the rubbery, athletic steps of the visitor returning.

He looked very grave, very neat, in his grey sideburns and grey-flannel double-breasted. He was wearing a club tie the bawd was too distracted to recognize. Overall, he appeared embarrassed.

Mrs Trist looked to Ada to leave them.

'Wasn't Bridie to your taste?' she asked.

'I'd better tell you straight,' he confessed, 'I came here, Mrs Trist, hoping to spend a few hours with the owner of the house.'

'Oh,' she said, 'I'd be delighted to get to know you, if that's what you mean. I'll ask them to bring up coffee. Do you take it black? With cream? Or perhaps you'd rather something stronger?'

He was looking at her, by now giving her his deepest attention; in other circumstances she might have been drawn to the

292

sideburns, attracted by eyes of a cold grey, not unlike Gravenor's, set in a less noble, but perhaps more revealing face. 'What I meant was, I'd hoped to sleep with you,' he said.

'Morning makes it sordid, don't you feel?' From a flicker of his face, a visual image of Bridie's room must have been passing through. 'In any case,' she said, 'I'm not in the habit of sleeping with my clients.'

'Lovers, then?'

She glanced down at the blotches on her withering hands. 'Not even lovers. No longer. I've learnt to suspect love, as you, apparently, suspect me.'

She really must manage her trembling.

'I don't suspect you.' He produced his card. 'We all know you're running a house of a pretty corrupt kind. How corrupt, Mrs Trist, we're not yet sure. You yourself might give the lie to our suspicions by being more frank about your own life.'

She smiled back, wondering if the bow of her lips looked too taut, and whether its magenta was flaking. 'Do you think a brothel will corrupt those who're already corrupted – or who'll corrupt themselves somewhere else – in their own homes – in a dark street – if overtaken by lust, in a parked car, or corner of a public park? All of us – even those you consider corrupt – I'd like to think of as human beings.'

In spite of her height, her presence, and the romantic sumptuousness of the dress she was wearing, her trembling hands were letting her down; while the Midlands three-quarter back was determined to break through her defences.

'Whatever you may think of me professionally,' she said, 'surely my personal life is my own concern?'

Always smiling back, he replied, 'I've been watching you long enough, Mrs Trist, to admire you as a woman. That's why I'd like to go to bed with you.'

'Oh,' she sighed, gasped, 'age apart, athletics aren't in my line. As for yourself, men often fancy what is withheld – and are less disappointed by going without.'

Her mouth, she felt, had dwindled to a rudimentary hole in her face. Her extravagant dress could only be doing her a disservice, the appliqué on its skirt grown garish, and where one of her hands rested, unstitched. From a window the normally benign light off the river was glaring at her so ferociously she found herself longing for the night lights of childhood, dipping and swimming in their chipped saucers on the borderline between sleep and waking.

How to extricate herself she could not think, when she heard a key in the lock, and footsteps approaching briskly over parquet before being subdued by carpet.

A visible melting had started in her inquisitor. 'Good to see you, Rod, after all this time.'

Gravenor measured out his words. 'And in a brothel, Hugh. Makes it an extra special occasion.'

Hugh might have invoked the officialdom of which Roderick knew him to be part, but didn't seem to know how to go about it. He laughed somewhat frenetically, exposing large, grooved teeth, and left after the least possible exchange of routine masculine geniality.

Eadith Trist might have wanted to reward her protector for his timely appearance in her house, but was stricken by such gaucherie she waited instead for him to leave; which he did on seeing she was suffering from too many incursions in one morning.

Whether the role Gravenor played in her life was that of saviour or evil genius, Eadith hadn't yet been able to decide. She both dreaded and counted the hours to their planned meetings. What appeared to be chance encounters she had sometimes induced, like dreams, by an effort of will, then if they proved to any degree requiting, she would panic, and break free before consummation of her desires.

On her blackest days she willed him out of existence. Perhaps he never had existed, except as a figment; only she had his letters, his signature on business documents, and in a silver frame, his photograph illegibly inscribed. Most tangible proof were her recollections of the squamous skin, pronounced finger-joints, stone lips fleshing out whenever her mouth consented.

He had told her once, while holding her knees between his, under the table at which they were dining, 'I've known you all my life, Eadith, but still have to teach you that you exist.'

She would have had to admit she had not existed in any of her several lives, unless in relationship with innocents, often only servants of ignoble masters, or for those who believed themselves her parents or lovers. She was accepted as real, or so it appeared, by the girls she farmed out for love, and who, if she were to be honest, amounted to fragments of a single image. Yet whatever form she took, or whatever the illusion temporarily possessing her, the reality of love, which is the core of reality itself, had eluded her, and perhaps always would.

Disentangling herself from the pressure of his knees, she said to her companion, 'Don't let me spoil your dinner, my dear, but I've an inkling I'm needed. Though Ada's thoroughly competent, you can't run a house and escape from the responsibilities.'

She got up, and had them call her a cab. She looked back and saw Gravenor concentrated on what he was eating, delicious enough in its sauce of mussels and lobster-coral and cream. The light had sharpened the bridge of his nose while softening the rest of his face. His lips as they moved unconcernedly appeared the blander for the cream anointing them. The coquettish little pink lampshades acknowledging their own reflections on the surface of the water were made to appear more frivolous, ephemeral, by the river's black, oily current.

She moved off, gathering her extravagant clothes round her, the whore-mistress diners were staring at. Or were they? Perhaps they did not recognize her existence any more than they suspected her desire to be recognized: this woman looking in her bag to see whether she had the change to spend a penny or tip the taxi — or simply look for reassurance as she crossed a desert plain.

For some time after, she did not see her protector, nor rustle up the courage or effrontery to make an advance; she was too ashamed of the musty smell her plumes exuded, a hint of verdigris in the settings of her jewels, and other more personal signs of decay — or was it the vapours rising from a river at low tide?

It was downright absurd to imagine she was less the woman they recognized: hair still kempt and naturally black except for a faint frosting of silver above the forehead; beneath the drifts of mauve powder, a bone structure time would probably never erode; lips immaculate, except when a stray camel-hair had remained stuck to the impasto. As she prospered, her jewels had become increasingly elaborate, tortuous, inspiring amazed gasps rather than passive admiration. Like her clothes, they delighted those who enjoy a touch of the bizarre in the uniform present. If she remained a joke for children, and affronted or frightened a majority puzzled by what they had not seen before and could never have envisaged, she was inured to the scorn of these comparatively simple souls, and worse, the hatred of others for what might not have been fully revealed.

Ladies, admittedly the more eccentric or raffish, began frequenting Mrs Trist's house. Two who considered it fun to be on 'darling' terms with a procuress were Diana Siderous and Cecily Snape.

One of the outwardly flawless English flowers, Cecily had been forced to leave the country for a while after an affair with an entire negro band ending in the death of a drummer and exposure of a drug ring.

Eadith found Cecily, for all her amoral swank, rather an insipid girl, yet touching in her desire to explore what she conceived to be 'life'. Her origins were never revealed, though she affected a vaguely aristocratic aura probably signifying Wimbledon.

Cecily confessed, 'Sometimes I think I'll become a whore — not for the money — just for the game.'

'Then why become it?' Eadith suggested. 'I'd say you'd be happier keeping on as an amateur.'

It nettled the pink Cecily. 'I detest amateurs in any department.'

On one or two occasions Cecily and Diana stood in for Mrs Trist's girls when someone had fallen ill or defected.

After one such experience Cecily grimaced. 'You were right, darling, I hated that. If at least I could have felt something for the paunchy brute riding me. Pity, or something. My trouble is I can't *feel*.'

Eadith was forced to reply, 'I guess you can't — if you didn't after an entire negro band.'

Cecily giggled. 'Who told you? Aren't people outrageous! Actually, it wasn't more than a couple — the one who died, and the one who did him in.'

She became weepy, and after that, perhaps genuinely sincere. 'I'd settle down in the country tomorrow if I could discover an honest man.'

(On losing sight of Cecily, Eadith had asked Gravenor's sister, Ursula, 'What became of Cecily Snape? It's ages since I set eyes on her. She told me she aspired to an honest man. Did she find one?'

'Poor darling, no!' A collector of rare objects, Ursula replied through her most exquisitely brittle smile. 'She's living with herself and fifteen dogs in a cottage near Saffron Walden. She goes for endless walks in the rain, and curls up in bed with the dogs without even taking her gumboots off. However, perhaps she's happier than she would have been with the honest man.')

Her equal in amorality, Cecily's friend Diana had ridden at life with less abandon, greater calculation, and in consequence had fared better, materially at any rate. If what her Orthodox forebears would have referred to as her 'soul' had suffered to any extent, Madame Siderous did not allow herself to consider; one was born with a soul, like that other hindrance a maidenhead, but any practical woman got rid of the one and forgot about the other as soon as was decently possible without damaging her chances of success. Of Smyrna-Liverpool extraction, she had married a rich Alexandrian Copt, but had left her husband and two rapidly acquired children, the better to circulate in the world, which in Diana's case amounted to London, Paris, and Antibes. She was liberally endowed by her Copt, and along with the settlement allowed to keep her jewels,, including a ruby necklet both friends and enemies claimed was in fact a present from somebody of vast importance.

Madame Siderous had a leathery voracious face, its complexion suggestive of tropical fruits in the early stages of going off. Perfumed expensively, her presence conjured up the scents of Egypt, predominant among them guava, toasted sesame, and cottonseed oil. The bracelets she wore from wrist to elbow of one arm were in the fashionable French paste, but rustled like the metal waves beaten out thin by smiths in an Eastern *souk*.

Looking in at Eadith's on an afternoon when Bridie was the worse for an orgy of Guinness and oysters, Diana volunteered to entertain a client who booked the Irish girl in advance because she understood his temperament. Though Diana's repertoire was extensive and included the game of whips and chains, she hadn't bargained for what she got; she had never been on the receiving end.

She emerged more than ever the bruised and rotting tropic fruit. *'Et la chambre de cette garce! Comme elle pu-ait!'* Disgust rattled at the back of her throat as she restored her lips at Eadith's rococo glass. 'This nauseating girl's oyster-shells and bottle-tops!'

'Bridie is a natural slut, which is why she is popular with certain men. The physical wounds they enjoy are only half of what they suffer morally.'

'But I was the one who suffered the physical wounds – inflicted on me by this species of pervert!'

What Mrs Trist did not disclose was that Bridie's regular had declined to pay for the services of an amateur.

Not until Madame Siderous had got herself back into the paste bracelets, her cabochons and pearls again nestling at her ears and throat, and doctored her nerves with a powerful slug of Armagnac, could she consider translating this gross physical outrage into an anecdote to amaze a dinner party of intimate friends.

She tried a little of it on the bawd. 'My poor hands, martyrized by oyster shells! My knees, crucified on the lust – of some little – civil *servant* – or mingy *professor*! *Mon Dieu*, my sweet, what these girls consent to! Does it excite their bodies? Does it stimulate their minds? Do you think they can enjoy an *orgasm*?'

'I don't expect so,' Eadith replied. 'They're too exhausted. Or too bored. They do it for the money, you know – as everybody does – politicians, butchers, most artists. Their professional skill or artistic dedication doesn't prevent them expecting a material reward. Isn't it natural?'

Madame Siderous grew thoughtful; her eyelids began flickering. 'Are you suggesting, Eadith, that I'm going to receive a material reward for my services? That would only be natural, wouldn't it? And I could buy some little nothing of a bibelot as memento of what I underwent one afternoon as a professional whore.'

Mrs Trist laughed. 'I shan't degrade you, Diana darling, by paying you money for your working holiday in a brothel. I'd rather give you – well, the little trinket you can remember it by.'

The bawd unlocked the wall-safe where she kept her less important jewels, and chose a ring on which an ancient black scarab was rolling in perpetuity a ball of agate dung.

'Pah!' Madame Siderous exclaimed and frowned. 'It's Egyptian, for God's sake!'

'Yes, and very valuable – if what I was told is true. You never can tell, of course.'

'No,' agreed Diana. 'You never can tell.' But she seemed cheered by the possibility that what she was fitting on her poor martyred finger was a priceless fragment of antiquity.

'It's very fine – very *unusual*.' Again her eyelids started flickering. 'I must show it to Ursula Untermeyer – without of course telling her how I came by it.' She raised her eyes. 'Ursula is so knowledgeable, but within the bounds of the museum.'

As in lots of other plain women, Diana's eyes were her best feature; they had procured her many of the benefits in what is known as polite society.

'Ursula would adore to know you. But perhaps we should wait for her brother to arrange it. As he will, I'm sure, because she never stops insisting.'

'I can't think why,' Eadith lied.

'You'll be the first madam she's met — and rare objects are her obsession. She'll add you to the Julius Untermeyer Collection.'

This was the way it went at the time, along with the hide-and-seek at Harrods and amusing hats (Ursula had been known to crown her own brittle carapace with a lacquered crab shell mounted on a doily in paper lace).

It was not Madame Siderous who introduced Mrs Trist the brothel-keeper of Beckwith Street to Lady Ursula Untermeyer. Gravenor the brother announced, 'My sister has decided she must meet you. Such is your fame, Eadith.'

If Eadith detected a trace of acid, she could not resent what she had induced.

As though by agreement, they had been seeing each other less and less. Whether they met in Gravenor's sleep as they did in hers, she had no means of telling. She was haunted by a Homburg and a furled umbrella, each of a black she had encountered in her waking life only in the paintings of Degas and the plumage of daws, rooks, and Australian crows. He was growing more cadaverous, more freckled; for a wealthy man his clothes were threadbare at knee and elbow in spite of a valet she knew had his interests at heart.

Gravenor appeared to be re-assessing his needs, as happens sometimes to those who are ageing and sensitive to social or political change. He might have been whole-hearted had he been an ascetic, or a voluptuary hell-bent on redemption, instead of a dilettante English gentleman. When in town he still lived in a dark rambling flat at Whitehall, and dined off crumbed veal and apple tart followed by a scooping of Stilton, its veins scrupulously tinctured with port.

Eadith hankered after tincturing his pale but unconsciously sensual lips. As she daren't, she said instead, 'Surely I'm accessible enough for your sister to approach? Her friends cultivate me — even her brother.' Her smile became a leaning tower of accusation.

'I'll tell her to come, then?'

'If she cares to. But won't you bring her — to help soften the fall?'

Eadith turned her back, to feel whether she had shaved that morning. A moment of panic persuaded her that Lady Ursula couldn't possibly find her acceptable, and worse, that the distance she had deliberately created between herself and Ursula's brother must widen as a result.

At least they agreed on a date and hour for Ursula's introduction to the house in Beckwith Street.

On the day arranged, Ada was dressed in her brown habit with white collar. Mrs Trist had given her deputy a pair of agate ear-rings which she felt added a touch of modest authority.

Perhaps out of diffidence on finding herself in the presence of a real live bawd, Lady Ursula was entranced by Ada. She could not compliment the servant enough, on her ear-rings, her pretty collar, the 'atmosphere' of the overcrowded office in which the visitors and hostess were awkwardly stranded.

Eadith remained by choice a minor figure, until Gravenor suddenly took her aside.

'Ursula is rather shockable,' he warned.

'Then why did she come looking for what she knew she must find?'

'She had to. Because her friends are coming. She doesn't approve of Cecily, still less Diana, but would like to emulate their daring — even their lack of judgment.'

Gravenor's lack of tact, which she should have welcomed, became Eadith's wound.

Ada was at her most serious answering Lady Ursula's questions, while the latter looked about her with bright birdlike glances, predatory if they hadn't been so nervously distracted, of a lady whose title and wealth allowed her to hold tradition and possessions between herself and the shoals of life. The possibility of drowning in some catastrophic flood was one that she could continue dismissing as too abstract to be entertained, whereas she felt all at sea in this minor social disturbance in which the three of them were floundering. For Ada, the fourth, was sufficiently conscious of her place to go below and organize tea.

Lady Ursula had finally begun a vague, hiccuping kind of dialogue, high in key, dry in tone, which her rank and circumstances could only make acceptable, '. . . must congratulate you, Mrs Trist — Eadith — I'd like you to call me Ursula . . .'

(actually, in her family circle, she answered to 'Baby') '. . . congratulate you on this very charming interior . . .'

On getting it out, Lady Ursula immediately suspected she was sounding 'old world'. She started smiling her apologies, or at least she parted her lips with their merest smear of tangerine, and narrowed her eyes behind the drift of eye-veil attached to her amusing little hat.

'Thank you,' said Mrs Trist with a humility she genuinely felt. 'It's always difficult to see one's own objectively.'

She, too, ended on a smile, but one which must have made her look like a horse; at the same time she was invaded by a burst of scents and images from the past: a landslide of chaff, a trail of rat-shit, leather armchairs in the Judge's study, documents tied with ribbon in disinfectant pink.

Ursula Untermeyer lowered her eyes from a hobbledehoy she might admire after she had accustomed herself to the eccentricity of Rod's friend. Gravenor himself was the victim of his own bones and a chair too narrow, too low, which had forced his knees higher than was natural. He was sitting, hands outspread, as though to disguise the shiny patches to which sharp kneecaps had reduced the cloth covering them. For an instant Eadith's glance was drawn in the direction of a pin-striped crotch.

She was at once shamed into blushing. But nobody could have noticed, or if they had, must have disbelieved. For most of those who came in contact with her thought they detected, from out of the tropic plumage and encrustations of baroque jewels, the glint of rectitude.

How Mrs Trist had overstepped the bounds of rectitude and devoted herself to satisfying the more vicious side of human nature was a subject for speculation amongst her employees, clients, and acquaintances. And why she herself never took part in the celebrations she arranged. There were a number who would have booked her if she had been willing, but it was not known whether anyone had ever taken Eadith Trist to bed.

Her friend and would-be lover Gravenor had tried to reconcile her continued affection for him, and even signs of sensual attraction, with her constant refusal of his propositions. 'You know, Eadith, I believe you have a savage nymphomaniac inside you, and a stern puritan holding her back. It's this unattractive mentor who forces you to look for consummation in the lusts of others.'

'How very ugly, but perhaps true! Truth is more often ugliness than beauty.'

Seated with Gravenor and his sister in the bawd's parlour she was reminded of his theory; it made her wistful rather than sad. She suddenly wished she were alone with her shortcomings.

Not a woman of sensibility or feeling, Ursula sensed an emotional dilemma strong enough to rouse her conventional strain of sympathy. All she could do to express it was to assume the brightness her governesses had taught her to parade. 'At least no one can accuse you, my dear, of leading a humdrum life.'

She raised her head to show off rather a fine throat. The glass on the wall opposite confirmed that she was looking her best, in fact a charming picture, the light glittering on still perfect teeth behind the faint tangerine of lipstick, her blue eyes widened under the little bronze veil. She could afford to be magnanimous towards one who deserved pity.

'None of life – shelling peas, peeling potatoes – digging holes for *fenceposts* – need be humdrum if you give yourself to it,' Eadith replied.

As one who had never shelled a pea or peeled a potato, let alone stopped to think that holes must be dug to accommodate fenceposts, Ursula could only toss her head and laugh for the extravagant answer she had just received.

(For no reason that she had time to consider she recalled an incident when she had dropped her passport and her keys down the hole between the footprints in a horrid Breton *toilette*.)

Rod was increasingly embarrassed, because poor Baby bored him, and he sensed his imagined mistress was bored too. From looking at Eadith's hand, he longed to take it and press it between his thighs.

Just then the doorbell rang, and Ada came to answer it. She admitted two individuals who would have claimed to be gentlemen. In the thin and thick of them, each looked exceedingly prosperous, with their Bond Street watches and signet rings, their club or old-school ties, and expertly tailored suits. They must also have lingered over lunch and were somewhat the worse for it.

Ada whisked them upstairs with professional aplomb.

Convinced that she was seeing life, Lady Ursula looked spellbound. '*Fasc*inating,' she breathed, but at once averted her eyes from her thoughts.

In rootling round for a theme with which to distract observers,

Ursula Bellasis' blue eyes, which had so successfully decoyed the elderly Julius Untermeyer, lighted on a ring the woman Eadith Trist was wearing.

'What an extraordinarily beautiful ring!' Lady Ursula exclaimed. 'Pigeon's blood, surely. Is it Indian?'

Eadith said it was while taking off the ring, its ruby carved in the form of a rose, and set in a cluster of silver leaves. '. . . given me by an Indian who carried off one of my girls. Into worse than slavery. I'm told she died of luxury – an over-indulged liver.'

The two women laughed, Ursula in envy of the ruby spoils, and delight at the ring's aesthetic perfection, Eadith more cautious, for a reminder of the cynicism behind a casually constructed human fate.

'I do hope you'll keep it, Ursula, if it appeals to you.'

Rod began mumbling, protesting, his sandy moustache growing sparser with the embarrassment caused him by these two women. At any moment he might drag himself out of the uncomfortable chair, and go upstairs, and fuck one of Eadith's girls to get his own back.

'But, darling, I couldn't – truly! Your ring!' Ursula was becoming ecstatic in her refusal.

She adored this rather peculiar woman.

'But take it. It means nothing to me.'

Ursula's hand closed on the formal Indian rose. In the blue eyes behind the scrap of a veil lurked the suspicion that she might be expected to give something in return, like on the rare occasions when Julius had got into her bed and started upsetting her hair. It was an agonizing moment, but looking into Eadith's eyes, a mosaic of experience and elusive beauty so unlike her own unblemished blue, she could detect no signal confirming her worst fears.

She was most relieved because, as her family and friends all knew, the millionaire's widow was pretty stingy.

Perhaps they should have expected it. As the prettiest of the Duke's daughters she had been reared to get them out of a mess. All those law suits. She was married off to old Untermeyer, a man almost her father's age, of unimpeachable honour and unfailing aesthetic instinct, whose only flaw was that of being Jewish. Ursula didn't care a jot about the Jewish, anyway in life as it has to be lived, and the family swallowed what pays off. An eldest son had been packed off to South Africa, leaving debts for which a car smash saved him further responsibility. Roderick the younger boy, dilettante, drifter, womanizer, though lovable fellow, could not be relied on. Of two elder daughters one was married to a decorative, impecunious German princeling; the other had taken an actor as the first of several husbands. Ursula ('Baby') was their saviour. It didn't occur to them that they were underestimating Julius Untermeyer when they did him the honour of accepting him into the family.

A decent enough creature, this Jew, who had made his fortune out of toothpaste and other toilet commodities – soap far commoner than Ursula was used to buying in Jermyn Street. Others of his race considered Julius simple-minded, or pretentious, not to have bought himself a title to trade against his wife's. Mr Untermeyer slept on a truckle bed, but bought the Kensington Gardens mansion to house his various admired collections. 'Wardrobes', the Wiltshire manor, was little more than an annexe to the principal museum, and the fat pony which jogged him on visits to his tenant farmers, an excusable Jewish conceit. (If he had a racing stable besides, a yacht, and a villa at Cannes, it would have been hypocritical of him to pretend not to be rich, and Ursula sold all those to help pay for her husband's death.)

She did love him, she believed, but was herself the rarest *objet d'art* of those the Jew had collected: a situation which tends to freeze love in the beloved. Though stunned by his death, she was harder hit by the death duties. She had no wish for another man. She had not desired her elderly husband in terms of flesh, because how can one surrender to a father without a vague sense of disgust? She continued to honour his name as a nominal director of the toiletry business on which the Untermeyer fortune was founded, and as custodian of the paintings, ceramics, porcelain, glass, which 'in due course' would go to the nation. Her mind would not dwell on her ascent, possessionless, into a comfortless Protestant Heaven, still less her possible descent into its alternative for having married the Jew. Nobody would have imagined Ursula's predicament, none of her rackety non-friends, not the writers, painters, *connoisseurs* she patronized, not even her brother Roderick, in London in the Nineteen-Thirties, but that was the way she had been brought up by Nanny and the governesses, and poor darling Daddy dying of a drawn-out bout with unconfessed syph.

On easing the Indian ruby in amongst her own rings, Lady

Ursula looked at Mrs Trist. 'We must keep in touch. I do hope, darling, you'll come and see me – in town – and at "Wardrobes".' Her voice and her charming tangerine mouth clamped down on every second word. 'I hope you won't find us *boring* after the interesting life you lead.'

An impasse might have occurred if two girls hadn't let themselves in through the front door. Their fresh, though rather blank faces immediately radiated respect for those they found in the office-parlour.

Mrs Trist did the honours. 'Audrey – Helga – Lady Ursula Untermeyer.'

Without the protection of make-up or jewellery the girls smiled nervously.

'Rod you know.'

The girls' eyes slid away from knowledge, and from that luminary with whom they were already familiar through *Tatler* and *Sketch*.

In Ursula's assessment, Audrey and Helga were charming simple girls in unpretentious floral frocks. It was such a normal occasion. The girls had been to an afternoon session at the Curzon, to a French film much discussed at that moment.

'It sounds most *significant*', the noble visitor murmured.

'Depends on what's sig-nificant.'

'Don't think I understood it.'

'Anyway, the seats are so comfy at the Curzon.'

The girls laughed in the pause which followed, Lady Ursula joining them in full agreement.

After that, Audrey and Helga ran upstairs, *pensionnaires* at a finishing school, or novices in a convent. Ursula found them 'unaffected – charming.' Charm appeared to be the yardstick she used in exercising judgment.

Gravenor was becoming so irritated by his silly sister and the grotesque totem he had been foolish enough to imagine as his mistress that he had to suggest in his driest voice,

'Inexperienced as yet.'

Eadith had grown sombre. She had a too heavy, almost a man's face, Ursula decided. She regretted coming. There were uneasy tremors besides, doors opening, voices breaking out disturbing the upper landings, the whole structure of this baleful house.

'Have you had enough, Baby?' asked her brother, suddenly fierce.

She had known him brutal, though never to herself.

'Why,' she said, 'no!'

She refused to be put upon. Even in the schoolroom, the nursery before it, she had been her own mistress.

'Eadith,' she demanded, 'won't you show me round?'

Ursula looked her coldest, her brittlest, her most imperious, her wealthiest. Gravenor hated his sister Baby because Eadith's eyes had taken on the most poignant tones in their whole fragmented repertoire. He was brought to heel; he loved her, even though his love were as grotesque as her grotesque beauty.

Eadith got up. 'If you want,' she told her guest. 'There's nothing I need hide.'

Everybody has his lie, and for that reason the others would not have questioned her remark. Gravenor hoped to preserve his grotesque ideal, Baby had decided to see life such as she had never wished to face.

Eadith was leading the way upstairs, one sinewy arm slid along the banister-rail for support, bracelets slithering, gliding, grating, wounding the already tortured woodwork. Ursula following. She tripped on one of the lower stairs, but recovered herself without assistance. It wasn't offered anyway.

Rod had stayed below. (Serve bloody Baby right if she'd bumped her nose and injured that perfect detail on the Heal's runner. Thanks to Baby's insistence their whole family came crowding into Mrs Trist's whore-house: darling Mums, selling off this one and that before dying of cancer, the Old Man, tradition's profile, perhaps no more than either of his unsatisfactory sons, or Deborah, Toto, Karl Heinz, Wally Miller and others, and others; those he respected, he not so suddenly realized, were Julius Untermeyer the toothpaste Jew, and his own non-mistress, Eadith Trist the bawd.)

As they approached the first landing, the two women on the stairs were subjected to the reason for those rumours only faintly heard in the office-parlour below. Several girls in a state of almost total undress were crowding into a renovated Edwardian bathroom. The object of their concern, as well as the cause of their alarm, not to say hysteria, was a stark naked figure seated on the blue-and-white porcelain lavatory bowl, or rather, slumped forward, arms lolling listlessly, in a faint or worse. The only live-looking thing about her was the torrent of glossy brown hair streaming floorwards from a head too heavy for its owner to raise, if indeed she was in possession of it.

'Who is it?' Mrs Trist called in a blatant voice such as her visitor had not heard during their politer conversation.

'It's Dulcie,' answered a tall honey-coloured girl in nothing but her high heels and a pair of chandelier ear-rings.

At the same instant Ada appeared from behind a door along the landing. She was carrying a huge white bath-towel. Her manner and the brisk sound of her cinnamon habit suggested that she had the situation under control.

'Yes – Dulcie – silly girl!' Her sigh was for human folly in any of its manifestations. 'Had a go at herself with the knitting-needle.'

'When I engaged her she swore she'd had the op!' the bawd exploded.

'It's what you can expect of amateurs.' As Ada reached the casualty, the girl's companions raised her up; the hair opened on a livid mask, a body the colour of bruises, the glitter of blood dribbled over thighs and ankles.

From neighbouring rooms the two business gentlemen were making a shaken getaway, one of them smarming his hair with a rigid, yet tremulous hand, the old-school tie slung round his neck, his companion forcing buttons into holes which seemed to have shrunk in the stress of the moment.

In the general commotion, and telephoning Dr Pereira, Mrs Trist quite forgot about her guest.

While Ada, who was wrapping the towel round the listless body, announced with conviction, 'She's not dead – only bled. I've seen too many of 'em.'

It started her helpers giggling in a shamed way, then laughing outright as they staggered, tits joggling, heels going over, in removing to an upper floor the figure shrouded in the bloodstained towel.

By the time Mrs Trist returned downstairs Gravenor must have carried off his sister. How much Ursula had seen of the aftermath of Dulcie's attempt at abortion, Eadith doubted she would ever hear. In her present state of physical exhaustion and moral despair she had no desire to see Ursula again. Nor, for that matter, Gravenor.

She was only deluding herself, she knew. More than ever before she longed for Gravenor's company. She was prepared to accept his silences, his censure, the disturbing aspects of proximity and repressed physical attraction. In her hopelessness she found herself scratching a buttock in a way which could only have shocked Lady Ursula. What the hell! She blew a fart at all Ursulas, at every spurious work of art. Herself included. In the glass a ravaged mess, a travesty no amount of lipstick and powder and posturing would ever disguise to her own satisfaction. A 'woman of character' to her clients and her girls, she continued swimming out of mirrors and consciousness, her elasticity her only strength, like a cat which refuses to drown.

Once at dawn she looked down over the parapet, and there was the corpse of this actual cat, fur opening and closing on patches of skin like blue-white scars, as the tide carried it, rolling and grimacing, rolling and grimacing. She might have chosen to join it had she been offered a choice by the blue-black immensity surrounding them. As she could not feel she was, she returned to the limbo of Beckwith Street, to the moaning and sighing of whores as the leftovers among their pseudo-lovers, the prickling pursy or smooth sinewy male animals, ground between their thighs or squelched against their buttocks.

On the stairs and on the landings it seemed as though the bawd alone must fail to drown in this loveless social orgasm. She could have been saved up for some event more tumultuous.

Several mornings after Ursula Untermeyer's visit and Dulcie's messy abortion, Eadith missed her early walk. She had gone to bed in broad daylight after a heavy night in which she had drunk too much while jollying or restraining, on the one hand the diffident and regretful, on the other the rorty drunken. She fell into bed recoiling from what should have rejoiced her: solid sunlight the other side of the curtains.

Physically exhausted, she felt herself reduced to moral slag. Most of her girls did their jobs without at least calling on their nerves. It was Eadith Trist the bawd who was the fucked-out whore. Ageing, too. In a professional capacity, she would have been fit only for meeting the late or early trains at Victoria Station.

She fell asleep in spite of the insomnia which at this time in her life had begun plaguing her. She must have been dreaming. She was standing in someone else's house, the furniture less pretentious, the real tables and chairs chosen by those who lead 'normal' lives.

She was waiting in a passage for some explanation of why

she was there, when she heard a voice calling to her from a nearby room. She went in. There was nothing to make her immediately aware of the room's function, except that a closeness, a warmth, a benign light converging on the centre of the carpet suggested an intangible cocoon. There was a young woman, her face softened by the light to a blur in which her features were lost, just as the details of the room were lost in a timeless blur. Everything about the young woman was familiar, but the dreamer could not identify her. She was kneeling on the fleecy carpet, bathing a recently born child. As the mother (so the dreamer sensed) squeezed the sponge, the child lay propped partly against the scuttle back of the enamel bath, partly by the mother's other solicitous hand.

The child was the rosiest, the most enviable the dream-walker had ever encountered. She dropped to her knees beside the bath, to join in the simple game of bathing this most radiant of all children. The mother seemed to have invited collaboration, but as their hands met over soap or sponge, resentment set in: the dreamer became an invader. She was warned back, at first not overtly, but by implication, till finally the fleece on which both were kneeling turned to grit, stones, road-metal. Dishwater, sewage, putrid blood were gushing out of the faceless mother from the level at which her mouth should have been. The intruder was desolated by a rejection she should have expected.

Eadith awoke. It was about lunchtime by the normal rule. She continued snoozing, protecting her arms and shoulders from the dangers to which they had been exposed. In spite of them, she could have chosen to return to her dream for the sake of the radiant child. She must recall every feature, every pore, every contour of wrists and ankles, and the little blond comma neatly placed between the thighs.

She must have fallen asleep again. She could feel the water wrinkling around her as she lay propped in her enamel bath. And finally awoke to the summer warmth of her actual sheets, and synthetic perfumes of the creams with which she anointed herself for synthetic reasons.

It had occurred to her in her half-doze: what if I adopt a child? The half-thought half-dream was still glowing in her when several miles down the dusty road of half-sleep she fell to wondering, almost aloud: what sort of questions would my child ask me?

She gathered her chest inside her arms, and was subsiding into the sheets again when Ada looked in to tell her employer that business already showed signs of becoming brisk.

Mrs Trist got out of bed to renew her mouth. Her body was still supple. It was also hairless, since the Arab woman came regularly to give her the wax-and-honey treatment. She sat on the bedside a moment, stretching herself, then pointing her elbows at the curtains which created what was neither gloom nor daylight, but an unnatural glow in which her figure had been posed, not necessarily by herself, a shell without echo.

On drawing back the curtains and the entanglement of net, she shouted at a dog, an English setter chasing a tortoiseshell cat down the street. She retreated from view on realizing from the dog-owner's face that he had witnessed something unmentionable. She covered her nakedness with a robe.

Ada returned in a waft of coffee and toast slightly burnt, on the tray she was carrying, the newspaper, and a clutch of mail for the most part bills.

Eadith Trist sat scratching herself. She might have felt more at ease had she heard the body-hair answer back. Her person, her life, her arts, constantly failed to convince her, though others seemed taken in.

She bit off a corner of toast and looked through the batch of bills. Sipping the blessed coffee, she tore open an envelope, the native toughness of its texture vying with discreet arrogance. A monogram of simple, yet withal, imperious design was cleanly incised in the opulent weave, the letter signed by a hand which promised warmth while remaining enslaved to its authority:

> Yours, with affection,
> Ursula

Eadith read the letter, chewing toast by ugly mouthfuls, or so she felt; scalding herself on coffee which had begun to taste of burnt beans. (The toast was even more repulsively burnt; she would have to tell that bossy know-all, the indispensable Ada.)

My dear Eadith,

We did agree, didn't we? that we should call each other by our first names. I do detest *formality*, and never feel at ease in it.

I am writing these few lines to say how much I enjoyed our meeting, our conversation, in your charming house. My brother is an old stick-in-the-mud. In spite of what some consider a wild life, he disapproves of practically everything. I adore him!

If you are not too busy, Eadith, and could bear the thought, I'd love you to come here to a cup of tea or drink, whichever you prefer. Please telephone me. It would give me still greater pleasure if you would come down to 'Wardrobes' and spend a week-end with a few chosen friends. Some of them you already know.

After adding that 'affection', Ursula had tacked on:

I was ravished by your tea-things — and scrumptious cinnamon toast.   U.

Eadith continued sipping her coffee as she re-read Ursula's parchment letter, from which nothing so vulgar as perfume arose, only a whiff of distinction. She mused over 'ravished by your tea-things . . . cinnamon toast . . .' She could not remember whether Ada had served tea as a prelude to Dulcie's abortion, yet they must have sat drinking it if this was what Ursula chose to remember. In spite of Ursula's ravishment, Eadith detected a common clinking from her honest, though aesthetically acceptable, cups and saucers. As for 'scrumptious cinnamon toast', she did remember, now she came to think, too much butter oozing out over delicate fingers.

She was too sensitive of course. The Duke's children as she saw them again, cheeks bulging, lips glossy, eyes glazed, were re-living life in the nursery while masticating the buttery toast in the whore-house in Beckwith Street.

Longing in and out of season for the cosiness of the nursery fire, with Nanny and a fender to protect them from its perils, in their still childish middle age they hankered after other, more perverse dangers which Nanny Trist was able to provide. Or so Eadith sensed in trying to explain why Ursula and Rod were attracted to her. They were excited by their own perverse behaviour, yet if her noble charges were to detect in Nanny a flaw they had not bargained for, she suspected they would not hesitate to reduce the whole baroque façade of her deception to a rubble of colonial wattle-and-daub; no compunction would save Nanny from the sack.

Mrs Trist dismissed her cab and rang the bell. There was a slight, cold wind lifting the edges of whatever stood in its way, an air of presage, a mould of green on the elms and the grass verges of the favoured gardens in the precinct. It was one of the chillier spring days, crocuses trembling, jonquils blowing but recovering themselves, like frail but erect Englishwomen.

The columned portico towered above the intruder, who felt wrong in a squirrel coat the rats must have gnawed the night before she put it on. She should not have worn her common, balding squirrel. Her lips were thickly coated with grease. Stalactites were dripping from her armpits. She must have looked everyone's idea of a woman who keeps a brothel.

Lady Ursula Untermeyer could still command a butler. He had a skull's ivory face with some hair drawn across the cranium.

Oh, *yes*! He must have heard about the madam.

He sat her in a small, not unsympathetic room, to await the august lady whose strange whims he was paid to obey.

Eadith shuffled about inside the squirrel coat she had made the mistake of wearing, in the small japanned room where the discreet butler had placed her. On the wall opposite, there was a small exact portrait of Ursula.

Eadith continued rearranging the collar of her unfortunate coat, and regretting she had come. There were no copies of the *Illustrated London News*, but the room was like a waiting-room at some fashionable doctor's or dentist's — or disguised abortionist's.

Ursula appeared. 'I can't think why Peacock put you in here!' Ursula, too, was possibly disguised; for a moment Eadith feared her hostess might administer a charitable non-kiss, but she went off instead into a high treble laugh.

She was plainly dressed. She looked like an exquisite plank with grain in it, her hair a perfectly incised helmet. She was wearing no jewels beyond a brooch in what was probably a rare, leached-out jade. Her manicurist must have been in constant attendance on the long pale nails.

She put out a hand at the end of its arm to encourage her amusing friend who was running that house in Beckwith Street, and smiled her tight little smile by way of encouraging herself.

Eadith was led back across the hall. This time she noticed a larger, more formal portrait of the mistress of the house in white satin, and long white gloves, the highlights and the blue shadows in satin, kid, and diamonds suggesting a noble icicle. Beneath the golden urn of upswept hair the face might have looked warmer if the painter had been interested as well as paid, or perhaps he had not detected warmth, or perhaps his subject was unfeeling.

The cheeks of a young Ursula looked like crisp little apples which had not been bitten into.

As they crossed the hall Ursula murmured incidentally the famous painter's name. The lowered voice did not prevent it bouncing off the chequered floor, to be reverberated by surrounding walls, before wrapping itself round fluted columns. Ursula added a dry little, mock-apologetic cough, and that, too, became echoed through what was virtually a Parthenon.

On their reaching an upper floor, Eadith was led through a succession of smaller though no less imposing rooms filled with furniture too valuable to be lived on. In every room hung a portrait, of varying importance, of the collector's widow. Halting for an instant in front of each, she paid the same mock-diffident homage, accompanied by what was half cough half laugh, and nervous hair-touching, as she named whichever fashionable artist. Her late husband must have schooled her in guiding the select tourist.

Though the painted reflection in each room showed Ursula herself to be the Athena of this Parthenon, there were other works of art as well, from Goya and Renoir to Lavery and Munnings, together with the inevitable signed photographs jostling one another in casual ranks: Marie of Rumania rubbing up against d'Annunzio, Lifar, Noel — not yet Eadith Trist, though Lady Ursula may have set her sights on such a prize. As for the books on the Untermeyer shelves, not one, you felt, could fail to reveal a personal inscription above the autograph of some mythical monster. Some of the monsters had even known Julius, and liked him enough to pander to a vice by which his widow continued doing her duty.

When at last the two women had reached a boudoir-cum-study, less constricting, more personal than the japanned waiting-room in which the butler had seated the visitor in the beginning, Ursula sighed and explained, 'This is where Wogs liked to sit.'

'Wogs?'

'My husband.'

His widow produced a small etching in a silver frame from somewhere in amongst the Baroness Popper, Sir Thomas Beecham, Gladys Cooper, James Elroy Flecker.

The toothpaste millionaire who had collected Baby the Duke's youngest daughter, was shown exposing a noble forehead, to either side a drift of startled hair, the nose's curve more benign than cutting, the eyes expressive of unfulfilled longing. Julius Untermeyer had everything of the artist *manqué*; he might have been Mahler's failed brother.

After treating the etching of her husband almost as though it were an oblation, she returned it to where it had been standing, with a moue which suggested, 'There, darling, we've got it over; I loved him, but . . .'

Peacock brought in a silver tray, followed by a maid with a second. The 'things' were arranged. Where Eadith Trist had been innocent enough to present Worcester, Ursula came out with Lowestoft.

'Cottage stuff,' she apologized.

She was short on the eats: a plate of Nanny's bread-and-butter, and a sponge hidden under a cushion of raspberry-embroidered cream.

The two women were beginning to feel cosier.

'I do admire you,' Ursula said, after nibbling for propriety's sake at a corner of her bread-and-butter, 'for your originality and independence – in choosing the life you wanted to lead.'

'In choosing? I'd like to think it, but never feel anything but chosen.'

Having introduced her theory, Ursula was not to be deflected. 'In our case – in mine, I mean – it's so much more difficult to break the mould in which one has been set.'

Here she deliberately hesitated, hoping for a clue to the mould in which her friend had been set originally, by fate, if not by tradition.

But Eadith was in no way helpful. She only mumbled a sort of agreement, and devoured the rest of her bread-and-butter, like a hungry man after a day on the moors.

Ursula might have been reminding herself that Eadith Trist was a woman of strong will.

'I mean,' said Lady Ursula, 'it's all mapped out for *us*. Marriage with someone desirable. Wogs – well, Wogs was a family necessity, but don't think I didn't come to adore him. He was my halfway house to freedom. I could never have kicked over the traces like Cecily Snape – God knows – or you, Eadith darling.' She hesitated, it seemed interminably. 'I'm told,' she said at last, 'you're from one of the – Dominions, which no doubt made it easier.'

Even she must have heard how terrible it sounded, for she seized

314

a knife and cut into the cake. It proved stale, but for the moment looked ghastly rich, with raspberry blood trickling down snowy crevasses.

Again Eadith was most unhelpful. 'Ah, the Dominions – yes,' she sighed, her voice dying on a note the English themselves might have approved.

She accepted a wedge of Ursula's cake, and wallowed in it, in spite of the staleness of the sponge. She was hungry, and perhaps also indiscriminate. She enjoyed a good blow-out when it offered itself, which may have explained Gravenor's remark about the nymphomaniac inside her.

She sniggered inexplicably. It made Ursula glance at this grotesque creature with cream and raspberry smeared over magenta lipstick.

Because of all she had been taught, Ursula was quick to ask, 'That lipstick, Eadith – tell me the shade, and where you get it.'

Only then Eadith came out with, 'I hate it! It makes me look old, ugly, and common.' She visualized her tongue sticking out from between her lips like that of some frilly lizard baited by a terrier bitch.

'Oh, but *darling*!'

'No. It's true.'

Ursula sat tossing her ankle in Alice-in-Wonderland style. She was reared an expert at ignoring. Eadith knew by now that Ursula would never refer to Dulcie's amateurish abortion.

'My dear brother is what I want to talk about,' Ursula said. 'You've been so good for him – darling. Women fall for Rod right and left. He's in perpetual danger of making a dire mistake. You, Eadith, save him by holding off. I want you to know I'm truly grateful.'

Surprising even to herself, Eadith replied, 'I love Rod, and for that reason, would rather remain his friend.'

Ursula looked startled as she studied the implications. 'I've always felt friendship, to a man, is something from which women are excluded – just as a woman can only rely on a woman as her friend. None of those *abnormal* relationships of course!' she was quick to add.

'True friendship,' Eadith decided after wiping off the cream and most of the hateful magenta lipstick, 'if there is anything wholly true – certainly in friendship – comes, I'd say, from the woman in a man and the man in a woman.'

Ursula's agitated ankle was stilled. She appeared aghast. Was her new friend perhaps more intellectual than she'd bargained for?

She came as close as Baby had ever got to a giggle. 'You make it sound almost perverse, Eadith!'

After which, she stood up, strolled round the bloody shambles on her Georgian tea-tray, and looking at herself in a minor glass, its frame studded with semi-precious stones, touched up her flawless helmet a little.

While Eadith glanced at a clock, equally exquisite, though less prominent than the studded mirror; not so inconspicuous, however, that it might not speed the lingering guest. By now she realized Gravenor would not appear, whether by his own inclination, or his sister's design.

'I do hope,' Ursula ventured on their reaching the chequered hall, 'that you'll spend a few days with me at "Wardrobes".'

She glanced at Eadith, and if earlier on, Baby had never come so close to a giggle, she had never come closer to a kiss than in the peck she bored into the cheek of her unlikely friend. 'Rod would love it,' she encouraged.

Mrs Trist went out, and after lowering her head, climbed inside the cab Peacock had called. Though the butler offered physical assistance, she was too ignorant, 'independent', or perhaps too colonial, to avail herself of his attentions.

Two or three weeks later Mrs Trist received a letter.

Dearest Eadith,
    You will remember we discussed your coming down to 'Wardrobes'. I am writing to suggest you choose your week-end – and do make it a long one – Friday till Monday – Thursday till Tuesday if you feel expansive and can tear yourself away from your *business*. (Ada appeared so competent.)
    Most of us lead such busy lives we need our little distractions. I'd particularly like you to come while Spring is still with us.
                                                        Yours affectly,
                                                                Ursula
PS. Rod would love to drive you down.

As the bawd had not set eyes on Rod since the afternoon he brought his sister to Beckwith Street she doubted he would love to drive her down. Yet there was evidence that she had not fallen entirely from grace in that she received indirect guidance from him at a moment when she most needed it.

Mrs Trist could have become involved in a tiresome scandal following the death of a brigadier, whose brother, a worldly cleric, had also been known to patronize her house (in discreet mufti, needless to say). Brigadier Blenkinsop, whose death might have caused Mrs Trist such vexation, had in fact died astride Jule the negress from Sierra Leone. Jule could not resist boasting, 'Had a general die on top of me last night. You should've heard the clatter his medals made as he left off spurring me on.' While Helga her lover grew tearful, hysterical, remorseful for the life they were leading, so far removed from her ideal of love between women.

It was Gravenor, Eadith gathered, who sent her a lawyer, as well as a man of some importance from Scotland Yard whose sympathy might have extended itself had Mrs Trist been willing.

In the circumstances she had not answered Ursula Untermeyer's letter. She was too distracted, not only by a scandal fortunately averted by the skill and sympathy of her advisers, and not a little of her own money. She was also emotionally unsettled by an episode of a different kind following on the brigadier's death and Ursula's invitation.

Mrs Trist had been to visit an aged, ailing prostitute known to her slightly from her sojourn in Hendrey Street. Elderly even in those days, Maisie specialized in meeting trains, but would sometimes venture as far as the Dilly and the scornful jeers of the plushy mob in their silver foxes, mink, and squirrel, whose beat it was.

Maisie had been let live in the attic of a house belonging to a rich benevolent queer, who was in the habit of siphoning off some of her rougher trade. On her patron's death, the house became the subject of endless legal wrangles, with Maisie a forgotten part of it. On the ground floor, in what had been the dining room, there was a claw-footed bath lying on its side, for no reason Eadith had ever heard explained. All the lower part of the house was unfurnished, the stairs uncarpeted and dry-rotten, rickety banisters with whole sections of the uprights missing. Only on the attic floor did life return, in a flowering of crochet and knick-knacks, the lank bodies of empty dresses hanging half-hidden by a faded cretonne curtain, face powder merging with spilt flour, tea becoming grit on an unswept floor. It was pretty much of a mouse-hole, but snug.

Eadith found Maisie toothless for her illness, though as she remembered, the Victoria Station prostitute had always been inclined to do without her teeth when not professionally engaged.

Now she cackled at Mrs Trist through the general squalor, leaking gas, and sickroom smells, 'Love isn't what it's cracked up to be, love – or is it?'

Eadith did not know how to answer, except by sternly mopping up Maisie's incontinence, and flushing its more solid parts down a grey and reluctant lavatory on a lower landing.

Maisie wheezed, 'Don't worry, love. I'll be at it again when I'm on me feet.' Lying side by side with an organdie hat and the grubbiest, most lifeless Arctic fox, the monstrous heels of her glacé shoes bore witness to the torments her feet must suffer. 'Won't ever let it get me down. I'll go straight up amongst those snooty molls on the Dilly. One of 'em, you know, has a wotchermecall – a chow-chow dog on the beat with 'er. Says the bloody dog brings the customers on by pissin' on their legs.'

Maisie paused to clear some phlegm out of her throat.

'Those girls are pros. My trouble is – I've always been an amatcher. Not that I don't give an honest-to-God professional fuck. And collect the money that's due for it. But I always done it – now don't laugh, Eadie Trist – I done it for love. Whether it was with some Hindu steward, or Gyppo stoker, or poxy British corporal. That was 'ow I built up me business. Anyways, I think it was.'

Her cheeks were growing flushed as her mind wafted her. If the five-bob tart was raised by her delusions towards apotheosis, the successful bawd was racked by the clearsighted view she had of her own failures, her anxieties, her disproportion. There was little more she could do for the present beyond leaving an assortment of notes beside the oiled carton in use as a sputum mug, and in the kitchen, a saucepan of soup she had brewed up. Maisie, if she ever awoke, would probably ignore the soup in favour of her gin.

Heading for 'home' across the great squares with their classical mansions and fuzz of elms, Mrs Trist was conscious of entering another world of make-believe. At a church the curtain was going up on a fashionable wedding; at a house the guests, both invited and parasitic, were boring into a reception for a Balkan princess. Mrs Trist had read about both these functions while still only projected, in newspapers which the ephemeral chic, including herself, read less and less for fear of what they did not wish to find.

In the central, proprietorial garden of one of the squares, a gang of men was digging a pit for what people had begun referring to as a 'shelter'. They paused in their work for a look at the woman passing the other side of the railings. Their expressions, half of them serious, half jocular, did not intimidate her. If she had turned on them and offered what Maisie would have called an 'honest-to-God professional fuck', these solid British workmen would have grown sheepish, too bashful to respond, at any rate by daylight, to a lady's improper suggestion.

So Mrs Trist spanked on her way, and on reaching a more populous thoroughfare, was faced with an incident involving another elderly woman, of a slightly higher social level than Maisie the sick whore.

The person in question was falling to her knees. She arrived on them just as Eadith Trist reached the opposite kerb. The woman landed with the dull thump of some commodity unrelated to her station or appearance: flour perhaps, or pollard, or even cement. Her handbag and hat were flung in opposite directions. Exposed by her fall, her hair was of a fashionable cut and tint, at odds with the veined face, the puffy body of a woman of substance rather than rank.

From kneeling, she had collapsed, and was lying on her side moaning and panting as Mrs Trist reached the opposite shore.

Too many rescues in one afternoon, Eadith would have liked to decide, till she caught sight of the woman's knee through a torn stocking, and felt she was to some extent responsible. (The nun inside her would not allow evasion, any more than Gravenor's 'nymphomaniac' could resist the perversions of her own brothel and Maisie's pavement life.)

Eadith stood looking down. The victim lay moaning, toadfish mouth smeared with coral lipstick, cheeks, for which the prescribed facials had done next to nothing, palpitating under their network of veins. Dimmed by glaucoma, cataract, or whatever, the staring eyes were not necessarily those of the toad but of any variety of stale fish laid out on the slab at an unreliable fishmonger's.

'Don't worry,' the rescuer, now the victim, advised; 'I'm going to help you.'

319

The woman, or she might have preferred 'lady', kept grinding her golden coiffure against the unresponsive pavement. 'Oh, what will become of us? I'm so grateful, my dear. I'd only like you to know I mustn't suffer any pain. Money is no object.' She stretched her arm in the direction of the bag from which she had been separated by an act of God; then began a disconnected whimpering against all acts human or divine.

Her rescuer helped her into a nearby chemist's, where she was treated for her few scratches and abrasions. What worried her most was the torn stocking, through which dimpled her milk-white knee, and her restored handbag, for wondering what she might have lost while separated from it. She kept rummaging through the bag, checking its contents: passport, keys, keys, passport; never satisfied, it appeared, until after patting the coils of flesh upholstering her middle, her ribs, her thorax, she hauled up a little chamois bag which must have been lodged somewhere between her breasts.

Reassured, she sat smiling, if tremulously, on the chemist's stool. 'You don't know what I owe you, darling,' she informed the one who had cut the strings trussing her as she lay, incredibly, on a London pavement. 'I am Australian,' she confessed between gasps, in case her saviour had got it wrong. 'My husband used to tell me that being Australian had given me an inferiority complex. Well, it isn't *true*! It's simply that one doesn't want people to mistake one's better nature for a worse.'

As on other painfully personal occasions the past began reaching out to Eadith through that shuddering of water which memory becomes visually, till out of time's wake, and this bloated body straining at the seams of its expensive black, surfaced Joanie Sewell Golson.

If memory troubled Eadith/Eddie/Eudoxia, there was only a slight presentiment of recognition in Joanie's blurred eyes and at the corners of her lipstuck mouth, of a colour someone like herself would have considered a 'pretty *feminine* tone'.

Joanie kept peering up. 'My eyesight isn't what it used to be. Actually, it's pretty ghastly. But I shan't go blind — though they've more or less told me that I shall. I've begun investigating Christian Science. A bore really. But if it works . . .'

She kept on blinking at her rescuer, eyes outlined in rheum, tears, and in spite of Christian Science, the drops with which she would be treating her ailment.

Old. Or at any rate, older than Eadith.

Inside her skin Mrs Trist recoiled from Joan Golson's predicament.

'Shouldn't I call you a cab?' she suggested. 'And help you home?'

Obsessed by the aura of her benefactress, if not her image, Mrs Golson must have forgotten what had happened, but suddenly remembered she was an object for pity, and slipped back too easily into the cloak of martyrdom.

'Oh dear, yes! If you'd be so kind,' she whimpered at the woman on whose goodness she depended; and when Eadith had telephoned the cab-rank, and paid for the call, 'Though my eyesight isn't what it was, I can tell you're kind, my dear. I can feel it.' In spite of her perception, a hand reached out in its black kid glove, a diamond bracelet rustling at the wrist — to touch, to reassure herself, to possess.

By the time the taxi arrived Mrs Golson had grown very old indeed. Wheezing, groaning, panting, hobbling, she let herself be helped into it. The burden fell on her nurse-companion; the chemist had had enough, and the casualty might have had enough of the chemist the way she shrugged him off.

When the two women were at last alone in the airless taxi, Mrs Golson told, 'Since my husband died, I seem to have been at the mercy of every-body and every-thing.' She might have thrown in God as well if she had known her companion better. 'Mind you, Curly — poor lamb — had his limitations. He was a man — but we need them, don't we?'

Had Mrs Trist tried to free her hand from the black kid vice grasping it, she might not have succeeded. For the present, she let things be.

'Are you married?' Mrs Golson asked on what seemed like an impulse.

'I expect you could call it that,' Mrs Trist answered.

'Like most of us.' Her fellow sufferer sighed; then she brightened. 'I always enjoyed our breakfasts together. At least I think I did.'

All the while the stale-fish eyes were directed at the figure beside her. 'I wish I could see better. I know I'd find something to encourage me to live.'

They were approaching the hotel Mrs Golson had named as her London address.

'I hope you'll come, my dear – and we'll pick a chop together.'

Only at this point did the black-kid hand relinquish a hand. 'I'll give you my card,' Joanie threatened, and began rummaging again in her overstuffed crocodile bag for the gold card-case. 'Telephone me,' the coral mouth, the blear eyes commanded, 'and I'll get them to keep us a table in the grill room. So difficult today, but Aldo and I understand each other. Curly used to say, "Got to make it worth their while. Have no illusions about the lower classes".' She laughed, exposing her gold bridges for this new and sympathetic friend. 'I hope to see you,' she added, without sounding over-confident.

After the stout person had been ejected from the cab and handed into the keeping of the porter as prolifically hung with brass as any dray-horse, Mrs Trist had herself driven away.

She sat bowed above the visiting card:

LADY GOLSON
38 MORWONG CRESCENT
VAUCLUSE
SYDNEY

She felt guilty she had not known enough to react appreciatively to Joanie's ladyhood. In itself an epitaph, she saw it carved in stone, rising above the couch-grass runners and paspalum ergot of a colonial democracy. Which of her own epitaphs would she choose if she had a say in the matter? Or would she settle for the anonymity of dust?

As she was driven away Mrs Trist could not bring herself to look back, for fear of being faced on the one hand with Sir Boyd and Lady Golson, on the other Judge and Mrs Twyborn, huddled round the Pantocrator on the steps of the Connaught Hotel.

He came to drive her down on the dot of the time specified. She heard his cold, precise voice asking Ada to announce his arrival to 'Mrs Trist', as though it had been a normal house. She was already downstairs, standing in the small office-parlour where she had received them the day he brought his sister.

Now he said he wouldn't come in; he'd wait in the sun. She could hear his feet, restive on the tessellated walk between street and entrance.

She realized she was trembling. She hoped she would be able to control her hands, her lips, not only at this artificial reunion with

322

her protector, but on meeting his sister's friends. Herself the whore-mistress. In its state of mid-afternoon sloth the house gave nothing away. It was a Thursday as Ursula had wished.

She went out carrying her own bag, not gushing and gnashing as she had rehearsed, and as she had seen and heard Diana, Cecily, even Ursula herself, though in the latter's case, the gush was a cold one, the gnash more the champing of an exquisitely poised Arab mare. Eadith felt in advance that the impression she would make on the one she most wanted to impress could only be sombre.

She arrived on the step without yielding the bag Ada had wanted to wrest from her. Gravenor did not attempt. His back was turned as he contemplated the car in which he was preparing to drive his sister's friend down to Wiltshire.

He did look at her as last. 'I haven't come too early, have I?'

'You couldn't be more punctual,' she assured him.

He had something of the school prefect, or undergraduate obeying custom by fetching a girl down for May Week, except that he was a middle-aged man in shabby, once expensive tweeds, and freckles on the pouches under his eyes.

He took his dressing-case from her. 'Is this all?' he asked, with the air of one who had vaguely expected hat-boxes and a wardrobe trunk.

'Yes,' she answered, 'this is all.' In her heart of hearts she was returning before she had arrived.

He threw the case, one could not have said vindictively, into the back seat, then fastened down the waterproof cover.

Rod was driving a sports-Bentley of ten years back, pretty shabby if its owner hadn't been in a position to indulge his taste in shabbiness. As well as eccentric women.

He did not look at her, or help much, beyond opening the door to admit her to the passenger seat. Crackled but still luxurious, the upholstery matched the shabbiness affected by the owner. The chassis, mudguards, and bonnet testified on the other hand to the pride in ownership of some anonymous minion still devoted to nobility.

They drove through the grey fringes of London, a reality which did not cancel out the more brilliant frivolous world of Gravenor and Ursula and their friends, or the half-world of Beckwith Street. Eadith herself might have claimed that Maisie, the bronchial septuagenarian prostitute, had for her a reality which the housewives of Lambeth and Southwark would never convey. Whatever compassion she had in her was roused by overtones of purple, not by grey surfaces. No doubt the grey world would condemn her for coldness and 'perversion'.

Gravenor appeared disinclined to talk and in her present mood she was happy to fall in with his silence.

Until as they whizzed through some mock-Tudor township, he turned to her and asked, 'How's business, Eadith?'

She admitted to being satisfied, then that she was doing very well indeed.

'You'll be able to retire and marry. Marriage is what I'm told successful whores and madams aspire to. I've heard of one — perhaps we ought to call her "courtesan" — who built a convent to her favourite saint in gratitude for her patronage.'

It was a conceit they could enjoy together, though she detected in his laughter a slight edge which was meant to cut.

'Unfortunately,' she told him, 'I wasn't born a Catholic, and conversions have never convinced me.'

'A pity. You might have set yourself up as the patron saint of chastity.'

A little farther on, in a peaceful stretch of road, he put out a hand and she accepted it. She must persuade herself to be grateful for the crumbs.

For a mile or two they remained gently united, when anger made him exert his strength, which she was forced to return. Their knuckles whitened into fists; her fingers developed a wiriness they should not have possessed.

She tore free.

She sat shivering, the scarf she had tied round her head for the journey by open car streaming out behind them.

She admitted to feeling nervous: nothing to do with Ursula, whom she now knew as well as one ever knows a woman of such fragile composition, but the prospect of facing Ursula's friends.

He laughed. 'You'll find "Wardrobes" more like a whore-house than Baby would ever let herself see.' Then he added, 'I don't guarantee it'll make you feel more at home, Eadie. But we'll have each other, shan't we?'

Whether spoken in irony or not, it warned her. 'I can't remember you ever calling me "Eadie". Why, suddenly, now?'

'To make you feel at home.' He spoke with perfect gravity, but still she suspected irony.

'Wardrobes' was less pretentious than she had imagined: no palace, not even a country mansion, but a compact, rather chubby manor embellished only by its gateposts and chimneys, and dormer windows set in the striations of its grey roof. Across one more sheltered wing, beech and birch had cast an afternoon shadow, like mauve lichen invading by creeping inches a stone shoulder of this house standing firm and grey in an altering landscape. For spring had swollen to early summer since Ursula issued her invitation, neglected on account of the barely averted scandal of Brigadier Blenkinsop's unseemly death.

Eadith could see at a glance that the house, if blessedly more modest, was as perfect as she would have expected of its owner. If there was a dash of complacency, that, too, was not unexpected.

More surprising were the two little King Charles spaniels wagging and swivelling, amiably sycophantic, as Ursula advanced to greet her guest. She was holding an old, ivory-tinted, ivory-handled parasol to protect her complexion from a watery sun. There was a scent of lavender from the dogs' brushing against its borders. Ursula looked down, frowning in the midst of her smiling welcome, drawing aside from the antics of her dogs who were obviously there only for effect, as were the borders of English and tussocks of Italian lavender, the clumps of white candytuft advanced to seeding stage by now. Ursula could have been frown-laughing as much for the no longer perfect candytuft as for the gambollings of her not-so-pet dogs. She herself was as unnatural in that casually devised work of art, an English garden, as would have been a meticulously executed Persian miniature fallen amongst a herbaceous border.

'Darling,' Baby's giggle had an ivory scroll to it, 'I can't tell you how honoured I am!'

Her brother turned back to attend to his car, leaving Eadith Trist to galumph as best she could beside her hostess while a servant carried the dressing-case. In the presence of so much management, perfection, contrivance, Mrs Trist felt she might have been wearing a surgical boot — or had sprouted a beard. At least Lady Ursula would not allow herself to notice anything peculiar.

The house was cool to cold, furnished with mock simplicity to disguise genuine luxury.

Ursula apologized. 'Country — you may even find it a bit primitive, Eadith darling. But isn't that the point?'

As they went upstairs, a peasant-woman hauling up a bucket from a well faced them on the wall of a half-landing.

'Could never make up my mind about Courbet,' Ursula murmured. 'Wogs adored him.'

Without waiting for the anonymous servant meekly carrying the Vuitton bag, the hostess broke open cupboards, tore open drawers, on the perfumes of lavender and verbena. Till on introducing her guest to the bathroom, she affected an akimbo stance, perhaps in keeping with her Courbet peasant. As in Mrs Trist's own house, the bathroom fittings were sympathetically antique, the lavatory bowl not unlike that on which Dulcie's faint had been witnessed by Lady Ursula.

'You'll be comfortable – and happy, I hope,' she enjoined the one who might be the catch of her house party. 'At least nobody,' she said, 'is arriving till tomorrow evening. In the meantime we can be together – *en famille* so to speak.'

With a last smile she left Mrs Trist to her meagre unpacking. A maid was prepared to take over, but she dismissed her assistant, not knowing what she would have done after turning on the HOT and COLD, flushing the antique lavatory, and feeling the bed to ascertain its temperament; it was hardly ascetic.

Rod appeared, and kissed her on the mouth with the cold gravity she could not accuse him of adopting since it was she who had forced it on him.

'They have tea for us,' he told her, 'in what Baby calls the library.'

They went down like an engaged couple, hand in hand, or stars of an operette from which the organdie frills were missing.

Baby was waiting for them behind silver trays better stocked than the ones in town. They were seemingly prepared for those who had been on a tramp through the woods, and returned smelling of leaf-mould, fungus, sweaty woollens, with an appetite for butter-sodden muffins. In addition to the muffins, there was a plate of little pink-iced cakes for Nanny's charges, and a fruit-cake which might have been the archetype, breathing brandy even at a distance, glittering with cherries and candied peel, and coagulations of moist black currants.

Although she claimed that a 'good old-fashioned tea' was her favourite meal and that the country air worked wonders with her appetite, Ursula remained almost as abstemious as she had been in town. She broke off a piece from the innocuous base of one of the small pink cakes while making a little face at the icing.

Gravenor tucked into the muffins after spreading a handkerchief over bony knees, then wiping bony fingers on a second. He gave up rather grumpily on noticing that he had spotted his none too spotless tweeds.

The guest alone did justice to the tea, sampling everything more than once, and emptying three cups to Ursula's languid half. Eadith left off only out of guilt, wondering how much her hosts could have noticed.

But they probably hadn't; they were too busily engaged in discussing family affairs: what to do about Nanny Watkins now that she was senile and all but paralysed.

'Something must be done,' Gravenor decided.

'Something must be done,' Ursula agreed piercingly.

'We can't abandon poor Nanny.'

'No, we can't abandon her. Or at least *I* can't – because I see that I'm the one who will have to do whatever is done.'

'For the moment you're in the best position.' Gravenor sat rubbing ever more furiously at the butter spots on his shaggy tweed. 'We can expect nothing from the Old Man – with Zillah draining him as she is.'

'Oh, *Zillah*! *No*!' Ursula tossed her immaculate helmet. 'I am the one – it is always I.'

'Well, Baby, you have the toothpaste money behind you.'

'Not in realizable cash. Most of it's invested in what will be left to the nation.' She waved her hand vaguely to indicate the objects in her house. 'That was what Julius wanted.'

'You can't tell me that an old fox like Wogs – and a vixen like you, darling – didn't allow yourself a few peanuts, golden ones, to play around with.'

'How horrid you can be!' Ursula was so put out by her adored brother she was only too glad of friendship however recent and superficial. 'Rod has never understood, Eadith, what I've been through. As if death weren't enough – on top of it the death duties! I can only believe it suits my brother not to realize. Having frittered away his own, he expects me to fritter what is left of what in fact I don't control.'

Perhaps as a relief from her exasperation she poured a saucer of milky tea for her unwanted decorative dogs, which, in their clumsiness, they slopped over a Persian rug.

All the perfection, the elegant contrivances against sordid life, seemed to be deserting Ursula. She had got up and was striding jerkily round the room.

'Nobody,' she moaned, 'can imagine my responsibilities. The tenants alone! Down in the village they expect me to install a *flushing lavatory* in every cottage. At the rents they pay!'

Rod remained preserved in calm. 'If you don't,' he suggested, 'your head will roll the quicker at the Revolution.'

'By now I don't care. And you, darling Eadith,' she had approached her friend and, bending down, embraced her almost passionately, 'what you must think of us! At least I know part of what you're thinking: how glad I am to have held off and escaped a monster.'

After this the lady of the house announced she was a wreck and must lie down before dinner.

Gravenor might have decided, not necessarily that he, too, was a wreck, but that he had had enough of an outsider who had seen and heard too much. He withdrew, smelling of gun-powder, Eadith thought, in an opposite direction from his sister.

Left alone, the guest went out on a paved terrace guarded by a balustrade, and urns from which trailers of a small white flower, suggestive of premature moonlight, were spilling over. Early though it was, the dark had begun gathering, or not so much dark as mist rising through a beech copse in a hollow. Ursula herself could not have planted such mature trees, though she might have deployed them thus if she had. They went with her, as did the white flowers and the deceptively unostentatious house, its grey now deepening to overall mauve.

Eadith wandered some distance from the house through the moist air of the gathering darkness and perfectly tended informal surroundings. Hungry for colour, she looked for the delphiniums Ursula must surely have had her gardeners plant, but on this evening of mist their few early spires seemed to have been drained, or infused with the prevailing white. The one sustaining note, she owed to memory: that of a crimson hibiscus trumpet which suddenly blared through the scoring of this lovely effete damp-laden garden.

The mist, the monochrome, warnings in her bronchial tubes, reminded her of failures. Failed love in particular. Her every attempt at love had been a failure. Perhaps she was fated never to enter the lives of others, except vicariously. To enter, or to be entered: that surely was the question in most lives.

As she turned back, someone was approaching down the lawn from the balustraded terrace.

'We shan't be dressing,' he announced, 'the three of us on our own.'

It was meant to encourage, and his leading her back towards the house they did not share.

They spent a rather boring evening, the Bellasis siblings yawning their heads off after a saddle of lamb large enough to feed a whole feudal household, followed by a cosy treacle pudding.

Ursula asked, while they were yawning their way up to bed, 'This Hitler – need one worry?'

Gravenor replied, 'Not while Neville's around.' Then he snorted. 'It's comforting. Whether it's morally desirable – that's another matter.'

Ursula sighed. 'Karl Heinz tells me not to worry.'

Suddenly she remembered her guest. 'Eadith darling, if you're hungry in the night . . .' With her lacquered nails she prised open a japanned tin on the bedside table; and smiled.

When her hostess had left her, Mrs Trist drew back the stiff curtains to let in some air, without which the room would have been suffocating. The night outside was cold and damp in spite of summer. The mist rising from out of the beech wood below had by now almost enfolded the house, nourishing its lichens. She remained leaning out the window, shivering as she breathed the foggy air, like one of those cheap prostitutes, she realized, breasts propped on cushions, on a sill overlooking the drenched brickwork of a side street.

She withdrew at last, chafing lean arms, a flat chest, and after taking a hot bath in the deliciously comfortable antique bathroom, furnished not only with silver fittings but every texture of warm towel, she went to bed.

She couldn't have been more restless in her sleep. Eddie Twyborn was pestering his sibling. She resisted, but was taken over, replaced. She was relieved finally to have the freedom of this other body, cropped hair bristling on a strong nape, and again the body hair for which there was no longer any need to telephone Fatma and submit to her wax-and-honey treatment (only a minor form of suffering, but painful enough).

As Eddie Twyborn tossed and turned in the white gulf of Baby Untermeyer's four-poster, the mists from the beech wood must have risen higher to be pouring in waves through the open window. Foolish to have forgotten the window. The cold was glacial. He could hear barking too, no brace of wobbly toy spaniels, but that of some large vindictive breed straining at leashes to scent, and on being released, to attack and destroy. In escaping through the first-floor window of what was no longer a hiding place. he suspected that escape can also mean extinction. Well he was committed to both, as the D.S.O. can be awarded to despair running in the right direction. He could detect a glint of boots as straight as beech trunks. The Judge was waiting for him below. Hand in hand they slipped between alternate slats of moonlight and shadow. If it were in fact the Judge, his thighboots were streaming with moonlit water or the slime from recently landed trout. It was not the Judge's hand, too freckled, the joints too pronounced, the skin too squamous.

He said if we lie down here they won't get us they'll fire over our heads Eddie.

Gravenor was forcing him down almost lying on him to protect him from the inevitable.

Not poor Edward, Eadie's husband.

Tears were falling for the past the present for all hallowed hell on earth.

The enemy firing on them from the rising ground beyond the trees the slaver of dogs pouring down into the hollow.

You aren't hit are you Eddie?

He could barely answer such a tender question.

Yes I suppose I am he managed.

It was pouring out.

Wounded in spite of the shield this freckled other body provided.

He tried staunching the wound with his hand as the blood continued pouring out into the hollow in what was no longer a beech copse but an ever darkening pine forest.

He looked down at his fingers and saw that the blood wasn't red but white.

Eadith awoke to find herself in one of the guest beds at 'Wardrobes'. Although disturbing, her mortal dream had also consoled as it ebbed from her. Drawing the nightdress round her naked shoulders, nursing a stickiness between her thighs, she turned her back finally, and after first nibbling, then devouring a Bath Oliver from the japanned tin on the bedside table, slept dreamless into a perversely sunny Wiltshire morning, to which she was introduced by a housemaid, anonymous and milky (she might have taken part in the dream), encouraging her to drink mouthfuls of tea (Ceylon for morning) in between consuming token slices of bread-and-butter.

War, death, and sex were the missing elements in this protected room.

Ursula, Roderick, and Eadith avoided one another till past eleven, when Ursula's friends, risen by supreme effort from their London beds, started arriving, trickling down the paths, clotting on the lawns, recoiling from smells, possibly those of mortality rising out of the beech copse below. Most of the guests looked out of place but seemed to enjoy the irony of it: Diana her melting mascara; returned from her exile at Saffron Walden, Cecily in flounces of crumbling-meringue organdie; an old bag of a Bellasis distant relation whose alter ego of a matted coat-and-skirt might have stood up without support like a similar garment worn by Eddie/Eadith's Eadie. The assortment of males was less vocal, but more important, the Mileses and Gileses who populate the F.O. and other Ministries more mysterious. Herself a whole entanglement of mysteries, Eadith did not intend to investigate anyone else's too deeply.

When those who had been inspecting their rooms (were they better or worse than last time?) had come downstairs, and those who had confidences to exchange had returned by trickles and driblets through the maze of garden, the guests were brought together, according to the law of quicksilver, on Ursula's paved terrace, laughing over their shoulders at the one who, technically their friend, was far more desirably their hostess. Those who had been opening tins of beans in an amusing mews, and dropping the alarm clock together with their gin into the pan in which they were boiling the spaghetti, looked forward to the vast saddles of lamb and bleeding barons of beef they hoped she would provide to feed the starving poor-rich.

On all sides were heard murmurs of 'Ursula darling . . .' if mostly followed by a snort.

Everybody was doing something: writing, painting, marrying a title, divorcing one, destroying a soul. Exposing their teeth, their long fingers clamped to their glasses, every one of them avid for the ultimate experience. If this were a war, their eyelids rejected it. Their glances lingered in rebuttal on the figure brought for their entertainment, speculating whether Mrs Trist, the accredited brothel-keeper, were not in fact a guardsman, a nun, a German, a Colonial, or the tail end of a dream nobody ever succeeds in arresting.

Mrs Trist could not have denied being their equal in crime and frustration, and was only less inquisitive because she might have had more to hide.

Most of Ursula's friends were born with that respect for the theory of discretion common to members of their class. Not so this young man approaching. He had the moist eye, the wreathed lips, the apologetic chin of one who intends to tell and be told all in the shortest possible time. In the name of friendship, naturally. Any confidences to be dished out in due course to the rest; isn't friendship a shared thing?

Dennis Maufey had written a play – indeed several, but this was the one which would be heard about. If all went well he had found backers, who were in fact expected at 'Wardrobes' – some Australians, he lowered his voice to apologize to Ursula's incongruous friend, who was none the less desirable because for the moment fashionable.

He looked at Mrs Trist, either to see how he stood in her estimation, or more likely, whether she should sink in his. He was wearing a rag hat (the Ursula set favoured hats in the garden: rag, raffia, rattan – anything provided it was old and tatty). Only Eadith and the elderly Honourable Bellasis lady in the smelly coat-and-skirt were going hatless.

Maufey congratulated Eadith on her success. 'Not that I've visited your house,' he said. 'I've only heard about it – and wouldn't go there unless you consented to take me on professionally.'

He did not leave off looking at her from under his rag brim, as though deciding how worldly she was.

She smiled back. 'There are too many applicants. One can't take on everybody,' she answered in her coolest English.

He giggled slightly, and looked at her closer than ever. 'I believe you've got something against us. I can tell by your tone of voice. I mean – you're not one of us, are you? The Dominions, possibly?' Always looking at her; he would have so liked to share a secret. 'Wait till you meet my Australians. That'll serve you right, darling. Frantic bores, but they adore the English.'

While Dennis Maufey and Eadith Trist stood about in increasingly disjointed attitudes, slopping the gin poured for them as the prelude to a country lunch, Maufey must have admitted his failure to have the creature confess to the shadow on which he had obviously trodden, for he began to concentrate instead on that other stone façade behind them.

'Ursula's house – *houses*,' he corrected himself, 'are the most ordered I've ever come across. Open any of the cupboards and I'm sure you'll find even the skeletons are catalogued.'

He was so pleased with his epigram, his snigger developed into an outright laugh, then subsided into thought. 'You must meet my Australians – well, you will, you can't avoid it,' looking at her always from under the frayed brim of his hat, 'because they're coming. Oh yes, they'll come. Titles and antiques are truffles to Reg and Nora Quirk. If they're sometimes taken in by puff-balls, they get a lot of pleasure out of the deception.'

'When will they be here?' She might have been making plans to leave.

'Possibly tomorrow. There was talk of polo with a prince today – or was it cricket with some grisly duke? Anyhow, they'll come. They've bought a left-over Turner.' He almost dislocated himself with his worst giggle yet. 'Nora's going to be presented if a war doesn't prevent her wearing her feathers to the circus. Poor darlings, I love them – such a *vigorous* country – I've great hopes . . . We'll always need plays, shan't we? particularly when the bombs are falling.'

After the hopeful playwright had cast her off, Mrs Trist was appropriated by the Honourable Mrs Spencer-Parfitt, who stood clutching to the grubby beige blouse worn inside her tailor-made a glass of the buttermilk Ursula provided specially for Muff.

'I can't think why I turn up at Baby's house-parties. I'm not wanted. And I don't want.' She looked sternly at the woman of whom she had heard tell. 'Are you? And do you?' she asked.

'I shouldn't have come if I hadn't been invited. Your second question is harder to answer,' Mrs Trist replied.

'You're as bad as any of 'em,' muttered Muff, whose christened names were Constance Grace Aurelia. 'People on the whole stink, I think – as the dreadful Americans say.' Then turning on what might have been intended as encouragement, 'Some of 'em stink sweeter than others.'

Muff by now was stinking of the buttermilk past and present she had spilt on her beige blouse, and the cats she slept with in Kensington. Increasing whiffs of Eadie Twyborn began to trouble Eadith Trist.

'I've heard all about you,' warned the honourable lady, slopping some more of the buttermilk, 'but only believe half of what I hear. Nothing is wholly believable today. Nothing is true. Except Dinky my old seal-pointed Siamese, and Dinky – but I shan't talk about that.'

Mrs Spencer-Parfitt started dabbing at herself with a grey, snotted-up Irish hanky.

'Purity . . .' she snuffled. 'That daisy at any rate is pure.' She pointed with the toe of an abraded brogue at a clump of pink-to-white daisies which had shot up since the lawn-mower razed Ursula's lawn to perfection. 'I'd like to think you were,' she turned abruptly to the bawd. 'In spite of what I hear, my instincts as a cat-lover tell me you may be. Too pure even for your own good.'

Eadith was aghast. 'I've never aspired to virtue. As for purity – truth – I've still to make up my mind what they amount to. But hope I may. Eventually.'

'Good for you!'

Somewhere an invisible servant was beating a gong, summoning people to a late lunch; a cold one considering the unreliability of the idle. It was no less sumptuous for being cold, and everybody tucked in, remembering what they would return to in their service flats, the eternal tins they would open in the mews, and the cockroach in the Charlotte Street *ragù bolognese*.

After lunch, and resumption of their hats, most of the guests returned to the garden and arranged themselves in deckchairs, to snooze, or continue their destruction of literature, art, and political careers, the dissection of adulteries they suspected or knew their friends to be conducting, and speculation on Hitler's next possible move in developing the Grave Threat to England.

With nothing to contribute beyond her incongruity Mrs Trist remained unnoticed. She was able to escape to her room. She could have been suffering from indigestion, or going to the lavatory.

Except for a sound of cutlery from the kitchen quarters, the house was heavy with silence, which did not prevent slabs of the past moving round in it. They pursued her as she fled upstairs past Courbet's peasant of the livery jowl. A cloying tortoiseshell light clung as insidiously as the misty future in her dream of the night before.

She stood bathing her face in front of the bathroom glass.

He burped back at her, out of the past or the future.

She felt the better for it, however.

Evening was as uneventful and discursive. The promised Australians, somewhat to Maufey's relief, hadn't arrived. The only incident to affect the displaced bawd was when Madame Siderous beckoned and drew her aside amongst the flower borders at dusk.

'Darling,' Diana began, and her perfume, her breath, overpowered the evening scents of the garden, 'do you realize how you fail to keep your promises?'

Mrs Trist could not imagine for what she was about to stand accused.

'You've never given me the Arab woman's number. The one who knows the wax-and-honey method for removing superfluous hair.'

Madame Siderous was looking at her intently at though expecting the coded reply to a coded question.

'She isn't on the telephone. We'll come to an arrangement next time I see her.'

It couldn't have been the correct answer, for Diana frowned, while seeming to offer a second chance. 'You're surely not one of those tiresome people who, when they discover something special, feel they've got to keep it to themselves.' A mole between her right nostril and the arch of a smoothly painted lip threatened reprisal.

'Yes and no,' Eadith replied; whatever the outcome in friendship or war, she would not be lured into surrendering her closer secrets to the likes of Madame Siderous.

Diana's exasperation returned them both to reality. 'These boring English house-parties!' She reached out and beheaded a delphinium with a quick flick of her brown fingers. 'All these F.O. pin-stripes and sculptured M.I. jaws! Not to mention the pansy artists! And noble crypto-Lesbians! Some of the women here would be more use than most of the men.' Suddenly Diana Siderous seized Eadith Trist by the nose with fingers smelling of nicotine, and sap from the slaughtered delphinium. 'Odd we never thought of doing it together . . .'

Almost at once she must have decided to reduce her gesture and remark to the level of the ridiculous.

'Don't worry, darling,' she screeched, 'I'm sure we'll never feel as bored as that. And disillusion poor old Ursula.'

She took her friend by the arm and was leading her back into what could pass for focus. '*Seriously*,' and Madame Siderous did apparently consider herself capable of seriousness, 'I believe you're Ursula's big disappointment. As a collector, I mean. When you should have been her *grand coup* – the whore-mistress of Beckwith Street, exposing her nipples, gnashing her teeth at the men – and here you are, as sombre as a nun.'

The bronze tunic Eadith was wearing, the skirt susurrating as it scuffed the ground, the long, fluted sleeves, did suggest a nun, or priestess, while the Siderous plastered to her ribs forced on her a stride more stilted than was normal.

When she answered her accuser, the gravity of her expression and movements seemed to have rubbed off on her voice, 'I like to think I'm sometimes capable of more than is expected of me.'

They continued towards the house and the nets of light which had by now been spread for them. The light caught their disappointments and illusions, and for a brief moment portrayed the wooden attitudes, the formal eyes, of a pair of worm-eaten Coptic saints.

Then Madame Siderous announced, 'I'm going to get myself a stiff gin – what else hardly matters – I can face the evening.'

But Eadith remained set in her sobriety.

During dinner she looked for Gravenor but did not find him. Without being asked, Ursula explained casually from down table that he had been called away; she expected him back later that night. Maufey's awaited Australians still had not arrived, which was cause for thankfulness as far as Mrs Trist was concerned.

She spilled some gravy on her bronze tunic and fell to rubbing surreptitiously. All the stains in her life were concentrated in this greasy emblem as she rubbed and rubbed with the spotless napkin. She reduced it at last enough to satisfy her conscience. More startling was the bloody mark left on the napkin by nervous lips; he hid it with such vehemence he might have been sitting with Prowse amongst the mutton fat in Peggy Tyrrell's kitchen.

Nobody could have noticed. They were all hanging on a story told to one of them by 'Ribb's closest friend'. Their eyes seemed to be probing the rather innocuous anecdote for a clue to their whole future.

Back in her cell, Eadith was afraid she might re-enter her dream of the night before. She heard what could have been the ten-year-old Bentley swirling over gravel, then rolling more evenly on the paving-stones laid as an approach to what were the stables in the days when life at 'Wardrobes' was sedate and indestructible.

During the night she heard laughter in the passages and on the landing, doors opening, closing, and opening. Her own door was tried several times, but she had thought to lock it. Whoever it was retreated after threatening to wring off the knob.

She fell into a sleep as blank as a paving-stone.

The warm, muzzy days might have been created expressly for the professional guests at country house-parties. At the same time they were too bland, too languid to refuse admittance to an outsider. She was free to disintegrate in the overall pointilliste haze of woods and fields, in particular the marigolden water meadows. The more demanding nights, the dinner table, the dressing, the door-knobs, the dreams were what made her apprehensive.

The following evening, those who showed interest enough were told that the Australians Reg and Nora Quirk had arrived.

On the terrace before dinner Eadith recognized the Decent Bloke and the Good Sort; she quailed for antipodal innocence exposed to hereditary expertise.

Introducing the new arrivals, Ursula was exercising what she understood as infallible charm.

As she called the roll, her friends were looking exceptionally grave. 'Diana — Cecily — *Muff* — Hugo — Waldo — Miles — Giles . . . Dennis you know, of course,' when what they knew was the least part of him.

On finishing the introductions, Ursula opened her cornflower eyes to their fullest, to beg a favour. 'I hope you'll let me call you Nora and Reg,' she appealed in a sustained whisper which revealed the transparent tips of her teeth.

The Quirks could only smile and mumble back to convey their humble gratitude, till Reg got up the courage to suggest, 'Names make it more homely, don't they?' and Nora, though hardly a girl, let off a corroborative, girl's giggle.

Like a ventriloquist not sure of his skill, Dennis Maufey stood mouthing his way too obviously through his dolls' performance. The Quirks could only be vastly rich to subject him to such agony.

In her unhappiness, Eadith Trist had remained on the edge of darkness. She was dressed even more sombrely tonight, in black, and for this reason perhaps, Ursula had failed to notice, till it could have been a glint from the cocks' feathers with which her long sleeves were edged, drew attention to her presence.

'And Eadith Trist – one of the friends I value most.' Her eyelids batted, not so much for an exaggeration, as to project her charm more shamelessly.

'How lucky I'd consider myself to be one of the friends Lady Ursula values most.' A small spry woman with a practical denture, Nora Quirk might not have been so innocent after all; the female of the species often isn't, Eadith remembered from her antipodal past.

While drinks were brought, the Quirks and Mrs Trist remained entangled on the outskirts, as though it had arranged itself thus, outsiders drawn to the arch-outsider.

Reg Quirk implanted his confidences more firmly by driving a shoulder into the person he was addressing (she was more or less his equal in height). 'I'm not apologizing for we Australians, but you've got the edge on us when it comes to culture– tradition. All this,' he nudged her and looked around. 'Democracy's right enough. The stuff's there for anyone to take if you grab quick. Then you sort of hole up. Out with us, the Lady Ursulas aren't gunner let you horn in without you have an English accent. They're the jealousest mob on earth.' He followed up his semi-indictment with a metallic laugh.

Nora muttered something like, 'The Australian twang'll get you in over here, but don't let it outstay its welcome.'

Eadith saw that the Quirks were recent vintage Golson. In the course of the evening she observed that although Reg normally wore the expression of a pole-axed bullock, he was revitalized at mention of investments, dividends, holdings, debentures, the magic word PROPERTY. This latterday Curly hankered after the paraphernalia of irrelevant living, at the same time dreaming on the image of the Gothic spire and myths such as Progress and Royalty.

'It was our greatest day, wasn't it, Nora? when we went down to Buckingham Palace, and stood outside the railings, and watched the King and Queen come out.'

Nora was moodier than Reg, less willing to join in the game. 'The little princesses are adorable.' She smiled an automatic, enamelled smile; Nora would most likely come clean with another woman while rinsing the smile under the tap after dinner.

Tonight Mrs Trist found herself seated between Dennis Maufey and Gravenor. The latter was smiling in almost any other direction, but Dennis touched her sleeve.

'How brilliant, Eadith, to have thought of cocks' feathers!' He stroked the sleeve in a purely abstract gesture of understanding.

She turned to Gravenor when there was a lull in his intercourse with cronies across the table, and on his left, Jill Watmore Blood, an aspiring actress who never let you forget she was also the Admiral's daughter. Jill had tickets on Rod, and was keeping an eye on the Maufey–Quirk relationship (she was on cheek-rubbing terms with Dennis) no doubt hoping for a part in the play.

Eadith aimed at Gravenor between mouthfuls of a consommé so exquisitely clarified there was no longer any substance in it beyond the several carrot stars shuddering in its transparent shallows. 'We thought we'd lost you,' she tried, 'when you swirled off, without giving us any sign that you might come back.'

'We? Us? I can't believe the gang was broken-hearted!'

He had deflated her with one slash. The tears were pricking behind her eyeballs, and at the back of her throat, where she was scalding her uvula with the routine soup. He must have known. Or didn't men experience the sensation of desperate, suppressed tears? She couldn't remember. Rod, a dry one, gave no clue, his lips pleating in apparent disdain below a clipped, sandy moustache.

'It was only a manner of speaking,' she said, 'to quote yourself and others.'

She could hear Reg Quirk in the distance hurling opinions heavy enough to demolish Ursula's table arrangements, 'Now, out with us . . . But you over here . . .' The bellows of the pole-axed bullock were ruffling the waters in which, as centrepiece, a dove carved out of white jade was gazing at her own reflection, while the little dishes of salted almonds and crystallized fruits glittered with increasing intensity.

Nora was more reserved than Reg. Eadith was conscious of eyes glancing in her direction, anxious to establish a relationship inspired by womanly sympathy as she understood it.

Whereas the more wordly Eadith Trist was all at sea in this

world of splintering light, cool, slanted accents, and oblique references, as she conducted her courtship of a lover who wasn't. In the circumstances Nora Quirk's sympathetic glances only assailed her, and each time Reg opened his big Australian mouth she was scarified: her flesh still reeked of the branding-iron which had seared it in her Australian past.

Dennis Maufey's claw had left off exploring the cocks' feathers; it was actually Rod's hand asking for assurance under cover of the table.

They sat holding hands regardless of the incised masks of the Mileses and Gileses, the Muffs and Cecilys, at Baby's party — all of them nourished on the boiled brains and milky rice prescribed by Nanny and rammed home by the under-nursemaids, the pap which under-housemaids, their cracked fingers black with coal dust, produced off trays, or in more impressive households, from the nursery hatch.

Rising out of a taut throat, Ursula's laughter rustled as minute diamond chips might have if released in a shower. She was no match for Diana Siderous, whose throatiness had the brazen clang of an Arab *fantasia*. Yet their targets were usually the same.

Hand in hand, Rod and Eadith sat looking at each other from time to time; perennial children, they could not believe in their situation however much they longed.

Jill Watmore Blood, who was falling out of her uppers, had to break up something, she wasn't sure what. 'A message from Daddy, Rod duckie: he hopes you'll join us at Cowes. Daisy and Buster will be there, so it's practically a royal command. But that's up to you. I probably shan't make it. It looks as though the piece at the Shaftesbury won't have folded.' She grimaced, picked at her canines with a vivid nail, planted a carnation in her cleavage, directed a smile at Reg Quirk, and a more virginal one at Nora.

Rod looked at Eadith. 'I'll never know what you think because you're not going to tell me.'

'Then I must have caught the English disease.'

She laughed. She was so happy watching the bristles of his pink moustache moving as he masticated, the chapped lips folding themselves around morsels of chicken, and finally, out-of-season peach. She knew there would be pockets of his body lined with soft peach-skin in contrast to the overall expanse of aggressive, male bristle.

340

She looked across, and found Nora Quirk looking her way, composing her blenched lips on her denture. Again Eadith looked, and Ursula suggested some oriental bird stilled by the eighteenth century on the surface of an English artificial lake. Attracted by a spectacle, cattle were descending the other side of a ha-ha, amongst them Reg Quirk, his Australian *museau de bœuf* parted.

Eadith was so in love with the unattainable Rod, she might have submitted to Reg had a beefy shoulder chafed her flank.

Glances had reached the interlocking stage at Lady Ursula's dinner table.

They served coffee on the terrace, where the English began breaking out, quivering with daring, brandy, and malice. They were discussing the Australian coo-ee, of which the more travelled and more generally knowledgeable among them had experienced or heard tell.

'Can you do it, Nora?' Maufey enquired of his still not fully controlled puppet.

'I'll say I can!' Nora nearly giggled her head off, snapping her denture shut in time to avert disaster.

Reg only muttered 'I reckon . . .' and plodded off in the direction of the copse below.

After ploughing through shaven lawns, shaggy with dew by this time of night, and reaching the descent into natural grass, beeches, and darkness, he turned and called, 'Come on, Nora, let 'em have ut!'

Nora filled her lungs, which everyone saw were considerable, and let fly through the Wiltshire dark, her navel straining at her Schiaparelli.

'Coo-*ee*?' she called.

And Reg called back, 'Coo-EE!'

The upright English were falling about inside their skins, while the Australians called back and forth like a couple of currawongs nourished on Wahroonga milk.

Only Eadith Trist had watched a currawong perching on an angophora's elbow, his free claw clenched on the finch whose head he was chewing.

The Quirks might have extended their performance longer than was expected of Maufey's amusing Australians, if the admiral's actress daughter hadn't declared, 'I'm sure I can do it – but from a distance. I'm going down to Reg Thingamy.'

At which, Currawong Nora failed to answer her mate's call. She had, in fact, that bird's vindictive eye. As Miss Watmore Blood glided over the shaggy dew before plunging into the natural grass, where the daffodils had been tied down at the end of the season, Nora Quirk's silence pulsated, as did her bust against the Schiaparelli, awaiting the cards fate might deal.

'Reg will teach me,' Jill burbled back, but failed to reach her goal for falling into the lily pond. 'Oh, God! Oh, Christ! Oh, *fuck*!'

Everybody was rushing to disentangle the actress from the lily-pads.

Though Baby ('. . . my precious lilies . . .') might have wished her drowned.

So lean, so loose-swinging, so weed-bedraggled, Jill was almost unrecognizable.

'Take her away, somebody,' Ursula commanded. 'What she needs is a hot bath. And a rub down with a warmed towel.'

'But I don't!' Miss Watmore Blood protested. 'It's a warm night. What I need is Reg – Rod – Reg – no bloody *towel*!' She was led away, her escaped breasts jumping like the frogs she had disturbed underneath the lily-pads.

After her too impulsive guest had been removed, Lady Ursula ordered beer to quench everybody's thirst, though perhaps more especially that of her re-united Australians. These stood on the perimeter of light enclosing Baby's disorganized party. Not ungratefully, the Quirks drank their warm beer. Reg might have been 'consuming' his. The demonstration and his climb back from the copse below had left him breathless. He should by rights have joined the British males, but was intimidated more than he would have cared to admit: they were talking shop, or same thing – foreign affairs.

He felt more at ease with this woman, this Mrs Trist – this Eadith – whatever they told you about her 'house'. (Might try it out some afternoon while Nora was at the dress shows.)

Reg confessed to Mrs Trist, 'The wife and I were saying only the other day, however much you feel at home in England it's good to hear your own language again. Just now you come across it all over London. It's odds on you'll run into friends. Last week it was Joanie Golson – next table at the Savoy . . .'

'No, dear, Claridge's.' Nora sighed.

'. . . Joanie – Sir Boyd's widow – of Sydney's most go-ahead store.'

If there was no holding Reg after a couple of warm beers, Nora only faintly preened.

'And yesterday on the Mall, it was Eadie — Mrs Justice Twyborn.'

'Hardly friends, dear — the Twyborns. Once or twice we shook their hands.'

'As you say, we've shaken hands, and I'm proud to have shook the Judge's hand — one of our most distinguished Australians.'

Mrs Trist dared ask, 'Is the Judge with Mrs Twyborn in London?'

Checking up on the menfolk! Well, it was her business.

Mr Quirk stood swirling the dregs of beer at the bottom of his glass with appropriate solemnity. 'The Judge recently passed on,' he had to inform her.

Flushed by social triumphs and the success of their little performance, death could have been the Quirks' least concern. There was not yet any sign that they would ever be threatened. The croaking of disturbed frogs, the clatter and splintering of human laughter at its most inhuman, a night bird calling more poignantly than the self-possessed currawongs of earlier, cannot have entered their consciousness. So why was this woman acting queer?

For the invisible bird, throbbing and spilling like blood or sperm, had brought Eddie Twyborn to the surface. Abandoning what the Quirks would still work into their travelogue as a cosy occasion, he started skittering across the lawn, the brutally illuminated terrace, into the house, in his ridiculous drag, the wisps of damp-infested cocks' feathers, trailing skirt, stockings soaked with dew.

At the foot of the stairs the reduced Eadith Trist was brought up against the one she most needed but hoped to avoid at the present moment.

'All this evening, Eadith, you would have avoided me if I hadn't practically handcuffed you under the table. I realize you must hate me.'

Again he put out a hand, as controlled as hers was trembling, and which she must resist whatever the hurt.

'Who's to decide — love and hate — not hate, *despair* — where one ends and the other begins?'

She pushed past him, continued up the stairs, and locked the door.

Early next morning Mrs Trist organized a car to drive her to the station. It was only Sunday. She left a note for Ursula. She would have a long wait for one of the rare Sunday trains. She preferred it that way: watching the cows munching through their idyllic pasture, alternate mouthfuls of veridian grass and pure English daisies. Perched on the platform beside her dressing-case she might have dozed if images of the past had not been slid between the brown barrels of the grazing cows, and as focus point of past and present Judge Twyborn's features melting like forgotten butter amongst the undulations of the placid field.

Mrs Trist might never have been away from home; she found her house in perfect running order: business thriving, accounts kept, no suicides or abortions, no cockroaches or rats. She might have felt jealous of her admirable deputy if it hadn't been for recent developments and information. In the circumstances Eadith was too distracted.

She began to wonder whether her life were a collage of fantasies: her profitable whore-house, her love for Gravenor, the romantic dresses, the elaborate jewels. On the other hand she could still practically feel the calluses got by crowbar and shears, experience the voluptuous ease of entry through the gateway of Marcia Lushington's thighs, the agonies of Don Prowse's thrust, hillocks of chaff crumbling around a salt-stricken mouth, pure contact with the Judge under the honeycomb bedspread of a circuit hotel.

And now Eadie, that squalid old drunk, Joanie Golson's ex-lover. The ex-lovers, the ex-husbands, the ex-lives were all weighing on Eadith Trist.

Since Ada had shown herself capable of managing the house, Mrs Trist had taken to walking, not only at dawn, the hour of forgiveness, but also by broad daylight, and farther afield, through scorching or soaking afternoons, in which newspapers blew in her face, or wrapped themselves in wet wads, like compresses, round her ankles and shins, as she shambled low-heeled over bottle-tops and broken glass, through dead kittens and vegetables, endlessly marching, round Islington, Stepney, Bethnal Green. What she hoped to escape or discover was not clear even to herself. At least nobody questioned her, but she was constantly accused of the worst sins by the graffiti she half-read in passing, and the face gnashing at her out of posters warned her what to expect.

344

After circling out east, she would be drawn westwards again, and her aim grew more palpable, more disturbing.

She first sighted Eadie Twyborn coming out of St Clement's, heading down the Strand past the great hotels and temporarily extinguished theatres. None of it looked to exist for Eadie.

She went into St Martin's. Eadith followed in her flat shoes, which long distances had worn down sideways.

In the otherwise empty church the two women sat at some distance from each other. Eadie was wearing dark gloves. She was holding what looked like a prayer-book. But did not pray, or gave no visible sign of doing so. Like Eadith, who was empty-handed, she simply sat.

Somebody was practising on the organ; the phrases of music unrolled rather jerkily, like the slats of alternate light and rattan in a blind. Somebody entering from the street let in a draught of air, a blast of light, whiter, more revealing than the illuminated slats of purely subjective organ music. The cold light from the street was trained for a moment on Eadie Twyborn. The blotched and raddled, leathery skin constantly boiling over in the past with emotion, resentment, frustration, curdled passion, had been washed white. Any ravines and craters were those of moonscape rather than skin.

Almost at once the church's padded door was sucked shut. The anonymous figures continued what amounted to a common vigil. If they were not brought closer together, the organ music, and beyond it the drone of traffic flowing into Trafalgar Square and distributed through the arteries, prevented that.

Eadie went out eventually, followed by Eadith, across the square, past the Gallery. On.

In the moil of the Circus Eadith lost sight of Eadie. As she raced backwards and forwards, down and up Pall Mall, hovering on the cusp of Regent Street, Eadith could feel herself looking like a drooping and distracted hen, beak open, throat extended, gasping amongst the horehound during respite from a doom she both dreaded and awaited.

For better or worse, she had lost Eadie the mother of her flesh and blood if not her spirit. She sensed that the loss was only temporary. Clutching the prayer-book with tenacious gloves, Eadie must recur during what remained of life.

In one last desperate attempt to face her mother, Eadith charged into St James's, Piccadilly. Outside the church darkness was clotting; inside, the candles were lit, for a small group gathered to avert by their prayers the war which was threatening.

Edith did not catch sight of Eadie. The possibility that she might never see her mother again forced her on her knees on a badly upholstered hassock. A waxen priest was comforting his flock. Eadith Trist plaited her fingers amongst her penitential rings. She focused on one striated agate in which she hoped to see the eye of God. But nothing worked. Perhaps if she had been Catholic, Orthodox, a humble charwoman — anything but a doubting Australian and the bawd of Beckwith Street.

Head bowed she left the church and started for home.

All down the Dilly the whores were drawn up in their irregular ranks. Some of them recognized Mrs Trist. They shrieked friendly obscenities. She should have felt rejuvenated walking amongst them along the Dilly under this translucent summer sky. But she wasn't. The shadow of Eadie Twyborn, prayer-book clamped between black gloves, was walking beside her, against this iron railing, beneath a greening sky.

Mrs Trist reached home. None of her girls or regular clients might have recognized her had she made her presence known. Ada asked no questions, but helped her mistress out of her clothes, or as far as the last layer. Ada had always respected any depths of experience her associates did not wish to reveal. She was as invaluable a presence in a brothel as she would have been in a nunnery.

The outbreak of war was to some extent a relief. The people could now assemble in the churches unashamed, asking for God's forgiveness and protection. Equally shameless were those who filled the brothels and pubs to indulge themselves as they had never dared, or more simply, fucked in the streets during the black-out. Someone had sprained an ankle by tripping over a couple in the gutter; someone else had been concussed by butting into a Laocoon group enlaced against the wall of Apsley House; one of Lady Ursula's elderly housemaids had gone out to post a letter after dark and found herself sticking it into a policeman.

Many of the rich crossed the Atlantic; others fled to the fells and dales, where they settled down to backgammon and gin while lamenting the intolerable boredom to which they were being subjected. Practically a national museum, Ursula Untermeyer set about organizing for herself at 'Wardrobes' a select team of scientists or scholars in preference to a rout of snotty children. The stories one heard were terrifying.

For the children were being evacuated. Taking a short cut across a railway station, Eadith Trist had come across one of the first of these contingents. Where children had gaped or hooted at her in the past, none of these seemed to notice the baroque figure pushing her way through their masses, as they stood silent, or were carried on variable, directionless currents in the girdered gloom of the railway station. They were too obsessed by the approaching journey, or tearful for a permanence they might never find again. Some of them bright and sharp as broken glass, others pallid and soggy as the layer between the pastry and the meat of the pork pies they were biting into. The piddle was already running down the legs of some, by rivulets, to gather in pools on the station grime. There were pregnant mothers, mothers giving suck, mothers flushed and aggressively jolly, others who mopped their own cheeks more often than their children's. Whether the mothers were accompanying the army or not, the whole operation was being conducted by a corps of selfless ladies, almost the antithesis of womanhood, in oblong dresses, hats in mole or rust tones, and in some cases coats trimmed with apologetic snatches of fur. Everybody slung with gas-masks. Surrounded by cases, bundles, parcels.

Mrs Trist fled through the expectant or smeary children, past the officers marshalling their platoons. She could not face the reflections in these women's spectacles, not so much reproachful as compassionate.

She regained the street.

After that, a miasma of inertia seemed to invade the lives of ordinary people. However Whitehall might tinker, and intentions gather beyond the Rhine, war was no concern of theirs, unless in the waking hours of night. At the same time, in their benumbed workaday consciousness, the faithful were scarcely less faithful in their devotions after being frightened almost out of their minds, or the sensual less licentious having dropped to the potentialities of licence.

In Beckwith Street Mrs Trist was doing a roaring trade. The boom brought with it an increase in minutiae. Whatever else, she must not relax the standards of her house in echoing the common cry, 'There's a war on.'

'Why wasn't it paid?' the bawd demanded irritably, while fitting a pair of enamelled macaws into pierced ears and wincing for the pain her weighty ear-rings inflicted on her.

'Because I slipped up,' Ada admitted.

As it happened, it was only the baker's bill, but her deputy's omission rankled in the bawd along with her own shortcomings.

In these unnatural times there were many other not unnaturally neglected details, such as the corporal's champagne which should have been chalked up to the banker (why not to those who were more affluent?) and compensation for Helga while laid off after the clap she got, she was pretty certain, from a colonel in the Welsh Guards.

In the lull after the outbreak of war, the minutiae might have made it appear that life had settled down to normal, had it not been for the barrage balloons, the sandbags, the gas-masks, and the exodus of children. As for the black-out, only puritans regretted what others saw as a cloak for normal human behaviour.

Mrs Trist was coming downstairs, a hand barely connected with the elegant polished rail, which over the years palms had clutched, seared, brutalized on the way up. She herself felt cool and detached, the dress she was wearing, its tropical leaves and archetype birds, collaborating effortlessly with her recently bathed and anointed body. She put up a hand in a purely conventional and quite unnecessary gesture, smoothing hair which the Mauritian devoted to its upkeep had worked on the day before. Her legs, her arms, her jaw, were as smooth as marble, for Fatma the Arab from Mansoura had spent the morning at Beckwith Street. So Mrs Trist was at her best, enjoying a confidence she rarely possessed unless in the eyes of others.

She reached the foot of the stairs, her dress floating agreeably around her figure, her own image greeting her in the glass ahead. His lordship, Ada had told her, with 'that nephew', and some other gentleman she couldn't place, were waiting for her in the small untidy room referred to as the 'office' or the 'parlour' according to the circumstances.

A sense of pleasurable anticipation made her linger an instant in the hall rearranging a bowl of florist's rosebuds.

Tonight she seemed to make a noticeable impression on Rod.

When she went in, they swam ahead of the casual greeting they exchanged as a matter of course from a distance. Without so much as touching hands they were at once united in a sober bliss unrelated to their sensual bodies or the period of time in which they were living.

The moment's perfection made her anxious to notice and include those Gravenor had brought with him. The nephew Philip Thring was a nice, inconspicuous youth, of fluffy cheeks, bitten nails, and nervous manner. Introduced to her house by his uncle, he had come there once or twice without taking part in its activities. He was too diffident, too effeminate. They served him supper, while upstairs, Gravenor was having one of the girls, or if later in the morning, they dished up bacon and eggs for the boy, without ceremony in the kitchen, where he sat friendly but aloof amongst a bunch of whores tearing into their food and the quirks revealed by their clients of the night.

On one occasion a certain drunken Guards' officer, a friend of the uncle's, exploded. 'I swear that boy's a bloody pansy. I wish, Eadith, you'd lay on one of your girls to find out.'

To which she replied, 'I can't, Hugo, if Philip himself isn't inclined. You can only lead a horse to water . . .'

'If you shove their noses in it, they'll sometimes see their way to drink.'

'He mightn't be able to afford it,' she suggested lamely.

'If that's what's biting you,' he fumed, 'I'll set up a fund – to prove my point.'

'Your point,' she said, 'is not the one that matters.'

This evening Gravenor's nephew was looking more diffident than ever, his cheeks fluffier, his complexion more noticeably English-roses blemished by thrip. His eyes appealed to her not to reveal a secret, the key to which she may or may not have possessed; while Gravenor ignored or accepted the boy as little more than an inevitable accompaniment, as family ends by being, or the overcoat he had left with the maid who let them in.

Still under the influence of this evening's reunion with the uncle, Eadith was all kindness for the nephew. Not that she could pay much attention to him after recognizing in the third man, Reg Quirk, the original Decent Australian Bloke. She was unnerved by the pale blue eyes, the texture of the tanned skin, most of all by the slight connection with Eadie Twyborn, even before the voice began to rasp.

'Glad to catch up with you again, Eadith. I've come to sample what you've got to offer. Nora won't have me around while she packs. I reckon she doesn't want me to count what she calls the few miserable rags she's picked up at the dressmakers'. We're off home tomorrow.'

There was no reason why he should mention Eadie Twyborn, and of course he didn't.

Reg Quirk was more intent on apologizing for their prudent retreat from a danger zone. 'Can't stay on eating our heads off in London while the English are up against it, can we?'

He glanced to see whether his excuse was accepted or condemned. He must have found her looking exceptionally grave, for he flinched somewhat.

Should she sound him on Eadie's whereabouts?

At the point of doing so, she couldn't. Instead, she led the party upstairs to her reception- or show-room, and assembled a handful of girls for her clients to choose from. Gravenor her 'lover' could only be numbered among the clients. Heavy lids and quizzical lips implied it was her own fault. He chose a new acquisition, a girl she hadn't taken to the moment after engaging her. She had not been able to rationalize her antipathy for Elspeth, who was slender, refined, diffident, submissive. Her insipid manner and milk-and-roses complexion were not unlike those of Gravenor's nephew, Eadith suddenly realized. She was unable to give further thought to what might have been a bitter situation, because she was busy accommodating the randy Australian.

Reg fancied Jule. 'As smooth a swatch of black velvet as I ever clapped eyes on.'

The two men were taken by the girls to their rooms. Everyone appeared satisfied, excepting Eadith, faced with entertaining the nephew in between receiving officers of the Armed Forces and turning away the rowdies bred by the black-out and wartime clubs.

In her own boredom, exasperation, and resentment at Rod's choosing Elspeth, she said to the youth she was landed with, 'How boring for you, Philip, to hang around unemployed in a thriving brothel.'

The boy blushed. 'I can't say it isn't a bore, Mrs Trist, and I shouldn't be here if my uncle didn't expect it of me.'

Irritation forced her to answer, 'You hardly live up to his expectations, I'd say.'

The young man might have been more embarrassed, and she regretful of her cruelty, if Gravenor hadn't returned to the room and beckoned the whore-mistress from the doorway.

'Surely one of your girls can take it from him. Do try, Eadith darling. We may all be dead a year from now.' He smiled his gentlest, most haggard smile, patted her arm, and was gone to enjoy the wilting Elspeth.

Eadith was torn by desire for revenge on those unconscious of their guilt, while dreading discovery by the lover she most desired.

On returning to Philip Thring she must have appeared agitated. He looked away discreetly.

'I mean,' he said, blushing again as he resumed their broken conversation, 'what I find at Beckwith Street interests me aesthetically – and for its perversity, morally. But it doesn't rouse me physically. Even if my uncle despises me for it – his friends do, and I think he must – I can't take part.'

Mrs Trist said, 'I believe you've almost told me a secret.'

The tremulous mirror he was offering her must have reflected the sympathy she felt for this boy. More than that: they were shown standing together at the end of a long corridor or hall of mirrors, which memory becomes, and in which they were portrayed stereoscopically, refracted, duplicated, melted into the one image, and by moments shamefully distorted into lepers or Velasquez dwarfs.

The tatters of diseased skin and hydrocephalic deformities were in the end what brought them closest.

The young man allowed her to take his hand. Ada passing along the landing opened Mrs Trist's own door with a superficial unconcern to disguise a celebratory gesture. Closing the door on the celebrants, she continued on her way to some other more mundane business of a bawdy house.

Gravenor and Reg Quirk had finished the eggs and bacon served them it seemed some time ago. Into the room where they were sitting, there floated a pallid London light through the rather sooty gauze protecting an equivocal interior from a curious outside world.

'Where the devil has the boy got to?' Gravenor complained.

Reg was extracting splinters of bacon with a gold toothpick. He looked older under his tan and not so much wiser as blank.

Ada assured the uncle, 'Mr Thring'll come when he's ready.'

'Which girl took it from him, Ada?'

But Ada was less communicative than ever. 'I'm not the one to tell your lordship. I only saw him go upstairs with Madam.'

By now Gravenor was quite tormented, his pink, clipped moustache prickling, his used, freckled skin jumping, most noticeably in the pouch under his left eye. This must have been where Gravenor's main pulse was located.

After Ada had refreshed their coffee and laced it with a liberal tot of brandy, he couldn't prevent himself blurting, 'Don't tell me my nephew is the only man known to have bedded Eadith Trist!'

'How am I to say, sir?' Ada answered. 'I've not known Madam all her life, and can't speak for every moment of the time I've known her.'

It was too reasonable for Gravenor not to accept, and his friend disrupted further speculation by interjecting, 'A fine woman – I wouldn't mind screwing 'er meself.'

Presently Philip came downstairs, his air so discreet nobody could have found fault with it.

'Shall I bring you some breakfast, sir?' Ada suggested.

Philip appeared undecided. He sank down, elbows planted in the table at which his uncle and this friend were sitting, the one surly, the other gross and drowsy from sexual repletion.

'Go on, Philip,' Gravenor ordered. 'Ada knows what's good for you. Get your strength back after a night in the whore-house!'

While the sound and smells of grilling bacon, tomatoes, and kidneys mounted from Mrs Parsons's kitchen, the uncle grew increasingly irritated, not to say maddened, at sight of his nephew's skin coarsening under the girlish down. So he imagined, or so it was.

He was goaded into calling out to Ada while the boy was devouring the plate of food, 'Isn't Mrs Trist coming down? To gorge herself on bloody kidneys?'

'I couldn't say, sir, but don't expect so,' Ada replied.

Gravenor became contrite, resigned, respectful of Ada's convention.

He paid up, and after recovering from his amazement at watching Philip lick the last vestige of bacon fat from the blade of his knife (there's a war on, Rod had to tell himself), asked for his overcoat.

The three men left the house and went their various ways.

A second golden summer accompanied the waves of invasion, the retreats, the numb scramble to defend what was left. Yet the People's War was still by no means everybody's. Figures strolled in the parks in their shirtsleeves, lolled in deckchairs at lunchtime, offering their cheeks to an indulgent sun. There were the letters from across the Atlantic, where the Dianas and Cecilys had installed themselves to their advantage in New York apartments. The Australians — who could blame them? — were returning home by droves. So there was, and there wasn't, a war. There were the barrage balloons, of course: amiable bloated cows, or sinister intestinal ganglia, depending on how one felt that day. The same applied to the sky-writing, which in the heat of a summer afternoon observers on the ground might interpret as an exercise on a blue slate. More disturbing were those old, indigent characters who had been overlooked, or refused to be evacuated, and who were haunting even the better streets to the discomfort of those who dismiss on principle, old age, ill-health, poverty, any phenomenon which threatens personal continuity. One might still succeed in dismissing other people's dead and wounded, but not these ancient harbingers, their wrinkles pricked out in coal dust or soot, who looked as though they had crawled from the ruins of a structure built for eternity. As indeed it had to be. There were too many sandbags around, to protect it from blast. There were all these uniforms. One could accept the smell of khaki and sweaty socks mingling with the stench of duck droppings and urinals when so many healthy lads from the Dominions had arrived to defend all that is most worthy of defending. In the circumstances, it was easy to accept adultery, perhaps even sodomy — more difficult their dreadful accents.

But the ancient harbingers remained haunting the streets. And night thoughts evading the golden days of what might be the last summer.

This was the London in which Mrs Trist reached the apogee of her career or fate. Not that she aspired to heights. Experience in her several lives had left her with few illusions. She was sceptical of history, except at a ground-floor level. She could not believe in heroes, or legendary actors, or brilliant courtesans, or flawless beauties, for being herself a muddled human being astray in the general confusion of life. (If she had been born all of a piece, she might have become a suburban housewife or, without those brakes which impede a woman's progress or downfall, a small-time down-to-earth whore.)

In her actual situation, she did not believe that people on the whole questioned her bona fides. Dennis Maufey might have as he gibbered snide compliments and stroked the cocks' feathers edging her sleeve. Philip Thring was an idyll so tender it would not have survived a second encounter. Gravenor could not suspect or he would not have continued making discreet demands. Dear Angelos Vatatzes had accepted the anomaly, but within the bounds of Orthodoxy and madness. Distanced by time, Marcia Lushington and Don Prowse could only appear as figments of Eddie Twyborn's lust when not clothed in a human pathos of their own. The Judge and Eadie: Eadie and the Judge. Nothing more difficult than to fit the parents into the warping puzzle without committing manslaughter and condemning yourself for the monster you are and aren't.

She must find Eadie. The Quirks had gone, as had Lady Golson, removing her blood pressure, her arteriosclerosis, her widowhood, and the chamois-leather bag of rings to the safety of Vaucluse Sydney.

Eadith could only feel that Eadie, the other widow, had remained, but where to find her she would not have known, and while wanting to, might not have wanted.

She continued obsessed by the image of her mother in a church pew, black gloves clamped to the prayer-book. She had heard of Italian peasant-women crawling as they licked the floor of the church commemorating their saint, and once in a half-sleep, Eadith visualized Eadie standing at the end of a platform in the underground, herself licking at the stretch of filth separating her from possible redemption. The crowd had parted to enjoy the spectacle of one engrossed in expressing an entertaining form of madness, but soon lost patience. They closed their ranks and started pushing to catch the train which would carry them home to their savoury mince, bangers, or poached eggs wafting veils as insubstantial as those of a first communion.

In the scrimmage the penitent lost her saint.

She must find her, even if finding doesn't necessarily reveal, nor was there any guarantee that Mrs Justice Twyborn would recognize either the elegant fiction or the down-at-heel frump with stubble sprouting from a violet jaw.

But Eadith longed to feel the texture of remembered skin.

She despaired of ever catching sight of her mother, when here she was, ascending by escalator out of the depths of the underground, Eadith herself descending, on a day of rain. All the faces on the up and down conveyed some purpose. Excepting Eadie Twyborn.

As on the first occasion, Mrs Twyborn was dressed in black, her clothes neat for Eadie, but in no way remarkable. Black gloves holding tight to the prayer-book. As she was carried higher, she was staring straight ahead, her abstracted face drained of any human expression.

For a moment of panic Eadith would have liked to think it was not her mother, that Eadie's weatherbeaten, blotched skin could never have existed under the mask of white powder, that her drunken, lipstuck mouth was in no way related to these meek, colourless lips, that the fire of a passionate disposition could not have been so thoroughly extinguished. And yet she knew that, under the ashes of resignation, the scars of retribution, the weight of grief, it had to be Eadie Twyborn.

Again seized by panic Mrs Trist wondered what on earth she could do about the situation. The climax was approaching: ascending and descending they would soon draw level. Should she lean over and touch her mother? She imagined someone like Dennis Maufey exclaiming, 'The hideous melodrama of it, my dear!' Whether melodrama or truth, intense emotion might bring on a heart attack, in an elderly, overwrought woman. And the embarrassment if it were not Eadie: 'I *am* sorry – so like somebody I used to know'; as they were carried apart, the relief, which finally was no relief. Alternately, the pain of, 'Oh, my darling, where can I find you? Tell me, tell me . . .' as they were carried upward and downward, out of reach.

Mrs Trist did not lean over to touch. Once more her will had faltered, the moment had eluded her. She would never find out. The answers were not for her.

She looked back at narrow shoulders in a damp black raincoat disappearing into the upper reaches.

A person on Eadith's present level, glancing sideways as they crossed on the down and up, was fascinated by the despair of a strong, but curiously violet chin, the mouth in a soggy face sucking after life it seemed.

Anyhow, the moment of longed-for, but dreaded expiation had once more been evaded, and was followed by one of passionate regret.

Mrs Trist was received into the lower depths and the desirable anonymity of all those who sojourn there.

Gravenor rang her. He hadn't made contact since the night of Philip Thring's consummation at the brothel in Beckwith Street.

He wanted her down for the week-end at a place he had in Norfolk (he used to refer to it as his 'folly').

'It's quite primitive,' he warned her.

'Comfortable-primitive, I'm sure.'

They enjoyed sharing a slight laugh.

'You never trust me, do you? or believe me, Eadith darling.'

She ignored that. 'But I've my "house" — my business.'

'We know.'

'And I'm no good at mucking in with the English in the country. They never get up in the morning.'

'Don't accuse us, Eadith. I don't want to feel a foreigner. Anyway, where you are concerned.'

There was a long pause on the telephone.

Finally he said, 'This call's going to work out hellishly expensive. I can only say I *want — you — to come*.'

She couldn't give him an answer.

'I'm going away,' he told her from a greater distance than before.

'To where?'

'Out of England.'

She still couldn't bring herself to accept his invitation, but said she would think about it.

When she hung up, the recording of his voice continued playing, just as Eadie Twyborn's apparition never quite left off haunting. From the window she caught a glimpse of those passive, silver cows tethered high above the city. Around her in the house the girls who were less and less hers lay steaming on their beds, prepared to open their legs to anyone in need of their services. One day, she felt, she might walk into the modernized bathroom and take up the razor instead of the toothbrush. (The razor itself, already of antique design, had been a present from Judge Twyborn to his son Eddie.)

She did, however, decide she must accept Gravenor's invitation. He said, 'I'll drive up and fetch you, Eadith.'

He had told her he was there 'sorting out his thoughts' till he went away.

'No,' she said, 'I'll come by train.'

'If you'd rather. I'll meet you at the station, darling.'

She tried to resent being called his darling like some whore-bride who had acquired the label along with an expensive diamond ring; yet she knew it was what she would have chosen.

She wanted to crush her mouth on the chapped-looking lips under the clipped, pink moustache of this emaciated, freckled man. Gravenor in the flesh, and her desire for him, might not have convinced a rational mind any more than would that apparition, narrow-shouldered in its black raincoat, as it was carried upward by the escalator.

Seated in the narrow slot in the train which was jolting her into the increasing flatness of East Anglia, she turned her face away from a landscape which seemed to be moaning at her. Where the latterday Eadie had been wearing gloves and carrying a prayer-book, Eadith's hands were naked and the pressure of her locked fingers was making her rings eat into her.

She hoped she would never arrive; but of course one does.

Rod was waiting for her on the platform, hair sparser than she remembered, legs thinner for a wind blowing his trousers against them. They kissed, his lips cold, thin, yet affectionate, against those which must have felt swollen, grasping, in their otherwise unconfessed desire to be comforted.

She followed up with a rather feeble attempt at rubbing her cheek against his, but he had already withdrawn and she was rubbing instead against a salt wind off the North Sea.

She had not been wrong in thinking the landscape was moaning at her as the train jolted her dispassionately towards her destina-tion. From the direction of the sea came a steady moan insinuating itself between a low sky and flat landscape. The expectations of those walking through a pale light were duly flattened.

Gravenor was holding her hand, chafing her rings with bony fingers. 'I'm so glad, Eadith, you could give me some time before I go away.'

'But where are you going?'

'I can't tell you.'

It increased the anonymity she had coveted intermittently. Yet Gravenor's refusal added another ominous note to a life which was becoming an orchestration of foreboding. Seated beside him in the car she visualized letters some of her girls had shown her from those they imagined to be real lovers, the dates, place names, sometimes whole lines, even paragraphs excised. Eadith was reminded of games Eddie had played under Nanny's supervision, snipping patterns out of folded paper, in a nursery sealed against draughts and asthma.

Turning to Gravenor she said, 'Anyway, Rod, I'm glad I came — that we'll have this time together.'

'If we do have it.'

They were driving through the East Anglian flatlands, which rose very slightly to seaward, protecting them from the forces beyond. As additional protection a straggling crown of black thorns. In one place she noticed an armoured car, dun figures of the military, concrete dragon's teeth and pillboxes, to remind that this low-keyed war was not entirely fantasy.

A flat landscape and preoccupation with war would not allow her to defer answering him for ever.

'Well, I'm here,' she said. 'Why shouldn't we enjoy being together?'

'That's for you to decide. You always close down on me.'

'I like to think we have something better than sexuality,' she half-lied. 'Isn't a relationship richer for leaving its possibilities open?'

She turned to see whether she was beating the English at their own game.

He said, 'Much as I enjoy your company, Eadith, I'd like to know you as a woman — because I love you — even if my temperament doesn't help me convey it.'

It was as difficult for him, she could see, as for herself. She would have liked to leave it at that, but couldn't; she must take more of the blame on herself.

'Day and night I'm surrounded by whores,' she offered as part excuse. 'Girls I'm exploiting, I should make clear. Even they like to think they have what they see as true lovers, sometimes only fellow prostitutes they can depend on for comfort and affection — above sexuality.'

Because she sensed she was causing him pain she was racked by her personal dishonesty. If she had been true to her deepest feelings she would have stopped the car, dragged him behind a hedge – and demolished their relationship.

At least what must be the house was beginning to take shape ahead.

'That's it,' he nodded. 'The camel couchant.'

The folly forming in the bleached landscape was every bit of that: its tower-neck in nobler stone patched with mortar, the body of humbler grey flint. Bits added on contributed a ribbed effect, the buckling timber only waiting for time, weather, or invasion to send it flying apart.

'I love it,' Mrs Trist announced with the glib spontaneity of a guest at an Untermeyer party.

No, she wasn't quite so dishonest; she didn't 'adore' it.

What appealed to her were aspects of its homely ugliness, the local flints, like the knobs of Gravenor's finger-joints. She resisted taking up the hand nearest her, which might have led to more and worse.

After the two of them had struggled inside with her bag, he resumed his apologies in an automatic silence-filling way, '. . . primitive as I warned you, darling.'

There was a fire burning in one room, then in a second. There was more than a touch of luxury, but of a subdued kind, such as the crypto-rich and the aristocratic hope will put them right with democracy.

In the same way the slaves who keep luxury in order may be discounted if they remain invisible.

Rod said, 'There's an old body comes over from the village and cleans up. Leaves a stew – a rice pudding. Otherwise, I do for myself while I'm here.'

'I look forward to seeing that.' She meant it tenderly, but he might have taken it as censure.

He left her after showing her her room, which looked out over the dyke, the crown of thorns, and the uncharitable light off a sea which, although invisible from where she was standing, must be lashing itself into frenzied action.

After living through the approach of one, and the early stages of a second and more equivocal war, she was sensitive to hysteria in the elements as well, yet probably, however many wars she experienced, she would not believe in their reality. Any more than she could believe in her own by now middle-aged face, in which every wrinkle was quivering as she repaired her lips in a fogged glass, driving the lipstick in as though committing a rape.

She glanced at her wrist, not so smooth as it should have been because Fatma had let her down that week. She found herself looking, she realized, for Eddie Twyborn's wristwatch: checking the time when we go over the top. The stench of sweat-rotted leather, mud, blood, and was it semen? rose disconcertingly through the concentrated perfume of French Fern.

She touched her hair and went down to find Gravenor, who called to her from the kitchen.

It was a small, improvised, littered room. She saw at first glance that the expensive utensils were dented or chipped — genuinely used, unless he threw them at himself when alone. Or at someone else if he weren't.

'I don't eat lunch,' he apologized, 'but we'll have something.'

They sat at a scarred table putting away lashings of indifferent cheese perilously perched on hunks of bread. She could see her violent lipstick coming off on the crust of a cottage loaf. They were both cramming in too hard the food which was, for Rod at least, another apology to common man; while Eadith's apology was for herself and that phoenix inside her which in the nature of things would never experience re-birth.

She put out a hand, and they were holding each other's, in her case holding off, fingers buttery, smelling of chain-store Cheddar.

He made coffee and they began listening — oh, no, she might have protested — to the *Grosse Fuge* on the gramophone. When they had descended — and it was no escalator, no apparition on the way up, only the dentist drilling at the ultimate in nerves — she got up out of the low-slung sofa, hoping he was not aware of what she heard as a strangulated fart.

She said. 'Rod, darling — I think I'll go for a walk — by myself. It's what I need.'

She stood above him, like a soubrette swinging the organdie hat, about to launch into a number, whereas in her self of selves she might have been preparing to drown in Wagnerian waves of love and redemption.

'You know what to avoid,' he told her. 'On the sea side, the Army. If they're not on hand to prevent you clambering through the barbed wire, there are mines along the beach.'

He had a coldsore breaking out. She could have fallen on it and sucked it dry. But contented herself with a few little half-coughs, half-sobs, which he probably interpreted as dispassion.

All through the grey-green landscape, the colour of succulents, samphire, dirty sand, lichened stone, blown cloud, war was gathering, she could feel. She could smell blanco, Brasso, male armpits, sergeant-majors' crotches, the phlegm in their screamed orders from away down beyond the uvula, as a prelude to the scream of shells.

Her clothes were almost falling off her as she struggled through the soft sandy soil held together by stones and the sea plants which struggle to maintain themselves between salt air and sand. Her ankles were swelling, she thought. She must struggle back to the lover she had failed, and would continue failing, because of the importance his illusions held for both of them. As she went, her expensive version of the tart's shoe was grinding the starved, dirty-pink pig's face, leaving a trail of inevitable desolation.

She avoided her host until having to face him at dinner. Looking out of her window, she was alerted by a smutch of bronze light glowering on this Anglo-Flemish landscape. Downstairs, Rod was working in the kitchen, wearing a waterproof apron edged with a fly-specked frill.

In what was part-library part-dining room he had lit candles, illuminating the spines of collected works, encyclopaedias, reference books, none of them, from what she saw, complete, certainly none relevant to an insoluble personal relationship, and not much more helpful in a universal context now that the accumulation of human wisdom had been withdrawn from circulation, the voice of percipience silenced, during a re-shuffling of the cards.

Rod came mumbling into the room. Rather than fiddle with black-out curtains, and to enjoy the lingering natural light, he pinched out the candle-flames with his fingers. The room was filled with dusk and a smell of dying candles.

Regardless of his waterproof apron, Lord Gravenor sat graver than ever at the head of the table while they ate the meal he had cooked for her: none of the village body's stew and rice pudding, but a soup so delicate she failed to identify its origins, chicken breasts in cream with slivered truffle, no sweet, but grapes which actually tasted of grape. Lord Gravenor's wartime dinner would have encouraged cynicism if it hadn't been for the air of last supper about it.

When what must have been the last of her lipstick had come off on the napkin, she looked at him and said, 'I'm touched that you should go to so much trouble for somebody so unresponsive,' hastening to add something, anything, to disguise the wound she had inflicted on herself, 'That's the kind of remark I'd have made to my parents if I hadn't been numbed by youth, cruelty — yes, a bit — and fear.' But it didn't help matters at all.

Gravenor didn't comment. He sat behind the shambles of their finished meal, hands clamped between his knees, a travesty in a moustache and a frilly waterproof apron. It was she who seemed invested with the authority and arrogance of manhood; till anger or regret forced her up. She gathered the dishes and started slinging them about in the sink.

Through the window a dollop of yellow moon had appeared in a slate-coloured sky above the black coils of protective wire. By moonlight the concrete defence measures were more than ever irregular teeth.

She plunged, and again plunged, her talons into greasy water. Whatever she handed him he meekly dried, then began to organize the black-out curtains.

The house became stifling.

She escaped to her room, though it wasn't by any means an escape, for she could not lock her door against this kindly man as she had locked it in his sister's exclusive whore-house.

He came to her of course. He lay beside her. The weight of his body tightening the bedclothes over hers, distressed her. She was moved to turn, but either way might have distressed Gravenor more. It seemed that his intention was not to possess her, but to give expression to what he saw as their relationship.

'You're what I always wanted, Eadith. Not that I can explain, exactly. Not that I'd want to. It might be embarrassing for both of us. Baby would be horrified.'

Eadith found some comfort exploring a whorl in the nape of his neck, and buried under the sandy hair, the crater of a boil extinct since little-boyhood. 'If you don't want to, don't tell me, then,' she tried to reason with him.

'Nanny might have understood. The jokes she had with Elsie were pretty borderline as I remember. Elsie did the dirty work of the nursery — brought the food from hatch to table — mopped up when we vomited those boiled brains. Nanny was in many ways an imitation of my mother, but touchable. She had a moustache. I used to put up my hand – and stroke this soft black – animal.'

He was drowsing by now in Nanny's bed. She held him to her.

How the Bellasis children if left to themselves returned to the nursery, in refuge from the noble parents, sycophant guests, and the hierarchy of downstairs servants.

She told him. 'Your fingers still smell of candle-wick. That was a big show-off downstairs in the dining room. I've always been afraid of burning myself.'

They were both more than a little drunk, but fortunately not drunk enough. When she suggested he leave her, he obeyed without protest, so that their relationship remained intact, which was how she must keep it.

She must have been awakened by protesting cries from other voices. It was the same room, except that all but the essentials of furniture had been removed. In this bare, clinical interior the light did not come from the bedside lamp, which she could remember switching on and off, nor was it related to normal daylight. As the room was windowless, she saw, the light falling around her could only have been shed from within, yet from no visible light fittings.

Throughout this flesh-coloured, infra-natural light, she became aware of a fluttering of the bird-voices, moth-like hands, of a brood of children she did not attempt to count. They were too many and too unearthly, also too frightening, in particular the eyes and mouths, which were those of flesh-and-blood children, probing, accusing the room's focal point, herself.

She understood by degrees that the children wanted out; the safe, windowless room (its walls even upholstered, she noticed) was the cause of their distress and she the one they held responsible for their unreasonable imprisonment.

'But my darlings,' her voice sounded as odd as her use of a term she had always tended to avoid, 'here you'll be safe, don't you see?'

But the children continued battering with flat hands on the unresponsive walls, a drumming to which was added, she could hear, sounds of gathering confusion outside, as of wind rising, waves pounding, and worse, human voices, screaming hatred and destruction as some monstrous act, explosive and decisive, was being prepared.

She, too, had begun screaming as she tore free from the hospital sheets pinning her down. 'Can't I make you realize?' She lunged among the milling children, trying to gather them into her arms as though they had been flowers. 'Safe – as you'll never be outside.'

Almost all of them eluded her. Only one little crop-headed boy she succeeded in trapping. She was holding his pink head against her breast, when he tore the nightdress she was wearing, and it fell around her, exposing a chest, flat and hairy, a dangling penis and testicles. To express his disgust, the pink-stubbled boy bit into one of the blind nipples, then reeled back, pointing, as did all the children, laughing vindictively as their adult counterparts might have, at the blood flowing from the wound opened in the source of their deception, down over belly and thighs, gathering at the crotch in such quantities that it overflowed and hid the penis. The dripping and finally coagulating blood might have gushed from a torn womb.

She awoke again, this time to the less hostile reality of Gravenor's guest room, her comparatively smooth body slimy with sweat inside an intact nightdress. A steely light of false dawn entering by a crack between the black-out curtains had replaced the sterile timeless light of her windowless dream. She got up chafing her arms. She could hear what was either a thunderstorm or gunfire, but far out at sea. Along the coast the black coils of wire, the white dragon's teeth, were beginning to materialize.

After dressing she walked some way through the Anglo-Flemish landscape, at each step experiencing the same struggle to withdraw her by no means exaggerated heels from the grey sand and mangled pig's-face.

She must have walked for over an hour. A red sun was rising out of a northern sea. At points along the coast one of the dun-coloured figures would train binoculars on the seascape. Obsessed by the prospect of invasion, they showed no interest whatsoever in what might have been a rewarding suspect in their rear.

When she got in she returned to her room to make up her face before going in search of Gravenor. Her natural lips tasted of salt; there were encrustations at the corners of her eyes, a mingling of sea salt, tears, the detritus which dreams leave.

She found him in his room doing press-ups in his underpants: the long form of an almost transparent, pink grasshopper.

'Why don't you join me?' he suggested. 'The exercise would do you good'; as he went on pressing his chest against the carpet, and up.

'I've taken my exercise. Along the coast. For quite two hours.'

'What a glutton! You might have been arrested by a captain. Or raped by a sergeant.'

'I think I've learnt enough to hold them off.'

Gravenor carried on with his press-ups. Feathered like a bronze cockerel on the shoulders, the pronounced vertebrae so exposed, the calves and Achilles tendons so strained, the heels polished almost as white as the bone beneath the skin, she was overcome by a tenderness which made her avoid them. She went and looked out the window at a view which was becoming hateful to her, as hateful as the blind room in her dream.

'I'm going to leave you today,' she said. 'It was foolish of me to come. And you to have asked me.'

'If that's how you feel, I'll run you over to the station.'

All the banalities of human intercourse were called into play in the kitchen as he served her with a coddled egg, Oxford marmalade, and burnt toast.

He told her she had made herself look 'extraordinarily attractive' and she cackled back at him in self-defence, like an ageing whore who would not have given up doing the boat-trains if the boat-trains hadn't been taken over.

For all that, he didn't seem discouraged.

Although unpunctual at the station, they arrived at the moment the train came in sight.

'I'll write to you,' he told her as they broke free from a hurried kiss.

She couldn't say she would reply because, from the little she had been able to gather, she wouldn't know how to find him. By the same token, he might never reach her.

She looked back out of the narrow window for a last glimpse of this sandy man, standing in his baggy, wind-blown clothes in a flat landscape.

Tentacles from a frayed and grubby antimacassar were trying for a hold on her hair as she lay back against the upholstery and closed her eyes to the press-ups, the pronounced vertebrae, the tense buttocks trembling inside cotton drawers, images she didn't succeed in shutting out; they were projected in even more vivid detail on the dark screen her eyelids had let down.

*

365

In Beckwith Street the train of events provoked the house's long-standing patrons to higher flights of lechery. Then there was a newer breed of client, his motives more obscure, often tortuous. If he was less dishonest than the regulars, it was because his unconscious reasons for disguising the truth were usually pure. These survivors of lost battles seemed intent on avoiding any accusation of heroism, let alone experience of transcendence, which some of them had evidently undergone. Those whose prayers had been answered no longer appeared to have faith, as though prayer were a drug which can outlive its virtue and fail to arrest future threats, more especially the constantly recurring disease of recollection. Now the survivors were falling back on brutishness; not only to absolve them of the sins of embarrassing heroism and shameful spirituality, but to dissolve memories of cowardice, authorized murder, dying friends, the faces of unknown families escaping with their bundles from the wreckage of their normal lives, the mummified death-throes of figures in a burnt-out tank, or a form shrouded in a parachute casually hanging from a tree.

In certain circumstances lust can become an epiphany, as Eadith Trist recognized while talking to some of those survivors of Dunkirk who frequented her brothel.

She was reminded of a man long forgotten, an Australian captain, who had met up with Eddie Twyborn during a lull in the First War. The captain was a Prowse before Prowse's advent, if Eddie had realized. They were sitting together in a poor sort of estaminet some way behind the front, drinking the lees of their watered-down wine.

When the captain suddenly confided, 'There's nothing like a good fuck, mate, when the shit's been scared out of you.'

He rinsed his mouth with the abysmal wine and squirted it out from between his teeth.

Eddie agreed. 'I expect you're right.' As he uncrossed his legs in a delicate situation, he thought he heard the chafing of silk, and blushed behind his dirt and stubble.

'I'll tell you something,' the captain said, 'I've never told it to anyone before — somethun funny that happened to me. We was over there a few weeks ago,' he pointed with his pipe in a vague direction, 'enjoyin' a breather on our way back for a bit of a spell. I started pokin' around where we'd halted. I was too nervous to stay put — we'd had it pretty tough the last trip. I went over to a farm that was still of a piece under cover of the next ridge. Always take a squint at what they're up to on the land. Got a place of me own at Bungendore. Well, I was pokin' round this poor sort of farm. God, it stank! of pig shit, like most of these Frog farms do. When I saw a bloody woman's face lookin' out of the winder at me. She'd every right, I had to admit. So I went in to apologize. We stood there sizing each other up. Couldn't say a bloody word of course. This big, white-skinned, fine figure of a Frog woman – and me. And we started takin' off our bloody clothes. You couldn't say which of us started. She took me by the hand and we got on a bed, not in another room, but on a sort of platform down the other end of the kitchen. You could hear the kids playin' in the yard. Where 'er husband was I couldn't ask. P'raps down the paddock diggin' up turnips. Otherwise, I reckoned, she wouldn't 'uv been so foolish. There was nothun foolish about 'er – *it* – US. Except that I was pretty feeble. I don't mind saying I was tremblin' all over from what we'd been through up the line. But I mounted, and she let me in. An' then this funny thing happened. It was not like I was just fuckin' a Frog woman with greased thighs. I reckon we were both carried, like, beyond the idea of orgasm. In my case, I was too fuckun tired. Just joggun along like it was early mornun, the worst of the frost just about over. As you doze in the saddle. The light as warm and soft and yeller as the wool on a sheep's back . . .'

The captain spat on the estaminet floor.

'You'll think me a funny sort of joker. But that's how it was as I fucked this Frog. And more. Wait till I tell yer.' If he could; he'd begun to look so uneasy. 'It was like as if a pair of open wings was spreading round the pair of us. Ever seen those white cockies pullin' down the stooked oats soon as yer bloody back's turned? Then sitting on a bough screechin' their heads off! Well, like the wings of a giant cocky, soft, and at times explosive. You heard feathers explode, didn't yer?'

By now the Australian captain had begun looking almost demented.

'You'll think I'm a shingle short! Don't know what the woman thought or felt. There was this language difficulty, see? When suddenly she let out a yell. Me – I thought this is it – it's 'er old man back from the turnips! So I jumped off, and started getting into me clothes – double quick, I don't mind tellin' yer. But she only lay there, poor cow, sort of smiling and crying — arm across 'er eyes. So it couldn't 'uv been 'er old man she'd heard.'

The captain was scratching in his pouch for a few last crumbs of dry tobacco.

'P'raps the husband was bloody well dead.'

He rammed the tobacco into the stinking crater of his pipe.

'Or she could 'uv been yellin' at the orgasm.'

He rammed and rammed.

'Don't know why I'm tellun yer this. About giant cockies. You'll think I'm a nut case.'

Eddie Twyborn had to rejoin his detachment down the road.

'An' don't think I'm religious!' The captain had followed him as far as the door. 'Because I believe in nothun!' he shouted after one he regretted taking for a temporary mate. 'NOTHUN!' he screamed.

The remembered scream rang in Eadith's ears as she listened to the men who had returned from Dunkirk, and as she walked through the warren of what was officially her brothel. She could not envisage leaving her house, or handing over to anyone else, for this was the life she had chosen, or which had been chosen for her. Yet her girls, her clients, seemed less aware of her presence than before. Ada had emerged as a person of abounding influence; her professional attitudes commanded the respect of those who had dealings with her; the brisk sound of her brown habit, the rustle of her bunch of keys, if not her rosary, could be heard in the corridors, the public rooms, and as they issued out of the individual cells under her charitable control.

That Ada might take over began to seem possible, at moments inevitable. The two principals accepted what their eyes and minds avoided, because theirs had always been a relationship of perfect trust. Now more than ever Mrs Trist relied on her deputy's support.

Eadith believed that sooner or later she must come across Eadie Twyborn again. She sensed that the conflict of individual destinies was as inescapable, and often as fatal, as the all-embracing undertow of war. As she waited, nervousness made her snip at the hairs in her nostrils; she even found herself picking her nose. Supposing the barbarians arrived before she and Eadie could be brought face to face? She went out and stood on the marble steps to repel the invader with what remained of her own strength, and the spirit-support of a father, husband, lovers, all of whom had been frail human beings, as frail in fact as Eddie/Eadith.

There was an evening when Mrs Trist was forced to defect temporarily from her over-organized, airless house. After strolling, by a great effort of restraint, some distance along the Walk, she sat down on a bench placed almost exactly in front of the Old Church. It was before the peak hour of activity at her brothel: when the armed services poured in, the politicians, the civil servants, the Law, the Church, refugee royalty, and those who had survived trial by fire. As she sat in the pigeon-coloured light she knew she had begun to renounce what Ada was better able to cope with: a world of fragmentation and despair in which even the perversities of vice can offer regeneration of a kind.

But perhaps she was what is called old-fashioned. Sitting on the bench on the Embankment, she saw herself as an Old Girl. Gulls flying up the estuary, wheeling above the incoming tide, were shitting on her dyed hair. She picked off a dob of white, while remembering that it was said to bring luck.

Whether that was so, she did in fact look round soon after and saw Eadie Twyborn come out of the church. She was dressed in the same black she had been wearing on recent occasions, her face as drained of human passion, the prayer-book held in black-gloved hands. If Eadith Trist was an Old Girl, Eadie Twyborn could have been the original She-Ancient.

To Eadith's terror, this timeless figure seemed to be approaching the bench on which she was seated. Should she make her getaway before her courage dwindled, her will left her? Or should she remain and be exposed as never before? Nothing was decided for her. She continued sitting, more passive than she had known herself in the moments of her worst despair.

The equally passive, outwardly unemotional figure of the elderly woman revealed no possible reason for her decision to sit on the already occupied bench. She didn't speak; she was not the traditional Australian looking for a stranger on whom to inflict a life story. No doubt she was only preparing to enjoy the last of the sun and the light on the river turning by now from dove to violet.

Eadith was so relieved, not to say disappointed, she could feel the tears coming into her eyes. She continued sitting, staring straight ahead, a stranger beside a stranger.

More than anything the evening light began establishing a harmony between them.

Eadith glanced sideways at the gloved hands, the skin showing white at the tip of one black forefinger pointed along the prayer-book's shabby morocco.

The hole in the glove, together with the scruffy leather, became more than Eadith Trist could bear. Perhaps it wasn't her mother, and she could leave without a qualm. Even if it *were* Eadie Twyborn, one shouldn't delude oneself into staying, out of sentimentality, compassion, or whatever.

The aged woman began to speak in what was indisputably an aged, drained version of Eadie Twyborn's voice. 'I'd been promising myself one of Gribble's brown-bread ices. I've only recently discovered them. But the light by the river is so delicious I've postponed this other delight, till now, I suppose, it's too late.'

Eadith had decided not to think of this woman as her mother. At the same time she was unable to move.

Mrs Twyborn turned to the stranger and asked, 'Do you know their brown-bread ices?'

Mrs Trist answered in her coldest English, 'I find them slimy.'

'Rich, perhaps. But a rich ice-cream or pudding is one of the few vices old age allows me to enjoy. Where I come from,' she added (now you were for it), 'they consider it a bit immoral to put too much cream in an ice.'

Mrs Trist failed to ask the stranger's inevitable question, but Mrs Twyborn didn't seem put out. She apparently took for granted a cold temperament in her anonymous acquaintance.

Presently she sighed. 'Another thing I've missed doing this afternoon is mending this tear in my glove. Ah well, it'll keep for this evening. I was never much good with my needle. I've always hated mending.'

Mrs Trist agreed that mending was a bore.

At this moment she was moved to look at Eadie Twyborn, even though she sensed the latter had turned and was looking at her.

They were looking into each other's eyes, Eadith's of fragmented blue and gold blazing in their tension, their determination not to melt, Eadie's of a dull topaz, the eyes of an old, troubled dog. The soft white-kid face, the pale lips, began to tremble so violently she had to turn away at last.

The women continued sitting side by side, till Eadie found the

370

strength to rummage in her bag, and when she had found the pencil she was looking for, to scribble on the prayer-book's fly-leaf.

Eadith was offered this tremulous scribble, and read, 'Are you my son Eddie?'

They were seated on this other bench inside the corrugated-iron shelter, sun blazing on black asphalt as the brown, bucking tram approached them.

'I do wish, Eddie, you'd stop picking that scab on your knee. Sometimes I think you do things just to irritate me.'

'Sometimes I think, Mother, you hate just about everything I do.'

Now in this violet, northern light, purged of her mortal sins by age, Eadie might have been prepared to accept a bit of scab-picking in others.

If Eadith could have unbent. But if she had, she might have broken. At least she couldn't have trusted her lips.

Instead, she seized the pencil and slashed the fly-leaf of the prayer-book with a savagery she did not feel.

Eadie Twyborn read when the book was handed back, 'No, but I am your daughter Eadith.'

The two women continued sitting together in the gathering shadow.

Presently Eadie said, 'I am so glad. I've always wanted a daughter.'

The searchlights had begun latticing the evening sky.

'How I look forward to our talks,' said Eadie. 'I'll give you my address. You'll come to my hotel, won't you? We'll have so much to tell now that we've found each other.'

'But aren't you afraid, Mother? This war. Shouldn't you be starting for home? The lull may break at any moment.'

'What have I to lose but the fag-end of life? Rather that than miss a last conversation with my daughter.'

Their harmony by now was a perfect one; until it occurred to Eadie, 'If I do go home, Eadith, is there any reason why you shouldn't come with me?'

The searchlights had woven their subtle aluminium cage.

'I mightn't be allowed,' Eadith replied.

She promised, however, to take her mother back to her hotel, and to visit her for conversations.

Eadie refused her daughter's company this evening. She said

she would take a cab. She could not have borne sitting in the dark cab with Eadith, falling silent, wondering whether they dare hold hands. But she did look forward to long talks on future occasions.

Or were they losing each other? she wondered, looking back through the window of the cab.

Back at Beckwith Street, Eadith and Ada avoided each other for unavoidable reasons.

In an attempt to clothe the silence, Ada called from a distance that Nonie had got herself engaged to a lieutenant in the Grenadiers, and that their wartime clientele was lifting the ashtrays, even towels, as souvenirs.

Eadith might not have heard. She locked herself in her room, and began brushing her hair, snuffling at herself in the glass. She longed to caress her mother, regardless of the embarrassment she would probably cause them both. She saw herself embracing Gravenor with a passion far removed from the austere, sisterly affection she showed her lover.

But Gravenor, since their last meeting, had been swallowed up by anonymity and Europe, while she remained trapped in this house, and the walls of that other prison, her self.

Eadith visited her mother the following afternoon, and then regularly. They had many delightful conversations, others more disquieting.

Eadie asked her daughter how she had been spending her life, and Eadith told her how she had drifted into becoming a bawd and running a brothel as a profitable business.

'Years ago,' Eadie said, 'I might have been interested in visiting your house. Yes,' she gave a short dry laugh, 'I'd have enjoyed investigating a brothel. Now I'm too old.'

She asked whether Eadith herself had enjoyed lovers.

Eadith admitted she had — if 'enjoy' were the word; she had run into such difficulties.

Eadie agreed that love was difficult. 'Quite a trapeze act in fact. I respected your father, and loved him, Eddie — *Eadith* — but never enough till after he died. I was fond of poor Joanie Golson — the friend I believe you disliked so much you always avoided. Joanie was too possessive. What one wants from a woman finally becomes suffocating. I only ever really loved, and was loved by, my little flea-ridden dogs. I could talk to them and they understood. Children and parents fail one another. Of course there are exceptions, but so worthy they're intolerable in a different way. No, dogs were my best relationship – until the last one of all, which I shan't attempt to explain. You might find my naked spirit as embarrassing as my shrivelled body.'

Seated in the characterless, neutral-toned cube of the steel-and-concrete hotel room, this woman of no longer alcoholic, but dotty, glittering eyes, who was also her mother, had for Eadith the fascination of anachronisms of most kinds. She was both personal and remote; those blotched hands must have pressed on her own belly to help expel in blood and anguish the child struggling out of it.

Eadie continued in the same tone of detached calm, of purged emotion, 'I can't see why you don't come home with me, Eadith . . .' she hesitated before allowing the word 'dearest' to pass her lips; it might have acted as a deterrent. 'As late as this perhaps we'd find we could live together. I can see us washing our hair, and sitting together in the garden to dry it.'

Yes, it was the most seductive proposition: the two sitting in the steamy garden, surrounded by ragged grass, hibiscus trumpets, the bubbling and plopping of bulbuls, a drizzling of taps. But as from all such golden dreams, the awakening would surely devastate.

'Do come!' Now it was Eadie's former voice issuing a command rather than making a plea.

'Mother, you don't realize how difficult it would be in wartime. You're a visitor. I am not. I have no passport. I had, but years ago. No, you must go, Mother.' It was becoming a feverish situation. 'Perhaps I'll follow eventually.'

'I'm sure there are no difficulties which can't be overcome,' Eadie countered, with a bright smile which disbelieved her own hopes.

'We'll see,' said Eadith as she gathered her belongings.

She had brought her mother a pomander, that pretty, perfumed toy people still offered one another in the last days of their idleness.

'You're not going, are you, Eadith?'

'Yes, Mother, I must make sure my whores are fed'; as though Ada wouldn't see to that.

Mother and daughter nuzzled at each other's cheeks; they might have been foraging for some elusive truffle.

Eadith left after promising to return next day at her usual time.

Ada the inscrutable, but understanding deputy had brought the mail to her Superior. There were the usual bills, protestations of enduring affection from the Ursulas, Dianas, and Cecilys, with a few letters of abuse from envious neighbours and disgruntled clients. There was the letter from Gravenor forwarded by courtesy of the Foreign Office.

Eadith laid Gravenor's letter on a corner of the dressing-table while hearing out Ada's tale of missing towels, torn sheets, and mice in the kitchen cupboards. Eadith remembered the mouse-catcher of grey skin and smelly socks in the flat in Hendrey Street. Rightly or wrongly, the young man was one of the many she had resisted taking as lovers.

She waited till Ada had gone before re-opening the discreet official envelope enclosing Gravenor's letter. There was neither date, nor address, the message brief, neat; done with a pin, one would have thought.

My dearest Eadith,

How I miss our unsatisfactory encounters. Unfulfilling though our meetings were, they would fill the void of wherever I am, surrounded by anonymous automata. I like to think those other automata you and I created for ourselves out of our inhibitions were human beings underneath, and that we might have loved each other, completely and humanly, if we had found the courage. Men and women are not the sole members of the human hierarchy to which you and I can also claim to belong.

I can see your reproving face, your explosive jaw rejecting my assertion. If I can't persuade you, I shall continue to accept you in whatever form your puritan decides you should appear, if we survive the holocaust which is preparing.

'Love' is an exhausted word, and God has been expelled by those who know better, but I offer you the one as proof that the other still exists.   R.

Several days later, as the proprietor came downstairs, the body of the house seemed pervaded by the torpor of reluctant flesh, except in the basement, where Ada, Mrs Parsons, and Tyler the houseman were stashing away the supplies they had brought back to withstand a siege by barbarians. Some of it had a glitter, almost that of precious stones, which the last of the loot always wears: brandied peaches, French plums, chicken breasts, caviare, none of it necessary, but all of it desirable as proof of the buyers' foresight or cunning. Not that humbler commodities on which they would depend, such as tea and sugar in bursting bags, tins of bully, bars of soap, a case of evaporated milk, even a carton of bandaids, were without an esoteric glow in the present light.

The independent servants were flushed with their perspicacity.

Mrs Parsons was telling, 'She said to me what do you think you're preparing for – a war? I said no the end of the world!'

Her helpers Maggie and Vi shrieked and giggled, Tyler rumbling in undertone, till Ada's gravity reminded them to carry on with their work in silence. None and all of it was important.

Hanging around in the passage he caught Ada's attention through the doorway, and she left her minions and came out to him at last.

He told her, 'I've decided to make the break tonight. I'm glad you're taking over, Ada, because you're a serious person, and practical seriousness is what a whore-house demands.' They enjoyed his joke, or she pretended to. 'My frivolous self will now go in search of some occupation in keeping with the times.'

This brown-habited imitation of the dedicated nun stood shuffling a bit on the basement flags.

'You know where to go if you need advice.'

'Yes, Eddie,' she answered.

But she averted her eyes from the pepper-and-salt tonsure.

Eddie himself felt uneasy, not as a result of their confidences, but in the cheap suit he had bought in a hurry, the shirt a size too small, and shoes which not only pinched his toes, but squeaked at every step he took. There was too much hasty improvisation about the current version of Eddie Twyborn, but probably no one beyond Ada and Eadie would notice.

He said, 'First I must go to my mother and tell her what you and I understand. She may, too. Yes, I think she does. Which will make it worse.'

Then he left, not by the kitchen stairs, but up the area steps, supporting himself on the bars of the railing as he stumbled into the street. Whatever his partially conscious plan for positive action, it could hardly take place in Eadith Trist's whore-house.

As he crossed this seemingly deserted city, a scapegoat again in search of sacrifice, his steely tonsure parried the steely evening light. He glanced sideways through the gathering dusk and saw himself reflected in plate-glass: the distorted shoulders of the shoddy suit, the pointed shoes, the cropped hair. He was disgusted to see he had forgotten to take off Eadith's make-up. The great magenta mouth was still flowering in a chalk face shaded with violet, the eyes overflowing mascara banks, those of a distressed woman, professional whore, or hopeful amateur lover.

She slunk, or rather, he squeaked past, grateful for the support of railings in this role which he had played so many times, yet almost forgotten. On Constitution Hill the chariot poised on its pedestal appeared on the verge of taking off. The Dilly ahead was an empty slope.

The squeaking shoes carried him along. He recalled those boots, mud clotting soles and eyelets as the guns opened their evening barrage. Where he had staggered under the weight of material equipment and exhaustion, now he tottered in a fever of fragmented intentions (must be age or something) trotting up the empty Dilly on a short but painful visit to his mother's womb. A metal confetti was falling around him, slithering on the pavement, rebounding. What if his monastic scalp were hit?

He giggled on envisaging a dish of brains a nursery-maid was serving the Bellasis children. No one around to share his joke. He would have liked it, but the whores with their fox capes, their chow-chow dogs, their straying fingers, their heels perforating ancient pavements, all were vanished. (It was safer nowadays to concentrate on the exodus from business lunches.)

He had almost reached Eadie's hotel when he noticed the east blazing with a perverse sunset, if not fiery razzle-dazzle, heard the chuffing of his own heart, a clangour of racing engines, the thump and crump of history becoming unstable, crumbling.

It was happening in the city its inhabitants thought belonged to them.

In a moment it seemed to Eddie Twyborn as though his own share in time were snatched away, as though every house he had ever lived in were torn open, the sawdust pouring out of all the dolls in all the rooms, furniture whether honest or pretentious still shuddering from its brush with destruction, a few broken bars of a Chabrier waltz scattered from the burst piano, was it the Judge-Pantocrator looking through a gap in the star-painted ceiling, the beige thighs hooked in a swinging chandelier could only be those of that clumsy acrobat Marcia, all contained in the ruins of this great unstable temporal house, all but Eddie and Eadith, unless echoes of their voices threading pandemonium.

Down one of the dark tributary streets came a young soldier in battle dress and tin hat. He reached the corner in time to fall head on, making almost a straight line on the pavement, with this character from a carnival or looney bin. The young man seemed to be trying to share the brim of his protective hat with one who could hardly remain a stranger. 'Something happening at last, eh?' At such close quarters he was little more than a white smile in skin as rough and red as a brick.

The next moment they were heaved up almost above the parapet.

Eddie Twyborn should have shouted, 'Time to go over . . .' but his voice failed him.

So he prepared to advance alone into this brick no-man's-land. This time could it be despair running in the wrong direction?

It might if he had been able to move from his position on the pavement. It seemed to him that the figure head-on was melting into the worn stone, the smile congealing, the tin hat no more than a cabaret prop.

A detached hand was lying in a stream of blood nor'-nor'-west of Eddie Twyborn's left cheek. It was neither of the soldier's hands he began to realize, for these were arranged on the pavement, a dog's obedient paws had it not been for blunt fingers with nails in mourning, still attached to bristling wrists.

It was his own hand he saw as he ebbed, incredibly, away from it. 'Fetch me a bandaid, Ada,' he croaked over his shoulder, while flowing onward, on to wherever the crimson current might carry him.

Mrs Twyborn had been waiting in her hotel room for the daughter she was expecting. There had been an unusually fine sunset, if to the east rather than the west it accorded with these times of illogic and apocalypse, so she had not bothered to question it.

Though a maid had drawn the black-out curtains, Eadie had dragged them open. The curtains made the room too airless and she loved to sit in the dark watching the changes in the evening sky.

She was sitting in this sterile room, a figure in seemingly

enduring marble which, again in accordance with these days of unreason, was draped in black.

She was barely shaken when the building moved in time with the crump, followed by an explosion, outside. From being a bland cube, the room for a shuddering instant became a rhomb, before settling back into its normal steel-and-concrete shape.

Outside, the clangour of chariots racing towards brassy sunsets.

She sat on. It had happened as Eadith had predicted. But she could not care. At least she did not feel afraid. Age had drained her of fear, along with her vices, doubts, torments.

Down the corridor a woman was hopping screaming, as though she still belonged to the present, some young person no doubt who had not yet suffered enough.

Now the kindly maid who had drawn the black-out curtains was tearing the door open, and no longer kind, trying to bully an aggravating old imbecile.

'Mrs Twyborn,' she shouted, 'you must come down. I'll take you to the shelter.'

'What was that woman screaming for?'

'Don't you know there's a raid? The East End's on fire. Now they're going for the railway stations.'

'But that screaming woman — was she hit?'

'No, she wasn't. She got a fright when the bombs fell. She jumped up and zipped herself into one leg of her siren suit. Now there isn't time to unzip.'

The old woman had dismissed bombs and their consequences; she sat contemplating the image of the hopping woman.

In her exasperation, the maid was hurting Eadie Twyborn. 'Please come — I can't wait for ever. Two men were killed at the corner.'

'It's too late — too late to die. I'll stay and watch. Besides, I'm expecting my daughter.'

'She'll not be so foolish to start out on a night like this. Or if she did, she'll have got in somewhere.'

Mrs Twyborn murmured, 'I'll wait. I'll watch. Edith will come.'

Frustrated by this stubborn old thing, the maid stormed off in pursuit of her own safety.

Overhead, the silver plane appeared to have been halted at an intersection of searchlights, its lovely abstraction far above human clangour and despair.

Now that night had fallen, all London could have been burning. But again, in abstraction.

What was real was the garden in which she was sitting. She had come out to dry her hair, and was sitting on the discoloured steps amongst the lizards and bulbuls and hibiscus trumpets, waiting for Eadith.

The towel she had brought with her was an old one, practically as old as her marriage, still serviceable, if thin. Things from then last for ever.

That drizzling tap. Nobody to mend it. Will Eadith, perhaps? Her man's hands. Eddie Eadith her interchangeable failure.

She had lost sight of the beautiful aluminium insect and would never know whether it had evaded those sticky feelers of light, or plunged into the destruction it had caused below.

You could never be certain, either sitting in the garden, or on the bench beside the river, or waiting for the tram in the blaze of Sydney.

Eadie said I must not fail Eadith now that I have found her Eadith Eddie no matter which this fragment of my self which I lost is now returned where it belongs.

Sitting in the garden drying our hair together amongst the bulbuls and drizzle of taps we shall experience harmony at last.

She loved the birds. As she dried her hair and waited, a bulbul was perched on the rim of the stone bird-bath, dipping his beak. Ruffling his feathers, he cocked his head at her, shook his little velvet jester's cap, and raised his beak towards the sun.

MORE ABOUT PENGUINS
AND PELICANS

For further information about books available from Penguins please write to Dept EP, Penguin Books Ltd, Harmondsworth, Middlesex UB7 0DA.

In the U.S.A.: For a complete list of books available from Penguins in the United States write to Dept CS, Penguin Books, 625 Madison Avenue, New York, New York 10022.

In Canada: For a complete list of books available from Penguins in Canada write to Penguin Books Canada Ltd, 2801 John Street, Markham, Ontario L3R 1B4.

In Australia: For a complete list of books available from Penguins in Australia write to the Marketing Department, Penguin Books Australia Ltd, P.O. Box 257, Ringwood, Victoria 3134.

In New Zealand: For a complete list of books available from Penguins in New Zealand write to the Marketing Department, Penguin Books (N.Z.) Ltd, P.O. Box 4019, Auckland 10.

Patrick White

VOSS

The plot of this novel is of epic simplicity: in 1845 Voss sets out
with a small band to cross the Australian continent for the first
time. The tragic story of their terrible journey and its inevitable
end is told with imaginative understanding.

The figure of Voss takes on superhuman proportions, until he
appears to those around him as both deliverer and destroyer. His
relationship with Laura Trevelyan is the central personal theme
of the story.

'A work of genius . . . *Voss* has an epic quality, the ageless sense
of the power and pride of man battling with his condition' – John
Davenport in the *Observer*

THE TREE OF MAN

This great novel could fittingly claim to stand as the Australian
Book of Genesis. A young man, at the turn of the century, takes a
wife and carves out a home in the wilderness near one of the
growing cities of Australia. There is the daily intercourse with
neighbours of their kind. And at the end death walks in the
garden.

and

THE BURNT ONES
THE COCKATOOS
THE EYE OF THE STORM
A FRINGE OF LEAVES
THE LIVING AND THE DEAD
RIDERS IN THE CHARIOT
THE SOLID MANDALA
THE VIVISECTOR

A Selection

OLD SOLDIERS

Paul Bailey

In flight from painful memories, Victor Harker encounters the
extraordinary Captain Hal Standish. Drawn together in an
uneasy alliance, the two men find they have unexpected ghosts in
common.

THE HEART IS A LONELY HUNTER

Carson McCullers

The story of a group of people in the American south which
explores their individual response to the gentle, sympathetic
appeal of a deaf-mute – and their common factor, loneliness.

FIRE ON THE MOUNTAIN

Anita Desai

The portrait of a strange relationship between two solitary
people, and a wonderfully observed picture of life in India by one
of her foremost living writers.

A CONFEDERACY OF DUNCES

John Kennedy Toole

'It is a masterwork of comedy', said *The New York Times* of this
Pulitzer prize-winning novel. Outrageous, grotesque, superbly
written, its Falstaffian hero is Ignatius J. Reilly, a self-proclaimed
genius in a world of dunces.

TESTAMENT

R. C. Hutchinson

Among the classic novels of the 30s and 40s, now rediscovered
and restored to print, *Testament* is a magnificent recreation of life
in Russia at the time of the revolution and, through the figure of
Count Anton Scheffler, a masterly study of the mentality of
heroism.